P9-DXK-925

TARGETS
OF
REVENGE

ALSO BY JEFFREY S. STEPHENS

Targets of Deception

Targets of Opportunity

TARGETS

OF

REVENGE

JEFFREY S. STEPHENS

GALLERY BOOKS

NEW YORK   LONDON   TORONTO   SYDNEY   NEW DELHI

Gallery Books
A Division of Simon & Schuster, Inc.
1230 Avenue of the Americas
New York, NY 10020

Copyright © 2013 by Jeffrey S. Stephens

All rights reserved, including the right to reproduce this book or portions thereof in any form whatsoever. For information address Gallery Books Subsidiary Rights Department, 1230 Avenue of the Americas, New York, NY 10020.

First Gallery Books hardcover edition February 2013

GALLERY BOOKS and colophon are registered trademarks of Simon & Schuster, Inc.

For information about special discounts for bulk purchases, please contact Simon & Schuster Special Sales at 1-866-506-1949 or business@simonandschuster.com.

The Simon & Schuster Speakers Bureau can bring authors to your live event. For more information or to book an event contact the Simon & Schuster Speakers Bureau at 1-866-248-3049 or visit our website at www.simonspeakers.com.

Manufactured in the United States of America

10   9   8   7   6   5   4   3   2   1

Library of Congress Cataloging-in-Publication Data

Stephens, Jeffrey S.
  Targets of revenge: a novel / by Jeffrey S. Stephens.
      p. cm.
  1. Intelligence officers — Fiction. I. Title.
   PS3619.T47676T375 2013
   813'.6—dc23   2012022211

ISBN 978-1-4516-8872-6
ISBN 978-1-4516-8873-3 (ebook)

Scott Sumner
for your enduring friendship, and
for never allowing me to abandon the dream

OVER LAGO DE MARACAIBO, VENEZUELA

Jordan Sandor was strapped into the small cockpit of the ASG-29 glider. The C-47 twin-engine that had been rigged to draw him up into the moonless night began its run down the tarmac. There was an abrupt tug as the towrope was yanked taut, then Sandor felt a second, more violent jerk as he was lifted into the air.

Sandor had piloted gliders before, but never at night and never toward a destination that was essentially in the middle of nowhere. As he was hoisted upward into the cloudless sky, he was reminded again how different a glider is than a powered craft. The basic aerodynamics are the same, but in the absence of propellers or jet engines gravity will ultimately have its way, which presents a different mind-set. Staying aloft depends in part on climatic and geographic conditions, but mostly upon the skill of the pilot. There is no other winged aircraft that joins a man so completely to the act of flying.

Sandor was clad in black commando pants and pullover, a Kevlar vest, and rubber-soled boots. He was wearing a helmet and had PNVG night vision goggles in place—the sooner he adjusted to the artificial lighting the easier it would be for him to navigate over the dark expanse of jungle. Through the goggles he could clearly make out the plane sixty yards ahead of him. It was an uncharacteristically helpless feeling for Sandor, knowing that for the moment he could do nothing but wait. He also knew his anxiety would have been far worse if he did not completely trust the three men in whose hands he had placed his life.

"You okay back there?" It was Bergenn, his voice loud and clear in Sandor's earpiece.

"Just like a ride at Disney World," Sandor replied into the helmet-mounted microphone.

"Get yourself strapped in tight, the best is yet to come."

Sandor ran through his mental checklist one last time, reviewing every detail from landing; to objective; to the arrangements for his escape. The operation was beginning with a flight plan that was as simple as it was fraught with danger. They were rapidly ascending to a high altitude, traveling northwest and then circling back to the south, toward the mouth of the Gulf of Venezuela and beyond. They would remain above the sea at all times, never crossing land as they veered in a southwesterly direction, taking them perilously close to the shoreline border between Colombia and Venezuela. They wanted to avoid wandering too far into the airspace of either country, and so, before making landfall, the C-47 would make a quick descent, release the glider, and then return to base. It would then be up to Sandor to guide the fiberglass craft southeast along the shore of the Lago de Maracaibo until he turned inland and reached his intended landing point in the jungle, south of the town of Barranquitas.

Bergenn's voice interrupted his reverie again. "Hang on," he said.

Doug Carlton, who was piloting the C-47, expertly banked a turn. Towing the glider required him to maneuver each roll in a wide arc.

"Still here," Sandor told them.

It was more than twenty minutes since takeoff when Bergenn said, "Almost time to go. You ready?"

"All set."

"When we bank to the port side again, hit the lever to release the towline."

"Got it."

"Good luck."

"The only kind to have," Sandor replied. "Going silent now." Then, as the C-47 made its slow turn to the left, Sandor hit the manual handle that released the towline from the nose of the glider. He saw the rope drop into the darkness, then watched as the twin-engine plane disappeared into the night off his starboard side.

He was alone.

The sound of the C-47 engines quickly faded into the night, leaving Sandor amid an exquisite silence. The quiet could be mesmerizing, but he busied himself with the task at hand.

At this hour of night he was not concerned about encountering other aircraft, especially as his altitude dropped, but he was alert to the dark sky before him as he took control of the instruments. Even a collision with a flock of large birds could pose a deadly hazard.

He had reviewed the navigation system with Craig Raabe. It was similar to the other gliders he had flown. A single stick controlled the ailerons, which governed bank and roll. This would have to be coordinated with the foot pedals that moved the tail rudder, regulating the glider's yaw. A hand lever worked the flaps that would reduce speed as he came in for a landing.

The first order of business was a controlled descent. The ASG 29 is an expertly designed glider with high-aspect wings, and Sandor instantly discovered how sensitive the craft could be when he made his first attempt to roll the plane to the port side and begin downward.

"Whoa," he said aloud as the glider seemed to take off underneath him.

He leveled out, then had another go at it. He was moving at more than 120 miles an hour and was rapidly approaching landfall.

This time he banked more slowly, making a smooth transition into a descent that took him within view of the enormous lake below— Lago de Maracaibo was the size of a small sea. He followed with another roll, this time to the starboard side, dropping even lower. As he pulled out of that turn he spotted a small formation of gulls coming toward him, off the port side. Not wanting to hit them, but not risking an unduly quick maneuver, he eased farther to starboard, taking him off course but averting the impact.

Sandor had a quick look at the LED readout of his digital compass. He needed to come back twenty degrees to port, which would return him to the planned route. The more populated areas were along the coast and, now that he was reaching the shore, he intended to move quickly west and get far enough inland so the chance of being spotted from the ground was, as Deputy Director Byrnes might say, within a tolerable degree of risk. The key to his mission was surprise—detection of any sort could prove fatal.

Sandor was over land and, as he turned the glider back on course, he began to make out the outlines beneath him. The night vision goggles were not all that much help in the open sky, but now the landscape below came into focus. He was passing over one town after another—Campo Maria, Rosario, Machiques, and finally Barranquitas. He struggled to maintain the precarious balance between staying below radar levels and keeping his altitude high enough to reach his landing area before gravity and wind currents brought him down. He repeatedly worked the controls to raise the nose of the glider, then lower it again, resulting in something akin to an untracked roller-coaster ride as he and his unpowered craft raced through the dark night.

South of the village of Barranquitas he made his final and most dangerous turn. At this low altitude, barely clear of the treetops, he would have to negotiate a 270 roll that would take him to the clearing where he intended to set down. Once again he was confronted with the difference between a glider and a conventional aircraft. There was no margin for error here, no second chance if he missed the landing. Sandor would have only one opportunity to get to the ground safely. If he failed, he and the glider would end up a shattered mess among the trees and vines below.

His vision was in constant motion, moving from the jungle ahead as it rose up to meet the glider—having a look at the compass in his lap as it helped keep him on course—then swiveling back and forth to check the wing flaps as he worked the levers and foot pedals to slow the plane.

Suddenly, as if an oasis had appeared in an endless desert, the clearing was visible among the dense, towering trees. Sandor pushed on the hand lever until the flaps were virtually perpendicular to the long, graceful wings. He held the foot pedals steady on a course of dead reckoning as he pulled the release switch for the water tank that serves as ballast beneath the fuselage. The rear of the aircraft released what might have appeared as some sort of liquid jet stream.

Even with all of this, Sandor knew he was coming in too high and too fast. He had simply not seen the clearing early enough.

Under the best of circumstances a glider this size would need more than five hundred feet of runway to come safely to a stop. Although the clearing appeared to be three times that long, Sandor realized that he was not going to get the glider on the ground until it was more than two-thirds of the way into the field, which would be too late.

He strained against the lever to hold the flaps down, but that was not going to work; there was not enough time. He knew he had only one remaining chance. Atop the wings were his fail-safe mechanisms, the so-called terminal velocity air brakes. They would create a forced crash, something just short of a complete nosedive. Sandor did not hesitate. There was no time to weigh options; there was barely enough time to react. He let go of the flap control and reached out with both hands, tugging hard at the two emergency loops.

The result was instantaneous. The glider shuddered as if he had hit a pothole in the sky. The nose of the plane dipped and Sandor felt himself careening headlong to earth.

He strained to pull on the main lever again as the ground appeared to race toward him at a breathtaking pace. At the last moment he yanked at the controls to pull the nose up, then pushed himself back in the seat and braced for the crash.

After flying in total silence, the sounds of the glider smashing to pieces all around him was deafening. The wings acted as land-based pontoons until they were finally shattered, and the torque of the violent impact caused the windshield to explode into pieces. But the reinforced cockpit held fast as the remnants of what remained of the glider skidded along the soft, vegetation-covered ground until it came to a jarring stop against a stand of trees at the end of the clearing.

Then everything became quiet and dark.

CHAPTER ONE

THE PREVIOUS WEEK, CIA HEADQUARTERS, LANGLEY, VIRGINIA

A WEEK EARLIER, SANDOR'S boss at the Central Intelligence Agency, Deputy Director Mark Byrnes, had not only refused to sanction the proposed mission into the Venezuelan jungle. He had specifically ordered Sandor not to undertake the operation.

Sandor had been careful not to make a formal request for approval when he discussed his idea with Byrnes. He had merely floated a trial balloon.

The DD shot it down without hesitation.

"We're not in the vendetta business," Byrnes told him. "We'll take care of this in due course."

It had been less than a month since Sandor and his team prevented an attack on American oil refineries along the Gulf Coast, but Sandor argued it was past the time for them to address the unfinished business of that mission. Although the main damage had been averted, several soldiers had died in the process of disarming one of the explosive devices. Before that, terrorists had taken down a commercial airliner in the Caribbean, followed by a deadly assault on a communications center. All told, those attacks cost the lives of hundreds of civilians and military personnel. And then there was the matter of a CIA operative, Sandor's close friend, who was killed in action during an incursion in North Korea where the terrorist plot was first uncovered.

The mastermind behind all of these calamities had never surfaced, keeping a safe distance from the action as he played out his murderous scheme. Rafael Cabello, a Venezuelan known in the intelligence community as Adina, had orchestrated the entire affair, never putting himself in harm's way as all of those innocent people died in the wake of his treachery.

Sandor was not inclined to wait for action in *due course,* as the Deputy Director suggested. He was determined to act now.

"Sir, there's no telling what Adina may be up to next. At the very least a reconnaissance mission could gather some valuable intelligence."

Byrnes fixed his subordinate with a knowing stare. "Reconnaissance? Come on Sandor, we didn't just meet this morning. I know exactly what you have in mind."

Sandor responded with the most innocent look he could muster. "Sir?"

"You're not thinking about intelligence gathering. You're thinking about liquidating Adina."

"Aren't you?"

Byrnes stood up, walked around his desk, and leaned against the edge, looking down at his agent. "Of course I am. But losing you or Raabe or Bergenn isn't going to help me right now, is it?"

"That would be impossible, sir. I'm your punishment from God. You'll never lose me."

Byrnes treated Sandor to one of his famous scowls, a look that was somewhere between indigestion and a reaction to a rotten odor. Byrnes was a patient man, but he was not renowned for his sense of humor. "Spare me your witty repartee. I'm ordering you to stay away from this. We've met with DHS and we're developing plans with the NCTC to deal with what happened. And, just so you know how far up the food chain this goes, the Director of National Intelligence is all over this as well. You're on a need-to-know basis, and right now you don't need to know."

"If plans are being made I think I've earned the right to be read in."

"I'll be sure to make a note of that in the file," Byrnes said as he returned to his chair. "Meantime, let me remind you that you're an agent of the United States government under my command, and you'll do as I say. Is that clear?"

"Completely."

"Venezuela is a hostile nation. If one of my agents were caught in an act of espionage within that country, the repercussions would be severe. Are you clear on that, too?"

"Not exactly. Are you saying that the key is not to get caught?"

"Sandor . . ."

"I understand."

"Is there anything else?"

"I'm entitled to some leave. I was planning to take a week, if that's all right."

"That's fine, you really should take some time. You've certainly earned that." As Sandor stood, the DD added, "But mark my words. You head off on some escapade of your own and I promise you, none of the good you've done will stop me from turning your world upside down. You read me?"

"Completely," Sandor said again, then turned and was gone.

———————

Bergenn and Raabe had been on the mission in North Korea with Sandor and they shared his views of Adina. When Sandor invited them for drinks that night and explained what he had in mind, there was no need to ask twice if they wanted in.

"You should know that Byrnes warned me off any nonsanctioned activities."

"There's a shock," Raabe replied.

Sandor then told them that the National Counter-Terrorism Center was already working out some strategies of their own, and that the DNI was also reviewing the situation.

"I doubt they're thinking what you're thinking," Raabe said.

"Just wanted you to know everything I know."

Bergenn said there was no reason for them to get in the way of the other agencies.

"By the time they put a plan in place we'll be all done and back home," Raabe said.

"My thinking exactly," Sandor agreed.

Bergenn said he would make the contacts Sandor requested. Raabe was still on a medical leave for the injuries he sustained during the operation in Pyongyang. He agreed to work from home, arranging for the equipment they would need. Then they planned to meet in three days in Curaçao.

Meanwhile, Sandor was going to take a short trip to visit a friend in St. Barths.

CHAPTER TWO

ST. BARTHÉLEMY, FRENCH WEST INDIES

SANDOR WAS GREETED at the St. Barths airport by Lieutenant Henri Vauchon. After a warm embrace Sandor took a step back and had a good look at his friend.

"Seems your shoulder healed up pretty well."

The Frenchman shrugged. "Not too bad."

"I take it you've been receiving the proper attention. Medical and otherwise."

"Several women I know have been most helpful with my recovery."

"I'll bet. You still a local hero?"

"Glory fades quickly."

Sandor smiled. "Isn't that the truth."

As they headed outside to the small parking lot, Vauchon said, "When you called you said you were coming down here for a short rest. I assume that's a lie."

"Why would you think such a thing?"

Vauchon grinned. "You booked yourself into Guanahani for only one night."

"Come on, Henri. A lie is not a lie if the truth should not be expected."

"Who said that?"

"A clever lawyer I know."

"Sounds like it might have been written by Voltaire."

"You're so French. More likely came from Machiavelli."

"What are you really here for?"

"Adina."

"As I expected, although I doubt you'll find him on St. Barths."

"You may be surprised what we'll find."

Vauchon responded with a skeptical look, but Sandor let it go.

They reached the parking lot, where Sandor tossed his bag into the backseat of Vauchon's car, then the two men headed into the port town of Gustavia. They parked along the main dock and made their way to the outdoor patio at Le Select. The lieutenant ordered burgers, grabbed a couple of bottles of beer, and led them to a small table on the patio.

"Look at you, Henri, drinking on duty in the middle of the day."

"Perhaps no longer a celebrated hero, but still enjoying certain privileges."

Sandor gave an approving nod.

"So tell me, what makes you think you will find Adina hiding here, of all places?"

"I didn't say he was hiding here," Sandor replied, then took a swig of his Caribe. "But we now know he was staying on a yacht here when he coordinated the attack on Fort Oscar. And he had men at that villa in Pointe Milou, both before and after the attack."

"So this is the starting place for your search?"

"In a manner of speaking. I believe you can help."

"You know I will if I can."

"I want to review the electronic tracking records, see if we can identify his phone calls."

Vauchon did not hide his pessimism. "Do you have any idea how many cellular calls are made in and out of here every day?"

"Of course," Sandor said as he held up his hand. "I'm talking about a very limited search. I want to see if we can trace any calls to and from his base of operations in Venezuela during that short time frame. How many calls into and out of Venezuela could there have been?"

"Not many," Vauchon conceded.

"We have some general intelligence about the area where Adina currently has his command center. If we can triangulate some of those calls from last month it might help to pinpoint the location."

Vauchon thought it over. "Why not work this through Washington?"

Sandor took a gulp of beer without responding.

"Ah, I see. You have come all this way rather than simply phoning in the request or sending an email." When Sandor remained silent Vauchon nodded. "Would it be fair to say that your visit is not official?"

"That would be fair."

"Would it also be fair to say that you have been told not to pursue this matter on your own?"

"*Fair* seems such a strange word in that context. Couldn't we just say that one friend is asking another friend for help?"

Their food came and Vauchon paid. "The least I can do," he explained. "Last visit you bought me dinner at Maya's."

"I'll buy dinner wherever you like tonight."

"Because you need this help. Unofficially."

"Because I enjoy your company."

"Of course." The lieutenant bit into his hamburger. Sandor waited. "Our systems are not what they were. The explosions at Fort Oscar were devastating."

"I understand. But you can do it?"

"I believe so."

"Without creating a problem for yourself?"

Vauchon drank some beer. "That's another matter entirely. As I have mentioned, I do enjoy a certain, how would you call it, standing. And I am still well regarded by the DGSE," he added, referring to the French intelligence service.

Sandor responded with an appreciative nod. "Don't tell me you're on a second payroll now, Henri."

Vauchon smiled. "Using your expression, let's just say they enjoy my company."

Given the unofficial status of Sandor's request and the anxieties of the local military after the recent invasion of Fort Oscar, Vauchon reminded his friend that subtlety in their approach to this fact-finding mission would be at a premium. Sandor agreed. He knew that if any word were leaked to Washington about what he was up to the consequences would be dire. He would be disciplined by Byrnes and CIA Director Walsh, but that was of no great concern. The important thing was that he would be put under watch and his operation scrubbed, and that worried him far more than any bureaucratic scolding.

"Just think of me as Mr. Subtle," he said.

Vauchon shot him a knowing glance. He had seen Sandor in action before. "All right, Mr. Subtle, let's see what we can do."

The destruction of the telecommunications center that had been secretly maintained in the lower levels of Fort Oscar had been damaging to the defenses in the Western Hemisphere, not to mention a horrific black eye for the French. It would be fair to say that no one in the world expected a terrorist attack on the glamorous island of St. Barths. And, since it came on the heels of the downing of a jetliner just outside St. Maarten, the lax precautions in defending the old fortress became a humiliation that reached from Gustavia to Paris. Vauchon told Sandor that enough heads were rolling to evoke historic memories of the Bastille in its heyday.

The lieutenant was the one man who had emerged as a hero from the debacle, having rescued a number of the fort's civilian personnel as well as military guards who were taken captive during the attack. Yet even for Vauchon, gaining entrance to the new computers and gathering the information Sandor needed was going to be difficult. Much of the replacement hardware had been relocated to Guadeloupe, where access was simply out of the question. Whatever technology remained on St. Barths was now temporarily situated in a makeshift facility above the hills of St. Jean, under tight security.

It was nearly five o'clock in the evening when Vauchon pulled up to the whitewashed stone building that housed the new telecommunications center. He left his car in a small parking lot below the building, then trekked up a steep path to the first checkpoint. Sandor was right beside him.

Vauchon knew the two sentries waiting at the entrance by name and, after polite greetings, their exchange became more formal.

"What brings you here, lieutenant?"

"Ah, this damned thing never ends. They want me to review some of the telephone records from before and after the attack."

The guards exchanged a quick glance. Then one of them asked if Vauchon had written orders.

The lieutenant rolled his eyes, as if to say that such things were beyond caring about. "No, just a call from Guadeloupe. The Americans again." He gave a tilt of his head and, although they were speaking in French, Sandor got the gist of the conversation.

Both sentries responded with knowing looks. *The Americans.*

"You really should have written orders."

"I'd just as soon go home, believe me. I'll tell them I couldn't get in, let them worry about it." Then he turned to Sandor and began to explain the problem in English.

"That's all right," the soldier said, not wanting to be criticized by a superior tomorrow because he had not cooperated with higher authorities today. And this was, after all, Lieutenant Vauchon. "Jean-Pierre is at the desk; he'll pass you through."

Inside the building Vauchon told the same story to Jean-Pierre, who, after a similar colloquy, granted them entrance. The real problem now became wrestling with the computers themselves. Vauchon had to be careful in requesting assistance because Sandor did not want anyone to know what they were looking for. On the drive over, Sandor made it clear that his demand for the utmost secrecy was not limited to his apprehensions about what would happen if anyone back in the States learned of what he was up to. Given all that had happened here, it was not impossible that Adina still had an informant somewhere on the island.

Vauchon issued an appropriate defense of his countrymen, insisting that they could be relied on for their discretion, but he realized that once Sandor embarked on this mission his life would hang in the balance between silence and betrayal. It was also not lost on the Frenchman that his friend had placed this sort of trust in him, and him alone.

Jean-Pierre directed the two men to a large room in the rear of the building. It was crowded with computers, monitors, and wall-mounted screens. As the steel door closed behind them the head technician walked up and extended his hand. "What are you up to, Henri?" Vauchon knew him well. His name was Philippe, one of the survivors of the attack on Fort Oscar.

"Just need to check some information for the Americans." He introduced Sandor. "He's been sent by the NTSB. Looking for telephone records before and after the attack."

"Anything specific?"

Vauchon turned to Sandor, who said, "We need to button down how the attack was coordinated. We want to see how it might have related to the downed airplane."

Philippe's English was excellent. He required no translation. "Through phone records?" he asked with obvious skepticism.

"We want to see if the man who took the plane down might have had communications with anyone here on the island."

"Haven't we shared all of those records already?"

"Maybe so," Sandor replied with a casual shrug. "I was sent to have another look."

Vauchon said, "We don't need to waste your time on this, Philippe. Just point us in the right direction."

"No, no, that's quite all right. Come with me."

Whatever suspicions the technician may have had, he was fully cooperative in sitting with Sandor and Vauchon at one of the computer stations and bringing up what seemed an almost endless list of incoming and outgoing phone calls for the week in question. Sandor asked whether the content of any of the calls might have survived, already knowing the answer was no. He knew the country code for Venezuela, but these records covered all of the calls into and out of St. Barths and, as they scrolled through thousands of contact numbers, he realized he would be here for days if he was going to allow this man to persist in displaying a random search. He could not hide his frustration.

"Is there any way to refine this search?"

"Of course. We can pull out different area codes, exchanges, any of that. But it's impossible to know what calls were made from whose phone unless we have the number," Philippe explained. "We've already been through this. We don't know if they were disposable cell phones, which they probably were, and we have no other parameter for filtering."

"I see."

"I am certain that your government already has several copies of this entire printout," he restated with some impatience.

Sandor reached into his pocket and pulled out a small paper containing a number. "This was the phone number of the cell used by the terrorist that was captured in Pointe Milou." He handed it to Philippe. "Can you try this?"

Sandor watched carefully to see how the technician targeted his search. The screen quickly changed, now displaying only a dozen outgoing calls. Two of the receiving numbers contained the country code for Venezuela.

"Can we get a printout of that activity?"

Philippe hesitated, then agreed. He hit the Print Screen command and a laser printer at the end of the table came to life. "Anything else?"

Sandor glanced at Vauchon, who said, "Philippe, can I speak with you privately for a moment?"

Before the technician could respond, Sandor offered them both a polite smile. "I'll be fine," he assured them.

As Vauchon led a reluctant Philippe to the far end of the room, Sandor went to work at the keyboard. Tracing the steps he had just seen, he revised the filter to ask the computer only for phone calls made to and from numbers bearing the country code for Venezuela during the week already entered in the field requiring a time frame. Almost instantly the screen provided a record of more than thirty calls. Sandor punched in the command to print the list, then returned the filter to its previous field.

Vauchon, meanwhile, was complaining to Philippe about how weary he had become entertaining these interminable requests for information and cooperation, all the while doing his best to position himself so that the technician had to stand with his back to Sandor. When Vauchon saw his friend reach out and pull the newly printed sheet from the machine, he brought his griping to an abrupt end. "Ah well, let's see if we can finish this, eh?"

Sandor stood as the two men approached. He had already shoved the second sheet in his pocket and held up the first printout for them to see. "Well, gentlemen, perhaps this will prove helpful. As you say, we already have the entire list of all calls made during that period, so my work here is done." He offered his thanks to both of them, then allowed Vauchon to lead him out.

———————

Back in the car, Sandor showed Vauchon the information he had taken.

"Is that what you need?"

"I hope so. Nice work in there, by the way. DGSE might have the right idea, getting you into the espionage racket."

"I didn't say they had."

"Come on, Henri."

Vauchon shook his head. "I don't think I'm cut out for your business. My nerves couldn't take it."

"You get used to it." Sandor paused. "By the way, I didn't like your friend Philippe."

"He's a bit of a tightass."

"Maybe. Could have been a little more helpful, since he was one of the crew you saved back there at the fort, am I right?"

"You are."

"Therefore I don't like him *and* I don't trust him."

Vauchon nodded. "All right. I will follow up for you."

"Thanks. So tell me, what happened to that cute girl who worked at the villa up on Pointe Milou?"

"Stefanie?"

"That's the one."

"The one you spent the night with at Guanahani?"

"How indiscreet of you to mention that. What kind of a Frenchman are you?"

Vauchon laughed. "She's been seeing one of my soldiers. Met him when we were finishing up our investigation."

"Pity," Sandor said.

Vauchon laughed. "Did you think you ruined her for all other men?"

Sandor stared out the passenger window. "It was a thought," he said. "Come on, let's have a drink, then I'll buy you that dinner."

CHAPTER THREE

HATO AIRPORT, CURAÇAO

THE UNITED STATES military has maintained a small air base west of the Curaçao airport since World War II. It began as a staging area for antisubmarine patrols and has gone through various incarnations over the years. Today it is used by the Joint Special Operations Command to support AWAC flights, as well as Colombia's anti-narcotics initiative and counter-FARC operations. There were three reasons why Sandor chose this airstrip as the base for his unauthorized mission.

First was the proximity to the coast of Venezuela. Second, an old friend was stationed there as commanding officer. Third, when he told Byrnes that Curaçao was the spot he had chosen for some R&R, it at least provided a credible story.

After spending the night on St. Barths, Sandor grabbed the early flight to St. Maarten and made the connection to Curaçao. He didn't bother to check into a hotel, instead taking a taxi directly to the air base. At the gate he asked for the man in charge.

When the CO got the call that Sandor was at the perimeter checkpoint, he jumped into his Jeep and drove out to meet his former platoon mate.

"Sandor, you old pretender." Captain Doug Carlton was a tall, muscular black man, with a personality to match his size, a deep voice, and a warm Georgia accent. He turned to the sentry. "Let this boy through," he ordered.

"Commanding Officer, pretty impressive," Sandor said as he

climbed into the passenger seat of the jeep. "What's the real deal with getting yourself stationed down here? You working on your tan?"

Carlton laughed. "Glad to see nothing's changed. You're still not funny."

During the short ride back to Carlton's office they caught up on a lot of names from the past, at the end of which Sandor said, "Bergenn's on his way here."

"I know, heard from him yesterday. When does he blow in?"

"Couple of hours. With Craig Raabe. Don't think you've met him."

Carlton shook his head. "Doesn't ring a bell." He pulled to a stop outside the squat rectangular building that served as headquarters for this small outpost. Before he climbed out he said, "I heard about what happened in Louisiana. That was nice work, guy."

Sandor shook his head. "Lost some good people there."

"Always the price we pay," Carlton said. "Always."

Inside the air-conditioned office Carlton handed Sandor a Coke. They sat facing each other across the captain's steel desk.

"So," Carlton said, "I've got these crates with your name on them inside the hangar, left it alone just like Bergenn asked, but I have several questions to go along with the delivery. The first, obviously, is what devilish sort of business brings you to my part of the world?"

"You want this on or off the record?"

Carlton gave him a hard, military stare, then said, "I think we've got enough history that I should get it both ways."

"Fair enough. Officially I'm taking some personal time. Unofficially, I'm going to track down the sonuvabitch responsible for all those deaths we just talked about."

"I see."

"Those crates contain the glider you're going to tow for me."

Carlton laughed. "We gathered that much, Jordan. You don't really think we stand out in the sun all day here, do you?"

Sandor smiled. "I'm going to pilot the thing into the jungle in western Venezuela. From there I'm going to hunt the guy down."

"And you expect me to have my men help assemble that paper airplane and then use one of my aircraft to tow it?"

"I do. And I expect to leave tonight."

"Which means, all things considered, you're as crazy as ever." Carlton nodded slowly. "Can't wait to hear what Bergenn has to say."

The captain did not have to wait long. Bergenn and Raabe arrived at the base a couple of hours later. After greetings and introductions were concluded Sandor got down to business.

"Those phone numbers Vauchon and I faxed you last night, were they any help?"

"They certainly were," Bergenn told him. "We triangulated the various coordinates and pinpointed Adina's location. It confirmed the intel we had."

"Hope he's home when you come calling," Raabe said.

"Where else would that weasel be hiding?"

"Caracas?"

"No way," Sandor disagreed. "He's still got to be lying low. Chavez is not going to risk having Adina seen anywhere near him. Not now, not so soon after the attacks. Chavez talks a big game, but he's as yellow as Adina. He's never going to give us an excuse to take his head off."

"Funny," Bergenn said, "I thought he already had."

"I agree," Carlton chimed in. "The way that bastard talks about our country, I reckon we've got reason enough already. I just wish someone'd give the order. Remember, I'm right here, staring across the water at that ugly sumbitch every day."

Sandor smiled. "You see why I love this guy, Craig?"

"But remember," Bergenn interrupted, "Craig may be right. Adina might not even be there; that's the one thing we cannot confirm."

"So I'll sit on his porch and wait for him to get home."

"Jim," Carlton interrupted again, "you've always had more sense than he does. You think this can work?"

Bergenn took a moment before answering. "I'd rather all three of us were going, but Jordan is right. This is a one-man job. All we can do is get him in there, then make sure we get him out when he's done." He stopped again. "If anyone can pull this off, Sandor's the guy."

———————

Carlton assigned his two mechanics to the detail, not telling them the why or wherefore, only that they were to assist in the assembly of a Schleicher ASG 29 glider.

While the plane was being put together under Raabe's watchful eye, Bergenn and Sandor spent time in Carlton's office going over the maps of the jungle area just south of the location where Adina was believed to be headquartered.

"So the bottom line is, once I set this baby down in the clearing, I'll be within three miles of the target."

"Exactly."

Carlton, who had been listening patiently, leaned forward. "I haven't heard a whole lot about how the hell you're getting out of there."

Sandor looked up from the maps. "We have several different scenarios. A lot depends on what happens when I get in."

"You've already told me this action has no official sanction," Carlton said. "If you get into a tussle, you understand I can't be sending a chopper into Venezuela to pull your butt out. My hands'll be tied."

"You're doing enough," Sandor assured him. "Jim and Craig should be able to pick me up if I get myself somewhere here, along the shore." He pointed at the map. "That won't start a war, right?"

Carlton shook his head. "Knowing you, I wouldn't be too sure."

CHAPTER FOUR

HATO AIRPORT, CURAÇAO

IT WAS NEARLY midnight when the four men conducted their final inspection of the sleek black glider inside the base hangar. They checked the newly assembled joints to see they were tight. Raabe went over the navigation options with Sandor. For the third time they looked to see that the towrope that would link the unpowered craft to the military transport was properly secured.

Constructed of carbon, aramid, and polyethylene fiber with reinforced plastic, the ASG 29 was an odd-looking craft with definite advantages for the intended purpose. The tiny cockpit had a bubble-shaped appearance, giving it enhanced visibility that would be crucial to the night landing. It had a glide ratio of more than 50:1, which would allow a gentle descent, but the optional wing-mounted air brakes—affectionately dubbed "terminal velocity"—could also bring her down almost as fast as a spin dive.

"Nice," Sandor said. "You're sure you didn't leave any bolts sitting in the bottom of the crates?"

Raabe's reply was a tired frown.

"You know what I'm talking about. Christmas morning, when you put together the train set and you forget one of the screws for the bridge. An hour later the whole thing is set up and the locomotive comes barreling down the tracks, then *boom,* the whole trestle falls apart. Hate to have that happen two thousand feet in the air."

"Try not to hit any trestles then," Raabe suggested.

"Ah. Good plan."

Carlton was staring at them. "You're out of your mind, you know that?"

Sandor nodded. "It's been said."

"I'm not kidding. You know the odds of making a safe landing in the dark? In the jungle?"

"Let me guess."

"Don't bother."

"You have any idea what the odds are of my getting there in daylight without someone spotting me?"

"Zero," Jim Bergenn said.

"Exactly," Sandor agreed. "So this is my best shot."

"What about a private chopper?"

"We've already been through that. Too easy to spot and too noisy. If they don't shoot it down when we enter their airspace, they'll spot us on the radar and launch a search-and-destroy operation before I even get close to their base. The glider is my best chance of getting in there undetected."

"He's right," Bergenn admitted.

For a few moments no one spoke. Then Raabe said, "Come here, let's go over the controls again."

CHAPTER FIVE

HATO AIRPORT, CURAÇAO

Bᴇʀɢᴇɴɴ ʜᴀᴅ ᴀ look at his watch. "Time to do this."

Sandor strolled to the side of the tarmac, knelt down, and opened his backpack to check the contents one more time. He had a satellite phone with a GPS function; two compasses, one traditional and one digital; a Smith & Wesson .45 1911 automatic with two extra magazines; a MAC 10 with four extra clips; and a US M24 Woodland portable sniper rifle with silencer and scope.

Carlton watched as Sandor went through each item. "You going in there to start World War III?"

"We'll see," Sandor replied. Then he held up a pair of bathing trunks, a T-shirt, and black flip-flops. "I guess I'm ready for anything," he said.

"Some disguise."

Sandor smiled. "You'd be surprised. Now where are the night goggles?"

"In the cockpit with your helmet," Bergenn told him. "Want to check them out again?"

Sandor shook his head. "No," he said, "I'm good to go."

———

Doug Carlton was going to pull the ASG 29 with a C-47. It was a military variation of the DC-3, one of the most reliable warhorses in air travel, but not an obvious choice for this purpose.

"Not exactly the ideal way to tow a glider," he admitted as they prepared.

Sandor smiled. "Beggars can't be choosers, right?"

"You just hang on," Raabe said as the three men watched Sandor climb into the glider.

"Roger that," Sandor replied.

Carlton was going to pilot the twin-engine transport himself, directing his second in command to make a log entry listing the flight as a "nighttime takeoff and landing exercise, IFR." There was to be no mention of the black glider he was towing or the two passengers he was carrying for the short trip.

It was after midnight, but Carlton ordered that the runway lights remained shut down until after takeoff, then turned on later for his return. Inside the C-47 he went through the preflight checklist with Raabe, who had settled comfortably in the copilot seat, prepared to assist. Bergenn was buckled in the seat behind them.

Once Carlton confirmed that all systems were operational, he revved the two engines, radioed his second that they were ready to go, then flashed a thumbs-up.

Less than an hour later Sandor's glider had been released over the Lago de Maracaibo, where he piloted it inland, south of Barranquitas, and crash-landed at the end of the clearing.

CHAPTER SIX

SOUTHWEST OF BARRANQUITAS IN THE JUNGLES OF VENEZUELA

AFTER THE CRASH, Sandor did his best to rouse himself. The reinforced harness had kept him in place. Now his training instinctively led him through an ingrained sequence of personal checkpoints.

First he took a few deep breaths to ensure he had not cracked any ribs or suffered chest injuries. Next he confirmed that his vision was clear, pulling off his goggles and moving his head slowly side to side to loosen his neck muscles. Then he moved his fingers and toes, finally uncoupling the seat belt so he could confirm his other extremities were intact.

He looked at his watch. It had only been a few minutes since he last checked the time, before he spotted the clearing and hit the ground.

It was just before 2:00 A.M.

Sandor climbed out of the seat and stood beside what was left of the mangled cockpit. His eyes had adjusted to the unremitting darkness, and he had a look around. He could make out the pieces of the demolished glider that were scattered across the entire field. Come sunrise the evidence of the crash would be evident from the ground, and possibly the sky, reminding him again that time was short. Reaching behind his seat he lifted the knapsack. He grabbed the night-vision goggles and digital compass and tossed both into the pack, then hurried off into the trees, just in case anyone had been near enough to see or hear the crash and might be coming by to have a look.

Safely in the thick of the jungle, he sat against the wide trunk of a large, gnarly kapok, pulled out his canteen, had a drink of water, then took out two 800 mg ibuprofen gelcaps and washed those down with a second gulp. The real pain he would feel was a couple of hours away and he wanted to head it off if he could. He placed the manual compass in his lap and had another quick look at his watch. He figured he had less than four hours before sunrise. In that time he would have to make his way through almost three miles of dense jungle, find Adina, send him to hell, and then make his escape.

Sandor nodded to himself. He was thinking clearly and ready to get started.

He removed his earpiece and zipped it into a side pocket of his vest. He was going to maintain total radio silence until the mission was complete—he didn't want to risk the chance of anyone intercepting even a one-word message letting them know he had touched down.

His Mark II combat knife, popularly known as the Ka-Bar, was in place on his right thigh. He reached into the knapsack for the S&W .45 1911 automatic in its holster and strapped it on. He placed the two extra magazines in another compartment of his vest.

He stood and hoisted the pack onto his back. When he put on the PNVGs the entire jungle became illuminated, as if a hazy, green-tinged light had been turned on. Then, compass in hand, he set off in a northeasterly direction.

The information developed by Jim Bergenn indicated that Adina's base of operation was southwest of Barranquitas. It was a typical choice of hiding place for a man like Rafael Cabello.

Barranquitas was a village of barely ten thousand people, but in medical circles it was famous for all the wrong reasons. Barranquitas has the highest per capita concentration of Huntington's disease in the entire world, with more than half the population testing positive for the fatal gene. Studies have been made, scientific expeditions undertaken, and the inevitable result, in the end, is that the small town has gained a reputation akin to a leper colony. Although there is no evidence that the misfortune of these inhabitants is in any way contagious to outsiders, people from surrounding areas simply stay away.

A perfect place for Adina to set up shop, seeking cover behind the misery of others.

Sandor moved as quickly as he could through the dense vegetation, but progress was slow. The ground was uneven and covered with a network of large twisted roots. The trees themselves were not a problem but the thick vines were. He would frequently have to reverse course and find alternate routes around these hanging obstacles.

The enhanced vision afforded by his goggles was invaluable as he avoided ditches and small ravines he might otherwise have plunged into, as well as fallen branches and dead roots he would have tripped over. It also helped him steer clear of the occasional curious snake that warily eyed this nocturnal interloper marching purposefully through its domain.

The backpack was heavy and his protective clothing too thick for the tropical humidity; although the night air was cool, he felt the clammy perspiration cover his skin beneath the microfiber shell he wore. He frequently wiped his face with the back of his gloved hand.

As he pressed on, Sandor continually checked his compass—he knew how easy it was to move off course on this sort of trek, and that would cost him precious time. After more than an hour of pushing himself through nature's unrelenting obstacle course, he saw a glimmer of light several hundred yards ahead.

He stopped at the edge of a small clearing, placed his pack on the ground, and sat. He drank some water, then reviewed his coordinates on the digital readout of the electronic compass.

This was it.

The satellite photos they received did not reveal much about the layout of the compound. Under the cover of so much large vegetation there was almost nothing visible from above. The entire area was a thicket of tropical trees with enormous trunks and wide, spreading canopies that blocked out aerial surveillance. This was thought to be Adina's retreat, a home away from the mainstream of the Venezuelan capital. However, the satellite heat sensors revealed a larger amount of activity than Sandor and his team had anticipated—perhaps this was also a base where Adina would plan and even equip his terrorist plots.

He checked his watch. It was just past 3:00 A.M.

Sandor opened the backpack and readied himself for the assault. He took his time assembling the US M24 Woodland portable sniper rifle, silencer and scope. Then he loaded the MAC-10, pocketed some extra clips and stood up. With the rifle strapped across his back, he left the backpack behind the tree, picked up the submachine gun, and moved out.

CHAPTER SEVEN

ADINA'S COMPOUND, SOUTH OF BARRANQUITAS

However carefully Adina laid out his secret home in the jungle, Sandor was certain it would also be carefully guarded, even in the dead of night. There might even be trip wires or land mines outside the perimeter, so his progress became even slower. He circled back using the trees for cover, moving with extreme caution until he saw another clearing just ahead.

He stopped and took out his night vision binoculars, removed the PNVGs, and crawled toward a wide jungle cedar to have a look around.

He saw that the light he had been following was one of four low-intensity halogen floods that sat atop metal posts at the corners of a large rectangle. There were no fences, which confirmed his suspicion there might be traps or some sort of laser sensors in place. The flood-lights were stationary, each directed outside and down, leaving the interior space almost completely in the dark. He could make out a few small buildings within the rectangle, each situated alongside a stand of the large trees that had blocked a clear satellite view. Most important, for the moment, he spotted a sentry off to his left.

The guard was leaning against one of the tall metal stanchions smoking a cigarette. He had an assault rifle slung across his chest and wore the look of a man doing a thankless job in the middle of the jungle in the middle of the night.

The trees would not provide much cover if Sandor chose to come at the man from here, leaving him exposed for too long when he emerged into the clearing. Charging from this angle would force him into the open for more than forty yards.

He could take the man out with a silenced sniper shot, but he preferred to get some answers first.

He had another look through the binoculars to see if other sentries were posted, but the trees and buildings made it impossible for him to see the other end of the compound. He decided he would circle all the way around to his left and then come at the guard from behind.

Just as Sandor prepared to move out, the sentry straightened up, threw down his cigarette, and began to walk toward Sandor's right. It appeared to be part of the man's patrol, a simple stroll along the edge of this large complex. Sandor placed the binoculars on the ground, crouched behind the large cedar, and waited. The guard moved slowly, passing across Sandor's field of vision toward the other light post off to the right.

As soon as the man's back was visible, Sandor did not hesitate. Leaving his rifle and submachine gun behind the tree he came out fast and low, his knife drawn.

By the time the sentry heard the sound behind him it was too late. Sandor hit him with the full force of his weight, driving the guard facedown into the soft earth with a thud, the sharp blade of the Ka-Bar already at his throat. With his left hand Sandor yanked the man's head back by his hair.

"Habla inglés?"

The sentry barely managed to say "No," the pressure of the knife already drawing a trickle of blood that ran down his neck.

"Bueno," Sandor said, then spoke to him in Spanish. "How many guards?"

The man tried to shake his head, but Sandor pulled tighter on his hair.

"You screw with me and I'll kill you right here. How many guards on patrol?"

"Two."

"You mean you and two more, or you and one more?"

"One more," the man told him.

"Where is he?"

"Other side."

"Any laser detectors?"

The guard did not respond.

"You understand laser?"

"I understand. No, no laser."

"Anything else, any alarms?"

"No, not here," the man said, then began to struggle against Sandor's hold.

"I told you, you move and I'll kill you." The guard stopped moving.

"Where are the alarms?"

"Some buildings."

"Which buildings?"

"Main house. The guardhouse above the laboratory," he said.

Sandor did not like surprises, so he was not about to admit he knew nothing about a laboratory. "Where's Adina?" he demanded.

The man's body tensed. "I don't understand."

"Hell you don't. Tell me which building? Where do I find Adina?"

The man suddenly began speaking very quickly, something about narcotics Sandor could not make out.

"Speak more slowly."

He did, saying something about cocaine, accusing Sandor of coming here to steal drugs. As the man rattled on he tried to move his left hand, which was pinned underneath him, reaching for something along his side. He made a sudden, desperate effort to break free but the pressure of Sandor's hold was too strong, the knife too tight to his throat. As the man tried to spin to his side, the razor-sharp blade sliced through his windpipe and carotid artery. Blood began pumping out of his neck as he gave up grasping for his gun, now clutching at his throat. He died facedown in the dirt without uttering another word.

"Damn," Sandor said through gritted teeth as he rolled off the man's back and raised himself to a sitting position. He looked around, but everything was quiet. He cleaned his knife on the guard's pants, replaced it in its sheath, then stood and, taking the dead man by his ankles, dragged him into the jungle.

Sandor knew it was not going to be long before the guard's disappearance would be discovered. He took the man's walkie-talkie, realizing there were probably regular check-in times.

"Damn," he said again.

His timeline had just been accelerated.

CHAPTER EIGHT

ADINA'S COMPOUND, SOUTH OF BARRANQUITAS

There was no way of knowing how much of what the sentry had said was true, but it was Sandor's experience that intel obtained from a man with a knife to his throat tends to be fairly reliable. Once he covered the body with some dirt and leaves, he snatched up his weapons and made tracks through the jungle again, this time circling the complex as quickly as he could to find the second guard. He discovered him on the other side of the compound, sitting against a tree. His automatic rifle was nestled in his lap and he appeared to be asleep.

Sandor moved quietly, not rousing the man until he was close enough to level the silenced barrel of his .45 at the sentry's ear and cock the hammer. The guard started, making a reflexive attempt to get to his feet, but Sandor clamped a strong left hand on the man's shoulder and whispered in Spanish, "Sit still or you're dead."

The guard eased himself back down. His hands remained in front of him as he glanced at his AK-47.

"Uh, uh, uh," Sandor warned, then grabbed the barrel of the rifle and tossed it behind him.

The man had a furtive look to his left and right.

"If you're expecting help you can forget it," Sandor said.

"Manuel?"

"He wanted to be a hero. Bad choice. Unless you want to end up like he did you'll answer my questions."

"You're going to kill me too."

"Not necessarily."

Unlike his deceased counterpart, this man appeared to have none of the hero in him. "What do you want to know?"

"Tell me about the laboratory."

The guard described an underground facility in the middle of the complex. Sandor's Spanish was good enough to catch the basic points. The main product was refined cocaine, but other substances were also being manufactured down there.

"Heroin?"

"No," he said.

"What then?"

"I don't know," the guard told him. "I only know it is very dangerous."

"Explosives?"

The man responded with a blank look.

"What do they do with the coke?"

The man responded with a confused look, as if the answer was obvious. "They ship it out of here."

"I understand that. To where?"

"Mexico, I think. Mostly to Mexico."

"Mexico's a big country pal."

"I don't know where in Mexico."

"All right. Anyplace else?" The guard began to give an instinctive shake of his head, but Sandor pressed the tip of the silencer into his ear. "Don't move, just talk."

"Not sure," the guard said. "There are men from somewhere in the Middle East; they come and go here."

"Where in the Middle East?"

"I think Egypt."

"Egypt?"

"Yes."

"And where's my friend Adina tonight?"

"The main house. To the right there, in the middle of those trees."

"Guards on duty there?"

"Always."

"Of course. What about the lab? Sentries posted there, too?"

"Yes."

"You have regular times that you have to call on your radio?"

"No. Only if there's trouble."

"That the truth?"

"Yes. We also have a button to push in an emergency." He began to point to the walkie-talkie strapped to his side, but Sandor stopped him.

"I get the idea. So, these drug shipments, how big and how often?"

"Every few weeks. Big." He did his best to describe the size of the packages that were placed on trucks, then taken west toward the shore.

"Okay. How many entrances to the lab?"

"Only one." He then explained the location of a small guardhouse that stood at the doorway down to the facility. "But you can't take any of the coke, man. No way to get out of here alive."

"We'll see," Sandor said, "but I must say, you've been very helpful." Then he abruptly raised the S&W and brought the butt of the handle crashing down across the man's temple. As the guard slumped to the side Sandor hit him again. He did not want him regaining consciousness anytime soon.

He had a look at his watch. It was nearly 3:45 A.M.

He decided to put his plans for Adina on hold for the moment and have a look at the laboratory.

CHAPTER NINE

ADINA'S COMPOUND, SOUTH OF BARRANQUITAS

SINCE THE LIGHTS on the four large posts at the corners of the compound were intended to illuminate the outside perimeter, the interior area was fairly dark at this hour. Now that Sandor had taken out the two guards, he encountered no resistance as he moved toward the center of this group of buildings. The entrance to the lab was just as the sentry had described, a small rectangular cement structure that served as the portal for the underground facility. The lab itself had a concrete roof at ground level.

Sandor crouched behind a large banyan tree not twenty yards from the guardhouse, his night vision binoculars in hand. He could see that it had windows on all four sides, and from the look of them it was possible they were constructed of bulletproof glass. He could also see the two men on duty inside, so any attempt to enter through this main access point was going to be a problem.

Beyond the laboratory entrance he spotted what he was looking for—the domed tops of the ventilation outlets that sat just above the laboratory's ground-level roof. Sandor stayed low, running in a wide arc to his left until he reached the pipe that was farthest from the sentries.

His watch told him it was nearly 4:00 A.M.

Sandor worked quickly and quietly, removing the circular cap from the ventilation shaft and peering down into the wide metal cylinder. There was a lateral shaft of light at the bottom, which looked to be about eight feet below ground level. The duct was approximately three feet in diameter and it appeared that it would be easy enough for him to shimmy down.

"Damn," he whispered aloud.

Sandor was a man without fear. All the same, tight spaces made him distinctly uncomfortable and, if he was not exactly claustrophobic, he certainly did not relish the idea of being wedged inside a large metal tube. All the same, the question was not whether he was going in; the question was, what would he find when he got down there?

He stood, arranged the US M24 sniper rifle across his back, and stared again into the hole. Since this appeared to be the duct farthest from the guarded entrance, it was logical to think that it would be connected to the remotest part of the lab. At this hour it was also hopefully the area most likely to be unattended.

He checked his watch. It was after 4:00 A.M. Whichever scenario he chose, time was running out. He had to act.

He clutched the sides of the duct and lowered himself into the shaft feet first. The fit was tighter than he anticipated. Bracing himself with his feet and hands he moved slowly, straining not to slip against the smooth metal surface while struggling to remain quiet as he made his descent. As he neared the bottom he reached out with his right foot and found the base of the dirt well, then allowed his weight to carry him all the way down.

Light was coming through a mesh grill to his right, around waist level, but he was jammed into the cylinder without much room to maneuver. Twisting himself around, he managed a contorted crouch, getting low enough to have a look through the vent.

It revealed a well-lit storage room that appeared unoccupied, at least for the moment.

The place had the appearance of having been hastily assembled without any care for appearance. If it was a lab it was certainly not designed for sterility. He waited to see if anyone might enter through the open doorway on the far side of the room, but from his vantage point saw no movement. The only noise he heard came from a large fan that stood on the floor in a far corner of the room that was circulating the air in his direction.

After a long minute of waiting and watching he began to work at the grill, which proved easy to force out of its frame with barely a sound. Like the cover to the air duct above, things here were obviously not constructed for the long-term.

Sandor turned the grill sideways and pulled it toward him, placing it on the ground beside his feet. Then, removing his .45 from its holster, he climbed through the opening and lowered himself to the dirt floor, glad to be out of the Iron Maiden the vent shaft had become.

———————

Once he hit the ground Sandor hurried silently across the room, stopping with his back to the wall, just to the right of the door opening. He leaned the M24 against the wall, then waited and listened. But he heard nothing above the whirring sound of the fan. He checked out the ceiling of the small room. There did not seem to be any surveillance cameras mounted in the corners. Beside him were several stacks of cloth-wrapped packages, each about two feet wide and deep, and a foot high. Pulling out his knife, he made a small incision in one of them.

A stream of white powder poured out.

He edged toward the open doorway and had a quick look into the next room. It was much larger, with two stainless steel tables running parallel along almost the length of the space. There were several industrial-looking stools, an array of glass tubing, portable burners, and numerous metal receptacles.

A bare-bones operation for refining cocaine.

Sandor could also see two doors, one on the far end that was wide open and the other, to the left, that appeared to be constructed of metal and more substantial than the other temporary installations he had seen up to now. It was closed. Sandor did not spot any security cameras in this room either, which surprised him. Adina was not the trusting type and leaving a crew of his countrymen in the midst of huge quantities of cocaine was not his style. There had to be some other means of monitoring activities within the facility.

Then Sandor spotted a man at the long table to the right. He had apparently been bending over and now sat up, engrossed in some sort of paperwork. Sandor strode into the room as if he belonged there.

By the time the man looked up Sandor was already beside him, the silencer attached to his .45 pressed hard into the man's ribs.

"You speak English?"

"A little," the man said, his startled expression quickly turning from surprise to fear.

"Fine. Then get up right now and come with me to that storage room in the back."

"I'm just a technician," the man protested, as if that might somehow excuse him from whatever this stranger had in mind.

Sandor responded by giving his pistol another shove.

"All right, I understand," the man said, then rose from the stool and walked ahead of Sandor into the back room.

He was shorter than Sandor, of slender build, with sad, tired eyes and a bookish aspect. He certainly looked like a lab technician. As soon as they were inside the storage area he said, "Please don't kill me. Take as much as you want. Take it all."

"And I suppose the guards upstairs are just going to let me walk out of here, that the idea?"

The technician did his best to conjure up a look of abject ignorance, as if the thought of Sandor being apprehended had never crossed his mind. "I have no argument with you."

"Sure pal, you're on my side all the way."

For the first time, the man had a good look into Sandor's dark, intense eyes. "Please don't kill me," he pleaded again.

"I have no interest in killing you," Sandor said. "What's your name?"

"Carlos."

"Well, Carlos, I just want some information about what's going on down here."

With this, the man began jabbering away in a mix of English and Spanish until Sandor raised the barrel of his .45 to eye level. That ended the chatter.

Sandor sighed. "If you knock off the bullshit you'll have a reasonably good chance of living through the night, okay?"

Carlos nodded slowly as he stared at the pistol.

"All you need to do is answer some questions. But you've got to answer them honestly. You understand?"

"Yes."

"Good. So for starters, tell me about the guards." When the man started to speak Sandor held up his hand. "Remember, honesty is the best policy."

Carlos responded with another slow nod.

"There are armed guards, yes?"

"Yes. There are armed guards all around us."

"They're posted outside the property and upstairs?"

"Yes."

"How many?"

"At this time of night, two men outside, two men at the entrance to the lab."

"What about Adina's house?"

"Always at least two men on duty."

"Uh huh. But no security inside this lab? No video? Nothing?"

He shook his head. "No need. They check us when we leave our shift. They also come in and make inspections from time to time. If we ever get caught using or stealing they'll kill us."

"A serious deterrent."

"Deterrent?"

"Disuasivo."

"Ah, yes."

"You're alone here tonight?"

"Another man is coming on soon."

"How soon?"

"Less than an hour."

"So what are you doing here by yourself in the middle of the night?"

"I was making arrangements for the new shipment."

Sandor gestured toward the piles of cloth-wrapped packages. "These being moved out soon?"

Carlos nodded. "This morning."

"To Mexico?"

"Yes."

"How do they ship the stuff?"

"Coffee. Inside large sacks of coffee."

"Throws off the drug-sniffing dogs."

"Yes," Carlos agreed. "Difficult to detect and easy to transport."

"Too much coffee is shipped around the world to check every sack."

The Venezuelan nodded again. *"Exactamente."*

"Okay, so other than this little cocaine refinery, what else is being manufactured down here?"

The man's expression changed from fear to sheer terror.

"Come on, Carlos," Sandor prodded him.

"Adina will kill me if I say anything."

"I'll kill you if you don't." For emphasis he waved the barrel of the Smith & Wesson a little closer to the man's face.

The technician's shoulders slumped. He said, "Shooting me will be better than what Adina will have them do."

Sandor shook his head. "You answer the rest of my questions and I'll make it look like I came to steal cocaine. The guard I left outside already believes that. Just stay with the story and you'll be all right."

"No. When they capture you they will make you talk."

"I won't be captured, trust me."

Carlos gave his head a vigorous shake. "You are wrong. They already know you're here."

"How would they know that?"

"You breached the perimeter, which means you had to come through the alarm system."

Sandor gritted his teeth. "What alarm system?" he demanded.

CHAPTER TEN

INSIDE ADINA'S COMPOUND, SOUTH OF BARRANQUITAS

CARLOS DESCRIBED THE laser security system that ringed the perimeter of the property.

"The alarm is silent," he added. "It registers in the guardhouse above us."

"Damn," Sandor said.

The CIA has a device known by various nicknames, but is technically referred to as a specialized electronic pack. About half the size of a pack of cigarettes, it serves various functions including the decoding of keypad locks, reading safe combinations, and detecting laser alarm systems. Unfortunately, Sandor could not risk taking one from the Farm before leaving D.C. Each of them has to be signed for and he feared Byrnes would find out.

"They must be out there looking for you now," Carlos was saying. "Eventually they will come here and we will both be dead."

"We'll see about that," Sandor replied. Then he had the technician tell him everything he knew about the manpower on hand, the vehicles on the premises, and the road out of there.

"Now you must go," the man urged him when he answered all of Sandor's questions. He had a quick look at the hole in the wall where the ventilation grill had been "Get out however you came in. I will say nothing."

"First I want to know what else is being cooked up in this place."

The man stared at him without speaking.

"Whatever it is," Sandor went on, "it's going on behind that closed door in the other room."

"Yes. But I am not sure what they are doing in there."

"You're a rotten liar, Carlos, not to mention that you must be a senior man here to be alone in the lab in the middle of the night." Sandor lowered the gun so it was trained on the man's left kneecap. "I said I had no intention of killing you, but I need some answers and I need them now."

Carlos gazed down at the lengthened barrel of the automatic, then looked up again. "Anthrax," he said.

"Anthrax?"

He nodded. "It's a secure area. Sterile. I don't even have access without a guard present."

Sandor thought it over for a moment. "What are they doing with anthrax?"

"Nothing yet."

"They have plans to ship it somewhere?"

"I am not involved in that part of these operations. I only oversee the extraction and refinement of the coca."

"You said you're involved in organizing shipments."

"Yes, but only from here to the shore," he replied, nodding toward the bags of cocaine.

Sandor knew the man was lying again, but time was running short. "Tell me about the men from Egypt. Then tell me how the hell people get out of here."

The two men in the guardhouse above the laboratory received the electronic alert that someone breached the perimeter. They expected one of the sentries to report in but too much time had passed as they stared into the darkness, waiting.

"They would never take this long without checking in. Should we report this to Alejandro?" the junior man asked.

"If it turns out to be nothing one of them is going to be in big trouble."

"Should I go outside and have a look?"

"I'll go," the senior guard said. "Give me five minutes, that's all. If I'm not back in five call the main house."

Francisco took his AK-47 and headed to the south end of the compound in search of Manuel. He held the weapon at the ready in case his concerns were justified, but he saw no one else in the darkness.

When he reached the end of the complex he called out Manuel's name but received no reply.

Warily he stepped into the dimly lighted area beneath the low-register halogens. He called out "Manuel," again.

Nothing.

Hurrying back into the darkness he reached for his walkie-talkie.

The junior man in the guardhouse picked up immediately.

"Manuel is not here. I'm heading for the other end of the property. Stay alert."

————

As Carlos explained the routes used to transport the narcotics, Sandor grabbed sacks of the processed cocaine and tossed them into the open vent, where they fell to the ground at the bottom of the shaft. He toppled one of the tall stacks of bags and used his Ka-Bar to rip open a couple of the fallen packages, letting the powder spill onto the floor. Then he returned his attention to the technician.

"I don't care what you say to them when they come for you," he told him, "but your best bet of living through this thing is to tell them we never spoke."

The technician looked at Sandor as if he were insane.

"Listen to me. When I climb back up there I'll replace the grill. You tell them you heard something in here, you came in and tried to stop me and I hit you."

"But . . ."

Carlos never got to utter another word. Sandor lashed out with his pistol and smacked him across the side of the head, knocking him to his knees. A second blow, to the back of his neck, rendered him senseless as he collapsed to the ground.

Sandor holstered the S&W, shouldered his M24 rifle and the

MAC 10, then, using the pile of cloth-encased narcotics as a plat-form, scampered up and into the air duct. Remaining in an awkward crouch he did his best to replace the mesh grill, figuring anything that might buy him a little time would be useful. He stood and, using his feet, did his best to cover the bags of coke he had dumped into the bottom of the shaft with dirt. He wanted to make it appear that some of the drugs had been taken.

Then he began the difficult process of hoisting himself up against the surface of the slick metal cylinder.

There was nothing to grab hold of, but his gloves and boots pro-vided enough surface tension to help him claw his way up. Bracing his back against the shaft he inched his way upward in a painfully slow exercise of arm and leg strength. After a couple of minutes he could finally reach out and hold the sharp edges of the duct. Pulling himself up, he stopped just as he was able to see above the level of the shaft.

It was difficult to make out anything in the darkness, and he could not reach the PNVGs in his pack, but he was certain there was a man running in the distance. Thankfully, he appeared to be rushing away rather than toward Sandor's position.

Heaving himself over the edge, Sandor rolled onto the ground and came to a stop in a kneeling position, his pistol again in hand.

It was dark and still all around him.

He had a look at his watch. It was nearly 5:00 A.M. Sunrise was not far off.

CHAPTER ELEVEN

INSIDE ADINA'S COMPOUND, SOUTH OF BARRANQUITAS

Francisco reached the far end of the compound. Once again he found nothing and no one on the perimeter, and he was not about to move beyond the lighted area into the jungle. It was uncomfortable enough standing near the halogen glare, an easy target for intruders who might be lurking amidst the trees. He was not going to make matters worse by venturing into the darkness.

He turned and took off for the guardhouse, grabbing his radio as he sprinted back across the complex. "Ramon?"

"What have you found?"

"Nothing," he reported into the mouthpiece as he continued to run. "Alert them at the main house."

———

Sandor was faced with several problems and little time to solve them. His principal dilemma was how he should respond to what he had discovered in the lab.

Anthrax was frequently threatened as a mode of terrorist attacks, and Sandor had spent time studying its production as well as its lethal effect. It is composed of three proteins, none of them independently dangerous until the ingredients are combined. It is relatively easy to manufacture once you have the components—specific instructions on how to synthesize anthrax are even available on a *jihadi* website— and once they are mixed the resulting exotoxin becomes deadly to the handler as well as the target. Sandor had no way of knowing what stage of fabrication had been achieved in the sealed-off room below, or how much of the noxious powder might be stockpiled there.

Some of the substances used to refine cocaine can be inflammatory—kerosene, ammonia, other chemicals commonly found in cleaning agents, and different forms of ethyl ether—but if Sandor found a way to destroy the lab by igniting these substances, they could launch a deadly anthrax cloud that would be a catastrophe for the surrounding area and suicide for Sandor.

As if that concern was not enough, Sandor realized that sabotaging the facility would be unlikely to derail Adina's plans. The operation would quickly be relocated and the trail of narcotics—and, more important, the anthrax—would grow cold.

Sandor reluctantly felt his priorities shifting under the weight of what he had discovered belowground. He had come here to assassinate Adina, but now he had a responsibility to determine where they were taking the toxin and what they were intending to do with it when it got there. And time was running out.

He had already left behind one dead guard and two unconscious men, all of whom were about to be discovered. The man who just ran the length of the complex was evidence of that. To add to his predicament, the sun would be rising soon, increasing the degree of difficulty for his escape.

It was time for him to move out.

———————

Sandor's thoughts were interrupted by the blare of a loud siren that cut through the night like a shrill announcement of danger. That noise was followed by the sudden glare of spotlights from atop the roof of the main house. Through the snakelike vines and branches of the banyan trees, the glare cast long and eerie shadows.

By the time a series of halogen lights outside the laboratory glowed to life, Sandor had already replaced the domed top on the vent and was on the run. He found shelter behind a kapok tree, where he knelt down and took the MAC-10 in hand. The time for silencers was over.

Even after the lights on the main house and laboratory were

switched on, most of the compound remained dark. Adina was obviously taking no chance of illuminating the entire area—it would then be vulnerable to a night sighting by air or satellite. From the looks of things, Adina was relying on his security forces to track him down.

From what the lab technician had described, those security forces were assigned to protect Adina first and the laboratory second. It was a limited contingent of guards according to Carlos, and Sandor had already taken two of them out of play.

As the rest of Adina's sleeping men were roused into action in the predawn hour, Sandor circled away from the laboratory and the main house. If these were the areas that would receive the most attention, he wanted to get to a safe distance where he still had a line of sight for both.

Sandor took cover behind a huge tamarind tree that was roughly equidistant from the back of the laboratory and the rear corner of the main residence. In the lighted area in back of the house he could see the four vehicles Carlos had described to him—a truck, a large SUV, and two Jeeps. He needed to get to one of them, and soon.

It was too late to consider an escape by foot, although backtracking into the jungle had been his intended route to safety. Sandor had expected to infiltrate this compound, locate Adina, take him out with the sniper rifle, and then disappear back into the tropical forest before his presence had been detected. The discovery of the lab and the activities belowground had changed everything, not to mention tripping the alarm system.

Subtlety, he ruefully accepted, was out the window.

He still wanted to do anything he could to make it appear that this was a raid on the cocaine rather than an enemy incursion—the less he did to disrupt Adina's plans now, the easier it would be to uncover them later—but at the moment, survival was the premium objective. He had information he needed to get to Bergenn and Raabe, and that required getting out of here alive.

———

Francisco had returned to the guardhouse.

"Everyone has been alerted?" he asked as he burst through the door.

"You heard the alarm," Ramon said. "I spoke with Alejandro. He's at the main house organizing the search."

"Good, good. Has anyone been in or out of the laboratory?"

"Not since Carlos went down there."

"I'll go check on him. You keep your eyes open, and do not leave here unless you receive orders directly from Alejandro. Or from the man," he added.

Ramon gave him a look that said the last directive was not required. "Right."

Francisco hurried down the stairs to the lab entrance. He opened the door with his passkey and stepped inside. The main room, which contained the two long, stainless steel counters, was deserted.

He pulled out his sidearm, then called out, "Carlos."

There was no response.

He stepped toward his right, his eyes moving cautiously from side to side as he approached the door to the secure area. It was locked tight.

This was not a room he ever wanted to enter, but he had no choice. Placing a magnetic card against the wall plate he heard the bolt release. He slowly pushed down on the handle.

The room was far smaller than the main refinery area. It was also well lighted, with glass and stainless steel enclosures lining the walls.

Francisco had a quick look around, confirming the room was empty.

He exited, shutting the door behind him with a sense of relief, then called out again. When he received no answer he walked toward the storage room in the rear of the facility, his weapon extended before him. Reaching the open doorway he saw the technician face-down on the floor, blood along the side of his head. He rushed over and felt the man's neck for a pulse.

He was alive.

Francisco straightened up and had a look at the scattered and torn sacks of cocaine.

"*Mierda,*" he spat into the silence.

Someone had gotten into the lab. Even worse, they had gotten out.

CHAPTER TWELVE

HATO AIRPORT, CURAÇAO

JIM BERGENN PACED back and forth in the cramped space of Doug Carlton's office. Raabe and Carlton quietly watched him since there wasn't much else to do at this hour of the morning. All their preparations had been completed.

"Crap," Bergenn said, finally coming to a stop, his arms akimbo, the muscles in his jaw tense. "We never should have let him go in without some means of regular communication."

"Too risky," Raabe reminded him. "He'll contact us when he shakes free."

"Not good enough," Bergenn insisted.

"How long you know Sandor?" Captain Carlton asked.

Bergenn stared back at him with a look that said, no matter how close Carlton and Sandor may have been in the service, working together in black ops was different.

Carlton understood. "Right," he replied to the unspoken statement. "Well, I've known him more than a dozen years, and I know he was doing it his way, no discussion, no edits."

Bergenn nodded. "Doesn't make it any less frustrating."

"Maybe not," Raabe agreed as he stood up and stretched his lanky frame, "but you'll just have to get yourself un-frustrated, buddy. It's time to rock and roll."

The three men stepped out into the darkness and climbed into Carlton's jeep, which was already packed with everything they would need.

At least they hoped it would be everything.

The captain sped off toward the dock, less than a quarter mile away.

———————

The seaplane waiting for them was a classic de Havilland Otter, chosen because it was fast and unobtrusive and carried no military markings. It was the sort of single-engine aircraft seen throughout the Caribbean, ready to take affluent tourists island-hopping, aerial sightseeing, or shopping. Borrowing it was another favor Doug Carlton had to call in.

"Sandor owes me big-time," he reminded the others with a wry grin.

"I'm sure you've been added to his list," Bergenn said.

Raabe laughed. "His extensive list, you mean."

Dawn was near as they stood at the water's edge, ready to go.

"What if he's completely off course?" Bergenn asked no one in particular as they climbed out of the jeep and headed toward the end of the short pier. "You guys have any idea how long the western shore of Maracaibo is?"

"I know exactly how long it is," Carlton replied, "which means Sandor better end up somewhere near your rendezvous point."

"Exactly," Bergenn snapped.

The other two stopped and turned to him.

"Sorry. Guess I should have caught a nap, huh?"

"Or switched to decaf a few hours ago," the captain suggested.

Raabe reached out and placed a hand on Bergenn's shoulder. "We're all worried man, but we'll find him."

CHAPTER THIRTEEN

INSIDE ADINA'S COMPOUND, SOUTH OF BARRANQUITAS

Sandor knew his only way out was to commandeer one of the four vehicles behind the main house, but he also knew he would first have to slow down their efforts to follow him. That meant he had to find a way to start one and disable the other three. With the entire compound on high alert there was no time to get under the hoods and rip out wires. That left him with the most direct approach—as soon as he got one of the vehicles running he would simply shoot out all of the other tires, hit the gas tanks, then take off.

He nodded to himself. That was the plan. Now he had to deal with the guards Adina would have assigned to watch over their transportation.

————

Francisco stood over Carlos as he radioed the situation to the guardhouse above.

"*Mierda,*" was Ramon's immediate response.

"Exactly what I said," Francisco agreed. "Report this to the main house, I'll wait here."

As the bad news was being relayed, Francisco began his efforts to revive Carlos. The technician was still lying in a leaden heap amid the toppled sacks and spilled cocaine, and he did not respond to being shaken or slapped hard across the face. Francisco took a moment to have a look around the room—bags had been moved and toppled with the white powder everywhere—and the knot in his stomach tightened.

In what seemed less than a minute he was joined by Alejandro, the head of security. He was tall and muscular, with a pockmarked complexion, coarse features, and a demeanor that seemed never to wander beyond a spectrum of angry and very angry. Other than Adina, there was not a man in the compound who did not fear him.

By way of greeting, Alejandro growled, "What the hell went on here?"

"Not sure yet," Francisco told him. "We'll know more once he comes to."

The two men turned to the technician, who was beginning to show signs of life, and watched as he struggled to roll onto his back. As Carlos made a move to sit up, Alejandro leaned over and roughly took hold of his shoulder. "Stay still," he ordered. Then he told Francisco to get some water as he grabbed two of the cloth sacks and shoved them under the man's head. "Lay back for a moment. Until your mind is clear."

Carlos felt light-headed but managed to focus enough to stare into Alejandro's dark, unblinking eyes. He did as he was told, leaning back and waiting.

Francisco returned with a clear beaker full of water. He knelt down, about to give the technician a drink, when Alejandro snatched the glass away and splashed the water into Carlos's face.

"He doesn't need a drink, you idiot, he needs to regain his senses." Looking back down, Alejandro watched as Carlos reflexively jerked his head from left to right and wiped his face with his hands. "You feeling more awake now?"

Carlos nodded.

Alejandro reached out and helped him sit up. "Tell me what happened. Everything." He handed the empty beaker to Francisco and said, "You can get him a drink now." Then he crouched down in front of the technician. "Tell me."

Carlos said he heard a noise in the storage room. Since there was no one else in the lab and no way for anyone to get past him without being seen he was not concerned. He thought perhaps something had fallen, so he came back to have a look. The next thing he knew, someone grabbed him and hit him across the head.

"Did you get a look at him?"

"No."

"Did he say anything to you?"

Carlos shook his head, the effort making him dizzy again. Alejandro handed him the water Francisco had brought. Carlos took a sip.

"Was it one man or more than one man?"

"I think only one."

"So," Alejandro repeated patiently, "you walked in here, found one man alone, he hit you over the head without speaking, and then disappeared. Is that what happened?"

Carlos turned his head slightly to the right and looked up at the ventilation panel. "Those sacks, he must have climbed up through there."

"And you just noticed that now?"

Carlos turned back slowly, struggling to meet his inquisitor's frightening gaze. "Yes. All these bags . . . ," he began, but Alejandro held up his right hand.

"Let's not say anything we might regret later, eh?"

The technician agreed, managing a nervous nod of his aching head. Then he watched as Alejandro stood, scaled the stack of toppled cloth sacks, and had a close look at the ventilation grill. "Somebody moved this," he said without turning back to the other two men. With minimal effort he shoved the grating inside the shaft. "Francisco, your flashlight."

The guard accommodated and Alejandro had a look inside the duct.

"Yes, I can see we had a visitor from above. Very clever." He switched off the flashlight and climbed back down. "But the question is, how did our visitor breach the perimeter without setting off the alarm?"

Now it was Francisco's turn to become flustered under Alejandro's accusatory glare. He knew the man well enough to realize lying was not an option. "There was a breach," he admitted. "We thought it was Manuel or Eduardo, using the latrine or something. Happens all the time," he added, as if this might excuse his carelessness in not acting sooner. "When they did not report in I went on patrol." He could no longer hold the man's gaze, dropping his head and staring at the ground. "You know the rest."

"Yes," Alejandro agreed. "And soon Adina will know, too. You can only hope for your sake that the others have caught this intruder by now. Come," he said as he bent down and grabbed hold of Carlos under the arm, pulling him to his feet. "Let's go."

———————

The intruder, Jordan Sandor, had made his way around a group of thick-trunked trees until he was within striking distance of the four vehicles. As anticipated, there was a sentry posted on the rear portico of the house, not twenty yards away, the veranda giving him the high ground and an excellent view of the surrounding area just as the sun began to make its appearance at the edge of the morning sky. The guard was armed with an automatic rifle that he held at the ready and his head was in constant motion as he scanned this section of the compound for any unwanted activity.

In the tradecraft of Sandor's profession, the high ground can sometimes be overrated. An early mentor pointed out that cover is often more important than position. "Finding your advantage is the key," he said. "Always remember, if you find yourself in a fair fight, you didn't plan well enough."

Sandor drew the .45 from his holster and gave the silencer a hard twist to make certain it was secure, then took aim. From a kneeling position he fired off two rounds, the first striking the man in the face, the second catching him square in the chest before he fell to the ground.

Sandor leapt to his feet and ran as fast as he could toward the four parked vehicles. He had a quick check of the ignitions and inside the consoles, then felt around the tops of the tires. There were no keys.

He had no way of knowing who might still be in the house, who might have seen the sentry go down, or who was already heading this way. One thing was certain—he could hear voices coming toward him.

He figured one of the Jeeps would be his best bet out of there.

Easy to hot-wire, agile through the jungle, and unlikely to have any sort of alarm.

He scrambled into the newer-looking model and, working under the dashboard, managed to get it started. He twisted the wires together so they would hold, then went to work on the remaining transportation.

Moving with haste and precision he shot out all twelve tires. Having already snapped the second magazine into his .45, he fired the remaining shots into the three gas tanks. The steel-jacketed rounds tore through the metal siding, causing gas to begin pouring out onto the ground.

The sound of the approaching security detail grew louder as Sandor jumped into the driver's seat of the running jeep and took off along the narrow path that lay dead ahead of him, the road that Carlos told him would lead straight into the jungle and toward the shore of the Lago de Maracaibo.

CHAPTER FOURTEEN

INSIDE ADINA'S COMPOUND, SOUTH OF BARRANQUITAS

Radio communications crackled across the compound as men raced to their designated positions. Two of them hurried through the dawn light toward the rear of the main house to reinforce the sentry posted there. As they drew closer they heard the sound of tires being popped, followed by the unmistakable rumble of a vehicle speeding off into the jungle.

One of them reached for his radio. "Back of the main house," he said.

"What is it?" Alejandro demanded.

"We're checking now," came the immediate reply.

The two men moved cautiously to the corner of the building, reaching there just in time to see Sandor's jeep kicking up dust as it flew down the dirt road and out of sight. After confirming that the lookout on the veranda was dead, they made a quick survey of the other vehicles.

"We've got trouble," one of them reported over his radio, then described what they found.

"No," Alejandro barked into his radio for every man to hear, "the *maricon* who did this is going to have trouble. The two of you go find those idiots Manuel and Eduardo. The rest of you meet me on the rear veranda. Now."

———

Sandor guided the jeep along the primitive jungle road, moving as fast as he could without losing control. There were huge bumps and large holes, low-hanging branches and exposed roots, all of which rendered the dirt path a lethal obstacle course. He negotiated these hazards as he formulated a revised strategy for meeting up with Bergenn and Raabe.

His plan had been to take out Adina in the dark of night, then grab the pack he left outside the perimeter of the compound and circle back through the jungle. He expected it to take him several hours on foot to reach the beach east of Barranquitas, which was their rendezvous point. Raabe was going to pilot the seaplane into the gulf, set it down, and await a signal from Sandor for pickup.

Now, however, Sandor was going to arrive at the shore a lot sooner than anticipated, a lot farther south than intended, and with a lot more fanfare. He could only hope his friends got an early start on their flight.

Carlos said there was a pickup of the narcotics set for this morning. He described a clearing near the shore where the drugs would be offloaded onto a Fountain twin-engine manned by the crew that would take the cargo north. Their speedboat was likely to be Sandor's best chance out of there if he could figure a way past the armed drug runners who would have already received word an unwelcome visitor was en route.

As he careened forward it was clear that this dirt road had no turnoffs, no alternate path through the jungle. He could ditch the jeep and make the last part of the trip on foot, but with Adina's men coming after him from behind and a welcoming party ahead the idea did not seem all that attractive.

He decided to improvise.

———————

Adina stood on the rear porch of the house, surrounded by his men. He was in his early sixties, tall, and trimly built with fine features, straight gray hair, and a dark, unfriendly mien. Even at this hour he was elegantly attired. He wore an expensive silk robe with brocade trim, his hair combed straight back and neatly in place, no evidence of sleep or panic in his reptilian eyes. When Alejandro began to give details of what had occurred and who was to blame, Adina held up his hand, commanding silence.

"I understand enough to know this is not the time for explanations or recriminations. This is the time for action." Pointing to Francisco and one of the others, he said, "Go and get this man. Now."

The two ran off to find a means to chase the intruder.

Adina directed his attention to Alejandro. "Come inside with me. Call ahead to our friends and tell them there is going to be a delay of a couple of hours in making our delivery this morning. Explain that we have had an intruder and ask for their help in apprehending this man. Alive if possible, yes?"

Alejandro nodded.

Pointing to two of his other men, Adina said, "You come in as well. And bring him," he ordered, gesturing toward Carlos, whom he had purposely ignored up till then. The lab technician was standing off to the side, his eyes cast down, the look of gloom evident to all. "The rest of you, you know what to do. There may be others in the area, but it does not seem likely. Help Francisco repair the vehicles. Patrol the grounds. Find out what happened here."

———

Sandor was keeping a close watch in the rearview mirror as he barreled ahead. He knew they would find some way to come after him, but he never expected them to come on motorcycles. He had not seen any bikes in the compound. Carlos had not mentioned them. He didn't even hear them as they approached, with the noise of his jeep and the bouncy ride. When he spotted the first one it was coming up fast. Then he saw the second. The agile, high-powered motorcycles were a faster means of transport on this hardscrabble road than his jeep, especially since the riders knew the terrain and Sandor did not. They were keeping to the outer edges of the road, where there were fewer bumps and holes, one man on each side.

Outrunning them was not possible. He had to stop them.

They were gaining on him from both sides, almost in range for them to begin firing. Knowing that control of his vehicle was more important than ever, Sandor could neither slow down nor could he risk accelerating beyond a speed where he could safely negotiate this teeth-jarring route. He reached for the MAC 10 that was sitting on the passenger seat beside him and laid it across his lap. Then, in one deft motion, he downshifted, jammed on the brake, and yanked the steering wheel hard to the left.

The jeep spun violently into a sideways position across the road, becoming a deadly obstacle for the two riders. They were coming at him too fast to brake in time and the road was too narrow and the jungle too dense for them to turn off. All they could do was ditch the bikes, but Sandor was not about to allow them that opportunity. Without hesitation he leveled the MAC 10 at the oncoming men and fired a spray of shots. The explosion of gunfire was followed by the crashing of the two motorcycles into the large trees as the riders were flung forward into the air. They slammed to the ground in front of him.

Sandor jumped out of the jeep and fired two more shots at each of the fallen men—he had to be certain they were dead. Then, after the explosive sounds of gunfire and the motorcycle collisions, everything was suddenly quiet but for the Jeep's engine. Sandor took a moment to listen, but he heard nothing else. No other motorcycles coming at him. No other vehicles.

Not yet.

He climbed back into the Jeep, straightened it out, and sped off again toward the coast.

CHAPTER FIFTEEN

INSIDE ADINA'S COMPOUND, SOUTH OF BARRANQUITAS

A DINA WAS HOLDING an impromptu council in the main salon of the house. This compound was designed to be his safe space, he reminded them. This was his retreat, his secure respite from the outside world. Now the sanctity of this haven had been violated and Adina wanted answers. The obvious starting place was his trusted lab technician, Carlos.

"So," he said calmly as he sat in a large, comfortable chair backed with a decorative arc of woven cane, "you had no conversation with this man."

Carlos nodded. "Almost nothing."

"Well which is it?" Adina asked with forced patience. "Nothing or almost nothing? As a scientist, I am sure you would agree that almost nothing is something. Am I right?"

"Yes, yes, of course."

"So then," Adina prodded him with an impatient sigh, "which is it?"

"Before he hit me, he said something about the cocaine. About taking the cocaine."

"What exactly did he say?"

Carlos was struggling. He wanted to look at Adina but could not. "I . . . I don't recall exactly. He struck me, so it's a bit unclear. But it was something like 'I'm going to take these sacks of cocaine and you're not going to stop me.' Something like that."

Carlos and the other men in the room were standing. Only Adina was seated. A large ceiling fan slapped gently at the cool morning air above them. Otherwise the room had become silent.

Now Adina rose and stepped forward. He reached out and took the technician by the chin, lifting his downturned face as one might do to a reluctant child. "Carlos," he said, "you have been loyal, you have worked hard, and you have never disappointed." He paused. "Until now. Because now I know you are lying to me."

Carlos began to speak, but Adina reacted by smacking him hard across the face.

"Allow me to finish." He grabbed the man's jaw, holding it tight so that Carlos could not avert his gaze. "I do not know what you are not telling me, or why you are not telling me. That is what makes this so difficult." Adina's tone made it sound as if the man's betrayal had wounded him. "I truly need you to explain this to me."

When Carlos began to protest Adina lashed out again, this time with the back of his hand.

"Please, do not insult me further and do not waste any more of my time."

Carlos was trembling now, tears flowing freely down the cheeks that had been reddened by Adina's slaps. "He asked me questions," he admitted, his voice barely a whisper.

"What sort of questions did he ask?"

"About the operation," Carlos said, speaking haltingly as he added, "Refinement of the narcotics. The security we have in place."

"I see. What else did he ask you?"

When Carlos did not immediately respond, Adina dug his fingernails into the man's face. "I suggest you tell me everything. And now."

Carlos attempted to nod, but Adina's grip made it painful for him to move. His cheek began to bleed. "He asked about the other room in the lab."

"Of course he did. And what did you tell our inquisitive friend in answer to these questions?"

Summoning what little courage remained, Carlos looked him in the eyes. "I told him nothing, Adina, nothing. That was why he hit me."

Adina let go of the man's jaw and shoved him hard in the chest. Carlos stumbled backward until one of the guards grabbed him and deposited him on a hardwood stool, where he sat with his face in his hands.

"So this man, whoever he was—I assume he did not introduce himself?"

Carlos shook his head.

"Naturally. Did he speak Spanish or another language?"

"A little Spanish. He was an American I think."

"So this American, he was not here to steal cocaine, he was here for other reasons. Am I right?"

Carlos nodded, still not looking up. "I think so."

"And you, being a scientist rather than a man of action, you saw danger, presumably a weapon of some sort, and so you told him everything he wanted to know. Am I right again?"

Now Carlos lifted his face. "No Adina, I told him nothing."

"Of course not. Yet he continued to ask you all of the questions you have described despite the fact that you continued to tell him nothing." Adina began pacing back and forth in front of Carlos. His voice louder when he said, "Just as you are telling me nothing right now."

"Adina . . ."

"Carlos, please, after all this time you do not take me for a fool, do you? You do not expect me to believe this little fairy tale you have concocted, do you?"

Carlos began to speak but Adina stepped forward, grabbed him by the hair and yanked his head back. "This intruder managed to get past two sentries, find his way into the lab, then make his way out, steal one of our vehicles while disabling the others, and you expect me to believe he could not persuade you to tell him anything he wanted to know?" Adina let go of Carlos and gestured to one of his guards. The man removed his gun from its holster and handed it to Adina. "Now tell me, Carlos, do you really expect me to believe that or do you have something else to say?"

The technician's eyes widened as he saw Adina take the automatic, his gaze following the gun as Adina held it at his side while he began striding back and forth across the room.

"The anthrax," Carlos blurted out. "I think he was here because of the anthrax."

Adina nodded thoughtfully. "And you told him."

"I had no choice, don't you see?"

"Yes, I see. Anything else?"

"He asked about you?"

"By name?"

"Yes."

"What did he ask?"

"He wanted to know if you were here. Which building you were in."

"And you told him. Because you had no choice."

Carlos replied with a vigorous nod. "I knew your guards would capture him."

Adina stopped his pacing and turned to face him. "And so they shall. But you, unfortunately, have proved yourself both a coward and a traitor." Adina leveled the automatic at the man's terrified face, waited a moment, then lowered the gun and returned it to his bodyguard. "Take him back to the laboratory," he told Alejandro. "Lock him in the secure room so he has time to contemplate his fate." He looked down at the weeping technician. "I'll deal with him later."

CHAPTER SIXTEEN

OFF THE NORTHWESTERN COAST OF VENEZUELA

CRAIG RAABE WAS piloting the Otter as they banked to the port side and headed toward the Gulf of Venezuela. Their course would take them directly above the inlet that led from the gulf into the large expanse of the Lago de Maracaibo.

Just before takeoff Doug Carlton offered to join Raabe and Bergenn on the flight, but they knew the captain would find himself in enough trouble if his involvement in this escapade became known. They told him not to exacerbate the situation by riding shotgun into enemy territory.

"We'll be fine. Anything goes wrong on your end," Raabe told him, "you can say we held you at gunpoint."

"How about you just bring Sandor and this seaplane back?"

"That's the plan," Bergenn assured him.

At first light they had taken off from the calm waters near Oranjestad and were now preparing to make their way to the shoreline near Barranquitas, where they would hopefully be able to retrieve their teammate.

The Lago de Maracaibo is populated by numerous oil rigs, so the area is accustomed to seaplane and speedboat traffic not typical for other large bodies of water devoid of commercial drilling activities. Men and equipment are constantly being shuttled back and forth from the large platforms, which made the flight less obtrusive and Sandor's exfiltration plan less dangerous.

Once Bergenn and Raabe entered the airspace over the Lago de

Maracaibo they would circle once or even twice. After that they would set down somewhere near the beach where Sandor was heading. They knew that repeated passes along the beach at low altitude would attract unwanted attention. They also knew they could not just sit offshore for too long without someone asking questions.

What they did not know was that things had already gone terribly wrong.

CHAPTER SEVENTEEN

SOUTH OF BARRANQUITAS

ACCORDING TO SANDOR'S rough calculations he was less than ten minutes from the shoreline south of Barranquitas. He also computed that he was more than twenty miles south of his recovery point on the beach.

Sandor drove on for another few minutes, then pulled to a stop and switched on the phone to activate the GPS. There was no longer any risk of the electronic signal revealing his whereabouts—Adina's men did not need a satellite fix to make his position, they already knew where he was. This was their road and there were no intersections.

Sandor confirmed that he was now less than a mile from shore. By activating the device it would also give Raabe and Bergenn the first signal that his plans had changed.

He turned off the GPS, pulled out his binoculars, and had a look ahead. The trail seemed fairly straight, but the vegetation was too dense to permit any view beyond a couple of hundred yards. He climbed out of the jeep, gathered together his pack with all of its contents, then stored everything in place.

He used his knife to tear a section of cloth from the jeep's ragtop. He opened the gas cap and forced the cloth down inside the tank with the help of a long branch he grabbed off the road. Using some vine and a couple of other broken branches, he rigged the steering wheel and the gas pedal. He tried not to put too much pressure on the accelerator, wanting the jeep to take a slow ride along the bumpy ground until the gasoline ignited. He did his best to set the small vehicle on a straight course, lashing the vines tightly through the spokes of the steering wheel and then securing them to the interior door handles, both left and right, for maximum leverage. Then he used his lighter to set the piece of cloth hanging from the gas tank on fire, ran to the driver's seat, and popped the jeep into gear.

He hoped the vehicle would get far enough and the explosion would be loud enough that it would get the attention of whoever was laying in wait for him at the end of the trail.

As the jeep pulled away he snatched up his weapons from the ground, then hurried off to his left into the thick of the jungle.

———————

"I've got something," Bergenn said.

"What've you got?" Raabe asked.

"It looks like he powered up his GPS for less than thirty seconds, but I've got a reading."

"Thirty seconds? You're sure it wasn't some crossed signal?"

"No, it was him, it tied into his code."

"So where is he?"

Bergenn punched the numbers into his tracking device. "Looks like he's just to the west of the shoreline, south of Barranquitas."

"Ahead of schedule and off vector. But why would he turn the GPS off if he's trying to let us know his position?"

"I don't know," Bergenn said. "Maybe he figured that quick hit was enough for now. Let's head south and see if he ties back in."

CHAPTER EIGHTEEN

SOUTH OF BARRANQUITAS

MOVING AS SWIFTLY as the terrain would allow, Sandor circled north into the jungle, his MAC 10 in hand, alert to any sounds or movements ahead. With the aid of his compass he traveled in an arc that would take him toward the shore. Hopefully he would end up behind the men there.

After he made a quick check of his watch he increased his pace, counting the seconds off in his head.

Then came the explosion.

It was loud and fiery, the gas tank igniting in a concussive ball of light and noise. The blast would have to be irresistible to the men who were waiting to ambush him.

What could it mean? they would have to wonder. *Had Adina's men caught the intruder from behind? Had he crashed his vehicle into the trees?*

Some, if not all of them, would have to go and check, which was all Sandor wanted. He would take any improvement in the odds he could get.

———

There were four men at the shore waiting for Sandor, but they were neither well-trained military personnel nor elite guards. They were drug runners, undisciplined and ruthless men who were there to pick up the latest shipment of refined cocaine, load it onto their speedboat, and take it to the next port of call.

Two of them were Mexican, two Venezuelan. They were dressed in shorts and sandals, one of them bare-chested, one in a tank top, the other two in T-shirts. They were all muscular, unshaven, and looked in need of sleep. It was barely seven and they had already been there for almost an hour. From their grumbling it was clear that this was way too early for them to be doing anything. The calls they received about the problems Adina and his men were having only added to their annoyance. They simply wanted to pick up their goods and be on their way.

The calls warned them of the approaching man and cautioned them that he was armed and dangerous. Alejandro told them of Adina's request that the man be taken alive.

The leader of this foursome scoffed at the notion. "What about our shipment?" he asked.

"It will be coming, but there will be a delay."

"A delay? You want us to do your dirty work for you, then you tell me about a delay?"

"We are organizing things. Just take this man and hold him for us."

"We don't take our orders from you."

There was a pause. Then Alejandro said, "You will take orders from me, my friend, because you know who those orders are coming from." He ended the call without giving the man a chance to reply.

So the four men waited, each with an automatic weapon in hand, each leaning against the side of the Fountain speedboat that had been pulled up onto the sandy shore. They were facing the opening in the jungle where the dirt road ended. It gave them a perfect vantage point for anyone emerging from the trail. There was no urgency in their attitude or position.

And then they heard the explosion.

The four of them rose as one, the leader saying, "You two, go have a look down there, see what happened."

The two men he had pointed to stared back at him as if he were insane. "Why?" one of them asked.

"Because I told you to."

"This isn't our problem, man. Why the hell should we get in-volved?"

"Because we want to get our shipment and get the hell out of here, that's why. If this *pendejo* blew himself up, we can let them know, maybe it'll get things moving a little quicker."

The man was not convinced. "This is not our fight, you agree?"

The leader shrugged. "Just see what happened, that's all."

The two men hesitated, then reluctantly trudged toward the opening before them.

———

Sandor reached the edge of the jungle shortly after the explosion. Standing behind a wide tropical cedar, he had a clear view of the four men. He watched as two of them hoisted their automatic weapons and marched slowly toward the trail, which was only fifty yards south of him.

There was no one else in sight.

Sandor understood that this was no time for finesse. He waited until the two advancing gunmen disappeared into the dense stand of trees, then allowed a little more time, estimating how far they would need to walk before they got near the burning jeep, before they realized there was no one there.

He reached for the .45 automatic, made sure the silencer was securely in place, then whispered to himself, "Three, two, one," and took off at a dead run toward the two men who were facing the trail, off to his right.

The MAC 10 was in his left hand, but he used the handgun in his right instead, opening fire on the two drug runners before they even had had time to turn toward him. The silenced shots from his S&W should have kept the other two men, now somewhere along the path in the jungle, from knowing there had been an attack. Unfortunately, the leader of this motley team managed to fire off a burst from his automatic rifle as he was tumbling to the sand under the barrage of Sandor's well-placed shots.

Sandor raced forward to ensure that both men were dead, then prepared to deal with the remaining pair. He hopped into the cockpit of the Fountain, relieved to see the key was in the ignition and lowered himself behind one of the cushioned seats.

He did not have to wait long. The other two came running back from the trail, weapons raised, then stopped in their tracks when they saw their friends facedown on the sand.

They just stood there, not knowing how to react, leaving themselves clear targets. *No discipline at all*, Sandor thought as he raised himself onto his knees and, protected by the starboard bulkhead, took out the man to his left with a fusillade from his MAC 10. Then he trained the weapon on the second man.

"Drop it or I'll kill you where you stand," he hollered.

The man hesitated for an instant, so Sandor encouraged him by firing several shots at his feet. The man tossed his semiautomatic rifle away with both hands and raised his arms above his head.

"What other weapons you carrying?"

"No comprendo, señor," the man replied.

"Really? Then I guess I'll just have to blow your head off."

"No, no," the man pleaded, his comprehension suddenly enhanced as Sandor leveled the barrel of the MAC 10 at his eyes. "Here," he said, lifting his shirt and revealing a handgun in his waistband.

"Good. Now lift it out by the handle and toss it away. Real easy," he added.

The man did as he was told, then watched as Sandor stood.

"You're going to kill me," the man said.

"No, *amigo,* I need you to help me push this little dinghy out to sea."

CHAPTER NINETEEN

SOUTH OF BARRANQUITAS

KEEPING AN EYE on his newly indentured servant, the S&W in his right hand, Sandor and the stocky Mexican managed to dislodge the Fountain speedboat from its sandy perch and slide it into the water. When the man tried to take a step back Sandor waved the gun at him.

"No, no, no. I can't leave you behind, and I'm only going to kill you if you insist on it. Now get in the boat." When the drug runner responded with something that was supposed to be a frightening snarl, Sandor said, "I can just shoot you in the knees and drag you aboard. Up to you."

The man hesitated, then stepped forward, his hands on his head. Sandor spun him around, grabbed him by the collar, and pushed him ahead.

"Move," Sandor told him, and so the Mexican scrambled over the transom, across the vinyl-covered rear deck and into the cockpit. Sandor followed, shoved the man onto his knees, and then, for good measure, smacked him across the back of the head and dropped him to the fiberglass deck.

It was time to move out.

––––––––

Alejandro returned to the main salon. The look on his face answered the question Adina was about to ask.

"The four men on the beach, have they reported back?"

Alejandro shook his head. "Nothing. We are calling but we get no response."

Adina permitted himself a grim smile. "This man is a professional, that much is obvious. But sent by whom?" The question was obviously rhetorical and Alejandro made no attempt to reply.

Instead he asked, "What do we do now?"

Adina ignored him. "Whoever he is, he's very good."

Alejandro waited.

"What was your question? Ah yes, what to do." Adina stood and clapped his hands together, as if suddenly energized by the task ahead. "He has obviously taken out those four idiots and probably has their boat. We'll need to call in a favor or two, see if we can track him down."

"Should I call Caracas?"

Adina responded with a vicious scowl. "And admit that I am surrounded by incompetent buffoons? How do you think that will go for all of you? Or for me?" He shook his head in disgust. "We have a laboratory to move. Get them working on that immediately."

"And this man . . ."

"Call our friend in Cabimas. Whoever the intruder is, he'll head north in their speedboat, trying to escape into the gulf. We want him alive and they will want their boat back. Have Monter get on it."

––––––––

The Fountain is a high-speed craft built for long-haul racing and, as such, has become the vessel of choice for narcotics smugglers who need to outrun both law enforcement and rival factions. Sandor fired up the engines, the loud, throaty sound of the twin inboards quickly harmonizing in a high-pitched whine as he threw the transmission into gear and surged forward.

The bow rose as Sandor stood at the wheel, guiding the boat into the gently rolling surf. He glanced back to be sure his new companion was still facedown on the rear deck, then placed his S&W on the seat beside him. Pulling out the satellite cell phone, he powered it up again. This time he would give Raabe and Bergenn enough time to pick up his GPS signal. Meanwhile he pushed the throttle forward and turned the boat due north.

––––––––

Cabimas is a port town on the northeasterly shore of the Lago de Maracaibo. It is a relatively busy harbor that is home to fishing boats and commercial traffic, and host to all sorts of maritime activity, legal and otherwise. The four men who had been awaiting Adina's shipment of cocaine near Barranquitas were scheduled to return the goods here, where the product would be transferred to an airplane and flown to Mexico.

Oscar Monter, the man in charge of arranging these exchanges in Cabimas, was handed the cell phone when Alejandro called and said it was an emergency. Monter was very disappointed to learn that there was going to be a delay in receiving the scheduled shipment. He was absolutely livid to discover that his four men and boat were missing.

"What are you telling me?" Monter demanded.

Alejandro was standing in the main salon and, with one eye on Adina, calmly explained the situation.

Monter was anything but calm in his response. "What is this, some sort of joke?" He was so angry he was having trouble spitting the words out. "You're telling me that one man has compromised your operation, killed four of my men, and stolen my boat? One man?"

He was hollering so loudly that Alejandro pulled the phone away from his ear. Adina could hear the man ranting, and he responded with a slight nod at his lieutenant.

"Yes," Alejandro said.

"And you want me to find him? One man, one boat, in a lake the size of an ocean? That's what you're telling me?"

Adina stood and took the phone from Alejandro. "That's exactly what we're telling you."

The sound of Adina's voice brought the raving to an abrupt end. "But . . . but . . . ," the man sputtered.

"But nothing, Oscar. I assume, at the very least, you want your boat back, eh?"

"Of course."

"Good. Because this man is probably coming toward you. Unless he's going to dock somewhere along the shore, which I doubt, his only escape is to head north through the inlet and into the gulf, am I right?"

"Well yes . . ."

"And nobody knows these waters better than you and your men. And you'll certainly recognize your own boat."

"Of course. But . . ."

"And I would think there will be a limited number of Fountains running full throttle at this hour, heading directly at you. You would agree?"

"What you say makes perfect . . ."

"Good. Then why are we wasting time talking? I want this man, and I want him alive. You understand?"

"Yes."

"Excellent. Now, if he is running at anything near top speed, he could already be less than an hour from you. So, it is time for action, yes?"

"Of course," Monter agreed, then heard the line go dead.

CHAPTER TWENTY

IN THE LAGO DE MARACAIBO

SANDOR WAS NOT running the Fountain at top speed. For one thing, he did not want to draw unwanted attention from any local authorities. He also did not want to make himself an easy target for anyone who might have organized a search. Finally, and most important, he wanted to give Raabe and Bergenn time to find him.

The GPS link would tell them he was at sea. All they needed to do was to fix his position and arrange a pickup.

If only things were that simple, he told himself.

Sandor steered a steady course to the north, making it appear he was approaching an oil rig he could see in the distance. He figured that was his best bet, appearing to be some sort of transport en route to one of the derricks, which is how he was going to play it until help arrived.

———

Bergenn picked up the signal.

"It looks like he's on the move."

"On the move?"

"And fast." Bergenn plugged in the coordinates. "He's on the water," he said as he electronically charted the path Sandor was traveling. "Looks like he's heading north-northwest."

"In a boat?"

"If he's swimming this fast, we're entering him in the next Olympics."

"Where the hell did he get a boat?"

"Sandor? You really want an answer to that?"

"Never mind," Raabe conceded. "How far are we?"

Bergenn did some math, then said, "If he keeps coming north and we stay on this vector, we're less than ten minutes out."

———————

Monter's men at the port in Cabimas boarded a Fountain 47 foot Lightning. It was fitted with a pair of Mercury 850 engines that could propel the boat at speeds reaching 120 miles an hour.

Unlike Sandor, these three men were not worried about attracting attention when they cast off. Situated at the far end of the marina, they were at the northern entrance to this enormous lake and they made fast work of negotiating the short canal that led out of the harbor. Once clear of the docks the man at the wheel promptly throttled up. The nose of the sleek speedboat rose in the air as the twin screws dug in. They lurched forward, accelerating across the top of the placid water.

They had no information about where their missing boat might be, other than the suspicion it would be heading north toward the narrows between Cabimas and La Concepcion. That was the only route leading into the Gulf of Venezuela and, ultimately, to the relative safety of the Caribbean. The sister boat they were hunting for was a forty-two-foot model of the Lightning, its bright yellow hull unmistakable on a clear day like this, providing they got close enough to spot it.

There was discussion about waiting, trying to ambush the hijacker once he came within range of the inlet, but that was risky. The narrows always attracted a lot of boat traffic, and a high-speed chase might become a problem. There was also concern about the sort of firepower the hijacker might have with him or how many other men he might have arranged to pick up along the way.

The decision was made to search for the boat in the open waters, hoping to spot him before he saw them. The pilot took the Fountain on a southwesterly course while his compatriots stood on either side of the small cockpit, balancing themselves and peering through binoculars as they raced ahead at more than eighty miles an hour.

Sandor did not have the luxury of a lookout, nor could he do much on his own to scan the horizon, except with the naked eye and an occasional look through binoculars. He had a half-conscious man on the deck behind him, unfamiliar waters to navigate, and a rendezvous to arrange. At the moment, his principal focus was the enormous oil rig that appeared to be just a couple of miles ahead, off his starboard side.

He checked his watch. It was after eight, and he knew Raabe and Bergenn had to be somewhere in the area by now. They had agreed that radio silence was his safest course, but now it was time to try to reach them.

He slowed the boat and made a quick check of the Mexican. The man was moaning but still seemed to be out of commission. Sandor grabbed some of the rope on board and bound the man's hands behind his back. He then reached for the binoculars and had a look at the sky around him. It was a bright morning, and he could make out a couple of high-altitude aircraft.

But no seaplanes.

Pulling the small satellite phone from his vest pocket, he switched on the power, waited for the keyboard to light up, and then punched in the code.

Out of the corner of his eye he spotted the Mexican crawling toward the port gunwale.

In two large strides Sandor reached the man, drove his heel into the small of his back, and sent him facedown again onto the hard fiberglass.

"You trying to go swimming with your hands tied? You must really be some kind of water-treader."

The man muttered something obscene in response.

"I'm not sure exactly what you said, but I think it's anatomically impossible, am I right?" There was no reply. "Look, I already told you I don't want to have to kill you, and I'd hate to give you a second concussion in less than fifteen minutes, but you're really testing my patience. Now, you either lie still for a few minutes or I'm going to have to rap you across the skull again."

The man understood enough to say, *"Tranquilo."*

"Excellent." Then, for good measure, he grabbed the end of the rope that was binding the man and secured it to the port railing. "You jump overboard and I'll keelhaul you. *Comprende?*" Just then Sandor's cell phone began to buzz. "Now shut the hell up and stay put." For emphasis he jammed his foot down on the man's ass again, forcing him flat on the deck. Then he hit the green button on the phone. "Vinny's Pizza."

"Funny man," Bergenn said. "You all right?"

"Peachy."

"Our friend?"

"Still among the breathing, unfortunately, but I have a lot to tell."

"Can't wait to hear it. Meanwhile we're working on your coordinates. You rent a boat for a day cruise?"

"Something like that."

"We'll be joining you in less than five minutes."

"Copy that. I'm less than two miles south of some gigantic drilling platform. Water's calm here, you can probably set down and not make a ripple."

"We see the rig coming up on the screen, we should be in your range of vision straightaway."

"Great. I'm bringing someone home for dinner with us."

"The man himself?"

"Sadly, no. But it's someone who should be helpful when I tell my tale. Now listen, I'm not sure what they might be doing to track me, but several of their people are down and I've borrowed one of their very pricey little dinghies, so you be careful coming in. I'm sure they're looking for me."

"Roger that."

"Look, in case I don't make it for any reason, you need to know why I aborted the mission." Bergenn began to say something but Sandor stopped him. "This is important. They have an underground lab there."

"Explosives?"

"No. Seems our friend has gone into the pharmaceutical business."

"Narcotics?"

"Yes, but it gets worse. Anthrax."

"I dread to ask the next question."

"What he's doing with cocaine and anthrax? I don't know yet. That's what we've got to find out. Since I raised hell, I'm sure he's already called in the movers, so we've got some work to do on this."

"All right. Keep your phone on; we're approaching the rig now; you should be able to have us in your sights soon."

Sandor gave his prisoner another quick look, then lifted his binoculars. Before he could make out the Otter flying toward him from the northwest, he saw the speedboat bearing down on him from the northeast.

CHAPTER TWENTY-ONE

IN THE LAGO DE MARACAIBO

I$_T$ $_{DID}$ $_{NOT}$ take long for Monter's men to locate their missing speedboat. They had a pretty good fix on the approximate time Sandor would have launched the forty-two-foot Fountain from just south of Barranquitas, right after they lost all radio contact with their team. Assessing his route was not complicated since there were limited choices that would ultimately lead to the narrows. Staying close to the western shore would have been too risky—there was the possibility of being spotted or even attacked from land. Heading east and then back north would have wasted too much time. That eliminated a substantial search area and sent them on the diagonal vector most likely to cross paths with their target.

When they spotted the speedboat, their only surprise was that he had not pushed it faster and was still so far to the south.

The pilot held his course as the other two men threw open the lockers along the bulkheads and prepared their weapons for the assault. They were told that the man was to be taken alive. They were warned that some of their own men might still be on the boat. And they were ordered to avoid destroying the speedboat itself, if at all possible.

That said, these were not men suited to tasks requiring finesse. They figured their job was to get this *maricon,* one way or another; to try to save their boat; and—most important—to survive the event themselves.

Sandor grabbed the cell phone again and hit the speed dial. "Mayday, mayday, we have hostiles bearing down from the east."

"Have they shot at you?" Bergenn asked.

"Not yet, but I don't think we're more than sixty seconds from the fireworks. They're not racing here at ninety miles an hour to have a chat." Hearing the discussion, the Mexican in the back of the boat began to stir. Taking the phone away from his ear, Sandor yelled, "You move another inch and I'll start the festivities by taking you out first." Then, speaking to Bergenn again, he warned, "You guys better chill until we see what kind of toys they have with them."

"Understood, but we're not about to stand down and leave you there to fry."

"No worries," Sandor told him. "I'll be right back to you."

Returning his attention to the prisoner on deck, he said, "Tell me what you have on board in the way of long-range weapons." When the man shook his head without speaking, Sandor lunged toward him, grabbed a handful of the man's hair, and shoved the barrel of his automatic into his neck. "Now, you listen very carefully. In about sixty seconds your friends are going to start shooting at us, which means you and I will suddenly be playing for the same team. So if you don't tell me what I want to know, they may or may not get me, but you are most certainly a dead man."

There was a slight hesitation, which was followed by Sandor leaning a bit harder on the S&W.

"In there," the man said with a very slight turn of his head.

Sandor's prediction, that he was only sixty seconds from being shot at, was not off by much. As he ran toward the compartment in the rear of the boat to see what munitions they had stowed away, the first spray of automatic fire whistled overhead. The other speedboat was closing fast, and the men on board began the attack by trying to hit Sandor before resorting to tactics that would destroy the speedboat in the process.

As the shots were fired Sandor dove to the deck, then crawled the rest of the way toward the cabinet and flung the lid open.

Meanwhile, the two men shooting at Sandor had some sort of long-range rifles, and they were not sparing the ammunition. Fortunately, they were still not aiming low enough to damage the boat.

Sandor was on his knees, rummaging through the store of armaments that were on hand. There were automatic rifles—likely the same variety as those being used against him. There was a grenade launcher. He found some sort of primitive flamethrower. And, most critical to his predicament, there was a rocket launcher with one projectile in place and a second wrapped and ready to go.

"You," he said to the Mexican, "what would their orders be?"

"How would I know?"

"You can do better than that."

"To blow your head off, what do you think?"

Sandor nodded. "I'll try not to take offense. What I want to know is whether they're willing to shoot up this boat in the process."

The man managed to roll onto his side just enough to have a look at his captor. "Not at first. They'll try and take you down. But they're not going to stay with that for long, man. Too many *federales* in these waters."

"As if the local authorities would care about some drug runners shooting at each other."

The Mexican shook his head. "They don't give a shit about narcotics; they're here to protect the oil."

Monter's men were rapidly losing patience. There was no purpose in firing if you're not allowed to hit the boat and you can't see the man on board.

"Report in to Monter," the pilot told them. "We could be here all day waiting for him to show himself."

The man on his left spoke into the radio and Monter instantly responded. "What have we got?"

The man explained their situation.

"So it really is only one man?"

"That's all we've seen. We came at him, he ducked down, now we've circled around, no sign of him."

"You have no shot at all?"

"Not without shooting at the boat. And we don't know who may be on there with him."

"Not our problem," Monter said without hesitation. "Anyone stupid enough to be captured deserves what he gets." He paused. "Any chance you can board? You have a three-to-one edge."

"Maybe. I don't know."

"He fire at you yet?"

"Not yet. Like I said, we circled back once we were in range. I don't think we hit him, but he's laying low."

Monter hesitated. It was an expensive boat and he was in no mood to have it blown to pieces.

"What if he finds the weapons on board?"

Monter had apparently lost four men already this morning. "All right," he said. "Take a run at him. He returns any fire, you lower your sights and get this done. We don't want the Armada on our backs, and you're too close to the southern rigs to stay out there for long."

——————

The Venezuelan navy, officially known as the Bolivarian Armada, serves as both coast guard and naval force, with authority on all waters surrounding or within the country. They run frigates along the coasts and engage in regular maneuvers to protect the nation's oil industry.

Sandor's concern, other than the obvious goal—to avoid getting shot—was the risk of being captured by the Venezuelan government. Given Adina's relationship with Chavez, it was no understatement to say that Jordan Sandor would never be heard from again if he was taken prisoner within the borders of this country. Once the Armada arrived, the capture of these drug runners would seem like a misdemeanor arrest compared to the apprehension of an American intelligence agent.

Sandor worked quickly to arm the rocket launcher; then he set it down beside him and reached for the satellite phone again.

"Go ahead," Bergenn said.

"I'm out of time here," Sandor told him, then gave a full assessment of the situation, available weapons, and his plan.

"Once you blow them sky-high we're going to have the entire Venezuelan navy after us."

"I have to figure they've already been alerted by security on that oil rig. Which means you'll have to come in for a landing right now or we'll all wind up like sitting ducks."

"Roger that. You going to cover us?"

"Like a blanket."

———————

The men in the other speedboat noticed the Otter for the first time as it circled in a descending path, just far enough away to be out of their range. Before they could decide what, if anything, there was to do about that, Sandor peeked over the gunwale and opened fire with one of the long-range rifles from the locker.

All three of Monter's men hit the deck, which is just what Sandor wanted. With the men in the other Fountain diving for cover and out of view, Sandor mounted the rocket launcher on his shoulder, steadied himself on one knee, and fired.

There was the customary instant of hesitation when he squeezed the trigger, then the *thump* of recoil as the rocket sped away, followed by a thin trail of white smoke. With Sandor's fusillade having temporarily abated, the three men peered over the side just as the missile was released. Their boat was still moving and, at the sight of the onrushing projectile, the pilot instinctively shoved both throttles forward and yanked the wheel to starboard. His two cohorts, having no way to control the speed or path of the boat, took the simpler approach and dove over the side into the dark waters.

For a moment it seemed to Sandor as if everything was happening in slow motion. It was quiet, with no shots being fired. The only action was the frantic attempt by the pilot of the attacking boat to avoid the path of the rocket.

But it was too late.

The projectile hit the port side of the boat with a loud crash, followed by an explosion of light and smoke and noise. The missile, which was heat-guided, found its optimum target toward the aft of the Fountain, detonating with full force as it struck the port engine, driving the stern of the boat into the air with propellers spinning helplessly as the fuel lines ignited, creating a pyre of burning gas, rendering the once sleek boat an unrecognizable tangle of destruction.

As Sandor got to his feet he watched the Otter complete its landing a few hundred yards away. He moved back to the cockpit, put the engines into gear, and headed toward the waiting plane.

"Get ready pal," he said to the man who was still tied to the railing, "you and I are taking a little trip."

CHAPTER TWENTY-TWO

CARACAS, VENEZUELA

As soon as Adina got word of the debacle in the Lago de Maracaibo he commanded Alejandro to speed up the work dismantling the laboratory and making preparations to relocate the facility.

His men crated and loaded the sacks of cocaine as well as the various apparatus. Then everyone was ordered out of the area as the final work was turned over to four specialists who had access to the segregated area where the anthrax was manufactured.

They pulled on their hazmat suits and went about the dangerous business of placing the deadly toxin in airtight containers and readying the encapsulated parcels for transport in a separate vehicle. They also gathered the various chemical components that had not yet been combined into the lethal concoction and placed those in the back of the same truck.

Then they doused the entire subterranean installation with gasoline and set it ablaze.

At Adina's direct instruction, Carlos, his trusted lab technician, was left locked inside the secure room, from which none of them could hear the man pleading for mercy, or later, begging for his life to end as he was engulfed in the chemical fire that melted his skin away before incinerating him beyond all recognition.

From a safe distance, Adina watched as the flames shot up from the laboratory. Then, accompanied by his two most trusted men, Alejandro and Jorge, he left for Caracas.

In recent years, Adina had spent as little time as possible in the Venezuelan capital. His role in various terrorist activities had made him a marked man, and surfacing in a heavily populated area was not an ideal situation. He actually preferred the controlled environment of his jungle retreat, where all of his needs could be met with minimal risk. There was an added benefit—for so long as he remained a phantom, he reduced the risk of embarrassing the administration he supported, obscuring the connection between his actions and the government at large.

Now, however, his sanctuary had been violated. Someone had breached his compound and escaped with knowledge of its location and purpose. He was determined to find out who was behind the invasion and to contain the damage. This required a visit to the intelligence facilities that served the Chavez regime.

His destination was a multilayered building known as El Helicoide, which houses the Servicio Bolivariano de Inteligencia Nacional, more familiarly known as the SEBIN. The architecture is an odd mix of spaceship and cliffside dwellings, the overall impression imposing, and the purposeful effect of intimidation not lost on anyone who has ever been there.

The impending arrival of Rafael Cabello was communicated well in advance as he traveled a secure and circuitous route, and he was welcomed with appropriate deference and formality when he and his two men finally entered the underground garage beneath the southern face of the building. From there Adina was whisked upstairs in a private elevator to the sixth floor. He was shown to a secure conference room where men at the highest level of this agency had already convened.

Greetings between the members of this group and their esteemed guest were respectful. Most of them had been acquainted with Adina for many years. Others, who knew him less well, were nevertheless familiar with his exploits and the closeness of his relationship with their president. Once the polite salutations were concluded they sat around the large table and Adina got down to business.

"I assume you have all been fully briefed on what occurred."

They assured him that they had.

"Then please tell me what, if anything, you have learned so far about this intruder."

Gilberto Bargas was a minister in the Chavez regime, the highest-ranking officer in attendance, and an old crony of Adina. "He was an American," he said.

Adina frowned. "That much I know from my own men. He spoke with two of them, a guard and a chemist. I thought you were all fully briefed."

The minister nodded and said, "Of course," then looked down at some notes before him. "It appears he was acting alone, at least with respect to this raid."

"Meaning what?"

"He was alone during the invasion. Others helped him escape."

This time Adina gave an impatient nod. "Is that it?"

"We received word through some locals. That night a small aircraft was spotted, flying low over the jungle."

"And?"

"We have already done aerial reconnaissance. These are photographs from a clearing a few miles from your compound." He reached into a file and handed over several prints. "Our analysts say these are remnants of some sort of glider. That was his method of entry."

"I see. So this American crash-landed a glider in the jungle in the middle of the night. Impressive."

Bargas held out another group of photos. "We managed to retrieve these shots of a seaplane, taken by one of our spotters, just north of Cabimas. We have enlarged them and have a partial identification of the call numbers. We believe it's privately owned and kept in Curaçao."

"Inquiries are being made?"

"Yes. Discreetly, of course."

"Any results yet?"

"Unfortunately there is no record of this plane having taken off or landing yesterday. At least not officially. If this was the plane, there was obviously no flight plan filed. It is owned by a company in Curaçao, used for shuttling tourists around. Likely took off and set down there. We are still pursuing the possibility that there were witnesses who saw it leaving or returning."

Adina sat back, hands folded in his lap, considering the information. "Gentlemen, would you all permit me some private time with the minister?"

The others, if insulted, offered no resistance to being dismissed. When Adina was alone with the only man in the room he trusted, he leaned forward and spoke. "So Gilberto, we are dealing with a man who risks his life to land in the jungle and find his way to my home, with no clear means of escape. I think it's obvious that the ruse of a narcotics robbery is nonsense, you agree?" The minister nodded his assent. "And, having found his way to our underground facility, he did nothing to destroy or even disrupt that operation. Which means that could not have been his purpose." Again, the other man concurred. "Leaving only one logical explanation." Bargas waited. "This man was an assassin who came there for me." Adina now tented his long, elegant fingers, tapping them together as he considered the likelihood of his conclusion.

After a few moments, the minster said, "But no attempt was made to reach you. Isn't that correct?"

"That is correct. At least as far as we know. Which can only mean that this man changed his mind once he discovered the laboratory." Adina sat back in his chair. "If this was someone who was determined to murder me for reasons that we can only guess at right now, once he stumbled upon what we were manufacturing he decided there were larger issues at stake."

The minister was clearly impressed. "As always, your powers of deduction are ahead of mine, Rafael."

"It's obvious, is it not? The man is an American. He was sent to liquidate me as retribution for the attack on their refineries. When he found his way into the lab he knew he had stumbled upon important information and he could not risk murdering me without greatly reducing the chances of his own escape."

"Of course," the minister agreed. "He wanted to do whatever he could to get out and relay that information."

"Just so." Adina allowed himself one of his thin-lipped smiles. "It was not fear of his own death that had him change course; he proved that by the risky means he used to enter the jungle. No, he was hoping to have us believe he was a thief and that we would leave our plant intact as he reported back to Langley."

"Langley?" the minister asked.

"Naturally," Adina replied, the smile still in place. "This man is a professional. He disabled one of my sentries and murdered the other. He got in and out of our lab and managed to escape my compound despite pursuit by two of my best guards and an encounter with several armed men waiting for him at the shore. He not only managed to deal with them, but he also stole their boat, then overcame another attempt to apprehend him and got safely away. Our intruder is a professional," he repeated. "It's now up to us to find out who he is and what he is up to."

CHAPTER TWENTY-THREE

CIA HEADQUARTERS, LANGLEY, VIRGINIA

MARK BYRNES WAS not a man easily amused, and this morning was certainly no exception. He was seated at his desk, staring up at Jordan Sandor who was standing there as if called to attention. Craig Raabe and Jim Bergenn were outside in the waiting room. The three men had arrived back in Washington late the preceding night and were promptly summoned to this early meeting.

After what seemed a long silence, Byrnes said, "I want to do my best to fully understand everything before I react."

Sandor nodded without speaking.

"I think it's only fair that I find out what actually happened before I explode into a homicidal rage. Would you agree?"

"Yes sir."

Byrnes drew a deep breath, puffed out his cheeks, and let out a long, unhappy sigh. "So, let's see if I've got this right. Without permission, without so much as a how-do-you-do, you flew to our Air Force base in Curaçao, infiltrated the jungles of Venezuela, sought out Rafael Cabello for the purpose of assassinating him, wound up in the middle of a narcotics operation, took out several foreign nationals, blew up a boat in foreign waters and almost got yourself and two other agents killed. Is that a fair summary?"

"You left out the anthrax lab."

"Ah, yes, the anthrax lab. Which you never actually saw, as I understand."

"I was inside the laboratory, but I never got into the area where they're manufacturing the anthrax, that's correct."

"Mm hmm. And when you organized this SMU with Raabe and Bergenn, you felt you had some special authority to do so, some mandate I'm not aware of?"

Sandor knew, of course, that he did not. Special Mission Units had to be authorized by the top echelon of the Agency. He also realized that his intention to keep the mission covert had gone up in flames with the explosion of the Fountain speedboat in the Lago de Maracaibo. "Not exactly, no."

"Not exactly? Do you recall the discussion you and I had last week, the one in which I refused you permission to hunt down Adina? You do recall that, I presume."

"I do, but I came across new information when I was on R&R in St. Barths. I got a lead on his whereabouts and I felt I was justified to act, sir. I was in hot pursuit."

"Hot pursuit? What kind of nonsense is that, Sandor? You weren't a state trooper chasing a bank robber down I-95. You planned and carried out an entire operation without sanction from or notice to this office. You even took a Mexican national into custody along the way."

"A drug runner, sir."

Byrnes stared at him as if they were speaking two different languages. "Do you have any idea what sort of trouble you're in? Do you know what kind of damage you've done to your career? In a best-case scenario you could be riding a desk in a cubicle on the third floor of this building until your infamous sense of humor is an ancient memory. Am I clear?"

"Completely, sir."

Byrnes shook his head. "God almighty, Jordan. What the hell were you thinking?"

"May I speak freely, sir?"

"A little late to play the ingénue, don't you think? Say whatever you want."

"I was thinking about the team that died when that bomb was ignited north of Baton Rouge. I was thinking of the people who were incinerated at Fort Oscar. I was thinking about the airliner they sabotaged as nothing more than a diversionary tactic. And then I was thinking about that bastard living under the protection of a scumbag like Chavez. When I got a lead on Adina's compound, my career was not even a consideration."

"You should have applied for authorization to proceed."

"Come on, sir, you know the Potomac shuffle. Getting permission for an incursion into Venezuela? Who was going to approve that? Even if I did, by the time we went up and down the chain of command where would Adina and his anthrax have been by then?"

"I understand your feelings about this man, I truly do. But there are protocols, damnit. And what about Bergenn and Raabe? How do you think it's going to go for them? And your pal down at the base in Hato Airport? Come now, don't look so surprised. You think we don't know Doug Carlton arranged your transportation in and out of Venezuela?"

"He had nothing to do with this. He thought we were acting on orders. And so did Bergenn and Raabe."

Byrnes almost managed a smile. "Sell that song and dance somewhere else." He stood up. "The Director wants to see us. All of us."

The reception they received in Director Walsh's office made the discussion with Byrnes seem positively congratulatory. Sandor, Bergenn, and Raabe had already been formally debriefed on the details of their rogue mission, and the Director had the report in front of him as they sat around his conference table. Walsh began by assuring each of them that they were in a world of trouble.

"You risked a serious international incident, which may yet bite us in the ass, and the totality of what you accomplished was to delay a shipment of narcotics that by now has likely been delivered anyway, despite your harebrained scheme."

"I don't think that's accurate," Sandor disagreed. "We gathered intelligence about Adina's operation, including a facility manufacturing anthrax and a multinational cocaine operation."

"Which leads you to what conclusion?"

"That this team should be permitted to travel to Sharm el-Sheikh to follow up on the information I gathered."

"Egypt? It's not enough that your escapade into Venezuela may ignite a melee with our most potent enemy in the Western Hemisphere. Now you want me to send you to one of the most volatile regions in the entire world to stir up trouble there?"

"That's where the trail leads, sir."

The Director shook his head in disgust. "That would be a definitive no, Agent Sandor. Meanwhile, what am I supposed to do with the Mexican you shanghaied?"

"Protective custody?"

"May I remind you, Sandor, this is the Central Intelligence Agency. Our primary objective is to gather intelligence in the defense of our country. We try to do our best, in that pursuit, to act covertly and not provoke wars all over the map."

The Director was interrupted when his assistant walked in and passed him a slip of paper.

"Well, gentlemen, in case you did not believe that these problems have already reached the highest levels of our government, the report of your exploits has been shared with the office of the National Director of Intelligence, and the NSC has arranged to join us for this discussion."

Walsh picked up a remote control and activated the videoconference screen on the wall. They all turned and waited until the image of the President's National Security Advisor, Peter Forelli, glowed to life.

Introductions were followed by the customary diplo-speak and expressions of concern over what Chavez might do in response to the shooting incident in the Lago de Maracaibo. Given Sandor's less than flattering opinion of the Venezuelan tyrant, he found himself wishing the hatchet-faced dictator would actually make some sort of retaliatory move. He remained silent on that as the others tossed around the usual back-channel options, with Walsh never missing the opportunity to make clear how the entire problem had been caused by blatant insubordination.

Sandor did not actually see a problem, which was why he was viewed as insubordinate. Fortunately, there was someone in the administration who agreed with him. As the NSA droned on about what needed to be done, the door behind him on the large screen opened and in strode the President of the United States.

Even though this was a videoconference, all five men around Walsh's table instinctively stood.

President Henry Forest responded with his familiar grin. He said, "At ease gentlemen," then sat beside Forelli as everyone else took their seats. "I got the headlines on this from Peter, fellas, so you've got two minutes of my time. What's the situation?"

Peter Forelli quickly reiterated the issues and Director Walsh chimed in with his concerns. It did not take long for the President to show them all the palm of his hand. Despite the carping of his worst critics, Forest was a deceptively quick study.

"So you're all bent out of shape because one of our boys blew up a drug smuggler's boat in the middle of Venezuelan waters, that the bottom line?" When no one replied, the President leaned forward to have a better look at his screen. "That you, Sandor?"

"Yes, Mr. President."

"You behind this mess?"

"I am, Mr. President. The mess is all mine."

The President nodded. "Never got to shake your hand after your work in Baton Rouge. I've got to be sure to do that real soon."

"It would be an honor, sir."

The President sat back and crossed his arms across his chest. "Look, men, they didn't capture Sandor, so they can't prove who did what. They can't even prove he was an American, am I right?" He did not wait for an answer. "Frankly, I've got bigger issues on my plate than worrying about that blowhard Chavez or some narcotics dealer in South America. So what say we skip all the State Department crap and let's hear what the man saw when he was down there?"

He was staring directly at Sandor.

"The narcotics operation was coupled with the manufacture of anthrax."

"I saw that in the report, son. Unfortunately, people are trying to make anthrax all over the world. What do you figure is special about this situation?"

"Rafael Cabello, sir. Adina has proved himself an avowed enemy of this country and an extremely dangerous man. I figure if we follow the narcotics we might find out what he intends to do with the anthrax. And hopefully we'll find him as well, Mr. President."

Forest nodded. "Anybody got a better idea than that, let's hear it." The President only allowed the clock to tick twice before he said, "Okay then, Sandor makes sense to me. What do you think, Mike?"

Director Walsh nodded at the large, flat screen. "Yes sir, I see the point."

"Good. Peter and I will talk it over, then he'll follow up with the NDI and get back to you all tomorrow. Meanwhile, if Chavez has a problem with a drug runner's boat getting blown up, let him take it to his leftist friends at the UN." The President stood, causing all the other men to scramble to their feet. Then he leaned forward and stared into the camera. "You're a good man, Sandor, and you do a helluva job for your country. But you know damn well that the business you're in is not about yesterday, it's all about today and tomorrow. So don't count too much on your past exploits to cover your ass, know what I'm saying?"

"Yes sir," Sandor said. "I do."

"Good, because if you go off the reservation like this again, I'll personally hand Mike the rope when he asks to string you up." Then the President smiled and, without another word, turned and headed for the door and out of the room.

CHAPTER TWENTY-FOUR

SHARM EL-SHEIKH, EGYPT

SITUATED ON THE southern tip of the Sinai Peninsula, the beautiful resort town of Sharm el-Sheikh has a storied and unusual history. Often referred to as the City of Peace, it was once a part of the Ottoman Empire. More recently, it became an Israeli-occupied territory. Then, in 1982 it was restored to its rightful inclusion in the nation of Egypt.

It has been the site of several Middle Eastern peace conferences, the location of a series of deadly shark attacks in 2010, the place where President Hosni Mubarak issued his resignation in 2011, and, tragically, the target of a vicious terrorist attack in 2005 by Islamic extremists who sought to destroy the Egyptian tourist trade, leaving eighty-eight people dead and more than two hundred wounded. Fortunately, this lovely seaport setting is graced by a surprisingly resilient population and, despite the turmoil in the region, it continues to flourish as a destination for foreign vacationers.

Sandor was familiar with the town, having used it on a couple of occasions as his exit point when heading home after completing missions in the Middle East. Famous for its long stretches of beach and world-class scuba diving, it is also a perfect location for nationals from different countries around the world to rendezvous. This is a place where Europeans, Asians, Hispanics, and Arabs regularly convene, and where meetings among and between them go largely unnoticed.

Unless one is looking for something or someone in particular.

Before he left Washington, Sandor had to endure another lecture from DD Byrnes, who picked up where Director Walsh and President Forest left off. Sandor did his best to appear chastened as Byrnes finished his tirade, which was not easy since the President himself had sanctioned the mission.

"Make sure you don't leave any footprints this time," was Byrnes's final admonition.

"I'll do my best."

"As for Bergenn and Raabe, try not to create any more problems for them, all right?"

Sandor insisted again that the idea and planning had been all his, explaining that the other men had merely come to his rescue when his exfiltration route was compromised.

Byrnes responded with a cynical stare. "You've got a better chance convincing me the Easter Bunny is real."

"Shall I give that a shot?"

"Zip it."

"Right."

"I'll deal with any of the diplomatic backlash here, you just keep a low profile."

"Will do," he said as he stood and headed for the door.

"Sandor!"

He spun around to face the DD.

"You let me know where you are. At all times."

"Of course."

"And what you're up to."

"Right."

"And I mean before the shooting starts."

"Of course, sir."

Byrnes fixed him with a stern look. "No vigilante nonsense. You got that?"

"Loud and clear."

Sandor left the DD's office and headed straight downstairs for an update on the interrogation of the Mexican drug runner he had escorted back from Venezuela. Bergenn reported that the man had been cooperative from the start, acknowledging he could never return home. His friends down south would assume he had given them up and would welcome him with an appropriate round of torture followed by an unceremonious burial somewhere deep in the jungle. He wanted asylum from the Americans and was willing to tell them everything he knew in exchange for that.

What he knew, unfortunately, was limited. The large drug cartels were careful about limiting the information shared with their rank and file—what the Agency famously referred to as a "need-to-know" chain of communication. He had learned enough along the way, however, to confirm some of what Carlos had told Sandor about the movement of the goods from Cabimas to northern Mexico, near the Texas border. He reported overhearing discussions about financial transactions in Egypt, just as Carlos had said, and heard Sharm el-Sheikh mentioned more than once, along with some banks there. He also gave them the names of two men that might prove helpful. One was a notorious drug lord who would almost certainly be involved in a shipment of this size. The other was a Russian financier. The Mexican was long on factoids and short on detail.

The three agents reviewed the balance of what they had gleaned from their debriefing. With help from the NCTC, Sandor confirmed there was evidence of financial activity in Sharm el-Sheikh consistent with the information he had gathered. They also helped him fill in some blanks.

He explained to Bergenn and Raabe what he was up to, insisting they remain in place until he had more specific intel. After that, Sandor made his travel arrangements and took the long flight that ultimately led him to the Ritz-Carlton hotel along Sharm el-Sheikh's Naama Bay.

———

Sandor checked in under his own name. Although he carried alternate identity papers in the liner of his carry-on, he did not want to raise any suspicions back at Langley by suddenly disappearing under a non-official cover. Using a NOC would be a red flag to the DD. He told Byrnes where he would be, and so here he was.

The room was a typically luxurious Ritz-Carlton room, and he immediately called the front desk and asked to have it changed. Old habits die hard, and tradecraft dictates certain precautions even in the most innocuous situations. The bellman waited with him as the woman at the front desk sent up a new electronic keycard for a room on a higher floor with a better view of the water. Once there, he quickly unpacked, took a cool shower, and prepared for action.

It had been a long flight, but Sandor had long ago developed the ability to sleep restfully on planes, a valuable skill when arriving at a destination refreshed was an absolute necessity. Which was all the time. After cleaning up he dressed in tan linen pants, brown loafers, and a black linen shirt with the sleeves rolled up to his elbows. He had no weapons, but he knew where they could be gotten—along with some of the information he needed—and that would be his first stop. He snapped on his stainless steel Rolex, pulled on his sunglasses, slung his black leather bag over his shoulder, and got started.

A short cab ride took Sandor to SOHO Square. He took his time in the area, walking in and out of a couple of shops, then circling around toward the back of the square, which was away from the water and the main thoroughfare.

Whether it was a heightened sense of danger after the clash in Venezuela, his years of training and experience, or a real threat, Sandor had the unshakable feeling someone was following him.

He hailed another taxi, took a ride down to the shore, then had the driver circle back to the square. Convinced he had shaken whoever might have been trailing him, he got out and found his way to Naama Heights Street. There he strolled at an unhurried pace, stopping twice to look in store windows as he confirmed no one was on his tail. Halfway down the block he walked into a shop called Red Sea Excursions. The only person in the place was an attractive, dusky-skinned young woman standing behind the counter. Sandor asked for Farrar.

"Farrar?" she repeated, as if she had never heard the name before.

"Just tell him it's Sandor," he replied with a knowing smile. The girl nodded, then disappeared through a door off to her right.

A few moments later she returned, followed by a man who appeared to be in his early sixties. He had a dark complexion, beaked nose, and a scar just below his right eye, all of which contributed to a surly demeanor that became incongruously brightened by the wide grin with which he greeted his old friend. "Jordan Sandor," he said, holding out his arms.

Sandor embraced the man, then took a step back. "Damn, you look as nasty as ever. Still scaring the customers away with that scowl of yours?"

Farrar gave his head a slight tilt to the side. "That's why I have Dendera here. She brings them in, I close the sale." He slapped Sandor on the arm. "What a surprise. It's so good to see you."

"And you."

When Sandor said nothing more, the older man nodded his understanding. "Come, we will go in the back, have some coffee, and catch up"

The rear of the shop was a cramped space filled with merchandise stacked against the walls, all of it surrounding a small desk and two chairs that served as a makeshift office. Atop a dented file cabinet was a Nespresso machine. Sandor laughed when he spotted it.

"Not exactly traditional."

"Ah well, you know my love of dark coffee. In the modern age, things become easier."

"Not all things."

"No, I suppose not," Farrar agreed. "So, I'm glad to see your skills have not diminished since we last met."

Sandor responded with an appreciative nod. "That was your man?"

Farrar smiled. "It was, and you managed to lose him even though he knew you were most likely coming here."

Sandor laughed.

Farrar opened a desk drawer and pulled out some capsules filled with ground espresso beans. "So, you will join me?"

"Sure."

The Egyptian quickly brewed two small cups, then the two men sat at his desk. "You are here on business."

Sandor nodded, then took a sip of the hot coffee.

"Just once I wish you would visit me and enjoy the pleasures of our beautiful port city."

"Someday, but not today."

Farrar drank his espresso down in one noisy gulp. "It has been too long."

"Since Bahrain."

Farrar paused, his expression turning to sadness. "I will never forget those we could not save."

Sandor nodded. "Hasani is well?"

At the mention of his son, Farrar looked down. It was the unbreakable bond between them, regardless of what either man felt about it. "I do not hear from him much. His mother still worries for him. I'm not sure what to feel." He looked up again, his eyes warmer than they had been before. "But he is my son. And you understand that."

"I do."

"His cowardice is a disgrace."

"No, my friend. He is young. And, as you say, he is your son."

Farrar could only sigh in response, then he changed the subject. "I heard about Traiman."

"Yes. And Covington."

"You did what you had to do, Jordan. They were evil men."

"The world is full of evil men."

"Too true. So, which of them brings you to Sharm el-Sheikh?"

"Adina."

"Ah, Rafael Cabello. This region is a bit far afield for the man from Venezuela."

"Not lately. Seems he did some business in Iran not too long ago. I have word that he now has contacts here."

"Financing?"

Sandor smiled. "As usual you're a step ahead of me."

"I prefer to think of myself as moving alongside you."

"What have you heard?"

Farrar sat back and rubbed his unshaved chin. "Narcotics from South America. Not a surprising commodity to be funded through our banks. The product itself does not pass through here, of course. Those who indulge locally have more convenient sources."

"That's my understanding. The movement of their goods is from South America into Mexico, then into the States."

"Yes. Which means one of the questions you have come here to answer is, why travel all the way to Egypt to make these arrangements?"

"It certainly is one of the questions."

"And the other might be, who is at the receiving end of these trades?"

Sandor grinned, then finished off his coffee and placed the small cup on the desk. "And you, as usual, are right again."

"The first matter is fairly simple. We have banks that welcome large deposits and ask very little. I can make inquiries."

"I have a head start," Sandor told him. "I have two names from my people. One is called the Bank of the Nile Valley. The other is the Sharm el-Sheikh International Reserve. We hear they welcome these accounts."

Farrar smiled. "Such grand names for the type of business they conduct. I know them both. How do you intend to approach them?"

"As a representative of a potential new customer."

"A large customer, I assume."

"Very."

"Then you will need to meet with the head of each of these banks."

"That's how I see it."

"I will make the contacts."

"Good. I also have two names, major players in this field."

"Are you prepared to share the names?"

"Jaime Rivera, from Mexico. One of the so-called drug lords. Ruthless. Feared even in his own violent world. Apparently he has a presence here."

"But not personally."

"No. From what I've learned he never leaves Mexico."

Farrar uttered a short laugh. "All that money and all that power, to end up a prisoner in Mexico of all places."

"Home sweet home."

"Yes, I know that name and I know that he has people who come and go on his behalf."

"I'd like to meet them if they're in town."

"I'll see what can be arranged. And the other name?"

"Sudakov."

"Yes, Ronny Sudakov."

"Ronny?"

Farrar shrugged. "He deals on behalf of the Russian syndicate, Moscow and New York. He's here now."

Sandor leaned back in the chair and folded his arms across his chest. "Then that's the man I need to find."

"Don't worry," Farrar said. "After you meet with these two bankers Sudakov will find you."

CHAPTER TWENTY-FIVE

SHARM EL-SHEIKH, EGYPT

Farrar stood, locked the door to the small room, then went to work moving some of the cartons stacked against the wall behind his desk. Hidden there was the entrance to a walk-in safe.

"Can't be too careful nowadays," he explained as he punched a combination into the electronic keypad and swung open the heavy door.

Inside was an imposing array of weapons.

Sandor got up and stood beside him. "Impressive. You expecting a major assault sometime soon?"

Farrar shrugged. "As I say, one cannot be . . ."

"Too careful, I got it. From the look of this arsenal I would say that business is good."

"I'm not complaining."

Sandor reached in and took hold of a hefty Glock 17. "Last time you helped me, everything you had could have fit in one of these cardboard boxes."

Farrar's smile revealed his tobacco-stained teeth. "At the time, it was all I needed to show you."

Sandor replaced the seventeen-shot pistol and picked up a Sphinx AT 380. It was smaller than most of the 9mm's and .45's and therefore easier to conceal. Swiss made, some Sphinx models are standard issue at Interpol. It was a safe, double-action weapon, with features similar to the Walther that Sandor favored, even a bit smaller than the PPK. He checked the magazine and action, then placed the Sphinx and some additional ammunition on the desk. "All right if I leave this with you for safekeeping?" he asked, gesturing to the black satchel he had brought with him.

"Of course. It will be safer here than at the hotel," Farrar assured him.

"My feelings exactly," Sandor replied, giving the soft leather an affectionate pat. "This bag and I have been through a lot together, wouldn't want to lose it now."

Sandor's "go bag" could sometimes be the difference between escape and capture, even life and death. He had refined the inventory of its contents over the years, anticipation being the byword that determined inclusion or exclusion. Some items were as mundane as a change of clothes, others as sensitive as counterfeit passports and cash that were secreted within the lining at the base of the bag. Sandor was not going to entrust the case to a front-desk hotel clerk or the easily breached combination safe in his room.

He unzipped a side pocket and placed the Sphinx and ammunition inside, then pulled it closed again and handed the bag to Farrar. "Thanks."

The Egyptian nodded, taking it and placing it on a shelf within the safe.

"I don't need a lot of firepower for now, but this might come in handy," Sandor said as he reached into the safe behind Farrar and picked up a Rohrbaugh R9, one of the smallest 9mm handguns made. It has no safety and holds only six rounds, but it weighs less than a pound and is easily concealed. Once again he checked the magazine and the action, then pocketed the weapon and sat down again as Farrar locked the safe.

"So the banks are in league with these drug smugglers," Sandor said as his friend also took his seat.

"Money has to be laundered, and the banks in this part of the world are extremely friendly. Terrorism has changed the Western world in many ways. From air travel to increased military spending to banking, yes?"

"Sad but true."

"They need bankers outside the United States, where the scrutiny is not so intense."

"What a world."

"But the reason you are here is beyond narcotics."

"Anthrax."

Farrar responded with a solemn nod.

"My goal is to stop a shipment of anthrax. If that shipment is tied to the cocaine it would seem I have to get to Rivera."

"Which will be no easy task. But as I say, you should start with the Russians."

"Isn't that swimming up the stream in the wrong direction?"

"Not at all. The stream, as you say, flows on a current of money. Rivera is a phantom as far as we are concerned in Sharm el-Sheikh, but the Russians are here. Their syndicate banks here."

"Sudakov . . ."

"Is the man you need to meet," Farrar finished the thought. "His yacht is at anchor in the harbor as we speak."

"All right. First the banks, then Sudakov."

"Yes. The Russians are a cutthroat bunch, but at least you can count on the fact that they are all about the money. It's another matter when you deal with the Islamic extremists, or the lunatics running North Korea or the socialists in Venezuela—they hate your country and your entire way of life. There's no reasoning with them." Farrar allowed himself a slight smile. "At least with the Russians you know you are dealing with capitalists."

———

Farrar suggested that Sandor do what tourists do in Sharm el-Sheikh—go clubbing at night and scuba diving in the morning. "That way they will be certain to find you," he told him again. Then he made a phone call and confirmed that a group from Sudakov's yacht had chartered a dive boat for the next morning. He got the details of the excursion and passed them to Sandor.

"I assume it's a private charter."

"Of course. When I spread the word that you are a wealthy American, here on his own, in search of fun . . . you understand. They like to, uh, what is the expression? Mingle?"

"Mingling is good."

Farrar stood, unlocked the office door, and called in Dendera. He told her to outfit Sandor with appropriate gear, wetsuit and tank. "We will have this available for you in the morning," he explained, "although I'm sure they will provide the necessary equipment."

"All I need to do is get myself invited, is that it?"

"Yes."

When the girl finished setting everything aside Sandor said, "Thank you," then waited until she left them alone again. "Can I buy you dinner someplace interesting tonight? Before I start trolling in the local bars."

"No, my friend, it is best we are not seen together. Not yet, anyway. Only a few people know of our history, and we should keep that to a minimum." As he said it, Sandor again felt the specter of Farrar's son enter the room. "For now you must be on your own. Especially when you visit these bankers."

Sandor nodded.

Farrar gave him the information on the two banks.

"You'll make the calls to set up the appointments?"

"Not I, but trust me, the calls will be made and the meetings will be arranged. I will phone your hotel and leave word of the times for each." Then he recited the names of a few clubs. "Tonight you should make the rounds, after your meetings. By then word about you will be out. And the Russians will be easy to spot," he added with a brief chuckle. "Look for cheap women, gaudy gold jewelry, and bottles of Cristal."

"Who's going to be wearing the gaudy jewelry?" Sandor asked with a grin. "The cheap women or the Russian men?"

"The men of course," Farrar said.

CHAPTER TWENTY-SIX

SHARM EL-SHEIKH, EGYPT

Sandor RETURNED TO the Ritz, where he rested for an hour, then changed into the white shirt and tan gabardine Dunhill suit he had the valet press while he was out. Sliding the sleek Rohrbaugh in his back pocket, he set out to make the acquaintance of the two crooked bankers Farrar had identified.

His first stop was the Sharm el-Sheikh International Reserve. It was headquartered in a modern building not far from SOHO Square. One of the many charms of this resort town is how everything is centrally located.

Sandor entered the bank, a high-ceilinged space defined by tall, smoked glass windows that did their best to contain the cool air that flowed in through numerous vents situated around the perimeter of the large room. The teller stations were located behind a long row of windows off to the right. Sandor approached a young woman seated at a desk to the left. He gave his name and told her he was there to see the bank president. She made a call, confirmed his appointment, then rose to show him to the elevator that would take him up one floor to the executive suite.

On the second floor he was greeted by another woman, who led him into a spacious office where the bank official was already standing.

"A pleasure, Mr. Sandor." He extended a friendly hand, then pointed his guest to a seat at a small, round conference table.

The woman who had ushered him in asked Sandor if he wanted

anything in the way of coffee, water or refreshments, but he politely declined. She nodded, said, "Very well, please let me know if you change your mind," then showed herself out and pulled the door closed behind her.

As the two men took their seats facing each other, the banker flashed a gleaming white smile that Sandor figured he must use quite a bit. He was elegantly attired in a dark gray suit, powder blue shirt, and dark Hermès print tie. "Well, Mr. Sandor, I must say you arrive with the highest recommendations." Sandor noticed that he did not mention from whom these recommendations had come. Whatever Farrar had done to set this meeting on short notice, he had clearly made an impression.

"As does your bank," Sandor assured him. "I am told that you operate with the utmost efficiency. And discretion."

The banker nodded appreciatively. "After security, of course, I believe discretion is the most important of the many services we provide."

"Excellent. I therefore take it that we can dispense with any unnecessary discussion about the nature of my interest in banking here."

The man sat back slightly. "Ah, the famous American bluntness surfaces at the very start of our relationship. Then I also say 'excellent.' It certainly saves time."

For a fleeting moment Sandor reflected on the fact that he was sitting across from a man whose illicit actions facilitate the movement of large funds among major drug sellers and drug buyers, criminals of various stripe and, ultimately, terrorists. Given the option, he would have enjoyed pulling out the compact 9mm in his back pocket and tapping the bastard twice in the forehead. For now he reminded himself that he was hunting bigger game. He forced a smile and asked, "How can we best move our relationship forward?"

The banker's eyes lit up. "Are you saying that you are prepared to open an account?"

"I'm saying that I am prepared to learn what will be involved in establishing this account so I might speak to the others involved and make an informed decision."

"Ah well," the man said with a hint of disappointment—he was well aware that his was not the only game in town. "I will do my best to answer your questions."

What followed was an oblique description of how the Sharm el-Sheikh International Reserve catered to unique customers for whom anonymity and a minimum vapor trail produced by the movement of their funds was an absolute priority. The man was smooth, Sandor would have to give him that. A recording of their conversation would not have yielded a single incriminating statement. He was a master of theoretical, vague, and noncommittal speech. Yet, by the time he was done, Sandor knew enough to satisfy himself that he was in the right place to begin tracking the flow of money generated by the narcotics trade emanating from South America. He was also convinced these criminals were smart to be laundering their funds in this small Egyptian town.

"Forgive a direct question," Sandor interrupted as the man was reciting a mind-numbing litany of bank regulations. "But are you saying that your bank does not make moral judgments about the nature of the businesses in which its customers engage?"

The banker thought that one over. "Let us say, our bank does not inquire into those dealings. We limit our involvement to the handling of our customers' financial transactions."

Sandor forced another smile, then said, "Good, good. Please continue."

When they concluded their meeting and stood to shake hands, it was difficult again for Sandor to resist his natural impulse—this time to rip the man's arm out of its socket and beat him to death with it. Instead he said, "This has been most helpful. You will be hearing from my man tomorrow." He then leaned forward and said quietly, "His name is James Bergenn, and he will produce the appropriate identification for you." Moving back, as if the utterance of that name was the most sensitive thing he had to say, he added, "Please provide him all of the courtesies and attention you have so generously given me. He will be the person with whom you will have most of your dealings on our behalf."

"Understood," the banker said without repeating the name. "Until tomorrow then."

As Sandor left he was not certain his performance had been completely convincing, but he did not care. The man might make calls, but he would learn nothing more about his potential new customer other than his scheduled meeting, later today, with the president of his institution's chief rival, the Bank of the Nile Valley. Hopefully that would be sufficient to convince both bankers that Sandor was a serious player, giving each of them motivation to keep their discussions confidential lest their indiscretion become discovered and their prospective client end up taking his business somewhere else altogether.

Consequently, when Sandor began his meeting at the Bank of the Nile Valley two hours later, he decided to begin with the admission that he was considering one of two local institutions and wanted to be candid in that regard. The official here was less friendly and more cautious, but the resultant discussion ended up yielding substantially the same information. When their meeting came to a close, Sandor felt he had enough of corrupt bankers to last him a lifetime.

He wanted to find his way to the nearest bar, where he could give his hands a good wash with hot water and then wrap himself around a cold cocktail, but he thought better of it and returned to his hotel instead. Using his encrypted cell phone he called Craig Raabe and gave him as much information as he had gathered to date. Then he changed back to a more casual outfit and prepared to head out on the town.

———————

Meanwhile, the rival bankers with whom Sandor had spent his afternoon were exchanging pleasantries in a brief telephone conversation.

"May the blessings of Allah be with you," intoned the man from the Bank of the Nile Valley.

"And with you," his counterpart replied.

"An interesting visit, was it not?" There was no need for further identification of the subject at hand.

"Interesting, yes. And a bit worrisome."

"His referrals were impeccable."

"A matter easily arranged, you agree?"

"I do."

"And no actual transaction was initiated."

"Nor with me."

"Which raises the delicate question of what we owe to our current clients."

"To warn them, you mean?"

"Let us say, to alert them to the possibility of competition."

"Or worse."

"Yes. Enemy action would be worse."

There was a brief silence, then the man from the Bank of the Nile Valley suggested they meet for a drink at their club.

"Excellent idea," came the reply.

CHAPTER TWENTY-SEVEN

SHARM EL-SHEIKH, EGYPT

Sandor began his pub crawl at Little Buddha, which, among other things, lays claim to a reputation as the longest continuously operating bar in the Middle East. It was the first place on Farrar's list of popular nightclubs.

Sandor asked for a small table in the corner of the restaurant area that allowed him to sit with his back to the wall and afforded a line of vision to both the entrance and the hallway leading to the restrooms. He ate sushi and drank mediocre sake served in a small ceramic carafe, then paid the check and made his way toward the real action. Finding a spot at the bar where he had a similar view of his surroundings, he ordered a Grey Goose, straight up and very cold, with a few slivers of ice to keep it that way and three olives to keep the vodka company.

As he took his first taste of the chilled drink he made a silent toast to Farrar and how he had organized those meetings on short notice, mobilizing his people to do whatever was necessary to convince the two bankers that they were being introduced to a major player. When that information spread through the proper circles it would become particularly helpful in dealing with the Russians. Sandor nodded to himself. Farrar was one of the few people who had never let him down. The reason for such loyalty, which in this case was driven by Sandor having risked his life to save Farrar's wayward son, did not matter. Most people tend to have short and convenient memories, a trait that never ceased to disappoint Sandor. He was grateful that his Egyptian friend was not so afflicted.

He replaced his glass on the bar and took some time scanning the crowded room. He was not at it for long when he saw her approach from his right.

"Hello," she said, which Sandor figured was the only pickup line a beautiful woman needs.

She was certainly beautiful, and perfectly balanced on a pair of narrow heels that were long enough to be registered as lethal weapons. Sandor was just over six feet tall, and the shoes lifted her to his eye level.

He said, "Hello to you too."

She didn't smile. Instead she continued to stare into his dark, intense eyes with an unblinking gaze that can only be managed with a fair amount of practice. "Buy a thirsty girl a drink?"

Sandor conceded the staring contest and had a look at the rest of her. She was wearing a reasonably short tan skirt and a reasonably skimpy white silk top, a combination that provided a reasonably good view of her considerable assets. When he finished the visual tour he returned his attention to her sea-green eyes. "Whatever you're thirsty for," he said, "I'm buying."

She didn't give in all the way with a huge smile or anything close to that, but she did part her lips enough to reveal very white, very even teeth that showed up quite nicely against her tan complexion. "Well then," she said, "whatever you're drinking I'm thirsty for."

Sandor called the bartender over and told him to shake up another vodka, then turned back to her. "I'm Jordan," he said, offering his hand.

She took it, her grip warm and dry and firm. "You can call me Lilli."

He stuck out his lower lip, as if what she allowed him to call her was something that deserved careful consideration. "I can call you Lilli? Is that because Lilli is really your name, or is there some other reason?"

Now she did smile, and he could see why she hadn't been in any rush to use that part of her arsenal. It was dazzling, and she had no reason to waste it early on. "It's actually Lillian," she said.

"Ah."

"It was my grandmother's name. Always felt sort of old-fashioned to me." Before Sandor had a chance to tell her what a lovely name it was, or something obvious like that, she added, "Maybe I'll use it when I'm a grandmother myself. What do you think?"

"I think a rose, by any other name, still looks pretty good."

"Thanks."

"So, Lillian a.k.a. Lilli, what are you doing in Sharm el-Sheikh?"

"You mean, why is a nice girl like me in a bar like this asking a stranger like you to buy her a drink?"

"As I recall, you explained that already. You're thirsty, right?"

She flashed some more teeth and said, "That's right, I did."

"What I actually meant was, who are you? Are you a tourist, an adventuress, maybe the director of hospitality here at Little Buddha?"

"How about two out of three."

The bartender placed a martini glass before her, filled to the rim with the clear, cold liquid. When she lifted it, her hand was as steady as a diamond cutter.

"Well," Sandor said as he hoisted his own glass, "nice to meet you Lilli." Then he watched her drink. Sandor always figured he could tell a lot about a person, especially a woman, by the way they take the first sip of a cocktail. Lilli was not shy about draining a serious portion of the vodka before replacing the glass on the bar, and that told him plenty. "So, now that we've dealt with your thirst, what else can I do for you?"

She appeared surprised by the question.

"Come on, Lilli, you didn't just happen to pick me out of this crowd by chance."

The girl's expression went as blank as a sheet of copy paper.

Sandor had another pull at his drink. "That's very good, you must work on that look." When Lilli did not respond, he said, "Can't let these get warm, can we?"

She picked up the cocktail, her long, slender fingers wrapped elegantly around the glass, and had another taste. "Vodka is lousy when it's warm," she agreed, not putting the drink down just yet.

He nodded. "So, how about you tell me who you are and who asked you to chat me up and where we're supposed to go from here?"

She took a moment before she said, "You're really all business, aren't you?"

"Me? That may be the first time a beautiful woman has ever accused me of that." He was staring into her aquamarine eyes again. "My guess, however, is that you're the one who's all business. At least as far as this discussion is concerned."

"Ooh, that's cold."

"Some people think my honesty is charming."

She gave her head a slow, purposeful shake, long auburn hair dancing across her shoulders. "There's a difference between blunt and honest, Mr. Sandor."

He responded with a knowing grin. "I see you have the advantage there."

"How's that?"

"You know my last name and I only know you as Lilli."

"You just told me. Jordan Sandor, right?"

"Right name, wrong play. I never gave my last name. So let's get back to why you're here."

For the first time he thought he saw something in her face that appeared authentic. She put the glass on the bar, then turned back to him and said, "I screwed that one up, didn't I?"

"New at this?"

"Totally."

"That's not necessarily a bad thing."

She responded with an embarrassed nod.

"So, who sent you?"

"I suppose there's no way around answering you."

"Don't worry, I won't tell."

Another nod. Then, "There's a group of Russians partying on a huge yacht down near South Harbor. I was on board with a few girl-friends. The man who owns it asked me to find you."

"Asked you, ordered you, or paid you?"

"Does it matter?"

"It does to me."

"He paid me."

"And you just happened to stroll in here and find me at the bar?"

She turned back to her drink and lifted the glass. This time she only took a small sip. "This is the third place I tried. Just came from the Fifties Bar."

"That was my next stop."

"That's funny, huh?"

"Hilarious. We almost became ships passing in the night."

"Except I found you."

"So you got that part right. Now what?"

"I'm supposed to get you to come to the party."

"That's it?"

"As far as I know."

"Well, I wouldn't want you to have to give the money back." Sandor drained off what was left in his glass. "We in any rush to get there?"

Now it was her turn to give him a once-over. After a long look and a brief smile, she said, "Not that I know of."

"Good," he replied. "Let's have another one of these. Can't fly on one wing."

CHAPTER TWENTY-EIGHT

SHARM EL-SHEIKH, EGYPT

Sandor decided it would be best to take his time before arriving at the party at South Harbor. There was no point in appearing too eager in accepting the invitation. For now he would focus on the comings and goings in Little Buddha, just in case Lilli had a trailer, or an unfriendly face appeared in the crowd.

Even as he kept an eye on things it was difficult not to keep returning his attention to Lilli. Her well-shaped legs were worthy of her height and the tight blouse she was wearing displayed enough of her smooth, full breasts to draw his gaze more than once. Putting all that together with her lovely face, it was easy to be distracted.

As Sandor knew only too well, however, decoys come in different shapes and sizes. It was not impossible that the girl was there to encourage him to become careless, or perhaps to draw him outside, where the festivities planned for him would be short-lived and violent.

They were well into their second drink when he asked, "So Lilli, what exactly did they suggest you do to convince me to show up for their little shindig?"

The girl shrugged. "I'm not enough?"

Sandor grinned. "That, as they say, remains to be seen."

"There are a lot of other pretty girls there. Does that help?"

"It might. Are they all as gorgeous as you?"

"I would say yes."

"'Yes' works for me." He had another look around. It did not appear they were being watched, but he was still not convinced. "You know, I have a terrific room at the Ritz, haven't spent any real time in it yet, but it has a great view. I think we should go have a look. Bet we can get drinks there, too."

"Jordan Sandor, are you propositioning me?"

"Absolutely," he said.

She treated him to another smile. "I wondered what was taking you so long."

He paid the check and they left the club, but not before Sandor tipped the girl at the front and had her get a cab to pull right up to the front door. When she confirmed the car was there he made a quick exit, his left hand on Lilli's arm, his right on the Rohrbaugh in his pocket.

If someone meant to take him out right here he saw no evidence of that, and the girl was not a good enough actress to fake the relaxed attitude she carried from the bar into the taxi. Still, whatever they did or did not have in store for him, he figured it would make sense to remove himself from public view for a while.

The cab dropped them at the Ritz-Carlton and they went straight to his room. He opened the courtesy bar, fixed them each a vodka rocks, then stood beside her at the large window, sharing a look at the glittering panorama of Sharm el-Sheikh at night.

"Beautiful," said Lilli.

"The view is better in here," he said.

She turned to him, an expectant look in her lovely eyes. He took the glass from her hand and placed it on the table. Then he put his arms around her and drew her toward him.

"You need to know something," she said after he kissed her gently on the lips.

"What's that?"

"This part was not paid for."

He drew back slightly and had another good look at her. "I didn't think it was."

"Good," she whispered. "I just wanted to tell you."

When they kissed again it was deep and long and passionate and, for what it was worth, he believed her. Then he told her so.

————

They spent the next part of the next two hours exploring some of each other's secrets—such as the sexy little flower tattoo just above the center of Lilli's firm ass, a couple of scars on Jordan's chest he promised to explain later, and a mutual affinity for long kisses, slow erotic movements, and each other. They finished creating a damp, tangled jigsaw puzzle of the sheets, which the maids would have to sort out later, then they showered and got themselves ready to leave. As Lilli was putting herself back together in the marble bathroom, Sandor had a quick look inside her purse.

Her credit cards and driver's license said she really was a Lillian, last name Mindlovitch, living on the Upper East Side of Manhattan—just across town from Sandor. There was nothing of help beyond that. He put the cards back in place, concluding that she was what she claimed to be—a party girl who had been sent to find him and bring him to the yacht in South Harbor.

During the taxi ride to the dock he asked where she was born.

"Moscow. But I've lived in New York for years."

"Sharm el-Sheikh is pretty far from New York."

"Got here this week. Some old friends asked me to come over."

"You're too young to have old friends."

She laughed.

"You enjoying this place?"

"It can be fun."

"So you've demonstrated."

She smiled. Then she took his hand and squeezed it.

"How is it your English is so perfect?"

"My mother brought me to the States when I was six."

"Your father?"

"Disappeared years ago. That's when we left Moscow."

"Your mother still in New York?"

"She died two years ago. Cancer."

"I'm sorry. She must have been young."

"Very."

"Sisters, brothers?"

She turned to him and, even in the darkness, he could see the answer in her eyes. "Only me," she said.

Sandor had a world of advice he wanted to share with her, but he said nothing. For now he had a job to do.

———————

It was not far from the hotel to South Harbor. They got out of the cab and she led him to the private dock entrance, punched in a code that opened the entry gate, then led him to a launch at the end of the pier.

There were two men waiting, one sitting on a wooden bench enjoying a smoke, the other standing in the cockpit of the motorboat. As Sandor and the girl approached, the man with the cigarette stood and, without a word, tossed the butt into the water and set about removing the docking line. The pilot started the engines.

There was no greeting, not to the girl or to him. They watched as Lilli slipped off her stiletto heels and let Sandor help her on board. Then they cast off and were on their way.

CHAPTER TWENTY-NINE

SOUTH HARBOR, SHARM EL-SHEIKH, EGYPT

There were times when Sandor's friend, Bill Sternlich, could not resist the reporter's impulse to ask about the *why* of the things Sandor did. He understood that Sandor would never share the specifics of *what* he did, but Sternlich remained fascinated that a man he knew so well could repeatedly put himself in harm's way with no apparent regard for the risks, seeming only to be concerned about the results.

As Sandor sat beside Lilli, saying nothing as the launch approached the enormous yacht looming ahead of them, he was thinking about Sternlich and how he had tried to answer his friend's questions. It was not that Sandor did not experience fear—only a fool would fail to recognize the dangers he faced. It was about putting those worries aside because there was something that needed to be done and he had the skills to do it.

Tonight he was going to confront men he believed to be involved in a scheme to import anthrax into the United States. It was up to him to do whatever was necessary to stop them.

As he would say to Sternlich, someone had to do it and he was that someone. It was as simple as that.

———

Sandor had been on any number of yachts, but the *Odessa* was certainly among the most beautiful he had ever seen. Even from a distance, in the moonless night, he could make out the elegant lines.

As they drew closer he looked up at the tall conning tower, which was set just ahead of a launching pad where a small helicopter sat at rest. The bow jutted gracefully forward and the transom had temporarily become the mooring point for several Jet-Skis and a Zodiac, all of which would be stored below when the ship was under way. The launch pulled alongside that aft platform, where they climbed out and made their way up a short flight of steps.

Sandor followed Lilli onto the rear deck, where they were met by a number of young women who had been watching the motorboat approach and now wanted to know what took her so long and where she had been. Sandor stood by in polite silence as they completed their feminine rite of greeting. Then Lilli introduced him around.

He accepted a glass of champagne, poured from a bottle of Cristal that was sitting in a silver bucket on the oval dining table positioned beneath a cantilevered overhang that covered half of the large outdoor area. The girls surrounded him, as if he were a curiosity, this new addition to the proceedings.

He noted that Lilli had been accurate in her assessment—each of the other women was indeed attractive—but at the moment he wanted to excuse himself from this circle of beauties and attend to the reason he had come.

As if reading his mind, a voice from behind him said, "A friend of Lilli's?"

Sandor turned to face a short, muscular man of about fifty with closely cropped hair, clear complexion, handsome features, and pale blue eyes that seemed capable of seeing through lead. Just as Farrar had predicted there would be Cristal on board, the Russian was indeed wearing a gold chain around his neck that was thick enough for use as a drapery pull.

"A very recent acquaintance, actually."

"Good enough for me. I'm Ronny."

Sandor took the hand Ronny offered, his grip so tight that shaking it felt like something of a contest. "Jordan Sandor."

"So glad you could join us," he replied. Sandor had been to Moscow often enough to place the source of his host's accent. "Come along, ladies, we are all in the main salon." Ronny took Sandor by the arm and led the group through glass doors into a richly furnished area that was roughly the size of a baseball diamond. The "we" he had referred to was a group of men seated on couches and chairs. In the center of the room was a glass-topped table that bore the unmistakable traces of cocaine that someone had made an unsuccessful effort to hide before he entered. None of the men rose.

"This is Mr. Sandor," Ronny announced to no discernible reaction. "Come," he said to his new guest without providing names for any of the members of his entourage. "Sit with me."

The salon was paneled in dark cherrywood, the floor covered with a plush beige broadloom, and the chandeliers were hung with enough crystal ornaments to make the designers at Baccarat blush. The fabric used for the upholstered furniture pieces was a coordinated mélange of silk, tapestries, and satins in a variety of earth tones. The accessories were dominated by glass and polished brass that glittered even in the muted lighting.

Sandor, his champagne flute still in hand, followed Ronny to an unoccupied couch, where they sat side by side, doing their best to face each other. "This is a magnificent yacht. I take it you are the lucky owner."

"I am, and I thank you. I take great pride in the *Odessa*."

"As well you should. Feadship, I imagine."

"Very good, Mr. Sandor. Wonderful shipbuilders."

"Yes, they are. And call me Jordan."

His host nodded in appreciation.

"Ronny is an unusual name for a Russian."

The man smiled, an exercise that clearly did not come easily to him. "My given name is Roman. A bit regal, no? Chosen by my father. My mother was a fan of the American actor Ronald Reagan, called me Ronny from the time I was born. One of life's little ironies, is it not? I am a Russian named for the man who brought down the Soviet Union."

"Which I assume you regard as a good thing," Sandor observed with a wave of his hand at their luxurious surroundings.

"Let us say that capitalism has been better to me than communism was to my parents." He was about to take a drink from his glass, then apparently thought better of it. "So what brings you to Sharm el-Sheikh?"

Before responding, Sandor had a look at the other men in the room. They were trying unsuccessfully to appear not to be eavesdropping on this conversation. When he smiled at them they all turned their heads away, as if on a single swivel. Sandor turned back to his host. "I've been traveling, had a few extra days, thought I might stop over and arrange some banking transactions. As well as some scuba diving," he added with a smile.

"You've been here before?"

"In fact I have, but always on business. Never had a chance to dive the reefs."

"Well you are in for a treat then. A few of us are heading out tomorrow morning. You must join us."

"That's very generous of you, but I already have plans."

The Russian waved that off as if Sandor's arrangements were of no consequence. "We thought we might go out at ten, then come back here for lunch. I hope that works for you, yes?"

Sandor managed a disappointed look. "I booked an earlier start, but thank you anyway."

Ronny's translucent gaze told Sandor that he was dealing with a man not accustomed to refusals. "Well, we can certainly accommodate a new friend. Eight early enough?"

Sandor had received an answer to his first question. They had gotten him here and were not about to let him go so easily. It took no effort for him to respond with a smile and say, "You make it very difficult to say no. Eight would be perfect."

"That's settled, then. Let me get you a real drink and some caviar." He snapped his fingers and a steward materialized, as if from the ether. "Bring us some vodka and a plate of the Osetra. How do you like your vodka?"

"Straight and cold would be fine," Sandor said.

They were served the food and drinks by two young men who took less time to set the table before them than it takes to draw a pint of beer. They were then left to drink Stolichnaya Elit poured from a frozen bottle, snack on the caviar that had been heaped with a silver spoon onto small blinis, and tell each other lies.

Ronny described his days as a star defenseman on the Russian national hockey team. He explained that his connections in sports led naturally to connections in government, since the Kremlin ran all the national athletic programs back then. His contacts eventually helped him to amass considerable wealth making oil deals once the USSR fell and the fever of capitalism spread throughout Mother Russia. "I have been very fortunate," he said, failing in the effort to sound humble.

Sandor already knew the story about hockey was true and that there had even been a series of oil deals in Sudakov's past. He was also certain that his host was neglecting to mention his most profitable enterprises.

When it was Sandor's turn, he used his customary cover, claiming to have spent time in diplomatic service for the United States government where he made his own international connections. The additional layer he added for this mission was a story about having become independently wealthy through hedge fund trading and related transactions. He then apologized, saying that the world of finance was simply too boring to spend any time discussing, especially since he had branched out into areas, as he put it, "that do not bear description." The best part for him, he said, was the extensive travel. He made it clear he had been to the Middle East many times. And, of course, to Russia.

"I'm surprised our paths have never crossed before. We probably know a lot of the same people."

Sandor shrugged. "It's a big world."

Ronny responded with a curious look. "Not so much, not anymore."

The tenor of their discussion and the relaxed attitude of the other men present—who had given up listening to their colloquy and again occupied themselves with the young ladies in attendance—provided Sandor an answer to his second question. There was no intention to do him harm, at least not yet. First they would want information. He watched as the steward removed his champagne flute, then replaced the first chilled glass of vodka with a second. He assumed that they were already running his fingerprints.

His involvement in National Clandestine Service operations for the CIA was a closely guarded secret, but no secret is completely safe in the modern order. After the treachery of Vincent Traiman, the turncoat station chief whom Sandor had dispatched a year earlier, it was not impossible that highly placed intelligence sources in other countries would at least be able to determine that Sandor's work for the State Department had transcended his pose as a diplomatic paper shuffler. His hope was that his cover would hold up, and that his allusions to shady dealings might actually help to impress the Russian.

"So," Ronny was saying, "you and our friend Lilli are recent acquaintances, yes?"

Sandor made a show of looking at his watch. "As I said, very recent," he replied with a smile. "In fact we just met a couple of hours ago, at a bar in town."

"Is that so?"

"Yes indeed. Lucky me."

"She is quite an attractive young woman."

"I agree. And imagine when I learned what she was up to."

The tilt of Ronny's head was almost imperceptible. "What she was up to?"

"I meant the fact that she was coming here. And that she invited me to join her. And to join you, of course."

"Ah, yes, of course. I am very glad you did. In fact, you will stay with us tonight."

"That's very generous, but I couldn't possibly. My clothes are back at the hotel and I've already arranged my diving gear."

"We have enough equipment for you here," he said with another dismissive flick of his hand, then took a turn at holding up his chunky gold wristwatch to show Sandor it was after one in the morning. "Look at the hour. The men who operate the launch are already in their quarters, asleep no doubt. I would hate to have to wake them." When Sandor began to protest again, Ronny added, "Lilli is staying with us too. This will give you a chance to get to know her better."

Sandor feigned a look of careful consideration, then said, "That would be nice, wouldn't it?"

"Of course."

"Well then, would it be all right if she showed me around the yacht a bit? I mean, I'm already dead on my feet, but I'd love to see some of it before I turn in."

CHAPTER THIRTY

ABOARD THE *ODESSA* IN SOUTH HARBOR, SHARM EL-SHEIKH, EGYPT

Ronny was having difficulty disguising his suspicions. He had offered Lilli's companionship as an inducement for his guest to stay, but he was not going to permit Sandor and the girl to roam the yacht on their own. He was not a man that easily played.

"Why not let me show the two of you my beautiful *Odessa*," he suggested.

Sandor smiled. "That would be such an imposition. It would be rude of me to take you away from your other guests."

"Not at all. Lilli," he called out. "Come, I'm taking you and Mr. Sandor on a private tour."

───────────

Meanwhile, Sandor's assumption about Sudakov's efforts to vet his background was correct.

Farrar had gotten out the word that Sandor was a wealthy man with something illicit to buy or sell and looking for an appropriate bank through which to run the money. In Sudakov's world, that news spread quickly, earning Sandor his invitation to the *Odessa*.

Now, as Sandor and the girl were being taken from cabin to cabin and salon to salon on a show-and-tell excursion led by their host, Sudakov's men were working to verify the American's identity—and his purpose in coming to Sharm el-Sheikh. His fingerprints had indeed been lifted from the champagne and vodka glasses and a background check was being run. By the time Sudakov escorted his two guests into the impressive control room on the bridge, the prints had been transmitted through a computer system in Moscow and communicated back to the *Odessa*.

Yes, his name really is Jordan Sandor. Yes, he really did work for the United States government. Yes, he had been assigned to the State Department after service in the military. As they reviewed the details about where he had been stationed and what he had done in those years, it was as if his dossier was too clean. *Sanitized* was the term of art. There were long stretches of nondescript bureaucratic service followed by time engaged in private enterprises they could not corroborate. And his finances could not be authenticated, at least not yet. Taken all together, this usually meant one of two things—either he was that rare peddler of contraband who had managed to successfully fly under the radar, or he was a poseur engaged in covert operations.

When the security staff gathered as much data as they could for now, a steward was dispatched to find Ronny. He caught up with him as Sudakov was bragging to Sandor and Lilli about the state-of-the-art electronics inside the wheelhouse.

"Worthy of the largest cruise ships on the sea. Even better," Sudakov said as he pointed out a variety of radar, sonar, and GPS screens. The captain had turned in for the night, but two other men were on hand. "We never have less than two crew members on duty," Sudakov explained, "even when the *Odessa* stands at anchor, as it does now."

"You can't be too careful," Sandor observed as he turned from the two crewmen seated at the control panel to the large Russian who had been accompanying them on the tour. He was one of the henchmen from the salon, who had wordlessly followed them since they began their stroll around the vessel. "Pirates, thieves, enemies, am I right?"

The steward had entered, but Ronny took no notice of him. He stared directly at Sandor as he said, "Yes, you are right. We live in uncertain times."

"I would guess, then, that your men are properly armed?" He shot another glance at the husky bodyguard.

"Are you the nervous type, Mr. Sandor?"

"Let's just say I'm the cautious type. Having worked in the State Department, I find it a healthy foreign policy."

For the first time tonight, the Russian uttered a laugh. It was not a pleasant sound, resonating more of irritation than mirth. Turning to the steward, he asked impatiently, "What is it?" The young man handed him a folded piece of paper. Ronny read the note, then placed it in his pocket. "Well," he said, "it's gotten late and I won't bore you with any more of this. Pavel here will show you to your staterooms." He gave a slight nod in the direction of his bodyguard. Then he looked at Lilli, whom he had ignored throughout the entire tour. "I have placed you in adjoining cabins. I hope you find that satisfactory." Without awaiting a response, he turned back to Sandor and said, "I am sure you will find the accommodations suitable. Sleep well." Then he turned and left.

———

Their spin around the ship was mildly interesting and well choreographed—Sudakov only took them to the places he wanted Sandor to see, which meant there was no place Sandor was being shown that he would have to bother about later. Now that he had an understanding of the yacht's layout he concluded that the activities he was interested in were being conducted on a lower deck—especially since Sudakov had twice pretended not to hear Sandor's request to visit below.

Pavel walked them to their adjoining staterooms. As he had no doubt been instructed, the tall Russian waited until they entered and closed their doors behind them.

Sudakov was true to his word: the accommodations were certainly suitable. The cabin was larger than Sandor's room at the hotel, and no less comfortable. He was just having a look around when he heard a knock on the door from the adjoining space. He opened up and Lilli walked past him.

"Is there any champagne in here? There's none in my room."

Sandor pointed to the ice bucket on the nightstand beside his king-sized bed. "I guess they expect me to be a good sharer."

The girl smiled. "Works for me," she said. "You want to open it or should I?"

———

As Sandor wrestled the cork out of the bottle of Roederer Cristal, Ronny was meeting with his security people in the communications room on the second level. They were standing around a highly polished teak conference table.

After describing the information they had compiled, the chief operative reported simply, "He's CIA."

"You are certain?"

"No. But everything points to that."

"What if he is who he claims to be? Could that be consistent with the data you've gathered?"

"It's possible. But after what happened in South America? I would say no, the timing would indicate otherwise."

Sudakov nodded in agreement. "Anything new from our friend in Venezuela?"

The burly officer shook his head. "Just what we had yesterday."

"Could this be the same man?"

"Not likely."

"Perhaps he's part of the same operation?"

"Possible."

"Possible." Ronny spat the word out as if it were a bad taste. "Why the hell would the CIA be interested in narcotics?"

"He could be from the American DEA, but I don't believe that."

"Why?"

"The profile doesn't fit."

Ronny shook his head. "If he's working for the United States government, regardless of the agency, that means they know he's here. Which means we can't just shoot him in the head and throw him over the side." The look in his eyes confirmed to the others what they already knew—that this would be his preferred course of action. "If he disappears while he's here that'll only bring more of them down on us."

"What could he learn from a night aboard the *Odessa*? That he saw the girls snorting coke? Why not just send him on his way tomorrow and be done with him? We can shove off as soon as he leaves."

"No, that doesn't feel right either. He came to Sharm el-Sheikh for something, and whatever it is I don't intend to let him leave with it."

The others waited without speaking.

"I believe you're right," Ronny said. "Whoever he is, he has something to do with the raid in Venezuela, I just feel it. Tonight you keep an eye on him. Tomorrow he's going to have a nasty little accident."

CHAPTER THIRTY-ONE

ABOARD THE *ODESSA* IN SOUTH HARBOR, SHARM EL-SHEIKH, EGYPT

LILLI HAD KICKED off her shoes, fluffed up some pillows, and was sitting on his bed, a glass of champagne in hand and a curious look on her pretty face. She watched Sandor pace the room, raking back his dark, wavy hair with the fingers of his right hand. "You upset about something?" she finally asked.

He stopped and shot her a look that said he had almost forgotten she was there. "I have a lot of nervous energy."

"I've noticed," she said, then flashed one of her genuine smiles.

He sat down on the edge of the bed. "What are you doing here?"

"Having some wine and waiting for you to wear a rut in the carpet."

"Very cute. I mean, what do you do back in New York?"

Lilli shrugged. "I'm trying to break into the fashion industry. You know that routine," she said in a way that made it clear she assumed everyone knows that routine. "Did some fit modeling, runway stuff, worked in a couple of showrooms. It seems like every good-looking girl in New York who isn't trying to make it as an actress wants to be in fashion." She took a gulp of the sparkling wine, then added, "And almost all of them end up waiting tables."

"But not you."

"Not me. Maybe I'm too clumsy to be a waitress, or maybe I just refuse to give in."

"So instead you hopped a flight to Egypt and ended up with the Russian mafia."

She looked away.

"I'm not making judgments," he said, "I'm just trying to figure you out."

When she turned back to him it was as if her features had softened. The world-weary attitude had melted into something far more vulnerable. "You worried about me, Jordan Sandor?"

"Actually I am."

"That's sweet."

Sandor smiled. "That's the second time you've called me something I never hear from an attractive woman." Then his grin dissolved into a look of real concern. He leaned forward and whispered in her ear. "You may not believe this, but when they chose you to find me tonight they put you in danger."

She pulled back from him and forced a laugh. "You haven't been dangerous so far."

Moving beside her again, keeping his voice as low as possible, he said, "I'm not kidding, and keep your voice down. They may be eavesdropping on us. My invitation here was not a social call. When they put us together, they made you expendable."

"You sound so melodramatic," she whispered. "They told me you were a rich guy who just got to town. They said they wanted to meet you, that's all."

Sandor nodded. "And all true," he lied.

"So?"

"These are serious people. There are things they want to find out from me, and when they're done, well . . ." He hesitated. "They're done."

She drew back slightly. "Who are you? I mean really."

He tugged her toward him again. "Let's just say that from their perspective I'm a person of interest."

She placed her glass on the nightstand and leaned forward, their cheeks touching. "Are you going to tell me what's going on here or are you going to keep talking in riddles?"

Sandor drew a deep breath and let it out slowly. "You've already said you have no parents, no siblings, no one to come looking for you if you disappear. If they told the other girls that we ran off together, none of them would give it a second thought. Am I right?"

"Pizdet," she cursed in a thick Russian accent.

"Well said." He sat back and thought for a moment. Then he leaned close to her again. "There are things I have to do that you cannot be any part of. So you've got two choices. One is to let me find a way to get you off this yacht so you can get the hell out of Sharm el-Sheikh as quickly as possible."

"And the other?"

"The other is to mess up your hair and rip your nightgown, then have you run out of this cabin, go back to the main salon, and make up some story about what an animal I am, how you didn't sign on for that sort of abuse and ask them to put you in another room."

This time, when she studied the look on his face, she understood how serious he was. "And they won't come here to do something bad to you?"

"Not likely. Not for that, anyway."

"And what if I tell them what you've just told me?"

"Then I would have made a mistake in judgment that I'll have to deal with. But you will almost certainly be a dead woman."

She gaped at him without speaking for a moment. Then she said, "I don't like them. I didn't like them from the time I got here. And that Ronny, he scares me."

"As well he should."

She thought it over. "I'd rather take my chances staying with you, if you don't mind."

"I don't mind at all. But you've got to agree to do everything I say. Understood?"

She nodded.

"I mean everything."

"Okay, I understand."

"All right. Then you sit tight for now. I've got some work to do."

———

An operator like Ronny would never use his own vessel to transport a large cache of narcotics or weapons. Or anthrax, for that matter. Sandor was not looking for contraband on the *Odessa*. He was searching for information.

He left Lilli in his cabin and ventured silently out to the passageway. It was pitch dark except for the ship's courtesy lights, and the deck was clear. He began to move to his left when he heard someone walking slowly around the corner behind him, sounding as if he was keeping a sentry's pace. Sandor reacted quickly, hustling forward until he reached a companionway leading above. He ascended, two steps at a time, until he reached the sundeck on the upper level.

He crouched down and had a look below. A man came into view, one of the large Russians Sudakov had neglected to introduce earlier that evening. Even in the dim light Sandor could make out the automatic short-barreled rifle slung across the man's chest.

As his host had mentioned, the yacht was patrolled by armed guards, but Sandor suspected this man had been instructed to pay particular attention to their new guest. That was confirmed when he stopped just outside Sandor's cabin, leaned over the rail, and lit a cigarette.

As the sentry looked out toward the harbor, Sandor had the opportunity to hurry back down the stairs, which were far enough behind the guard to be out of his view. He moved quickly aft, seeking access to the lower decks. Around the first turn he found a narrow set of stairs that led him down, into the large galley. Everything was quiet there, so he continued swiftly on, past the assortment of stainless steel counters and high-end appliances, until he found himself in a corridor that headed toward the bow.

Sandor figured the communications center of the yacht would be positioned just below the bridge. Ease of access would dictate that the bulk of the electronic equipment would be found there. He checked to see that the passage was empty, then went on.

He passed a number of doors on his left that were set close enough to suggest smaller cabins, not what he was looking for. He pressed on until the corridor ended in a T, where he found what he was looking for. To the right was a short jog that turned forward, to the left a passageway that would lead to the port side of the yacht. Dead ahead was a door that he calculated to be just below the command deck.

Sandor felt for the compact 9mm in his back pocket. If this was the communications center it was likely to be manned 24/7 and, at two in the morning, he could hardly claim to be lost and searching for his own cabin. He decided to improvise, reached out for the handle, and opened the door.

Sudakov was seated comfortably at a small conference table bracketed by Pavel and another of the men Sandor had not been introduced to earlier in the evening. "Come in, Mr. Sandor," Sudakov said. "We've been expecting you."

CHAPTER THIRTY-TWO

ABOARD THE *ODESSA* IN SOUTH HARBOR, SHARM EL-SHEIKH, EGYPT

SANDOR STEPPED INSIDE and closed the door behind him. "Expecting me?"

Ronny pointed to a bank of monitors to his right. "We've been watching you as you were exploring my yacht just now. I take it my guided tour was not enough to satisfy your curiosity."

"Let's say it was a lot to absorb in just one viewing."

Ronny nodded. "So what did you think of our galley? Worthy of a five-star restaurant, is it not?"

"It certainly is."

"You didn't take much time to look around."

Sandor shrugged. "Never been much good in the kitchen."

"I take it our all-seeing nerve center here would be of more interest to you."

Sandor had a look around without replying.

"Impressive, yes?"

"Very."

"So then, have a seat. I would feel far more comfortable if you were sitting on that peashooter you carry in your back pocket. Come, come, don't look so surprised. And don't make the mistake of underestimating me. There is a scanner on the rear deck. We knew you were armed as soon as you boarded."

Sandor took the chair opposite the three Russians. There was another man present, his back to them as he worked at a large control panel. "But you didn't ask for my weapon."

"Please be assured, if you had so much as sneezed in the direction of that little automatic, you would not have had the chance to draw another breath."

With that, the men on either side of him responded with confident smiles.

"Well then," Sandor said, "I'll be careful not to sneeze."

"Let's just say you would be well advised not to suddenly reach for a handkerchief."

"I'll keep that in mind." Sandor had another look at the array of LCD screens. "I assume you have the cabins bugged as well."

"Some of them. I am told you were quite careful in keeping your voice low in speaking to Miss Lilli, but our technician is working on a retrieval of your conversation right now." He nodded in the direction of the techie working the keyboard.

"Not very gallant of you, intercepting a romantic tête-à-tête."

Sudakov responded with a knowing look. "Something tells me that romance was not the topic of your discussion. But we'll soon know, won't we?"

"Do I seem worried?"

"No, you don't. But something tells me you are not a man who worries easily. Am I right?"

Sandor smiled.

"Why not save us both needless gamesmanship by simply telling me who you are and what you are doing here."

"The girl invited me to your party, remember?"

Sudakov sighed. "I was hoping you would surprise me and dispense with pointless banter."

"I'd be happy to. You just asked me a question and I answered."

"Then how about this—what were you looking for just now?"

"I was trying to find your communications center and it appears I have."

"To what end?"

"You claim to be an oil trader. I suspect that's not the truth. At least not all of the truth. I wanted to find out who you really are and how you afford a yacht like the *Odessa*."

"And you thought you would find that in here?"

"I thought I might."

"You could have asked."

"You've already lied to me. I tend not to ask a liar a second question."

Sudakov sat up a little straighter. "You take liberties you should not, Mr. Sandor."

Sandor shrugged. "Maybe so, but as you said, I don't worry that easily. And you're the one who wanted to dispense with pointless banter."

His host forced a tense grin. "All right. What causes you to have such interest in me and what I do?"

"Someone mentioned that you might be a person with whom I could do business."

"I see. And what sort of business might that be?"

"Narcotics."

For a moment no one in the room moved or spoke. Even the clicking of the computer keyboard suddenly stopped. Then Sudakov made a loud chortling sound, something between a wheeze and a gasp. "You are quite a character, Mr. Sandor, you know that?"

Sandor treated each of Ronny's goons to a broad smile and turned back to his host. "It's been said."

As quickly as he had erupted into laughter, Sudakov resumed his severe manner. "You have the nerve to come aboard my yacht, a total stranger, drink my wine, sneak around in search of who knows what, and then ask if I want to engage in an illegal business transaction with you?"

"In a word, yes. I mean, if I could have thought of some indirect approach I would have tried, but as you say, you've caught me looking for information and you've asked that I answer your questions without playing games. It's a little late for you to pretend you're offended, don't you think?"

The Russian glared at him but said nothing.

"I was told you could arrange for the shipment of large amounts of product. And that you might be helpful on the financial side as well."

"And who told you this?"

"Carlos. A Venezuelan."

"No last name?"

"I didn't think it was important. He gave me your name and told me I could find you in Sharm el-Sheikh."

"I see. And you thought you would march in here, without a reference or any proof of who you are, and inquire about the transport of contraband as if you were ordering dinner from a menu, do I have this right?"

"No, in fact I thought we might find time to have a private discussion about business, but you have me at something of a disadvantage here. Since you asked for candor, I've provided it."

Sudakov gave his head a slow, deliberate shake. "Mr. Sandor, I don't know who you really are or who you think I am, but you have made a serious error in judgment."

"Nothing that we can't repair, I hope."

Sudakov studied him for a few moments. "That remains to be seen. For now I suggest you return to your cabin. My two friends here will show you the way so you won't need to retrace your indirect route." On cue, the two bodyguards got to their feet, so Sandor also stood. "We have gotten off to a bad start, but perhaps you are right, perhaps it can be repaired. We are diving in the morning, you should get some sleep."

The two large men came toward him. One of them pointed to the door. "Time to go," he said, his accent thick and his voice stern.

As Sandor turned to leave, Sudakov added, "I must confess, at this point I will sleep better if you relinquish your weapon. It will be returned to you tomorrow, of course."

"Of course," Sandor said, but as he reached for his pocket the man on his right grabbed his wrist with a backhand maneuver that was surprisingly fast and uncomfortably tight. Without a word the second man reached in and pulled out the gun. "I don't let just anyone put their hand in my pocket," Sandor said, "at least not on the first date."

No one laughed.

––––––––––

Lilli was still sitting up on his bed when Sandor was shown into his cabin by his two escorts. When they shut the door behind him he listened, but there was no sound to indicate they had been locked in. Having taken his automatic and with surveillance cameras all over the ship, there was no need.

"So?" she asked.

There was no reason to tell her anything. He said, "It's been a long night. Let's get some rest."

Then he turned out the lights. Whatever happened in the dark would happen in the dark.

CHAPTER THIRTY-THREE

ABOARD THE *ODESSA* IN SOUTH HARBOR, SHARM EL-SHEIKH, EGYPT

THE NEXT MORNING Sandor rose, showered, and dressed well before sunrise, then had Lilli get ready. When she emerged from the shower wrapped in a large Hermès bath sheet, he sat her on the edge of the bed and leaned over, whispering in her ear one more time. "Once I leave, you've got to get off this yacht."

"Can't I wait for you to come back?"

He shook his head. "I'm not coming back. And these people do not leave loose ends. They will want to know what we discussed, anything I told you. I want you to tell them anything and everything I said."

Lilli appeared puzzled. "But you haven't really told me anything. Except that I should be afraid of them."

Sandor pursed his lips, as if about to say something, then thought better of it. "Tell them that." He drew back and looked into her nervous, aquamarine eyes. After a moment he leaned toward her again. "Just repeat for them anything I said. The point is to get off this boat and out of Sharm el-Sheikh. You understand me? And I mean to get off as soon as possible."

She said she would, though she admitted that she still did not understand why.

A short time later the yacht's entourage was served an early breakfast on the rear deck. They were seated at a racetrack-shaped table large enough to accommodate thirty people and sturdy enough to support a brass sculpture in the center that looked to weigh half a ton. Sudakov was seated at the head of this enormous expanse of polished mahogany, nearest the stern, accompanied once again by the two brawny escorts who had shown Sandor to bed. Sudakov was an early riser, and not a man to be kept waiting, so he had seen to it that everyone was up just after dawn. He appeared to be in very good spirits and Sandor gave the man high marks acting as if nothing had transpired between them just a few hours before. His men, on the other hand, were far less convivial, some of which Sandor chalked up to his nocturnal wandering, some to their hangovers.

As for the women, they wore that look young women tend to have the morning after a night of too much wine, too much revelry, and too much of whatever else it was they had indulged in, particularly when they did not have the time necessary to recover their bearings and put themselves back together. The girls had been obliged to dress quickly, hair piled on heads and held with clips or pulled back in ponytails, their makeup not as carefully applied as it had been the night before.

Either that or the sunlight was not as favorable as the moonlight had been.

Sandor thought Lilli looked just fine, and he said so. He also announced that Lilli was interested in a small shopping spree in town while he was diving. He said that he would fund the expedition.

"Sounds delightful," Sudakov said with a knowing smile. "All of the girls should go into town and pick up some new things for tonight, don't you think?"

"Absolutely," Sandor agreed.

The women voiced their excitement at the prospect.

"Consider it done," Sudakov announced. "And I will be the one financing the venture, I insist. I will see to everything myself."

Sandor could feel Lilli's gaze bore into the side of his head, but all he did was smile at their host and say, "Perfect."

————————

While Sudakov and his guests were finishing their eggs and croissants, two of his men were belowdecks, filling the four scuba tanks that would be used for the dive that morning.

A standard air tank mixture is 21 percent oxygen and 78 percent nitrogen, the balance made up of inert gases. Changes in that combination, or the introduction of other substances, could become dangerous. Or fatal.

A tank low on air would not guarantee death. No matter how deep the diver went there was always the chance he could jettison his pack and make it to the surface once he discovered his supply was spent.

A nitrogen-rich mixture would ensure a fatality but the postmortem would reveal it had not been an accident—an autopsy would disclose the unusually high concentration of nitrogen in the lungs.

Loading a tank with pure oxygen was far more cunning. A diver would not be able to discern any problem at the start of the dive, but in less than a half hour at 45 psi or more—just one hundred feet or so below the surface of the water—the pressure in his lungs caused by the pure oxygen would cause a seizure without warning, and death was assured. The postmortem would be unlikely to disclose anything to suggest foul play. As the diver convulsed, his tank could be removed and dropped to the floor of the sea with extra weights, the evidence of tampering effectively destroyed.

Oxygen was the smart move.

Sudakov's men loaded one of the four tanks with pure oxygen, placed a small blue appliqué on the metal cylinder, then went about organizing the other equipment.

It would not be long now.

Less than twenty minutes later Sandor stood on the platform that hovered just above sea level at the stern of the *Odessa,* watching as the dive boat came about. A lithe young woman in a black one-piece bathing suit tossed out a bowline from the dive boat. One of Sudakov's crew caught it and tied it off on a transom cleat as the girl dropped white rubber bumpers over the side.

The boat appeared to be about thirty-six feet long with twin outboards. It was piloted by a dark-skinned Egyptian who looked to be about sixty, wearing khaki shorts and a tropical shirt in a loud print featuring silk screens of palm trees and coconuts. He killed the engines, climbed forward, and jumped up to the platform.

"Morning," he said with a wide smile that revealed a set of uneven teeth.

The man standing beside Sandor issued a grunt in response, then held out a hand and helped the girl onto the platform.

"I am Captain Sadiki," the Egyptian told them. "Everyone ready to go?"

As if on cue, the two men who had been in the equipment room emerged through a door to the starboard side of the transom. They were carrying four tanks, fins, regulators, wetsuits, weight belts, and other diving paraphernalia.

"Seems you won't be needing our equipment," the captain said with an unmistakable hint of disappointment in his voice.

Sudakov stepped forward. "Not a problem captain," he said. "We prefer to use our own equipment, but we have agreed to your rate." Then with a chuckle he added, "Do I look like a man seeking a discount?"

"You certainly do not," the captain replied with his own laugh, obviously relieved that he had not carted tanks out here only to be chiseled on his fee. He took the hand Sudakov extended, gave it an energetic pump, then climbed back into his boat.

As Sandor watched the gear being loaded, Sudakov moved beside him. "A beautiful day to be on the water, is it not?"

"Or under it," Sandor said. He was wearing a new Vilebrequin bathing suit and crisply pressed white tee, both on loan from his host. He turned to Sudakov, who was still in the black gabardine slacks and cotton polo shirt he had worn at breakfast. "A bit overdressed for this adventure, aren't you?"

Sudakov offered him an indulgent smile. "Unfortunately I cannot join you. A childhood injury to my ear prevents me from diving. A pity."

"It certainly is." Sandor returned his attention to the young woman to whom the Russians were passing the diving gear. He was far less interested in the girl than the four steel air tanks she was handling. They were all made by the same manufacturer, identical in size and markings.

"I envy you the experience," Sudakov was saying, "but I look forward to the stories you'll have to tell when you return."

Sandor turned back to the Russian. "And I certainly look forward to seeing you again."

"Good. You all enjoy yourselves," he said, slapping Sandor on the back.

The women on the yacht were above them, leaning over the railing on the rear deck, jabbering about their upcoming excursion to the shops in town at Sudakov's expense. Lilli, however, was watching Sandor without speaking.

He looked up and smiled at her. "And you be sure to enjoy your little shopping spree."

She nodded.

"Of course she will," Sudakov assured him as he witnessed the unspoken exchange between Sandor and the girl. "We'll take good care of her."

"I hope so," Sandor said, looking directly into the Russian's cold blue eyes. "I really hope so."

————————

When Sandor boarded the dive boat he was not surprised to discover that his companions on this excursion would be three of Sudakov's men.

"They love to dive," Sudakov called out to him, answering the question that had not been asked.

Sandor looked up from the deck of the smaller vessel. "Can't convince you to just come along for the ride, can I?"

The Russian shrugged, then pointed to the girls and flashed a smile. "Business before pleasure."

Sandor nodded. "Till we meet again, as they say."

"Till then."

————————

Captain Sadiki's destination for the dive was beyond the sandy island in the national park known as Ras Mohammed. A nature preserve off the tip of the Sinai Peninsula, it is a popular location for underwater explorers and snorkelers alike. As they got started Sandor moved forward and stood beside the captain.

"Nice boat," he said as Sadiki navigated his way across the deep, calm waters.

The Egyptian said nothing.

"Beautiful day for a dive."

That earned him an indifferent nod.

"Not much of a talker, are you?"

Now the swarthy face turned toward him. "No," the captain said, his unblinking gaze holding Sandor's for a moment, then letting it go as if dismissing an unpleasant thought.

"Well then," Sandor replied, "I'll try to keep my questions to a minimum." He made his way aft, where the young woman was organizing the equipment. "Good morning."

That earned him the first smile he had seen since he came aboard.

"Ah, a friendly face."

"You probably found that my uncle is not very sociable."

"Your uncle? Yes, I noticed. Seemed a lot happier when he came aboard the yacht."

"He's always nice to the people who pay him."

Sandor laughed as he extended his hand. "I'm Jordan."

She took his hand, said, "I'm Nadia," then went back to work.

"This unusual?"

"What?" she asked over her shoulder.

"People bringing their own tanks and scuba gear?"

She stood and looked at him, her lower lip jutting out as if this required some thought. "Most tourists rent from us. But some of the bigger yachts have their own equipment."

He waited, knowing that sometimes saying nothing is the best way to evoke a response.

Nadia hesitated, then added, "Wealthy people tend to do things their own way."

Sandor nodded. "Your English is perfect."

"I studied in London," she explained. With the roar of the twin engines, their conversation could not be heard by the others aboard. Even so, Sandor noticed that the captain had given her a quick, disapproving glance. "I need to get this done," she said, then knelt down and returned to sorting out the equipment.

Sandor could feel the three Russians watching him as he crouched beside her. "I'm curious. Is there any real advantage in using your own equipment? I mean, I assume you do this almost every day. I'd think it would be safer with you preparing things."

When she turned back to him he thought he detected a change in her demeanor. "I'm sure these tanks are fine."

"Just the tanks?" he asked.

When Nadia fumbled for a reply, he held up a hand. "Only kidding," he assured her. "I'm just getting in your way here. Let me give you a hand."

Before she could utter a protest Sandor grabbed one of the tanks and stood it in the hard plastic rack along the railing. By the time he had moved the second canister she took hold of his wrist.

"This is my job," she said quietly. "You're a guest on our boat, and my uncle will be upset if . . ."

"No need to explain," Sandor said as he stood. "I understand completely. I'll let you get back to work." Then he turned to the three Russians, who were seated along the port rail, gave them a brief wave to which they offered no reaction, then climbed atop one of the starboard lockers and sat down.

CHAPTER THIRTY-FOUR

CARACAS, VENEZUELA

WHEN WORD WAS released that the health of President Chavez had taken another bad turn, the Venezuelan government was thrown into its latest round of turmoil. Players within the administration jockeyed for position, ever mindful that so long as Chavez remained alive he also remained in power. Which also meant, for so long as Chavez was in charge, none of these aspirants was going to extend less than the fullest cooperation to the nation's deadliest terrorist. The current maneuvering was all about the future order of things.

For now, therefore, Adina was still safely ensconced in the fortress known as El Helicoide, a guest of the Servicio Bolivariano de Inteligencia Nacional. He was meeting again with the minister, Bargas, who was the only one within SEBIN who knew of the laboratory where the anthrax had been manufactured. Beyond that, the minister knew nothing of the plot Adina was implementing, and neither he nor any of the others at El Helicoide was asking.

"I will need you to follow up on certain arrangements I have made in New York," said Adina.

"However I can help, of course."

Adina was about to review those plans when an aide knocked on the door and was told to enter. The young man delivered an encrypted message from Egypt, then left the room.

Adina took several minutes to decode the text, then looked up. "My associates in Sharm el-Sheikh have been approached by a man they believe to be an American agent. They identified him as Jordan Sandor."

Bargas was about to ask what associates Adina had in Egypt, then thought better of it.

"You recognize that name? Jordan Sandor?"

The minister nodded. "Wasn't he responsible for, uh, interfering with your plans in the Gulf of Mexico?"

Adina placed the message down on the large conference table and looked at Bargas. "Responsible for interfering," he repeated. "You make it sound so benign."

"I didn't mean to . . ."

"That's all right. We're interfering with Mr. Sandor's plans as we speak. My associates assure me that he will be neutralized. A tragic diving accident."

The minister did not respond.

"He is of no further consequence. The only concern is what re-criminations might come from this."

Again there was no reply.

"I have to assume it was Sandor or one of his cohorts who infil-trated my compound. We have no way of knowing how much they learned or what information they might have passed on. My opera-tion near Barranquitas was utterly secure. Now it has been compro-mised. We did not need these complications nor did we want to accelerate our actions. Unfortunately, we may now be forced to make some adjustments both in timing and approach."

"What can I do to help?"

Adina thought it over. "There are arrangements I am making in New York. We must move up our timetable."

"Of course. I will make whatever contacts there you require."

"Good," Adina said. "Let me share some information with you."

CHAPTER THIRTY-FIVE

ON THE RED SEA, OFF THE COAST OF THE SINAI PENINSULA

THE CAPTAIN SLOWED the boat as they approached the reef he had chosen for them.

"This is a good spot," he announced as he throttled back, leaving them to rock to and fro atop the gentle waters.

It was still early, but there were a number of other boats in sight. The morning sun hung above the horizon, the rays glistening across the sea. The captain nodded to the girl and she told the four men it was time to get ready.

The three Russians stood and made their way aft, followed by Sandor. They began the process of climbing into their wetsuits and inflatable vests, snapping on their weight belts and arranging their masks, fins and regulators.

The captain joined them, pointing off the port side. "Some of the best scenery is over there. You'll have to get down a hundred feet or so, but I'm told you're all certified."

The Russians gave no reply but Sandor smiled. "A hundred feet, should be interesting." He stared at the Egyptian, wondering if he had already been told he would be returning a passenger short.

"The waters are safe," Sadiki said, averting Sandor's gaze as he pointed to the other vessels. "You'll find it quite rewarding."

"Oh, I'm sure I will," Sandor said. "Now where do I get a knife?"

They all looked at him as if he had posed a riddle they could not solve.

"A knife, boys. I don't ever dive without a scuba knife. I don't care

how safe the water is, there's no telling what the hell is down there."
Then he pointed to the thigh of the tallest of the three Russians. "He's
no fool, he strapped his on already."

For a moment no one spoke. Then the big man shrugged and said,
"Sure. Give him one."

Once Sandor attached the serrated knife to his belt it was one of
the Russians, not Nadia, who lifted a tank and handed it to Sandor.
It bore the blue appliqué. Sandor took it and placed his arms through
the straps. Then the other three cylinders were passed out and the
men were ready to go.

"Stay together," the captain told them. "We'll lower this rope with
the yellow beacon. Try to stay in sight of this at all times, yes?"

The men all nodded, then one by one they adjusted their masks
and went over the side.

———————

Sandor had to admit the scenery was spectacular. A swarm of colorful
fish swam around the four divers as if they were a natural part of the
environment, and the closer they came to the reef the more it had the
look of a fascinating geometric sculpture. As they slowly descended
Sandor felt the water becoming slightly colder, but his wetsuit kept
him comfortable.

They continued downward and Sandor kept an eye on his three
companions as they constantly shifted their positions to maintain
something resembling a circle around him. It was evident the Russians planned to keep him surrounded that way, just in case he tried
to make a move up, down or sideways. Sandor concentrated on
moderated breathing, maximizing the air in his tank for whatever was
to come. When one of the men signaled, Sandor nodded his understanding, then hit the release valve on his vest and the four of them
continued farther below the surface.

Sandor knew his companions were in no rush. They wanted him
down there as long and as deep as possible. Time moved slowly as
they floated near the vibrant coral and among the larger denizens of
the deeper water. Then somewhere below one hundred feet Sandor
saw what he had been waiting for.

When he was speaking with Nadia, Sandor noticed that only one of the four tanks bore a small blue appliqué. Whatever they had done to the tank, Sandor wanted no part of it. With his back blocking the equipment from the view of the three Russians, he had made a deft switch of the adhesive patch from the deadly tank to another. Then, when the captain killed the engines and one of the Russians passed him the tank bearing the marker, he knew he was safe. He was not certain which of the Russians drew the short straw when the other tanks were passed out, nor did he care.

Now he saw the man off to his right suddenly clutch at his own throat and spit out his regulator, a dense cloud of oxygen bubbles releasing into the water.

Instinctively, the other two swam as quickly as they could to his aid. Sandor, instead of using the moment to escape, also rushed forward. The others did not see that he had already unsheathed his scuba knife.

As the two men tried to help their dying comrade, Sandor came up from behind and, in two swift cuts, slashed their air lines.

It happened so fast, with their attention on their choking friend, they had no chance to counter Sandor's attack. They were more than a hundred feet below the surface and now their own survival was in question. One of them reached for his own weapon, but it was too late. Sandor had already distanced himself, swimming furiously away, his own air supply intact.

The dying man was convulsing and had begun inhaling seawater. The others ignored him as they attempted to draw air from their own severed lines. They scrambled to drop their weight belts and began the climb to the surface as Sandor continued to paddle away from the yellow beacon that marked the location of the dive boat above.

CHAPTER THIRTY-SIX

ABOARD THE *ODESSA* IN SOUTH HARBOR, SHARM EL-SHEIKH, EGYPT

J UST BEFORE THE group of young women boarded the launch for their shopping spree in town, they were told that Lilli had decided not to join them after all. Only the girl who had invited Lilli to Sharm el-Sheikh voiced any concern.

"Should we wait for her?"

"No, she's decided to stay here until her new friend returns from his diving adventure," Sudakov explained pleasantly.

The young woman was obviously surprised. "But Lilli loves to shop."

Sudakov shrugged. "They seem to have bonded very quickly," he answered with a knowing smile as he helped the girl onto the launch. He remained there to see all of the women off, then returned to Sandor's room. Lilli had stayed behind, but it was not to await Sandor's return. She was in the company of two armed guards.

"Please leave us, gentlemen," Sudakov ordered. They vacated the room and shut the door behind them.

Lilli was seated on the bed. She had obviously been crying.

Sudakov pulled up a chair to face her, not more than a couple of feet away. "What is the problem, my dear? You seem upset."

"Why didn't you allow me to go into town with the other girls?"

"And not wait here for the return of your friend Mr. Sandor?"

She stared at him without speaking.

"Let me be frank with you so you may be spared any unnecessary unpleasantness. You are going to tell me everything Mr. Sandor said to you since the moment you met him last night. You can do that willingly or you can do that, how shall I put it, under duress. That choice is yours."

"What he said to me?"

Sudakov nodded. "And don't waste time playing the fool. I want to know what he said about me or anything that relates to me."

For a moment, anger replaced fear. "He said you were dangerous."

"Ah, you see. And now you realize that to be true."

She glared at him.

"What else did he say?"

She studied his unblinking face for a moment. "That I should get off this yacht and not come back."

"Now why do you think he would have said such a thing? I mean, such a beautiful yacht. Such fine food and great wine. Why would he tell you to leave?"

She drew a deep breath. "I told you already, he said you are a dangerous man."

"Yes, yes. You've said that. But dangerous how? I mean, what danger could I possibly be to a beautiful young woman like you?"

"I don't know."

Without warning, Sudakov lashed out and smashed her across the face with his right fist. Lilli let out a shriek, grabbing for her jaw as he sat back again, appearing as if nothing had happened. "You see, that's just the sort of thing I was talking about." He sighed, then reached in his pocket and handed her a handkerchief to wipe the blood that was dripping from the corner of her mouth. "I promise you that I am not going to hit you again. Those men outside are much better at such methods. I also promise you that I will send them in here the next time you fail to answer one of my questions. Do you understand?"

She wept quietly as she pressed the handkerchief to her face.

"Do you understand?"

She managed a nod.

"Good. Now, what did Mr. Sandor say?"

She drew back slightly, then said, "He wanted to find something on this boat."

"And what was he looking for."

She cringed even before speaking. "I don't know. I really don't know."

Sudakov stood and pushed back the chair. "Well, as I promised, my men are about to find out if that's true. And if it is, I am sad to say that you will have outlived your usefulness here."

Then he turned and walked out of the room.

CHAPTER THIRTY-SEVEN

ON THE RED SEA, OFF THE COAST OF THE SINAI PENINSULA

Sandor had no way of knowing if Captain Sadiki was involved in the plan to murder him, but he was taking no chances. Using his underwater compass he continued to swim west as he slowly ascended, moving as far away as possible from his assailants. When he could make out the sunlight above him, he unhooked his straps and shrugged off the air tank. Then he swam straight up, breaking the surface of the water just enough to gasp for air and search for the only man he wanted to see out there.

Without any sort of homing device it was going to be difficult for Farrar to locate him. Sandor had called his friend last night from the yacht, using Lilli's cell, keeping the discussion casual, assuming it was being intercepted. He said he would be going for a dive in the morning and gave him the approximate time. Then he said, "I'll see you for cocktails at sunset," expecting Farrar to understand that meant his plan was to keep moving west once he had shaken free of his captors. At the time he had no way of knowing what they had in store for him—a contaminated air tank, for instance—but he assumed they would be making a move against him and figured his best chance of breaking free would be out on the water. Farrar had told him yesterday morning that he knew which local skipper had been chartered to take passengers from the *Odessa* for a dive. All Farrar had to do was follow that boat from a safe distance and position himself west of it for a pickup.

Easy as that, Sandor told himself as he caught his breath, treaded water, and tried to get his bearings. He marveled at how the sheer expanse of the sea can so quickly become disorienting. It is difficult to appreciate its overwhelming enormity until you are alone in its midst with your head barely above the surface. The slightest swell blocks your line of sight in virtually any direction and, even in bright daylight, a sense of helplessness can grow quickly.

Fortunately, there were even more boats on the water than when Sandor began his dive, which helped as reference points since he was too far out to see the shore. He was not going to be able to find Farrar; Farrar would have to find him. He turned east, attempting to locate Sadiki's dive boat, but with all the other vessels around even that was impossible. He decided his best chance was to continue west, away from the sun, and hope that Farrar spotted him on the move. At worst he could seek refuge in one of the other vessels out there.

Without his weight belt and tank it was easy enough for him to swim through the calm water, his vest providing extra buoyancy. But the risk in movement was that he became more visible, not only to Farrar but to the men who would now be searching for him.

Sandor hoped the two Russians were inexperienced enough to rush upward too quickly once he cut their air hoses. In a panic they might create their own decompression issues and the captain would have no choice but to speed them toward the Sharm el-Sheikh Hyperbaric Medical Center for immediate treatment.

Sandor swam a hundred yards or so, but when he stopped to have another look around he thought he could make out a boat motoring toward him from the east. He knew that could mean trouble.

Without the air tank he would not be able to submerge for long, but invisibility was presently his best defense. He dove just below the surface and stayed there as long as his lungs would allow. When he came up again he could see that whoever had been on course toward him was now heading toward shore. Sandor could not be sure, but it certainly looked to be the dive boat carrying the two Russians. He submerged again and kept moving west.

———————

Farrar knew which skipper had chartered the *Odessa* excursion. It was Sadiki and his niece Nadia. That was easy to determine for a man with his local connections. He borrowed a fast boat from one of his colleagues, headed out early, spotted the dive boat, and then slowly motored to a position off to the west, per Sandor's instruction. Using binoculars he had watched Sandor and the other three men enter the water. From that point there had been nothing to do but wait.

Now came the difficult part. He could approximate the time when they would surface, figuring somewhere between thirty and sixty minutes, but he had no idea how many of them would come up. Or if Sandor would still be in the company of the other three men. If Jordan had not managed to shake free there would be nothing for Farrar to do but follow them, likely back to the large yacht. If Sandor had been successful in separating from them he would try to swim away from their boat, hopefully closer to where Farrar now rocked back and forth.

But even in these placid waters a man alone out there was going to be tough to spot.

It was more than forty minutes into the dive when Farrar saw activity on the other boat. He grabbed for his binoculars, watching as two men boarded and removed their gear. He could see that neither of them was Sandor. There was a heated discussion between the two returning divers and Captain Sadiki, then their boat began to move.

The deductions were obvious: one of the three Russians was not coming back—Sandor was the reason—and Sandor had managed to escape, at least for now.

When Farrar agreed to help his friend, he knew this was not going to be a simple reconnaissance and recovery mission. *It never was with Sandor,* he thought with a grim smile. So, before he put the twin engines of the motorboat into gear, he placed his assault rifle on the seat beside him. With the weapon nestled comfortably within reach he began to circle at an unhurried speed toward the north, holding the wheel in one hand and the binoculars in the other.

When Sadiki's boat turned for land it was also motoring slowly. Farrar nodded to himself—it was the obvious move. Once Sandor eluded them, they had to assume he would keep his tank on, stay below the surface, and make for shore. They would be attempting to track his progress.

Farrar maintained a steady speed, doing his best to remain unobtrusive among the other craft out there. These men were looking for Sandor, and he had no interest in becoming a secondary target.

Farrar steered wide around a couple of other vessels, then lifted the binoculars to have another look for Sandor. When he also took a look toward Sadiki's boat he saw that one of the men had his binoculars trained on him.

————

Sandor had no idea what Farrar's boat looked like, but as he bobbed up and down amid the gentle swells, he could make out a small craft off to the west that had begun moving in a large circle. He was close enough to see there was only one man aboard, and although he could not be sure it was Farrar, for now it was the best bet he had. He was about to start swimming that way when he took another check on what Captain Sadiki was doing. He had been moving south, toward shore, but now his boat was turning and seemed to be gaining speed as it came his way.

————

When Farrar and the Russian locked on each other through their high-powered binoculars, it might have been a coincidence. Just two men out there, looking for their divers or checking the seascape.

But Farrar had not survived this long in a violent business by believing in coincidences. His natural cynicism was vindicated when he watched the burly man drop the glasses and point in his direction. Then the dive boat turned north and began to accelerate.

Farrar still had not spotted Sandor, but he at least had a general idea where his friend intended to rendezvous with him. He also had his assault rifle. And, most important of all, he knew he had the faster boat.

He pressed the throttles forward, the need for stealth having suddenly vanished. Turning quickly to port he came about, charting a course he felt most likely to produce a sighting of his stranded friend. As he turned past two other vessels, which up to then had been peacefully riding the calm surf, he was greeted with angry shouts to slow down as his wake sent them rocking wildly back and forth.

Farrar ignored them as he negotiated the tight turn, then came to starboard. That was when he caught a glimpse of Sandor who, having been able to make out some of the action, was now waving with both arms. Farrar slowed the engines, made another turn, and did his best to get close.

"Hurry," Sandor shouted out, then pointed to the oncoming dive boat.

Farrar was aware of the pursuit and maneuvered into position as fast as he could. When he was close enough, Farrar tossed out a line, and Sandor grabbed it on the second attempt. He was still pulling himself over the railing when Farrar pushed the levers forward again. The boat surged and Sandor tumbled onto the fiberglass deck.

"Get up here," Farrar called out to him.

Sandor scrambled to his feet and took his place beside the Egyptian as they headed on a northerly route, out to sea. Farrar was in the captain's chair. Sandor was standing, steadying himself by taking hold of the stainless steel rail on the instrument panel. "Good to see you," he said as he pulled off his vest and tossed it on the deck.

Farrar nodded.

"You know this Captain Sadiki?"

Farrar shot him a quick glance, as if to say that he knew everyone.

Sandor checked behind them. The dive boat was still several hundred yards away as they passed the last of the other craft sitting above the reef on this sunny morning and continued out to sea. "They tried to pass me a contaminated tank. Any chance he knew what they were up to?"

"Sadiki? No. He's a prick, not a murderer."

"Even for a lot of money?"

"No. Not even for a lot of money."

Sandor checked over his shoulder again. "Then why the hell are they chasing us?"

Farrar handed him the binoculars. "What do you think?"

Sandor had a quick look. One of the Russians had some sort of handgun. The other was holding what appeared to be an Uzi, and he had it pointed at the captain. "It seems their duffels contained more than scuba gear," Sandor said.

"I don't want Sadiki or the girl to get hurt."

"Of course not," Sandor agreed, "but in case you haven't noticed, they seem to be gaining on us. You purposely letting them get close?"

Farrar looked up at him. "Just close enough," he said, then slid the M-16 toward Sandor, keeping it low enough so it remained out of sight. "We can outrun them, but that doesn't solve the problem."

"They might kill the captain and the girl, head back to the yacht for reinforcements, and we've got a small war on our hands."

"That was my thinking."

"Plus they'll be able to identify you as the man who came out here to get me."

"Yes, that too. If we run them to the open water and take them out right there without Sadiki or his niece being hurt . . ."

"Then we solve a lot of problems, provided Sadiki can be trusted to keep his mouth shut."

"We'll be saving his life. What do you think he'll do?"

Sandor shook his head. "I wish people were that easy to figure."

"You have a better plan, I'm willing to listen."

"No, stay on course, let them think they have the faster boat, let them keep coming."

CHAPTER THIRTY-EIGHT

ON THE RED SEA, OFF THE COAST OF THE SINAI PENINSULA

Captain Sadiki stood at the wheel, piloting his boat near its top speed. Nadia was seated beside him, as ordered by the two armed men, where it was easier to keep an eye on both of them.

"Faster," the Russian holding the Glock 9mm demanded.

"We're almost at full throttle now," the captain said.

"All the way then," the man hollered.

"You'll be sorry if one of these engines blows."

The Russian ignored the warning. "I want to get alongside where we have a clean shot. Now!"

Sadiki and Nadia exchanged a furtive glance. The captain knew these waters and the vessels on them. He knew the boat he was chasing was faster than his. And he had a fairly good idea who was at the helm. "When we come abeam," he whispered to Nadia without looking at her, the roar of his engines covering his warning, "you dive to the deck."

"Faster," the Russian bellowed.

———

Farrar stayed just enough in front to draw them well out into the open sea, where his quicker, more agile boat would have the advantage. And where there would be no witnesses.

"You ready?" he asked.

"Always," Sandor said. He was holding the M-16 at waist level. He checked the magazine and made sure one round was already in the breach. "You know what to do, right?"

"What is that expression you have? 'This is not my first rodeo.'"

Sandor laughed. "You going to be able to turn this baby quickly enough?"

"Don't you worry about me, you just make sure you don't miss."

Captain Sadiki had pushed his twin inboards to the limit. Farrar had a quick look in his direction, gauged the distance, then cut his port engine slightly, forcing a turn to that side. Then, as the gap between the boats narrowed, Farrar throttled up the port engine, cut the starboard and made a violent turn, heading directly at the dive boat.

The Russians reacted with confusion and then alarm. They both opened fire, but neither the sidearm nor the Uzi had the range nor the accuracy to be a threat from this distance. They had not come out here prepared for an open-water battle.

Meanwhile, Sandor lunged toward the port railing and braced himself against the bulkhead as the two boats appeared to be on a collision course. He opened fire with the M-16, taking out the man standing in the bow with his second shot. The other ducked below the railing, out of sight, then crawled across the deck to grab Nadia, who had taken cover behind the captain's chair.

Farrar cut back on his engines and Sadiki did the same. The two boats, which had moments ago been careening at breakneck speed toward one another, were now swaying side to side amid the waves they had themselves created.

For a moment everything was still, and then Nadia shrieked. Sadiki turned and saw that she had been tugged to her knees by her hair. The large Russian was holding the heated barrel of the submachine gun to her head, burning her skin.

Sadiki spun and instinctively kicked at the man, but the Russian growled at him. "Move again and I'll kill you both." He nodded toward the other boat. "Tell them to throw down their weapons and jump into the water where I can see them."

"What?"

"Tell them," the man snapped.

Sadiki stood, his arms raised in the air, although no one had asked him to do that, and stepped toward the bow. Calling across the water, he told them what the man wanted.

Farrar was hunkered down between the wheel and chair, well out of sight. Sandor was also protected, and still out of range from the Uzi.

"I've done enough swimming today," Sandor said to Farrar.

"You were supposed to take them both out."

"I know," Sandor agreed with a disgusted shake of his head.

"He has Sadiki's niece. What do we do?"

Sandor nodded, then raised his head just high enough to see Sadiki standing with his hands up. "Here's the deal," he hollered out. "I don't give a damn about you or the girl, but if he throws down his gun we won't kill him. Otherwise I'm going to use this rifle to take out both of your engines, and maybe even blow up your boat if I can arrange that. And then I'm going home. So what's it going to be?"

When Sadiki turned to repeat this to the Russian, he was told, "Shut up. I heard him."

For his part, Sandor was not waiting for a reply. He fired three shots into the casing of Sadiki's port outboard. It immediately began hissing and emitting a stream of oil and a cloud of steam. "What's it going to be?" Sandor repeated.

The Russian got to his feet. He was using Nadia as a shield, his left hand clutching a large clump of her hair to keep her in place, his right still pressing the barrel of the Uzi against her face. Then, without warning, he pointed the submachine gun at Sadiki and fired a three-shot burst at his legs. The Egyptian screamed in pain and crumpled to the deck with a thud. "I will kill them both before I give up my weapon," the Russian shouted across the water.

With each of the boats rocking it was difficult for Sandor to get a clean shot, but the man was taller and broader than Nadia, which at least presented a narrow target. The situation being what it was, Sandor's options were limited. He took dead aim and fired at the man's right shoulder, an area exposed as the Russian tried to crouch behind the girl. The shot hit the girl in the soft part of her shoulder, but the high-caliber round had sufficient velocity and power to pass through her and rip into the Russian. It knocked him backward on the rolling deck, causing him to lose his grip on both the submachine gun and the wounded girl as he struggled to keep his footing.

The weapon tumbled from his grasp and Nadia collapsed onto the fiberglass deck, giving Sandor the opportunity to fire off two more rounds. The Russian had fallen to his knees so the rounds sailed high. Sandor stood for a better angle, but before he could take aim he heard a loud burst of gunfire and saw the Russian's chest and face rip open. Only then did Nadia manage to get to her feet, her right shoulder stained with blood, the Uzi in her left hand.

CHAPTER THIRTY-NINE

SHARM EL-SHEIKH, EGYPT

THE SITUATION WAS complicated, even by the murky standards of Farrar's world.

Ronny Sudakov had chartered a dive boat from Captain Sadiki, sending out three of his men and Jordan Sandor. His expectation was that the boat would return with those three men carrying Sandor's corpse and a tragic story about the American's horrific diving accident.

Instead, one of the Russians was missing somewhere in the depths of the Red Sea, the other two had been shot dead—one with his own weapon—and both Sadiki and his niece were now in the local hospital being treated for wounds sustained in the battle.

And Sandor was missing.

As Farrar towed Sadiki's boat to shore and Sandor tended to the wounds of Nadia and her uncle, the four of them dealt with the obvious problem—how they would explain what happened to the authorities.

They agreed that Sadiki and Nadia would say their boat was boarded by armed men in masks shortly after the divers went over the side. When the four divers returned, all three Russians were killed in the struggle, one of whom was thrown overboard, and the assault team then drove the boat out to sea where they met their own vessel and made off with the American. Sadiki and his niece were shot in the crossfire and left for dead.

Sandor did his best to keep the details simple, knowing that Sudakov's men would ultimately get to Sadiki and his niece. Inconsistencies, hesitation, or even reluctance to tell their tale, could be fatal.

Convinced they had done the best they could, and with Farrar's boat coming within sight of the dock, it was time for Sandor to disappear. Just before he slid over the side to make his own way to shore, he apologized one more time to Nadia.

"He was going to kill me," the girl said. "I know that. You did the right thing."

Sandor nodded. "Sorry I had to hit you first. It was the only shot I had at his chest."

"Well then," she said with a weak smile, "I suppose I should be grateful you weren't aiming at his head."

———————

Word of the shootings had spread all over town by the time Farrar met with the police and harbor patrol at the hospital. He answered their questions, staying with the script, then asked if he might go get a change of clothes. Since he was not accused of firing on anyone and thus far had been described as the person responsible for rescuing Sadiki and Nadia, they let him go for the time being.

Despite being released Farrar assumed he was being watched—by the authorities or Sudakov or both—so he made a phone call and arranged for one of his associates to meet him a couple of blocks from the Ritz-Carlton. They passed on the street and, without exchanging a word, Farrar handed off the keycard to Sandor's hotel room. Then he hailed a cab and returned to his shop on Naama Heights Street.

Sandor, who had made his way there on foot by a circuitous route through the backstreets, was waiting in the small office, anxious for news.

"So far we are all right," Farrar told him.

"What about Lilli? Is she at the hotel?"

"We'll know soon enough. I gave the job to Malik."

"Reliable?"

"Very. Although I trust you left nothing of value in your room." He shrugged his shoulders. "Malik is a good man in his way, but everything has its price. Whatever you left behind you will certainly never see again."

"The least of our troubles," Sandor conceded. "My go bag is in your safe, so I'm fine. Right now I could use a chilled vodka or an aged bourbon. What have you got?"

Farrar called in the girl and arranged for two Stolis on ice. Then they spent the time reassessing their risks.

"I didn't expect things to get so far out of control," Sandor said. "I never meant to put you at risk."

The Egyptian forced a smile. "I knew very well who I was dealing with."

Sandor forced a tired smile. "You mean the Russians, of course."

"Yes, of course."

"And you did have the foresight to bring the rifle."

"Praise Allah," Farrar responded with a rueful nod.

Sandor fixed him with a serious look. "At some point Sadiki will either cave in or louse up the details. Sudakov is going to find his way to your door."

"Perhaps," Farrar said, trying to sound less worried than he felt. "You're the one he wants. By the time he gets to me you'll be long gone and I will be of no consequence."

Sandor stared deep into his friend's ebony-colored eyes. "I hope you're right, but remember that we took out three of his men. Sudakov is not the type to suffer that kind of loss without demanding payback."

"Please, stop trying to cheer me up."

"Just tell me what you want me to do."

"I want you to stop worrying about me. I have many powerful allies here who will intercede on my behalf."

Farrar's cell phone rang and he took the call. He listened without speaking for what seemed a long time, then issued some instructions in his native language and rang off. When he looked up his expression told Sandor what he did not want to hear. "That was Malik. He could not get into your hotel."

Sandor waited.

"He says the police are all over the place. The girl. They found her in your room. She is dead."

CHAPTER FORTY

CIA HEADQUARTERS, LANGLEY, VIRGINIA

WHEN SANDOR LEFT Washington two days before, he told Deputy Director Byrnes that he would keep him apprised of where he was going. He had done that. He also assured him that he would let him know what was going on before the shooting started. On that score he had failed badly.

Byrnes knew that his agent was tracking a lead to Sharm el-Sheikh. Now his office was receiving intelligence reports from the station chief in Cairo about a violent incident on the Red Sea that might have involved men from the yacht *Odessa,* believed to be owned by the suspected narcotics dealer Roman Sudakov. Added to that was the murder of a young woman whose body was discovered, as a result of an anonymous tip to the local authorities, in a hotel room booked in the name of Jordan Sandor.

Byrnes's attempts to reach Sandor had been unsuccessful so he called in Craig Raabe. He did not even give his agent time to sit down. "You have intel on Sandor's contacts. I want you to reach out and let them know I expect to hear from him within the hour."

Raabe did an about-face and returned to his office. Less than forty-five minutes later contact was made and the DD's assistant put the call through.

Byrnes's first question was "Are you secure?"

"I'm in Egypt," Sandor replied.

"All right, what can you tell me that I need to know right now?"

"There's another stop I have to make on the way home."

"Do you want us to bring you in?"

"No, I'm fine."

"What have you learned about our Russian friend?"

"Absolutely in the path of this thing."

"I see. When will I have details?"

"Already en route to the usual recipient."

"What about the murder of this young woman?"

There was silence for a moment. Then Sandor said, "It was completely unnecessary and I intend to do something about it when that opportunity presents itself."

"What you need to do, Sandor, is your job."

"Understood. I'll handle this on my own time."

"There's no such thing, not for you."

Sandor offered no response.

"I need you to stay in touch."

"And I will," Sandor said, then hung up.

Byrnes immediately summoned Raabe back to his office.

"Sandor was not in a position to communicate much, but he did indicate that information is already on its way. He's passing it through you."

"Yes sir."

"Get it to me as soon as you have it."

"Of course."

"That's all for now." Then, before Raabe turned to go, Byrnes asked, "What happened with this young woman? Do we know yet?"

Raabe shook his head. "We're still putting it together."

CHAPTER FORTY-ONE

SHARM EL-SHEIKH, EGYPT

When Sandor finished the call with Byrnes he angrily broke the disposable cell phone into pieces and tossed the remains into the trash can beside Farrar's desk.

"We've got to get you out of the country as soon as possible," the Egyptian said. "I have friends among the police, but there are just as many on the force who will be counted among your enemies after the obligatory bribes are paid by Sudakov. We cannot take the chance of you being placed in jail." He paused. "You will not survive," he predicted with characteristic bluntness.

Sandor nodded his understanding. He had been operating on pure instinct since hearing about Lilli and, despite his visceral desire to storm Sudakov's yacht, he knew Farrar was right.

They retrieved Sandor's leather bag from the safe and, as the two men talked, Sandor changed into the clothes he had packed. Gray flat-front slacks, a black polo shirt, and black rubber-soled loafers. He had two more disposable cell phones, one for use in the United States, the other set for international calls. He reached into the bottom of the bag, separated a finely sewn Velcro strip, and pulled out three passports. He chose the one issued to Scott Kerr of the United Kingdom, bearing Sandor's photo, then carefully replaced the other two. He pocketed two credit cards issued in the name of Scott Kerr, some of the cash hidden there—a small stack of euros—then resealed the lining.

While Sandor went about his business, Farrar made some calls to follow up on what Malik had told him.

Looking up, Sandor said, "Let's have it."

Farrar told him that a warrant had already been issued for Sandor's arrest. He also had some details of the girl's death. She was badly beaten—her face, arms and shoulders bore numerous contusions—and her throat had been slit. The crime scene indicated that the fatal wound, if not the assault, had occurred on the bed in his room. How she was brought into the hotel was not clear since they had yet to locate a witness. Farrar suggested that she had likely been drugged and brought up through the service lift, access being facilitated by a payoff to some maintenance worker who would not have guessed her intended fate.

"Your room, with your fingerprints all over the place," Farrar said.

Sandor nodded. "An old KGB ploy, setting someone up for murder."

"Yes," Farrar agreed. "Brutal but effective."

The problem for Sandor was not the flimsy attempt to implicate him in the crime, it was the sheer senselessness of Lilli's death. She knew nothing. She had never heard of Jordan Sandor until last night. The Russians obviously learned that he was an American operative. What chance was there that he had shared any information with this complete stranger, a party girl sent on a mission to entice him onto Sudakov's yacht?

Sandor lived in a world of brutality and deception, but even in the context of that shadowy existence there were still boundaries. This was depravity, pure and simple, and Sandor was going to be sure that the man responsible would be made to pay for the girl's life with his own, regardless of what Byrnes or anyone else had to say about it.

Farrar sighed and then, in a soft voice, said, "You cannot be thinking about the girl now."

Sandor responded with a blank stare.

"It is too late. Or too soon, depending upon what you are planning."

"I'm planning to take care of things so you'll never have to worry about Roman Sudakov. You have my word that I'll take care of that."

Farrar nodded. "But now it is time for us to go."

"All right," Sandor said, "but first I have a stop to make."

———

It would not be long before the local authorities linked the fugitive Sandor to the local Farrar, and so the Egyptian was adamant they move quickly. Although the murder investigation had just begun, Sudakov would doubtless be funding his own expedition for the prompt apprehension of the American suspect.

Farrar was going to drive them north, where they would pick up another vehicle and Sandor could proceed from there on his own. Farrar offered to continue on with him but Sandor refused.

"Right now you need to stay with the story Sadiki and his niece are telling. You get caught with me and you'll have a whole new set of problems."

Farrar reluctantly agreed. "Although I cannot come back here, not for several days. Things need to cool down a bit."

Sandor agreed.

Armed with the Sphinx automatic Farrar had given him the day before, together with additional ammunition, they headed out the back door to a small Fiat.

"Dendera's car. No problem," Farrar explained. "You just keep your head down and let me get you out of Sharm."

"I told you, I have a quick stop to make first."

"Do not be foolish."

"It's not as if there's a dragnet out for me, Farrar."

"Where do you want to go?" the Egyptian asked warily.

"The first bank I visited, the International Reserve."

"What do you expect to gain from this . . . this lunacy?"

"I need to deliver a message."

"A message?"

"Just drop me off a block away, then come around the corner. I'll be in and out in three minutes."

Farrar shook his head. "I don't suppose you could send this message by email?"

Farrar brought the car to a stop just around the corner from the bank. "Three minutes," Sandor said. "When you drive by, if I'm not walking out then you just keep going. Got it?" He did not wait for a reply, swinging the car door open and climbing out into the bright sunlight and into the flow of pedestrian traffic along SOHO Square.

It never failed to amaze him how ordinary life maintains its ordinary pace even as extraordinary events are unfolding all around. The police were looking for him. Undoubtedly Sudakov's men were as well. Lillian Mindlovitch lay dead in his hotel room, and three Russian thugs had just been executed—two still aboard Sadiki's boat and one floating somewhere in the depths of the Red Sea strapped to an air tank meant to kill Sandor. Yet here he was, calmly strolling along until he made a quick right and pushed his way through the glass doors of the bank.

When he marched swiftly past the receptionist to the left she began to stand, uttering a protest.

"It's all right," Sandor told her as he pushed the elevator button. "Just a follow-up visit with your boss. Only take a minute."

The doors to the lift slid open and he got in and pressed "1," then rode up to where he was greeted by the same woman he met yesterday. She had obviously been alerted that he was on the way and was not quite as happy to see him today.

She began to say something along the lines of "May I help you," but he brushed by her without comment, making a straight line for the president's office. The door was open and the man was already standing. He remained behind his desk, as if that offered some measure of safety.

"Mr. Sandor, I, uh, have just heard . . ."

But Sandor cut him off. "Save it," he barked, still striding toward the man. Before the Egyptian could react Sandor had a tight grip on his left wrist which Sandor twisted until the banker's arm was behind his back and his face pressed down onto his desktop. "Now you listen to me, you dirtbag. When you call Sudakov, which I know you'll do as soon as I walk out of here, you tell that Russian sonuvabitch that I'm coming for him. And tell him it's not for me, it's for the girl. You got that?" For emphasis, Sandor lifted him slightly, then smashed his face onto the desk. "Tell him he better start sleeping with his eyes open, because I'm coming for him."

As the man uttered a groan, Sandor heard something and looked toward the door. The secretary, who had been standing there in mute disbelief, was being shoved aside by a bank guard who had charged into the room with gun drawn. Sandor, in what appeared to be a single motion, yanked up on the banker's arm, dislocating the man's shoulder with a dull, sickening crack as he pulled him into position as a human shield, then drew the Sphinx from under his shirt with his free hand and leveled it at the guard's head.

Ignoring the banker's cries of pain, Sandor hollered, "Drop your gun!"

The guard hesitated.

"Do it!" Sandor shouted. "Unless you want to die, right here and right now, drop your weapon. I'm not going to tell you again."

The guard had no clear shot and was not about to risk hitting the president of his bank. He had a look at the barrel of the automatic that was aimed at his head. Then he looked into Sandor's eyes.

An instant later his gun clattered to the floor.

"Now the two of you," Sandor ordered both the guard and secretary, "turn around and stand facing that wall." When they did as instructed he dropped the banker, who fell to the floor like a sack of hammers. Sandor hurried forward and drove the butt of his automatic into the back of the guard's head. The man's legs buckled and then he collapsed onto the carpet. When the secretary began to scream he had no choice. He hit her hard across the back of her neck with the side of his left hand and watched as she also crumpled to the floor. Then he raced out, found the staircase, and hustled down to the lobby and out onto the street as Farrar waited with the motor running.

"What happened?" the Egyptian demanded as Sandor climbed into the Fiat and they took off.

Sandor told him.

"You really are insane."

"Not so much as you may think."

"You're going to get us both killed."

Sandor turned to his friend. "Maybe," he said, "but not today."

CHAPTER FORTY-TWO

CIA HEADQUARTERS, LANGLEY, VIRGINIA

CRAIG RAABE LOWERED his tall, lean frame into the chair facing Deputy Director Byrnes across the small conference table.

"So," the DD said, "you're prepared to give me a report?"

"I am."

"Something that will make sense of this debacle?"

"Yes sir."

"I'm listening."

Raabe peered down at his notes, then looked up at his superior before he began. "I intend to convey all of the intel I have from Sandor. I hope that it will be received in a, how can I say this . . ."

"An informal basis?"

"At least for now."

Byrnes nodded. "Go ahead."

"You're aware of Sandor's objective in Venezuela."

"To assassinate Rafael Cabello. No need to go over that again."

"And you know that he aborted that mission when he discovered that Adina—Cabello—was refining cocaine as well as developing biological weapons."

"When you say 'mission,' you attempt to give Sandor's actions the imprimatur of an authorized incursion into a foreign country."

"That was not my intent."

Byrnes frowned. "Proceed."

"Faced with this situation, Sandor made a determination in the field that it would be more valuable to track the path of these toxins than to liquidate Adina at the time. He felt that any attempt to take out Adina, successful or not, would cause them to relocate their operation and leave us without a trail to follow."

"I understand that."

"There was also the possibility that Sandor would not survive the attack on his target, which would mean that he would not have had the time or the means to pass on the information he gathered."

"That was almost the case anyway as it turned out, is that not right?"

Raabe resisted the impulse to smile. "It became a close call, yes. The point is, he did what he could to make his invasion appear to be motivated by the cocaine, nothing else."

"Unfortunately his escape was something less than discreet."

"That is true. But he learned that these transactions involved money laundering in Egypt, through a group of Russians apparently connected to the transport of narcotics into the United States, and possibly the Mexican drug lord Jaime Rivera."

"But he has yet to find anything that would reveal the intended use for the toxins."

"Not yet."

Byrnes pursed his lips in disapproval. "Need I remind you that we are not the DEA, at least not the last time I looked. And despite Jordan Sandor's best intentions, satellite photos confirm that the day after his jungle escapade, the compound was burned to the ground anyway."

"Understood. But he has now made contact with a man named Roman Sudakov, known as Ronny, in Sharm el-Sheikh. I have his dossier here." He passed a manila file across the table. "His game seems to be moving narcotics, not terrorism, but he does appear to be another link in the chain."

Byrnes put on his reading glasses and had a quick look at the life and times of Ronny Sudakov. When he looked up he said, "The problem, as you say, is that Sudakov is a drug smuggler, not a terrorist."

"Agreed. But Sandor believes there are still two possibilities that could prove useful."

"And I, of course, hang on his every word."

This time Raabe could not fight off a momentary grin. "Sudakov is the type who would make a deal with the devil if the price was right," he said, pointing to the folder. "There's no way of telling how much he knows of Adina's plans for the anthrax, but he might look the other way if it became profitable enough. He's already tried to kill Sandor, and he murdered a young woman for no reason at all."

"No reason at all?"

Raabe nodded. "She was a messenger sent by Sudakov to bring Jordan to his yacht. Nothing more. She didn't know a thing about any of these activities. Her offense was spending the night with Sandor, which Sudakov set up, by the way."

Byrnes shook his head. "All right. What's Sandor's second theory?"

"That Adina would hide packages of the toxins within the shipment of narcotics."

"Without Sudakov and his cohorts knowing."

"Exactly."

"But the cocaine might then be contaminated, or the anthrax opened by mistake. I can't imagine that Adina's plan is to murder a group of unsuspecting drug dealers."

"There are numerous variations on how the toxin could be packaged. As you know, the Colombian and Mexican cartels have opted for larger shipments lately. As much as a ton or more of product at a time. Packages of anthrax could easily be added to the cargo in sealed containers."

"All right, so the conclusion is that Sudakov is either in league with Adina or is an unwitting transporter of a large amount of anthrax to a place or places unknown. Where do you suggest that leaves us?"

Raabe hesitated. "We need to determine where this shipment is going. That much is obvious. Then we can prevent the attack and hopefully neutralize Adina in the process."

"How do you propose we manage that?"

"Sandor wants to continue tracking the situation on his end. He has an idea about getting help from the Russian government."

"The Russian government? Why am I suddenly getting a knot in my stomach, Raabe?"

"We also feel that Bergenn and I need to be on site in Mexico."

"Working through the DEA, I hope?"

"Yes sir. Knowing what we do about Adina, I think you would agree that there is only one logical conclusion about the ultimate intent for those toxins."

"An attack somewhere in the United States."

"The goods are almost certainly going to be moved through Mexico before an attempt to bring them here. As far as everything we have been able to check, Adina has gone to ground and we have no trace on him anywhere. Unless someone is prepared to authorize military action against Venezuela, I think you should let us run with this."

"Should I?" Byrnes let out a long audible sigh. "I've got to brief the director and the NDI."

"When you do, there's a collateral matter that needs to be addressed."

The DD waited.

"This woman, Lillian Mindlovitch, was murdered in Sandor's hotel room. The locals have issued a warrant for his arrest and we're concerned about Interpol becoming involved."

"You think it might put a crimp in Sandor's travel plans."

"Yes sir."

"I'll speak to the director about that as well. We'll also have to get State and the NSA involved."

"Thank you sir."

"I want Sandor back here, and fast. Where is he?"

"That's a little hard to say. Right now he should be somewhere just south of Cairo."

CHAPTER FORTY-THREE

CARACAS, VENEZUELA

Adina received the bad news from Egypt—his Russian colleagues had taken Jordan Sandor, but somehow he had eluded them and was again at large.

"That man is becoming more than a nuisance," he said to no one in particular. He was seated in a conference room in SEBIN headquarters, attended by his two bodyguards and Minister Bargas.

"So," the minister said, "this man Sandor. We must assume your first analysis of the situation was correct. He is a member of the American intelligence service."

"Yes," Adina agreed solemnly.

"Which means he may have information that . . ." The minister paused, choosing his words carefully. ". . . would be detrimental to your plans."

Only Bargas knew what the others at SEBIN did not—Sandor had learned of the production of anthrax in the laboratory within Adina's compound, which meant that the information was now in the possession of the CIA.

"It would be enlightening to know exactly what he has learned. I will concede that. The sooner we have taken him out of play the better."

The minister sat up a little straighter now. "You may need to abort your plans," he suggested, his tone respectful but firm.

"No," Adina disagreed as he eyed the minister with obvious irritation. "We merely need to make some adjustments."

CHAPTER FORTY-FOUR

ON THE ROAD TOWARD TABA, EGYPT

SHARM EL-SHEIKH IS located on the southernmost tip of the Egyptian portion of the Sinai Peninsula, which does not lend itself to a wide variety of departure options. There is the sea, of course, but given all that had just occurred outside the harbor it was not a viable choice. The small airport was also likely being watched by the authorities, not to mention Sudakov's thugs.

Which left the roads north as the only practical option.

When it comes to travel by car, Egypt is notorious for having one of the world's highest fatality rates per miles driven. Organized rules, signs, and policemen are few and hard to find. When an officer does appear, he will tend to direct traffic with the slightest, almost imperceptible motion. A mere tweak of his forefinger may be intended to have traffic either stop or go—and if a driver is confused by the gesture, a collision is almost inevitable.

But those dangers were not the concern for Sandor, not even with the erratic and heavy-footed Farrar at the wheel. The potential hindrance to their journey was the government ban on the use of the main Sinai roads by foreigners. Given the volatile nature of the region, the authorities had imposed these restrictions years ago and, unlike traffic violations, they were strenuously enforced. If Farrar's vehicle were to be stopped and searched they would both be arrested.

Their journey north, just to the west of the Gulf of Aqaba, required them to make use of the secondary roads in the hope of putting some miles behind them before they would ultimately have to risk entering one of the restricted highways.

"Perhaps if you had not felt the need to break the banker's arm we might have drawn a bit less attention leaving town," the Egyptian suggested, not taking his eyes off the road as they surged ahead.

"I see. So murdering Lilli is not as offensive as assaulting a prominent banker?"

Farrar grunted in response.

"If it were up to me I would have stayed in town long enough to take care of a few other people."

"And you'd already be in an Egyptian prison."

"Point taken."

"I don't think so," Farrar said, turning toward him. "The point is that someone outside the bank may be able to identify this car, which means we are in far greater peril because of what you did. *That* is the point."

"I did what I had to do."

"No, my friend, that is nonsense. You did not have to do it, and it was unprofessional of you to allow your emotions to interfere with your responsibilities."

Sandor was about to reply when a loud horn blast caused Farrar to quickly turn his eyes forward, giving him just enough time to yank the steering wheel and avoid an oncoming truck. For a moment neither man spoke. Then Sandor laughed. "Looks like I may have more to worry about than the Egyptian police."

Farrar scowled as he always did when criticized about his aggressive driving. "Just remember, right now I'm the only chauffeur you have."

"I appreciate that, I truly do, even if you are one helluva scary wheelman. Let's try to get somewhere near Taba in one piece and I'll take it from there on my own."

"Even if we manage to get you close to Taba, you'll have no way to deal with the border guards, not to mention the other authorities that might be looking for you in connection with the girl's death."

"She had a name," Sandor snapped. "It was Lilli."

"Fine. Her name was Lilli." Farrar shook his head again and blew out a stale lungful of air. "Listen to me Jordan, because I speak to you now as if you were my own son. Please have the respect to hear what I say." He paused. "You have chosen a life where you are not entitled to give free rein to your feelings. Such behavior is not just a liability, it is a death sentence. I realize you know this, but right now it appears you need to be reminded."

"They murdered an innocent young woman."

"But that's not really why you're so angry, is it? They murdered her because she spoke with you, and you feel the guilt that comes from that knowledge."

They rode on a little way in grim silence until Farrar spoke up again.

"Innocent people die every day," he said. "Children die of hunger and disease and even for want of clean water. Hurricanes and earthquakes take countless lives. Extremists conspire to kill people who have never done them any harm."

"What's your point?"

"My point is that you have chosen a profession where you have sworn to do all you can to stop that last type of injustice."

"Is that not what I want to do with Sudakov?"

"No," Farrar responded, his voice as loud as a shout in the confines of the small car. "Avenging the death of one girl, of Lilli, is not your mission. If that's all you accomplish then she will have died for no reason and you may well end up joining her, which would be even worse."

After another interlude of sullen quiet, Sandor said, "Well, I guess you told me."

Farrar, still facing straight ahead, allowed himself a sad smile. "I hope you listen better than my own son."

"You haven't said much about Hasani," Sandor pointed out, pleased with the change of subject. "How is he?"

"Ask him yourself. We should reach him in less than twenty minutes."

––––––––––

Sandor had not seen Farrar's son in more than three years, not since the tragedy in Bahrain. Sandor was running a mission that was compromised by the rogue agent Vincent Traiman together with a mole within the CIA. When the operation imploded, Hasani chose to flee rather than fight, leaving the other local agents behind. Sandor attempted a rescue of the remaining members of his team, but he arrived too late. They had already been captured and were later killed by a Libyan-led group of assassins sent by Traiman.

Sandor understood the pressures of combat better than most. He empathized with the grip of fear that had overtaken Hasani, a young man on his first mission, acting in a nonofficial capacity, whose actions ultimately had no effect on the grizzly outcome. More important, Sandor felt he owed something to Farrar for all of the older man's loyalty and help over the years. Eventually Sandor hunted down and liquidated both Traiman and his accomplice, but the sting of Hasani's cowardice was still keenly felt by the proud Egyptian Farrar.

Today he was giving his son the opportunity to redeem himself.

Less than twenty minutes later Farrar pulled off the dusty road and, after negotiating his way around an assortment of potholes, animals and pedestrians, he came to a stop behind a small, one-story building where another car waited.

Without a word, Farrar turned off the engine, pushed his door open and got out. As Sandor also climbed out of the small sedan he watched Hasani emerge from the other car.

The two Egyptians strode toward one another, then stopped as they drew near. Before either of them could speak, Sandor moved past Farrar and extended his hand.

"Hasani," he said with a warm smile, "I see you've been called back into action."

The young man was not yet thirty, taller and better built than Farrar, with a handsome face and his father's dark, wary eyes. Hasani took Sandor's hand and said, "Please believe me when I say that when my father telephoned me this morning he did not have to ask twice for my help."

"I believe you. So, where do we go from here?"

Father and son exchanged a look that spoke for generations of fathers and sons who never had to say a word in order to communicate. Then Farrar turned to Sandor.

"Israel," he said.

CHAPTER FORTY-FIVE

ON THE ROAD TOWARD TABA, EGYPT

THERE ARE BUS tours that make a three-hour run between Sharm el-Sheikh and Taba. They carry tourists in air-conditioned comfort to a border exchange that takes them from Egypt into Israel and back. It is a journey that traverses an ancient region where two nations sit side by side, characterized by deep political, religious, and cultural divisions. The crossings from one country to the other require passage through armed encampments worthy of a Cold War hostage swap.

Hasani's scheme was to have Sandor pose as one of these travelers and depart the dangers of Egypt for the safety of Israel.

"I'm listening," Sandor said with obvious skepticism, "but I'm sure you've noticed we're already halfway to Taba."

"More than halfway," Hasani corrected him.

"Don't you think it's going to be a bit suspicious if we flag down a bus in the middle of nowhere and I get on?"

"That would certainly be a mistake," the young man agreed. "There is no way we can get you onto one of the tour buses without creating unacceptable risk. And we certainly cannot drive all the way back to Sharm el-Sheikh and have you board there."

"Definitely not," Sandor agreed.

"Our intention is to get you to Taba. A friend of mine drives one of the buses. He will have your name added to his manifest. When he arrives there you will simply mingle with the other tourists and make your way into Eilat."

"And this friend of yours . . ."

"Is trustworthy. All he needs is the name you will use. Something other than Jordan Sandor, of course." Hasani looked to his father, then back to Sandor. "You have an, uh, alternative passport?"

"I do."

Hasani lifted his shoulders and then dropped them, as if to say it would be as simple as that.

Sandor turned to Farrar for a reaction. The older man tilted his head slightly to the right, then asked his son, "This driver, is it Awan?"

"Yes."

Farrar nodded approvingly. "He is a loyal friend," he told Sandor.

"Loyal enough to trust with my life?"

"Yes," Hasani said.

Sandor shook his head. "All right, let's go over everything from the beginning, then we'll make a decision."

———————

The tour bus in question was a classic-style coach, about halfway full today as they learned from Hasani's cell phone discussion with Awan. As usual, all of the window seats were occupied, the riders hoping to have a view of something worth seeing as they traveled north, with the Sinai Desert stretching out to the left and the sea to the right.

The important thing, Hasani explained, was that the passengers tended to take little notice of each other, and certainly none of them would have any reason to make a head count of those aboard. That should make it easy for Sandor to work his way into line as they disembarked at the bus terminal.

So much for the good news, Sandor thought.

The problem lay in the inescapability of the situation he would face once he placed himself in the hands of the Egyptian officers that monitor the crossing from this side. His photograph might already have been obtained and circulated; his British passport in the name of Scott Kerr might be spotted as a forgery; Interpol may have already been alerted; or, despite Hasani's confidence in the scheme, someone on the bus might point out that Sandor had not been on the ride north. Any of these, or a handful of other hazards, could cause the guards to draw their weapons and take him into custody.

With the responsibilities before him, it was not a result he could afford. "I need to get through," Sandor told them.

"They're searching for an American," Farrar observed as he studied the grim look on his friend's face. Then he gestured toward his son, who reached into his car and removed a small bag from the backseat. "And we have a few items to alter your appearance."

Sandor managed a smile. "Glad to see you're on the case, but I still need to look enough like myself to match my passport photo."

"Of course," Farrar said with a patient nod. "We don't intend to make you look like a Bedouin. We'll just make you a little older."

CHAPTER FORTY-SIX

TABA, EGYPT

They finished their journey in Hasani's car, since no one had any reason to be looking for his small sedan. Sandor was slumped low in the backseat, not quite hiding but doing his best to stay out of view. Farrar rode shotgun. If there was a serious manhunt under way to find him, Sandor spotted no evidence of it as they sped north along the main highway. Given that Sharm el-Sheikh exists almost exclusively for the tourist trade, he figured the local authorities would want to place a lid on the entire affair as soon as possible.

Murder in a high-end hotel room tends to be bad for business.

Nevertheless, Sandor and the Farrars remained alert and were taking nothing for granted. After a couple of phone calls back and forth, Hasani caught up with the bus being driven by his friend Awan. Then, instead of following the large coach off the highway into the heart of town, they veered off one exit earlier and made their way through the backstreets of Taba that circled around toward the parking plaza where the passengers would disembark.

"Better this way," the young man explained without being asked. "It would be too obvious for us to pull up right behind."

As arranged with Awan, they arrived before the bus, giving them a chance to park around the corner.

"After you get rid of me, I want you to be careful yourself," Sandor said to Farrar. "As you said, they're going to make a connection between us, which means you need to keep out of Sudakov's way for now."

"He can stay with me," Hasani said. "He'll be safe."

"All right," Sandor said. "As soon as I can I'll provide a permanent solution to that problem. I already promised you that."

Farrar placed a hand on Sandor's shoulder. "What was it you once told me? Wait to worry?"

Sandor nodded and was about to say something else when Hasani told them it was time to go.

They got out of the car and, with the Egyptians on either side of him, Sandor slung his black leather bag over his shoulder and wandered into the midst of what was thankfully a busy midday scene. They had considered various means of Sandor feeding into the line of people as they filed off the bus. It was agreed that Hasani should head directly toward the driver.

Awan was the first man down the steps. After half a dozen passengers followed him onto the street, Hasani approached and made a loud show of greeting his old friend. Their pretense at surprise was followed by a hearty greeting and an affectionate hug, which drew the attention of the surrounding passengers. Farrar advanced into the growing crowd of tourists climbing down to the street. He said something pleasant in his native tongue to one of the older men there, then prodded Sandor to step behind the gentleman.

Without another word, Farrar sauntered off. Moments later Awan informed Hasani that he had to get about his business, so the young men shook hands and said goodbye. Then Hasani also walked off, in the direction opposite the one his father had taken.

There were no goodbyes for Sandor, one of those small but conspicuous peculiarities of a profession that relies on the integrity of relationships which, by its very nature, it is compelled to distort. Not even a glance or smile could be exchanged.

———————

As he sidled up beside the elderly gentleman, Sandor found that Farrar had made an excellent choice. The man was alone, friendly, and spoke some English, which made him a good candidate for the casual conversation that would give the appearance they were traveling companions. The man would also move slowly, which was just what Sandor wanted. He had no interest in appearing anxious or in a hurry. He would be pleased to shuffle along as the authorities went through the tedious process of passing them through the checkpoint.

Awan led his group to the entry point of the crossing, where he presented information to the first guard they encountered—a manifest that now included one more visitor than he had departed with from Sharm el-Sheikh. He bid his passengers farewell and the group of some thirty people entered the holding area ahead of them.

Two large rectangular buildings face off across the border, one in Taba and the other in Eilat, bracketing an area set up as a demilitarized zone. Moving through these gray, officious-looking structures, people pass either east or west, explorers who are made to endure the requisite screenings, baggage searches, body checks, and state-of-the-art metal detectors.

Politely waiting his turn, Sandor was finally called forward. He placed his black bag on the conveyer that drew it through a screener which disclosed nothing sinister or even interesting. His weapons had all been left in Hasani's car. The additional passports and money were secreted in the bottom of the satchel and could not be distinguished from the lining and structural base of the bag. The only thing that might raise a question was the presence of two cell phones.

Indeed, the question was asked.

Sandor, faking a serviceable British accent, said, "One domestic, one international."

The soldier nodded as he began to scrutinize the passport.

This, Sandor knew, was the critical moment. Any issues with his papers and he would be pulled aside without rights or reason. If they suspected the passport was a forgery they would not even need to connect him to the murder of Lillian Mindlovitch to detain him. He would be charged with espionage and held incommunicado until they sorted out who he was and what he was doing there. His mission would be in jeopardy, not to mention his safety.

All this, and Sandor without so much as a Rohrbaugh 9mm in his pocket.

"So," the Immigration officer said in perfect English, "you were visiting Sharm el-Sheikh?"

Sandor affected the relaxed manner of a Brit on holiday, someone who was used to standing in lines and having his personal life poked and prodded. "I was," he replied.

"How did you enjoy the diving?"

"Not my sport, I'm afraid."

That earned him a curious look. "Sharm is famous for its reefs," the man said, seeming a bit annoyed that someone had come all this way to visit his country and not at least have a look.

"Ah yes, so I understand. I prefer the beach."

The young officer responded with a slow nod, then looked down and stamped the passport, handing it over without another word.

———————

Crossing the large courtyard under the blazing afternoon sun was the next ordeal. If his photo had been circulated and they were watching for him, someone in the tower above might spot him through binoculars. He did not want to walk with his head down or do anything suspicious that might draw attention. The makeup applied by Hasani had actually done a decent job of aging him a bit, running a little gray through his hair and using a cream that dried up into some temporary wrinkles around his eyes. He would have to rely on that and the hope the search for him was not as intense as Farrar had feared.

The elderly man in front of him had gone through the security line first and now waited. Sandor caught up to him just as they were about to leave the building. Once again the man seemed pleased to have the company. They made their way outside and trudged across the neutral area toward the Israeli border compound.

Sandor made comments about the bright day, the efficiency of the Immigration officers, all the usual banal chatter one expects from a total stranger. Then the old man turned to him without altering his pace.

"Have we met before?" he asked.

"Before today? I don't think so."

He studied Sandor's face as he continued to walk on. "Strange, isn't it?" he asked with a smile. "After you reach a certain age, you begin to think you've seen everyone, at least once."

"My grandfather used to say something like that."

"Your grandfather was a wise man. Were you close?"

"Very," Sandor said, then paused. He and his mother had lived with her parents after his father was killed, but he was not about to share that much with a complete stranger. Instead, he replied, "He lived a long and full life."

"Well," the man said, still without breaking stride, "I only hope you also live long enough to experience that feeling, Mr. Sandor. For now, I will do my part to see that you do."

CHAPTER FORTY-SEVEN

EILAT, ISRAEL

SANDOR HAD HOPED that Farrar was feeling proud of his son. Not only had Hasani organized a means for him to leave Egypt, but the young man and his father had also arranged an escort. Sandor allowed himself a slight smile as he and his elderly companion were herded by guards along the paved roadway that stretched ahead of them. The sea was to one side, and Mount Tallul loomed above them on the other, a no-man's land separating two hostile nations.

"It seems we have common friends."

"No," the old man corrected him, "we have uncommon friends."

Sandor nodded. "Who am I to argue?"

As they neared the Israeli checkpoint Sandor knew he was about to undergo a different level of inquiry. He had just exited a country that had no particular concern about letting people leave—not unless an all-points alert had been issued to apprehend a murderer on the loose. Now he was seeking entry into a tiny nation where the fear of enemy infiltration was a national obsession, but refusal was not an option—being sent back to Egypt would be a death sentence.

Allowing his new friend to go first again, Sandor was then beckoned to a table by a young man wearing a military uniform and a serious mien.

The questions began at once. Where had he been? Where had he come from? Why did he want to visit Israel?

The routine was more intrusive and more intense than on the Taba side of the crossing. He had been to Israel more than once and he was prepared, determined to maintain his casual demeanor. He answered each inquiry in the unhurried pace of a man on vacation.

After the Israeli soldier took a moment to read through the passport he held it up with his thumb and forefinger, waving it at Sandor as if it were some filthy piece of business he did not want to handle. "I saw you speaking with that man over there. You traveling together?"

"No, just met on the bus. Nice fellow."

The soldier nodded. "Where are you staying in Eilat?"

"I'm not, actually. Thought I'd have a look around this afternoon, then fly to Tel Aviv."

"And where are you staying in Tel Aviv?"

"At the Hilton."

"You have a reservation there?"

"If I don't, there'll be hell to pay with my travel agent," Sandor said with a weary smile.

The man paused, as if considering whether he should call the hotel to see if there was a reservation in the name of Scott Kerr. "What flight are you taking to Tel Aviv?"

"You have me there," Sandor said. "Figured I would wait to see how much time I spend in Eilat. Must be enough flights I would think."

The soldier locked eyes with Sandor, then pointed at the bag he had already gone over twice. "You travel light for a man on vacation."

Sandor nodded. "Only way to go, really. Had some things shipped through. Just hate luggage, don't you? Especially when I'm going to be sightseeing all day." The man did not reply, so Sandor added, "Thought I might do some shopping too." Then he waited out their staring contest until the man finally relented.

"All right," the officer said, stamping an insert he then placed inside the passport. "Welcome to Israel."

———

When Sandor was finally allowed through, he made his way to the exit door and out to the street. He took a deep breath and exhaled slowly. His elderly friend was there.

"Everything all right?" the man asked.

"Everything is fine. Come," Sandor said, and they began walking toward the taxi stand across the street. "Where do you go from here?"

"There's a very nice restaurant down by the shore. I thought I would have an early dinner. Care to join me?"

"I have a flight to catch. Another time perhaps."

The Egyptian nodded.

"I appreciated your company on our short journey. I believe it was very helpful."

"I was glad to do it. Uncommon friends are rare."

"They certainly are," Sandor agreed. "I'm going to grab a taxi to the airport. Can I drop you someplace?"

"Better not."

"I understand." They reached the line of cabs and Sandor held the door so the old man could get in the first one. "Thank you again," he said.

"May God grant you a safe journey," the elderly gentleman said, then climbed inside and the cab drove off.

Sandor got into the next taxi and, still employing his British accent, told the driver to take him to the airport. Then he sat back and stared out the window, realizing he had never even asked the old man's name.

CHAPTER FORTY-EIGHT

BEN GURION INTERNATIONAL AIRPORT, TEL AVIV, ISRAEL

SANDOR CAUGHT THE first flight he could get to Tel Aviv. When he landed at the large, modern airport he used his credit card to gain entry to a first-class lounge, found a quiet corner, and powered up his international cell phone.

He knew the first call he should make would be to Langley, but he decided that would have to wait. Instead he called an old friend from Special Forces who was now a senior official with the DEA, stationed in Texas. After negotiating his way through a receptionist and personal aide, he finally reached Dan LaBelle.

"My God," LaBelle said, "when your associate called earlier to say you'd be in touch I couldn't believe it. It's been what, three years?"

"At least," Sandor agreed.

"How the hell are you?"

"I'm okay. What're you up to these days?"

"The usual. Trying to monitor a fifteen-hundred-mile border that can't be monitored. Trying to stop illegal drug traffic that can't be stopped. Dealing with impossible politicians and bureaucrats. What else is new?"

"Like you said, the usual."

"What about you?"

"Same old, same old."

"Still pissing off your director?"

"Just as a hobby. It's not my main line of work."

"I suppose I shouldn't ask you what your main line of work is these days." LaBelle paused. "Or maybe I should. From the sound of this connection I'm going to take a wild guess that you're not in the neighborhood."

"Correct."

"Should I ask where you are?"

"My line is reasonably secure."

"So is this one."

"I'm in Tel Aviv."

"Then dinner tonight is definitely out of the question," LaBelle said with a laugh. "Your man told me you need some information."

"What I need is deep background about Russian involvement in the drug trafficking business."

"When you say Russian, are you asking about their government or the black market?"

Now it was Sandor's turn to laugh. "Is there a difference at this point?"

"You're talking about a complicated area, geographically and politically. You want to be a little more specific?"

"What do you know about Roman Sudakov? Calls himself Ronny."

"Sudakov? He's on the transportation end, runs more drugs through this country than Johnson & Johnson, but he's a shrewd operator. We don't have so much as a traffic ticket on the guy. Haven't been able to get near him."

"I have," Sandor said.

The response was silence. Then, "I'm listening."

For now, Sandor was not going to mention Adina or the involvement of anthrax, not on an international cell phone call, secure or otherwise. Sandor only provided the headlines of what happened in Sharm el-Sheikh.

"You've been busy," LaBelle said when Sandor finished. "Given Sudakov's reputation you're lucky you made it out of Egypt standing up."

"I had help from some old friends."

"And now you're calling another old friend for help, is that the deal?"

"That's the deal. I need as much intel on his operation as I can get. Especially as it ties in to drugs coming out of Venezuela."

"Venezuela? Our sources say his trade routes come from Colombia and then through Mexico."

"Always or just most of the time?"

LaBelle thought it over. "We've had some recent play in Venezuela. Not a big percentage of the action."

"I'm looking for a small percentage play."

"And you have reasons you're not going to share with me now."

"It's one of the beautiful things about longtime friendships, Dan. Some things need not be said."

"Right."

"I want to know how they move these drugs, and I figure you would know who I to ask."

"The 'who' is Vassily Greshnev."

"You're kidding me. That old KGB warhorse?"

"He's the man. Still the same corrupt Politburo phony, just working a new angle."

"Money talks and bullshit walks."

"You got it."

"Still comfortably ensconced in Moscow?"

"Where else?"

"Will he see me?"

"Only if I call him. He's sort of my Russian counterpart in the war on drugs."

"Except they're not fighting quite as hard as we are."

"Not when it comes to narcotics flowing into the States, no. He couldn't care less. But I know he won't speak with you over the phone. He'll want a face-to-face. For many reasons."

"I figured I would have to pay a visit, just didn't know it would be Greshnev."

"He's the man."

"And I assume money is one of the reasons he'll want a face-to-face."

"You got it."

"But you think he'll help me."

"I know he will. He despises Sudakov. They have a lot of history and Sudakov has been a thorn in Greshnev's side. Greshnev is probably jealous too."

"Because Sudakov is cashing in on a large scale."

"Give that man a stuffed animal."

"So, you'll make the call?"

"I will. Anything I can do to help someone jam a stick into Sudakov's spokes I'm happy to do."

"I hope to be that guy."

"I'll reach out for Greshnev. You're serious about going to see him?"

"I can get a flight to Moscow from here."

"You're in the airport?"

"I am."

"You're a beauty, you know that. Call me back in an hour."

An hour gave Sandor the time he needed to book a flight to Moscow and then make the next call, this one to Craig Raabe.

"How did Byrnes react?" he asked.

"Let's say he's gone from ice cold to lukewarm," Raabe told him. "I called your friend in Dallas."

"Just spoke to him. I'm onto something here."

"What you were on, buddy, was the Interpol list for fugitives."

"I need that to be cleared, and fast."

"Byrnes already took care of it through back channels, but he wants you back here, and I mean pronto."

"I'm practically on my way home."

"When you say practically . . ."

"I have to make a stop first."

"Where?"

"Moscow."

Raabe could not suppress a chuckle. "Moscow. Well, sure, that's basically on the way home."

"Look at a map. It is."

"So is Bali, but you're not stopping there for a massage, are you?"

"Funny."

"When you said you had to speak with the Russians I didn't think you would actually have to go there."

"Answers I want aren't going to be found in their D.C. embassy, pal."

"Okay, but time is tight. What's your ETA?"

"With flights and time changes I should be home day after tomorrow. I can listen to Byrnes do his song and dance then."

Raabe paused, then said, "What happened with the girl? We got a general report, but we're short on details."

Sandor took a deep breath, started to say something, then thought better of it. "I'll call tomorrow," he repeated, then hit END.

CHAPTER FORTY-NINE

MOSCOW, RUSSIA

Sandor found that he was already too late for the last nonstop flight from the Ben Gurion Airport to Moscow. He had to book a milk run that stopped in Kiev and did not reach the capital until almost noon the next day. He did his best to get some rest en route, then used the time in the Kiev-Zhulyany airport to organize his plans and make a reservation at the Hotel Metropol. Still posing as a traveler from the United Kingdom, he had no trouble with Customs in Kiev. He reached Moscow without incident, grabbed a taxi, and headed into the city.

The Metropol is a classic, old-school *gostiniza* located on Theatre Drive, near the center of the city. The desk clerk accommodated Sandor's early arrival by finding him an overpriced but available suite. It gave Sandor the opportunity to rinse away the hair coloring and peel off the facial cream Hasani treated him to outside Taba. Then he showered, shaved, and had time to visit a men's shop inside the old GUM on Red Square, where he picked up an appropriate outfit for that evening. The days of long lines of people hoping to find a pair of black boots in their size had long since given way to international boutiques such as Cartier, Ralph Lauren and Ermenegildo Zegna.

Sandor returned to the hotel to change into his new white shirt and navy blazer for the early dinner Dan LaBelle had arranged with Vassily Greshnev. Unarmed and feeling particularly vulnerable in Roman Sudakov's hometown, he left the Metropol and walked to the nearby Café Pushkin on Tverskaya Street.

The Pushkin is renowned for its great history, rich food, and people-watching. A popular spot for many decades, it is a bustling, energetic venue. The main level is a casual if costly eatery, the upstairs a formal setting with elegant décor and an extravagantly priced menu. Since Sandor was paying, Greshnev reserved a corner table on the second floor.

As a young man, Greshnev had been a KGB agent with a penchant for common sense that served him well amid the complex politics of the USSR. That pragmatism also served him well when failed socialism morphed into corrupt capitalism. Greshnev always found a way to get along with his countrymen, whatever government was in power. He also did well with his American counterparts. Dan LaBelle had come to know him since Greshnev became a director of the Federal Drug Control Service of the Russian Federation, or FSKN. Similar in its authority to the American DEA, the FSKN shares concurrent jurisdiction with the FSB and the Ministry of Internal Affairs over matters involving the trafficking of illegal narcotics. More important for the purposes of this evening's inquiry, the FSKN has sole responsibility over foreign investigations into such activities.

Sandor and Greshnev had met twice before. Once was by happenstance, when they were introduced at a diplomatic function at the American embassy in Moscow. The second time was during a mission in Kabul, where they found their interests aligned. They had not seen each other since then, more than five years ago.

When Sandor arrived at the restaurant he was shown upstairs. The maître d' escorted him to a table at the far end of the room where Greshnev was already waiting. The Russian stood and extended his hand as the waiter politely retreated.

"Jordan Sandor. What a wonderful surprise it was to receive the call from our mutual friend."

Sandor took his hand. "I was glad that you could accommodate me on such short notice, Vassily."

Greshnev was a tall, burly man somewhere in his sixties, with a well-furnished middle, an affable style, and a look in his eyes that rarely relinquished a sense of cynical amusement. His hair had grayed but was still full and combed straight back. His features were lined but strong—a wide mouth, broad nose and prominent forehead. He thrust out his lower lip as he gave Sandor the once-over, then said, "The fit of your clothing is not up to your usual sartorial standards, eh? A recent purchase, no doubt."

"Moscow's finest," Sandor said. "Unfortunately without time for proper alterations."

"As you say, you are working on short notice. Traveling without a change of clothes, rushing here from Tel Aviv. You must be hot on someone's trail, as you Americans like to say." When Sandor responded with a knowing smile, Greshnev gave his shoulders a slight shrug. "We have our sources, of course." He gestured to their chairs. "Please, sit. It seems we have much to discuss."

The Russian explained that he had already taken the liberty of ordering a chilled bottle of Russian Standard—the au courant vodka in Moscow, which sat in an ice bucket on the table—and that caviar was on the way.

"Excellent," Sandor said as Greshnev poured them each a shot of the icy liquid into the crystal glasses provided.

"To friendship," Greshnev said.

"And capitalism," Sandor responded.

The Russian laughed as they clinked their glasses and threw down the drinks. "So, allow me to save us some time in the preliminaries. I understand that you have come here because you want to know about Mr. Sudakov, who has only recently attempted to murder you and, failing that, attempted to frame you—another quaint American expression—for the murder of a young woman. This much I have learned through, uh . . ."

"Your sources?"

"Yes, yes. My sources. What they cannot tell me, however, is whether you want information from me to assist in some sort of personal vengeance against Sudakov or whether there are larger issues to consider."

"You're asking me if I'm here on company business or on my own dime, is that it?"

"Precisely. It may affect some aspects of how we approach this discussion."

Sandor grinned, but held his reply as a waiter appeared, refilled their glasses and moved away. "Such as the price," he then said.

The Russian raised his eyebrows slightly and tilted his head to the side, then picked up his glass and the two men drank again. "I do not want to be tactless. To the contrary, I want to be sensitive to your situation. But let's be candid, Jordan, you are not a drug enforcement agent and so I am more than a little curious about why you and Ronny Sudakov would have crossed swords."

"A fair question. Let's just say that I have reason to believe he is not only a drug runner, but also a terrorist."

Greshnev's lower lip came forward again as he leaned back to think that over. After a few moments he said, "If that is true, it would be inconsistent with his past practices."

"That may be so. In fact, it's possible that his involvement in a plot against my country may be unintentional."

"That is almost more incredible. Sudakov, as you have apparently seen, is a very purposeful individual."

"Yes, he is. But he is also greedy and ruthless and, like so many of his ilk, blinded by the insular nature of his circumstances."

"He is out of touch with things because he must, by necessity, exist in such a protected environment if he wants to survive."

"Yes."

Greshnev nodded. "So then, are you here with the full faith and credit of your government to seek my assistance?" He permitted himself a brief laugh. "Another American expression I have always loved. Full faith and credit. Sounds like a motto for a bank, no?"

"Yes it does. And no, I'm not. At least not yet. I need to piece some things together first, to confirm my suspicions."

"Ah, Jordan," the Russian said with a vigorous shake of his head. Then he topped off their glasses again. "You toast to capitalism and yet you come here empty-handed. What am I to do with you?"

"You're supposed to let me buy dinner, give me some information, and then we'll decide how to do business." His dark eyes became serious as he leaned forward and took hold of the man's gaze. "In Kabul did I give you reason to doubt that I will do the right thing by you?"

The humor gone from his own expression, Greshnev shook his head. "No my friend, you did not."

"Our intentions with respect to stopping Mr. Sudakov, whether as a drug lord, terrorist, or both, are identical, are they not?"

"They are."

When Sandor leaned back, it was as if he had released the Russian from a firm grip. "So then, since I'm paying this bill I assume you ordered the Beluga."

Greshnev allowed himself another of his cheerful laughs. "Jordan, you know the Beluga is no longer legal, even here."

"But I assumed you . . ."

Greshnev showed him the palm of his hand. "Please, I'm an official of the government," he reminded him, the smile still spread across his large mouth.

"Of course."

"But the Osetra is excellent, I assure you. Let's have them bring it on."

CHAPTER FIFTY

CARACAS, VENEZUELA

Adina was becoming impatient, feeling more a prisoner at the SEBIN headquarters than a guest. He was determined to move his plans forward regardless of what had been discovered at his jungle compound outside Barranquitas. None of his men there had the slightest idea what he intended to do with the biological weapons they had been manufacturing or where they were being transported, not even those in his inner circle. One of the principal tenets of his guerrilla philosophy was compartmentalization—it guaranteed secrecy and prevented betrayal. Even the most loyal soldier would be tempted to give up what he knew in exchange for the promise of sufficient money or to avoid death or torture. The frailty of the human condition is almost always the undoing of great plans, but no one can be persuaded to tell what he does not know.

Having been summoned from his comfortable living quarters inside El Helicoide to the secure conference room, he expected more political chatter with no likelihood that it would be of any help in his efforts to move forward. He was surprised to find only the minister waiting for him.

"So, Gilberto," Adina said as he took a seat opposite his old comrade, "do we have news?"

"Yes, we have some things to discuss."

The minister was not displaying his usual genial demeanor, so Adina simply said, "I'm listening."

"The president's health has taken a bad turn," he said.

"How bad?"

"His brother is seizing a more active role in governing the country."

"Ah," was all Adina said. As close as his relationship was with Chavez, the president's brother was not counted among his supporters. The younger Chavez was always suspicious of Rafael Cabello—both his methods and his motives. He also harbored a poorly disguised jealousy of the bond Adina shared with his brother.

The minister was well aware of the issue, hence the importance of this information. He was not particularly fond of the president's brother himself. "He may end up too much of an appeaser of the United States."

"Yes," Adina agreed.

"If he has the power, he will likely order that your plans be stopped."

Adina sighed. "Just one more reason for me to hasten the process."

After a silent moment, the minister said, "That would place those of us here in a very awkward position. Giving assistance to you, once he has ordered that your operations cease, would prove embarrassing."

Adina showed him his reptilian grin. "I understand, of course."

"I am not sure that you do. His ascendancy is happening as we speak. The president is too weak to object and those around him see his brother as the only viable alternative to a complete loss of power by the administration."

"What are you saying, Gilberto? That I should go to this jackal and seek permission?"

The minister winced at the pejorative, saying, "Careful Rafael, you are speaking about the man who may succeed our leader as the president of this country."

"Bah. Stop the political nonsense and tell me what's on your mind."

The man could not look at Adina now. Instead he stared down at his hands. "I am saying that you should leave here. As soon as possible. For your own good."

Adina allowed the statement to wash over him. He was nothing if not disciplined, always capable of gathering himself in the face of adversity. He would never act in anger or fear or, as in this case, in response to surprise. The moment having passed, he actually laughed his hollow, brittle laugh. "I see. You all want the right to plausible deniability. You can say I was here, that you determined I was up to no good, and so you showed me the door, is that right?"

The bureaucrat said nothing.

"Won't our esteemed acting president ask why you did not detain me under house arrest?"

Now Bargas looked up. "There are some who advocate that very thing. That is why I have come to you before it happens."

Adina's smile had vanished. "I see. So you really do suggest that I leave as soon as possible."

"Listen to me, Rafael. There are many here including myself who are loyal to our cause and who will give you help, but not with you working from within, it is simply not possible. Not until the president recovers."

Adina nodded. "If he recovers, you mean."

Bargas nodded slowly. "Sadly, yes."

"All right. I will leave here with Alejandro and Jorge. But I need a means to contact you, outside the normal channels."

"Of course." The minister paused. "There is one more piece of information we received that you might find interesting."

Adina could not imagine anything to compare with the treachery and cowardice of this man and his cohorts, but he maintained his composure. "Yes?"

"The American agent, Sandor. When he fled from Egypt he did not return to the United States. We received word that he traveled to Moscow."

"Moscow?"

"We have confirmation that he is staying there under an alias."

"You have the name? And his whereabouts?"

"I do." He reached into his pocket for a slip of paper and handed it across the table.

"Good. I need a favor before I leave," Adina told him. "Whatever this American has or has not learned, we would do well to be rid of him. I want you to make contact with someone for me."

CHAPTER FIFTY-ONE

MOSCOW, RUSSIA

Sandor and Greshnev ate and drank and talked. The caviar with blinis would have been enough for Sandor since his focus was on information and not food, but the Russian had done the ordering. One course followed the other as he educated Sandor about the nefarious world of Roman Sudakov and his cohorts.

"The cartel controlled by the Colombians has altered its methods in recent years," Greshnev explained. He described how, in the past two decades, the cabal known as the *hermandad* headquartered in Cartagena had opted for large shipments of product. Strategies such as "mules" hiding plastic bags of cocaine in their stomachs or couriers stuffing carefully wrapped bricks of narcotics inside the floorboards of cars passing across the border from Mexico to Texas had been left to the small-timers. Given the risks, rewards and expenses, it made better business sense to transport cocaine by the ton. They use customized ships, or planes that fly under the radar. "The business has simply become too big to be left to amateurs," the Russian said as he used his cloth napkin to wipe a bit of creamed herring from the edge of his mouth.

"You've got to love the global economy."

Greshnev nodded. "Small shipments became impractical. Too many people involved, too many details to manage for just a few kilos getting through at a time. The product itself is cheap to produce. If a large shipment is lost there's always one right behind it. Their new approach to transportation is sophisticated, modern and technologically advanced. They refit old tankers and make exchanges of cargo at sea." He paused to spear a piece of gravlax. "Of all people, I don't need to remind you how vulnerable we are in our ports." He took a moment to chew the salmon. "They bring in the goods using double-hulled containers that have false compartments and pass them right under our noses."

"And our dogs' noses."

That provoked a loud guffaw. "How right you are. The best drug-sniffing canines in Vladivostok never get a whiff of the stuff."

"Once the narcotics enter the United States, it seems there are any number of distribution networks that become involved, including the Russian mob."

"Centered in New York City. Brighton Beach."

"You've been there?"

"I have," Greshnev said. "A dangerous group, I can tell you that. Russians at their worst can be a vicious people."

"Only at their worst," Sandor said with a grin.

"Of course."

"So how does Sudakov fit into the hierarchy?"

"He told you he made his fortune in oil. That is partly true. He was in the shipping business, moving crude from here to there, but he was not a major player. Among the new Russian oligarchs he was no Prokhorov. He wanted more money and found a way to get it."

Sandor nodded.

"When the Colombians revised their tactics and decided on bigger paydays, they had to be cautious about looking for ships. That type of purchase carries a paper trail, and retrofitting old freighters has to be done with complete discretion. Who better to ask for help than someone on the other side of the world? Who better than a greedy neocapitalist from Moscow?"

"You've become quite the capitalist yourself, Vassily."

Greshnev offered up a sad smile. "Socialism was always nonsense, anyone with an ounce of sense understood that. You cannot deprive man of motivation and then expect him to perform." He shook his large head as if dismissing a bad thought. "The concept of expecting each to contribute according to his ability only works if the man or woman using those abilities is going to be rewarded, am I right? Otherwise he might as well sit under a tree while someone else plows the field."

"No argument here."

"Worse than that is the foolishness of giving to each according to his need. What rubbish. That becomes a tired idea very quickly, especially for the people doing the giving. This is the very problem you have in your own country today, is it not? The principle that is destroying your economy." He put his fork down for the first time in an hour and leaned forward on his elbows, his hands folded in front of him. "In a capitalist system, the rich become rich because they work smarter, they innovate, they hire others, and they ultimately create wealth. It is human nature that the poor will resent this, but as long as the lower classes have the incentive and opportunity to pull themselves up and create their own success, the system works. That's the point of the American Dream, is it not? Invent something. Start your own business." He shook his head. "It's when the underclass becomes entrenched in its own poverty that things go bad. When the state hands out more and more in the way of welfare and benefits it ultimately destroys the impetus for the poor to work. They have food stamps and health care. They are given subsidized apartments. I hear they even receive free cell phones." He chortled, then picked up his fork and went back to eating. "What a sad irony for the world's greatest power. You have created a society where the poor have no reason to improve themselves. Or to educate their children. And what are you left with?"

"Class warfare."

"Precisely," Greshnev said with a satisfied look, as if Sandor were a talented pupil he had finally reached. "The underclass in America has given up the dream. They complain about the rich, but who really suffers? The middle class, of course. They end up working harder and paying more taxes. This way the government can go on paying benefits to those who don't deserve them and the middle class takes it in the neck, as always. So, my friend," he asked with a throaty laugh, "which of our countries is socialist now?"

"I appreciate the civics lesson, and admit I cannot disagree with anything you've said. But what does this have to do with Sudakov?"

"Ah yes, the subject at hand." Grehsnev nodded. "In its purest form, capitalism should work for everyone, up and down the food chain. But then there are villains like Sudakov who operate outside the law, outside the conventions of decency. The problem on Wall Street is not with the honest traders and money managers. They may be overpaid, but at least they play within the rules. The problem is a thief like Madoff. He represents the underbelly of the entire system, and that's where we find Sudakov."

"I'm loud and clear about his morality. What I need is some practical information to stop him."

Now it was Greshnev's turn to hold the American's gaze. "What I need is an honest answer as to why Jordan Sandor is chasing after a man trafficking in narcotics."

"I told you, I have reason to believe he's also a terrorist."

"Yes, but you did not tell me why you believe that."

Sandor smiled but said nothing. This evoked another guffaw from the Russian.

"Jordan, you come here and expect to buy my assistance with nothing more than a dinner at the Pushkin, but you disrespect me by refusing to share the reasons for your mission."

"You have to admit, it's quite a dinner."

Greshnev frowned.

"I don't mean to be disrespectful, Vassily, only cautious."

The Russian waited, taking time to pour them each some of the Puligny-Montrachet he had ordered.

"Your intelligence sources no doubt told you what happened in the Gulf of Mexico last year."

Greshnev lifted his glass and drained a mouthful of the Pauillac he ordered for the next course, then smacked his lips. "The attempted sabotage of an oil refinery."

"That's right."

"I understand you were instrumental in preventing that disaster."

"That's not important. What is important is the identity of the man behind the attack."

"Rafael Cabello," the Russian replied without hesitation. "The

Chavez henchman known as Adina. Yes, we know. The KGB may be gone in name, but the spirit lives on."

Sandor responded with an admiring nod. "I think Adina is working with Sudakov, or at least with the people Sudakov does business with."

"So your concern is that Sudakov may be arranging to smuggle something into the United States other than cocaine."

"Correct."

"Arms?"

"Nothing that conventional."

"Biological weapons then."

"High marks."

The lower lip was thrust out again as Greshnev took a moment to put it all together. "Yes, that would be Adina's style. And I see how it could work with a cocaine shipment."

"As you are so fond of saying, precisely."

"That's why you believe it is possible Sudakov is not even aware he is organizing a contaminated shipment?"

"It's possible."

Greshnev shook his head. "Sudakov is a psychotic, but he's not a fool."

"No, he's not, but I'll bet he's never done business with anyone like Adina before."

CHAPTER FIFTY-TWO

CARACAS, VENEZUELA

ADINA WAS NOT a man who had to be asked twice to leave. Once Minister Bargas made clear that it was no longer wise for him to remain at the SEBIN command center, Adina took the elevator down to his living quarters and made arrangements for a hasty departure.

He was also not a man who deluded himself with a belief in loyalty, friendship, or even discretion. As far as he was concerned, they only exist insofar as they serve someone's purpose at a particular moment in time. He and the minister went back many years, and as long as Adina was safely entrenched inside El Helicoide it was useful for him to sketch out the general parameters of his assault plans for which he needed help, while carefully omitting key details and contact information. Having the support of the minister might have become important at some point.

Now, however, the man had proved himself just another spineless bureaucrat. The political winds were shifting as a result of Chavez's infirmity and, rather than stand up for Adina and his strategy, Bargas had joined the chorus of weaklings too afraid to pursue an aggressive policy against the United States. When he advised Adina that he was no longer welcome, he couched it in terms that made it appear he was still a friend giving fair warning. Adina thanked him, adopting the same pretense of fraternity.

Back in his room, Adina received the call he was awaiting. The minister had done as he asked, he had reached Adina's contact in Moscow. The man was put through and a brief discussion ensued.

Once that business was completed, Adina summoned his lieutenant Alejandro into his room.

"Call the minister's office. Tell him I want to see him upstairs in the same conference room. Ask him to meet me there in five minutes. Alone. Tell him I must pass on some vital information before I leave."

Despite what little he had imparted to Bargas, Adina was not about to leave even a general description of his intentions behind.

The call was placed, after which Adina gave Alejandro additional instructions.

The minister was not surprised to hear back from Adina so quickly, expecting to be informed of the result of the call with Moscow. However, when he arrived at the conference room he was surprised to find that only Adina's man, Alejandro, was waiting.

"I have been asked to express Señor Cabello's apologies, but he is in the middle of packing for our departure. He requests that you accompany me to his room."

"Of course," Bargas said, and followed Alejandro to the elevator.

Three floors down they stepped into the corridor. When they reached Adina's room Alejandro knocked, opened the door, and moved aside to allow the minister to enter. He then pulled the door shut, remaining in the hallway as a sentry.

Inside, Adina was seated in a desk chair. "I am preparing to leave," he said without wasting time on cordialities, "but before I go I am compelled to express my disappointment at the lack of support for my efforts."

The minister remained standing, staring down at a man he knew to be the most dangerous in all of Venezuela. "You understand, my old friend, it is not I who created this uncertain political climate."

"No, of course not. Was there ever a bad deed that was not an orphan, Gilberto?"

The man had no response.

"Well, what a shame for our proud country. And what a shame for you."

As Adina got to his feet, Jorge emerged from the bathroom, moving purposefully across the room in three swift strides. The minister turned to him, suddenly realizing that the man was holding a knife with a long, curved blade. Before he could react, Adina's man drove the blade hard into the minister's midsection, driving it upward in an arc that tore through his stomach, lungs and heart. The assault was so painful, the internal injuries so devastating, that all Bargas could manage in response was a futile effort to grab at the weapon as he exhaled a deep, guttural sound of primal anguish.

Adina studied the look of agony in the man's eyes. He said, "You disappointed me, Gilberto," then walked to the door, opened it and called Alejandro inside. "Quickly," he said as he locked the door behind them, "before there's blood everywhere."

Jorge still held the handle of the knife in place with his right hand, doing his best to contain the growing stain of blood on the minister's chest, his left arm supporting the weight of the dying man as Bargas's knees gave out and he began to sink to the floor.

"Quickly," Adina said again.

Alejandro brought two plastic garment bags from the closet and placed them on the carpet. Only then did Jorge lower the minister to the ground.

"Wrap him up as best you can," Adina ordered.

They used towels and a small blanket, transforming the minister into a manageable package.

"Is he dead?"

Alejandro leaned over and felt for a pulse along the side of his neck. Then he looked up. "Yes."

"All right, you know what to do."

They had earlier loosened the cover to the air vent. Now Alejandro removed it and the two large men lifted the body, covered in plastic and cloth, and hoisted him above their heads. Then they shoved him into the duct.

"Get on the chair and make sure he's far enough in there, where he won't be seen."

Alejandro did as he was told, then replaced the vent cover and returned the chair to the desk.

Adina had a look around and was quite pleased. "Well done," he said. "The car is waiting for us downstairs?"

Alejandro nodded.

"Good. Get your bags and take mine. We're leaving right now."

The two men went about collecting the luggage as Adina checked the room over one more time. He knew they would find the man's body in the next few days. Even as the cool air of the air-conditioning system passed over him, the odor would eventually give him away. But by then it would not matter, by then Adina would be a national hero and all would be forgiven.

He nodded, confirming his own thoughts. Even if his rivals in the government were foolish enough to try to move him aside, they would not be able to stop him now. No one could, because there was not enough time and because no one knew enough of all the pieces he had already put into play. He should never have shared as much as he did with this old crony, but the mistake was simply a reminder of what he already knew.

Trust no one.

Now he had effectively rectified the error. And he had also made arrangements to rid himself of the Jordan Sandor problem.

He nodded again. A good day, he told himself. All in all, a good day.

CHAPTER FIFTY-THREE

MOSCOW, RUSSIA

SANDOR SPENT THE rest of dinner debriefing Greshnev on every imaginable aspect of Russian involvement in the narcotics business in the United States, especially where Sudakov might be involved. As Greshnev made his way through a perfectly prepared rack of lamb and a pile of mushroom blinis, he provided Sandor a thorough education in the workings of the Russian group in Brighton Beach.

"They are almost certain to be the recipients of whatever Sudakov is shipping."

Sandor reminded him that Adina was his real concern.

"I understand that, but whatever Adina may be orchestrating is your area of expertise, not mine. What I can help you with is the connection between Sudakov and my countrymen in New York." He went on to describe methods of importation, distribution and protection. He also focused a great deal on their abject ruthlessness. "They will kill you for nothing more than a suspicion that you are an enemy. And they will kill you in ways that no man should be made to die."

"I understand."

"I'm not sure you do, but my conscience is clear since I have warned you."

"Well," Sandor said as he lifted his glass for yet another toast, "here's to a clear conscience."

At the conclusion of the meal, after far too much vodka, wine and

after-dinner drinks, Greshnev said, "You can attribute my cooperation in part to professional courtesy."

Sandor grinned. "I realize that sort of generosity goes against your
better nature."

"Perhaps I am getting soft in my old age, Jordan. But I must confess, it would delight me to see you bring down Sudakov, even if he is
not your primary target here."

"I appreciate the information, not to mention the sentiment."

"Just remember, I said professional courtesy was only a part of my
motivation."

"I understand that I still owe you."

"Yes, you do," Greshnev said, "and I mean to collect."

"And I take it you do not regard this as a long-term voucher."

Greshnev treated him to the largest smile he had managed all
night. "Precisely!" he exclaimed.

Sandor paid the exorbitant bill, which was certainly going to raise
some eyebrows when he submitted it to accounting in Langley. Then
the two men stood up to leave.

"You need to be careful with these people, my friend."

"So you said, and so I will," Sandor assured him.

The Russian responded with a long, searching gaze that was, for
the moment, less drunk than concerned. "I hope so," he said, then
came around the table and wrapped Sandor in a bear hug.

———

Outside the Café Pushkin, Greshnev offered Sandor a ride back to
his hotel.

"Thank you, but I think I'd better walk off some of those desserts
you ordered."

"Not to mention the vodka, eh?"

They said their goodbyes and Sandor started back toward the
Metropol, using the night air to clear his head. Sandor reviewed everything Greshnev had shared by creating a mental outline, a device
he used to memorize data and organize it into categories he could
draw on later. He was becoming convinced that Adina meant to use
the shipment of cocaine to conceal the anthrax. Ideally, Sandor would

find a way to intercept that cargo. Worst case, he had to determine how and where Adina meant to use those toxins, and then stop him at the point of attack.

He strode at a brisk pace around the circular center of Moscow. He reached the intersection of Tverskaya Street and Tverskaya Boulevard and turned on to Theatre Drive.

Greshnev had repeatedly cautioned him not to underestimate the Russian mob in Brighton Beach. "There are murderers and there are zealots, but these men are sadists who use their atrocities to rule by fear." Sandor understood that murder, by definition, is a unique offense—once the action is taken it is irreversible. As obvious as that notion may be, there is no other crime against man, no matter how heinous, that cannot be survived. Sandor had seen men and women suffer unimaginable injuries from combat, natural disasters and terrorist attacks, yet somehow people struggle to go on.

Which led him inexorably back to Lilli Mindlovitch and the suffering she was made to endure before they slit her throat. She never had a chance, and that thought caused the anger to rise in the back of his throat like a wave of acid.

But Farrar had been right when he criticized him for acting unprofessionally in attacking the banker in Sharm el-Sheikh. Even Greshnev saw the rage of vendetta in his eyes. It was time to put all that aside, at least for now. He had a job to do.

There would be time later to settle other scores.

———————

Inside the hotel lobby Sandor bypassed the front desk and headed for the elevator. He didn't stop to ask for messages since only Craig Raabe knew where he was, and Raabe would make contact via cell phone if he wanted to reach him.

He rode the lift up to the fourth floor and headed for his suite. Inside, he bolted the door and pulled off his sport coat, tossing it on a chair. Then he went to the minibar for a nightcap.

He was leaning over the credenza, looking into the small refrigerator, when he sensed the man rushing at him from behind. Sandor sidestepped as he rose, then braced himself for the assault.

The man charging at him was stocky, a few inches shorter than he, and clutching a wire garrote tightly in both hands. He had obviously intended a swift and lethal stranglehold from behind, but Sandor had avoided that fate.

The attacker dropped the metal cord and reached for the gun inside his waistband.

Unarmed, Sandor had nevertheless taken away the man's advantage of surprise. He leveraged his weight and sprang forward, coming up with the heel of his right hand, aiming for the man's chin. Properly executed, the blow would have been concussive, but Sandor instantly learned he was dealing with a skilled professional. The man used his left forearm to fend off the uppercut, executing an agile counterstrike even as he continued to reach for the weapon with his right hand.

Thrown slightly off balance, Sandor was still moving forward enough to drive the crown of his head into the man's chest while he grabbed for his right wrist, stopping him from pulling out the automatic and sending both of them toppling to the floor.

Sandor had now seized the upper hand, landing on top and knocking the wind out of the man. He drove his right knee hard into the man's groin, but the attacker answered with two quick jabs into Sandor's right kidney as he struggled to withdraw his automatic. Sandor responded with another head butt, this time directed at the man's nose. The intruder managed a quick turn of his head, but not enough to evade a blow that sent blood streaming from his right nostril. A painful hit, but not enough to stop him.

Still pinned beneath Sandor, the man effected a powerful scissor kick in an attempt to turn them over, but Sandor responded with another head butt that caught the man flush in the face this time, dazing him for an instant, which was all Sandor needed. He scrambled to get his weight onto the man's chest as he drove three punches in rapid succession into the side of his head.

The assassin was not done. Giving up on his weapon for the moment, he worked his arms free and grabbed for Sandor's neck.

It was exactly what Sandor wanted.

Now it was his turn to reach for the automatic, and he realized instantly why the man was having such trouble unholstering the weapon—it had a silencer fixed to the barrel and required a long pull.

The assailant's eyes widened as he understood what had happened. As he was attempting a choke hold, Sandor was drawing the gun. He let go of Sandor's neck and, using both hands and all of his strength, tried to wrestle free.

But it was too late. Sandor had managed to withdraw the automatic, a Glock 9mm, and smashed the butt across the side of the man's head before shoving the tip of the elongated barrel into his left eye.

"You move you die," Sandor warned through clenched teeth.

The man said something in Russian that Sandor did not understand. Sandor pressed the barrel deeper into the man's eye socket.

"Don't say you don't speak English. It'll be the last lie you ever tell."

The man responded with an invective that was unmistakable in any language.

"Ah, good," Sandor said. "At least we understand each other."

Another string of obscenities followed, these in Russian.

"Who sent you?"

The man attempted to shake his head, but Sandor had him pinned down. The end of the silencer was now drawing blood from the perimeter of his eye.

"You keep moving and this popgun of yours is going to go off." He stared into the man's other eye, which returned a look filled with as much hate as he could muster. Sandor was not impressed. After leaning a little harder on the gun, he said, "If you understand me, just say yes."

The man groaned, then said yes.

"Good. So, I asked you a question. Who sent you?"

"Drop dead."

"You have no interest in surviving this botched attempt to strangle me, is that it?"

"You'll kill me anyway."

Sandor used his right knee, which was jammed between the man's legs, giving him another painful jolt as he said, "You're dead for sure if you don't answer my questions."

The man seemed to be thinking it over. After a moment he said, "I was called, that is all I know."

"By whom?"

Another pause. Then "Vassily Greshnev."

"You're lying."

"How can you be sure?"

"Because it's what I do. I separate lies from the truth. But I have to admit, it's a nice try on your part. Now, tell me who called you or I'm going to shoot you."

When the man went silent again, Sandor made a sudden move, removing the barrel from the man's eye, aiming it at his shoulder and firing, then shoving the hot, smoking silencer back into his left eye socket.

The shot had made a quick, hissing sound and the man convulsed in pain. His torso contracted upward and he made a move with his right hand to reach for his left shoulder, but Sandor had all of his weight on him and the gun in his eye, keeping him in place. The searing heat of the silencer against his eye socket added to the man's anguish, but Sandor was not interested in his cries.

"You listen to me now, you sonuvabitch. You came here to kill me, and I take that personally. You either answer my questions or you're going to die right here, right now."

The Russian assassin did not hesitate, making a move even before Sandor finished his threat. He shoved upward at Sandor, using his core and legs, while at the same time twisting his arms in an effort to get free. But Sandor's finger was on the trigger of the Glock, which was honed for light action, and when the man made that final, desperate attempt to shake free, the gun went off, the shot exploding into the man's eye. His body twitched several times, then he collapsed in an inert mass, dead on the floor.

"Damnit," Sandor said as he got to his feet.

Sandor stared down at the body, assessing what little he knew—that this attempt on his life had almost certainly been set up by Sudakov or Adina, or perhaps both—that they had tracked him to Moscow—that they had somehow learned of his meeting with Greshnev—and that they had gone to a lot of trouble to get him out of the way.

How the hell did they know I was here?

He stood up, found his way to the armchair in the corner of the room, sat down, and took a long, deep, calming breath. He shook his head and had another look at the corpse, which lay in the middle of his hotel room floor. "What the hell do I do with you now?" he asked out loud. Then he picked up the hotel phone and placed a call to the private number Greshnev had given him.

CHAPTER FIFTY-FOUR

CIA HEADQUARTERS, LANGLEY, VIRGINIA

THE NEXT AFTERNOON, back in Washington, Sandor was seated in one of the small but secure conference rooms in the headquarters of Central Intelligence. Also in attendance were Deputy Director Byrnes, Craig Raabe, and Jim Bergenn. On the large video screen, Dan LaBelle joined them from his office in Texas.

"Any backlash from your counterpart in Moscow?" Byrnes had just asked the man from DEA.

"None at all," LaBelle reported. "Greshnev has been cooperative. His team identified the dead man as an enforcer for a local mob. Criminal record of assaults and narcotics."

"That's who they sent? I'm insulted."

The other men in the room turned to Sandor. It was evident Byrnes was not amused.

"In the past three days you've left dead bodies in hotel rooms in Egypt and Russia," the DD reminded him. "If you see something funny about that Sandor, I need you to let me in on the joke."

"You know who's responsible for the death of Lilli Mindlovitch, sir. And that punk in Moscow was trying to kill me, just in case that part of the story got lost in translation."

"That doesn't make it a source of amusement, does it?"

"No sir."

"I've spent too much time over the past three days cleaning up the mess you left in Sharm el-Sheikh, including removal of your name from the Interpol list. You can thank me for that later. Right now we've got the embassy in Moscow working with a cleanup squad from the FSKN doing a Harvey Keitel imitation."

"There's been purpose to my actions, sir, and the fact that they've twice tried to take me out should be a fair indication that I'm onto something."

Byrnes turned back to the screen. "What about the intel that Sandor has developed? The prospect of a large narcotics shipment that's being used to conceal anthrax? Make any sense to you?"

LaBelle nodded at the camera. "I've seen too much to rule out anything, Director Byrnes. It's a bit far-fetched on some levels, and yet it might also make some sense."

"Explain please."

"If you're going to the trouble of importing a large cargo of cocaine—and believe me, they go to incredible lengths to get these shipments past us—it could be used to piggyback some other illegal substance."

"Go on."

"It would pose several potential issues for us," LaBelle continued. "The obvious threat is having a large quantity of anthrax in the hands of terrorists within our borders, which means we should do everything possible to follow Sandor's lead to intercept the goods. But what if the shipment itself is booby-trapped, rigged so that if it's seized and opened the toxins will somehow be released or exploded? Or what if the poisons have already been mixed with the cocaine, creating a lethal compound for anyone who comes in contact with the narcotics?"

"That last possibility would mean that Adina is double-crossing the drug runners themselves. That makes absolutely no sense to me."

"Yes, the least likely scenario, I admit. But as I say . . ."

"You've seen too much to rule out anything," Byrnes completed the thought. "Do you have anything on your radar screen about a large quantity of cocaine?"

LaBelle could not stifle a sigh of frustration. "We get tips every day, most of them useless, some of them outright disinformation. America is a big country with huge borders, hundreds of ports, and small airports everywhere. Trying to anticipate what these smugglers will do next is our job 24/7."

"So there's no credible information about a current play?"

"Only what Sandor learned, and whatever else you might get from the Mexican he brought back with him from his vacation in the jungle."

"That mission was classified," Byrnes said defensively.

"After the shootings outside Barranquitas and the explosion of that boat in Maracaibo, I would say keeping anything about that mission classified would be impossible."

Byrnes shot Sandor a quick glance but said nothing.

"From a diplomatic point of view, the whole thing might be a disaster if it weren't for the fact that the Venezuelans don't want to admit there are drugs being run out of Cabimas. But this is the era of cooperation among our own agencies of government," LaBelle reminded them with a wry smile. "No secrets, right? Our sources tell us the guy Sandor brought back is a low-level drug runner with nothing more useful than the headlines from yesterday's *Washington Post*."

DD Byrnes frowned. "You're not wrong. The man told us what he knew about the narcotics operation, but he's worthless to us as far as Adina's plans go."

"Information about their plan for the cocaine could certainly be useful if it's tied to the biological weapons."

Byrnes was shaking his head before LaBelle finished. "When you described this man as 'low-level' you were exaggerating his importance. We've been at him for a few days now and it's clear that his job was limited to getting the product from Barranquitas to Cabimas."

"Maybe you'd let us have a shot at him."

"With pleasure."

The group fell silent until LaBelle asked, "Anything else I can help you with today, Director?"

"You could find this shipment," Byrnes said, forcing one of his uncomfortable smiles.

"We'll be working on it."

"You understand, of course, that our agency has no jurisdiction over domestic issues."

"I do."

"And I understand," Byrnes added with special emphasis on those three words, "that you and Sandor have a relationship that he has already called upon to lead him on his excursion to Moscow."

Since no question had been asked, LaBelle decided not to respond.

"My point is, Sandor has no authority to undertake any sort of domestic investigation of these leads. Your agency, the NCTC and Homeland Security have the jurisdiction here and we intend to honor that fact."

"We'll do the best we can."

"I know you will," Byrnes said, then terminated the teleconference and turned to his agents. "Are you three also clear about what we can and cannot do and where we can and cannot do it?"

Sandor responded with an unblinking gaze. "Are you telling me we're supposed to sit back and take no action?"

Byrnes let their staring contest go on for a few moments, then gave it up and said, "No, I'm not, although Director Walsh would certainly be pleased to have you on the sideline. You can imagine what he has to say about your adventures over the past week."

"Wait'll he sees the bill for my dinner at the Café Pushkin."

Byrnes shook his head in obvious frustration. "Unless you can develop intelligence within our jurisdiction, which means outside this country, our hands are tied and we have to leave this to the DEA, FBI, and Homeland Security. Am I clear on this?"

Sandor nodded. "I've been at this too long not to understand the politics. I'll just have to—how did you say it, sir?—develop intelligence within our jurisdiction."

"Sandor, I'm warning you."

Raabe and Bergenn remained silent as Sandor looked to them and then back at the Deputy Director. "No need sir, I'm loud and clear."

When Byrnes left, the three agents remained in the conference room to review the events of the past several days.

"If we go after Sudakov," Bergenn said, "Adina will just pick another guy to deliver his goods."

"That's my thinking," Sandor agreed. "He might have already made that switch, figuring we're tracking Sudakov."

Raabe disagreed. "This isn't like changing from UPS to FedEx. When you hit Adina's compound it may have forced him to move up his timetable. The cargo may already be in transit."

"That's my biggest concern," Sandor said. "Timing."

The other men nodded.

"The problem is that everything points to a shipment coming into the States, and Walsh is going to order us to stay away. You know how he feels about jurisdiction. He is not going to want to start a turf war."

"You think there's still a shot we can intercept it outside the country?"

"There's always that possibility," Sandor said, leaning back and staring up at the fluorescent light fixture. "Right now I wish I'd blown up the entire facility when I had the chance."

"Easy cowboy, that would have been a little easier said than done," Raabe reminded him. "You didn't have the goods to take the place out, you were armed for a sniper mission. And in case you forgot, you thought it would be better to track the shipment and end a terrorist threat. Even if you managed to take out that lab, they would have set up another one within the week."

"Thanks, mom, I feel a whole lot better."

"We need to present something to the DD," Bergenn suggested, "a game plan within our jurisdiction that won't send the Director into orbit."

Sandor sat up again. "One of the key things I learned from Vassily Greshnev was how and where the narcotics will likely end up. Our best opportunity is to come at this thing from both ends. You guys need to find the point of embarkation."

"In Mexico."

"Exactly. Go see LaBelle, he's a solid citizen. He'll give you some good contacts, and he'll point you in the right direction from there."

"I'll actually feel better once we're south of the border," Raabe said. "Byrnes doesn't want us doing anything inside the home fifty."

"Whatever they're bringing in and whenever they're bringing it, most roads for this sort of contraband run across our favorite border. Byrnes should have no problem giving you the green light, especially if you're sharing the intel with DEA."

"Makes sense," Bergenn conceded.

"Jaime Rivera is a major player in the Mexican drug trade, and his name keeps coming up in this deal. I need everything you can put together on him. Dan LaBelle should be able to help with that too."

"What about you?" Raabe asked.

"I'll start in the other direction and swim upstream."

"If you're going after the Russian mob in New York you'll be butting up against the same jurisdictional problem," Bergenn reminded him.

"Don't worry, I'm going to call a guy with the NYPD, narcotics. He'll take the lead. I'll just ride shotgun."

"When do you ever ride shotgun?"

"Leave this to me, it's no problem."

"No problem," Raabe repeated. "Where have I heard that before?"

"Go see Byrnes right now and get his okay so the two of you can start moving."

"Where should we say *you're* going?"

Sandor thought it over for a moment. "You shouldn't."

CHAPTER FIFTY-FIVE

NEW YORK CITY

T HE TIME HAD come for Sandor to meet with his friend Bill Sternlich. He caught the shuttle to New York. On the cab ride into Manhattan he made plans for dinner.

Sternlich was an articles editor for the *New York Times,* having managed to rise from his post as a city reporter and to maintain that position despite the problems occasionally posed by his relationship with Sandor. Over the years, their private philosophic debates some-times spilled into open controversy. Most recently, Sandor stopped just short of choking a staff reporter for releasing information that might have imperiled Bergenn and Raabe. Sternlich was left to smooth out the ensuing mess without losing his job.

Their close friendship endured these various highs and lows, as well as Sandor's frequent absences.

"So, I guess you government spooks have given up using cell phones and emails and all of that."

Even this offhand reference to his profession caused Sandor to make a reflexive survey around them. They were comfortably se-cluded in the back corner of the Osteria Morini on Lafayette Street. The neighboring tables were empty and Sternlich was speaking in an appropriately muted tone. "We use smoke signals nowadays," Sandor told him. "Budget cuts are a bitch."

"Of course. Well next time you take off for points unknown, send up a puff or two when you have a minute."

Sandor nodded.

"All right, I haven't seen you in more than two months, you give me an hour to meet for dinner, and now you look as distracted as I've ever seen you. What do you want to talk about?"

Sandor looked down into his glass of ice and Jack Daniel's. "You remember Bob Ferriello?"

"Sure. Good cop. Straight shooter. Assigned somewhere in Brooklyn."

"Not just somewhere, Bill. He's one of the top dogs in narcotics."

"That's right, I remember that now."

"I'm going to need his help."

"Narcotics? Isn't that outside your area of influence?"

"That's why I need to reach out for Ferriello."

"Uh huh. And you want me to make the call."

"That'd be helpful."

"Didn't you step all over his size twelves last time you two met?"

"Something like that."

"So you want me to make nice for you."

Sandor smiled. "You're like a psychic, Bill."

"You going to tell me what this is about?"

Sandor picked up his glass and had a drink. "You remember what happened down in Baton Rouge?"

"Of course."

"A lot of good people died that day."

"I know. But you prevented a major catastrophe."

"A lot of people had a hand in stopping it." He had a look at his glass, then placed it back on the table. "We never got the bastard who was behind it."

"So you told me. The same guy responsible for the downed airliner."

Sandor nodded.

"And the attack on that fort in the Caribbean."

"Yes. Rafael Cabello," he said, then lifted the glass and had another swallow of the caramel-colored liquor. "That's what this is about."

Now Sternlich picked up his cocktail. "I'll make the call."

"Thanks Bill."

"You going to ask me how I am now, anything normal like that?"

"How are you Bill?"

"I'm hungry," Sternlich said as he pointed to the menu, which lay on the table. "Just so you know, I'm starting with the *stracci* and wild mushrooms. And you're buying."

Sandor managed a smile. "I might as well. Whatever we order it can't come close to the damage I did in Moscow."

———

As Sandor was meeting with Bill Sternlich, DD Byrnes was seated in the office of CIA Director Walsh reporting on recent events and outlining the intended operation he was recommending. Walsh was more a politician than an administrator, the responsibilities of which he left to his deputies. He was committed to the underlying mission of the Central Intelligence Agency, primarily the safety of the United States. His focus as he listened to Byrnes, however, was the diplomatic fallout that had already occurred and was yet to come.

"They are well aware of the limitations of their authority," Byrnes insisted. "Bergenn and Raabe will be meeting with DEA in Dallas, then heading to Mexico."

"What about Sandor?" Walsh asked, managing to pronounce the name as if it were a contagious disease.

"He'll be pursuing other leads."

"Other leads?" From across his large desk, Walsh stared at the DD as if the man had just claimed that two plus two is actually five. "I realize you have a great deal of confidence in Sandor, but compared to him a loose cannon looks like the Rock of Gibraltar."

"He gets results."

"The ends do not always justify the means, Mark."

"Not always, but in this business they do, or at least far more often than we care to admit."

Walsh grunted in response. "To the extent this intelligence gathering is to be conducted within the United States, it's a job for the FBI, DHS, and perhaps the DEA. It is not within the jurisdiction of this agency."

"They are all well aware of those constraints."

"I truly hope so, because I do not want to hear that Sandor is running around the countryside wreaking havoc on citizens, guests, or even illegal aliens."

"Understood."

"I think it's time for you to call DNI and bring in all the other agencies. Put together a joint task force. If Sandor is really onto something we should have everyone involved."

Byrnes nodded. Spreading the blame was just one of the many Potomac dance steps. He opened the file he had been holding in his lap. "Would you like me to provide the details of the operation?"

"No," the Director said, getting to his feet as if he just recalled there was a train he had to catch. "You have my total confidence and I trust you will do what needs to be done in the proper manner."

"Thank you," the DD replied, having also stood. Then, without another word, he headed back to his office to try to track down Sandor and find out what the hell he was up to.

CHAPTER FIFTY-SIX

DALLAS, TEXAS

D AN LaBELLE ARRANGED to meet Bergenn and Raabe at the Mansion on Turtle Creek, located in uptown Dallas. The Mansion is a stylish complex featuring a renowned restaurant with an adjoining cocktail lounge that is understated and elegant, the walls lined in polished wood awash in muted lighting, the ambience reserved. It provided an ideal spot for a private discussion, the exorbitant cost of drinks ensuring that none of LaBelle's subordinates would be inclined to stop by. He was waiting at the bar, nursing a glass of club soda, when the two agents arrived.

The teleconference in Byrnes's office did away with the need for formal introductions. After shaking hands LaBelle led them to a table off to the side, where they took their seats and ordered drinks.

Raabe asked, "Is your office a mess or are you just embarrassed to have the likes of us visit?"

LaBelle laughed. "Even in this age of interdepartmental cooperation there's no way to eradicate petty jealousies."

"We're stepping on toes by getting involved here, is that it?"

"Stomping is more like it."

"Too bad," Bergenn said. "Our DD gave us orders to tread lightly. I guess we're screwing up already."

"Nah." LaBelle shook him off. "It'll be fine. Fact is, we can use the help. It's just that the guy you'll be going after has been our public enemy number one for some time."

"And you boys want to be there for the kill."

"Something like that."

"We talking about Sudakov?" Raabe asked.

"No, I'm talking about Jaime Rivera. He's the kingpin in moving goods from Mexico into the States."

"That's why your agents might feel we're poaching."

LaBelle nodded. "Rivera specializes in the transportation end of the business, getting the product from Mexico into the U.S. In the past three years we've done everything we can to stop him, but it's like fighting a phantom."

"We're here to help."

"Understood, and I wish I had more to tell you. We don't have so much as a photograph of the man. He moves his operation around more often than I change my socks. He obviously puts the fear of God in his people, because the ones we've captured haven't given us anything that's brought us so much as a step closer to the guy."

"Maybe you haven't gotten to anyone high enough in the food chain."

"One of our concerns, certainly. The amazing thing is how Rivera seems to anticipate every move we make to intercept his shipments. We think we're close to grabbing a major haul and end up with an empty container or truck or what have you."

They became quiet as their waitress arrived with three beers. When she walked away LaBelle continued.

"Once in a while we get lucky. You hear about that shipment of marijuana we grabbed coming out of Tijuana a few weeks ago?"

The two agents nodded. "Something like eight tons," Raabe said.

"Not quite that much, but a banner day for us here. We're convinced it was one of Rivera's cargos." He stopped to take a long drink of his draft.

"Any leads from that?"

"No," LaBelle said with a frustrated shake of his head. "None of the runners we took into custody had a thing to say about the man in charge. The best we got was an admission from one of them that he'd rather rot in prison than give up the big boss. Said his people would get to him wherever he was, and he wasn't going to trust us to protect his ass."

"When we deal with Al Qaeda we're dealing with extremists willing to die for their cause. Sounds like you've got the opposite problem. These people are afraid of dying and they know there's a limit to what you can do to them legally."

"Welcome to my world."

"What about the guy Sandor brought back from Venezuela? His people must think he died in the boat explosion. That would leave him safe from their reach."

"He's likely off their radar, it's true, but he's a bit player, as we already discussed. Our people have begun interrogating him in Washington. He wants to make a deal, but he doesn't have enough information to trade for a Big Mac."

"Bottom line this for us."

LaBelle nodded. "Whatever Sandor found in Venezuela, you can be certain a shipment of cocaine from that region would be heading for Mexico. It's the perfect transit point since the enforcement there is about as airtight as a screen door. They bring it by sea or fly it in on a private plane. From there they move it by ground. Then they load it aboard a ship heading north or pack it on trucks and use their network of tunnels to get it across."

"We know the problems you have covering the border. Tell us about the shipping option."

LaBelle nodded. "It's our worst-kept secret that the ports in this country are as vulnerable as hell. No telling where they might try to send one of those double-hulled boxes on a container ship. There are more ways to hide dope on those things than you can imagine."

"They load it in Mexico?"

"Just look at a map of the Mexican coastline. Their choices are endless. And they don't even have to make the transfer inside the harbor, they can do it out at sea."

"Far enough out that they're beyond any patrol boats?"

"Of course. We use satellite surveillance, but try spotting a single maneuver like that somewhere out in the Pacific or the Atlantic, especially at night. It only takes a few minutes and then the delivery vessel is gone."

"But you've got the entire crew on the cargo ship witnessing the exchange," Raabe said.

LaBelle let go with another of his easy laughs. "Man, you have just put your finger on the biggest problem we face. There is simply so much money in narcotics, you can afford to pay off everyone and their brothers. Anyway, when the crew gets to port they're not responsible for knowing what's in the containers. They go ashore and leave it to Customs to do random inspections. The Coast Guard helps and Homeland Security has placed radiation scanners in a lot of our major harbors, but they're not going to detect cocaine. Or anthrax, for that matter. A large container ship holds up to three thousand containers. We receive over six million containers a year in this country. Just think about the expense and logistics of tracking and examining each one. We actually spot-check less than five percent of the goods that arrive, and only around two percent are opened and physically inspected."

Raabe was painfully aware of those statistics. "What about the ship's manifest that lists the number of containers aboard? Wouldn't someone notice the discrepancy?"

"These people are evil but they're not stupid. They shove off with a container filled with nothing but junk. When the delivery shows up they use the crane to hoist the decoy and drop it overboard, then load the new one."

"Beautiful."

"The other way is to come in by plane, fly the stuff right into some private airstrip in the States, or even a flatland where they have a truck waiting. It's fast, effective, but risky. We have our best shot at stopping the air transports with radar and satellite. And they lose a plane in the process," he added with a grin.

"That it?"

"Those are the headlines. Obviously a lot of variations on those themes are possible."

"So you think the way we get to the shipment from Adina is to find this Jaime Rivera, or at least infiltrate his operation."

"That's my take. One of the biggest problems we have in a situation like this is that Venezuela is a hostile country."

"So we've heard."

"But how much have you heard about the way the South Americans hang together when it comes to the narcotics trade?"

"We're listening."

"You remember when the Colombian government captured Walid Makled Garcia?"

"Venezuelan businessman, working out of Bogotá," Bergenn said. "Suspected of involvement in cocaine trafficking."

"Suspected? He was a loudmouth, openly claimed that some of the top officials in the Venezuelan government were on his payroll. We wanted a shot at him, could have helped us fill in a lot of blanks. So what did the Colombians do? Instead of turning him over to us they sent him back to Venezuela, claimed he was wanted there for murder and they had to honor the extradition. Nice way to cover their asses for letting him operate right there, in the middle of their capital. And the best part was that the Obama administration still gave Colombia the free-trade agreement they wanted while Chavez gave Colombia the economic concessions they were after." He shook his head in disgust. "When you've got corrupt government officials in the mix, finding a way to ship narcotics into the U.S. is that much easier."

"I'm guessing not much has been heard from Señor Garcia recently."

"Not much, no."

Craig Raabe lifted his glass and had a long drink of beer. "All right," he said, "where do we start?"

CHAPTER FIFTY-SEVEN

NEW YORK CITY

Bob Ferriello was less than thrilled to receive Bill Sternlich's call. It would be an understatement to say his experience with Jordan Sandor had not been among his favorite memories in nearly twenty years on the police force. It would not be an overstatement to say he hoped never to see the man again.

All the same, Sternlich was a solid contact in the media, and there were times when a New York City narcotics detective could use that sort of friend. So he agreed to meet with Sandor, but refused the invitation to have a drink or engage in anything else that might suggest this was a social reunion. He knew Sandor well enough to know whatever he wanted was all about business, and he was fine to keep things that way. He invited him to stop by headquarters in Brooklyn.

Ferriello's small office was on the second floor of a decades-old precinct house not far from Court Street. He had been coming to work here for so long that he lost sight of what a grimy, haggard appearance the place had. The walls had not been painted since Ferriello was transferred here more than ten years before, and were plastered with torn administrative notices, old and new wanted posters, and an array of different sized and colored papers containing information on cases, both pending and cold. The metal filing cabinets were gray and dented. His metal desk was also gray, a solid, heavy rectangle that was also dented. His chair was comfortable, gray metal with a vinyl-cushioned seat and a back that tilted on strong springs, the casters allowing him to roll around the linoleum floor. The two guest chairs were less inviting, institutional uprights with hard seats and curved backs of wooden slats that encouraged short meetings.

"Sit down," he said when Sandor was shown in by one of the uniformed officers, who then did an about-face and pulled the door closed behind him.

Sandor stood there for a moment, but it was clear that Ferriello was not getting out of his seat. "What, no team hug?"

Ferriello stared up at him. "Last time we met I ended up having to take a four-week leave to recover from my injuries. Not to mention the time I had to spend with my superiors dodging questions I couldn't answer because your bosses in Washington told me to dummy up or else. So I'm not in the mood for your warped sense of humor and I'm not interested in a long discussion, if you catch my drift. You stand or you sit, that's up to you. Just tell me why you're here so we can get this over with as quickly as possible and you can get the hell outta my office."

Sandor nodded, then lowered himself into one of the chairs facing his host. "You left out the part about my saving your life."

"I'll give you that, even if you're forgetting that you weren't supposed to put my life in danger in the first place."

"You're a narcotics detective with the NYPD. Your life is in danger every day."

"Not from a terrorist lunatic trying to blow me to pieces."

"As you would say, I'll give you that, but we got the job done and that's what counts."

Ferriello took a deep breath and exhaled as if he were blowing out the candles on a birthday cake. "All right, enough of this bullshit. You didn't come here to reminisce, I have no official orders to sit with you, and I only agreed to meet because Sternlich is a straight shooter and wouldn't have asked if it wasn't important. So what do you want?"

"Ronny Sudakov."

"Ah." He gave Sandor an appreciative nod. "Still aiming high, I see."

"We have reason to believe he's involved in moving a large shipment of cocaine into this country."

"Tell me something I don't know."

"The shipment I'm interested in is either contaminated with anthrax or is being used to conceal anthrax so it can be brought into the States."

Ferriello let out a low whistle. "And why would a player like Sudakov contaminate his own goods?"

"He wouldn't, I agree. He's either being paid a huge amount of money to do it or, more likely, he's unaware that the shipment is part of a terrorist plot. Either way, not good."

"Either way, not good for the home team, you mean."

"Exactly."

"What do you want from me?"

"The way I understand this business, a shipment arranged by Sudakov is probably going to end up with the Russian boys in Brighton Beach. True?"

"As you say, probably."

"I want you to give me a rundown on how that works. Then I want you to get me to the top dog over there."

Ferriello could not help himself. He paused for a moment, then burst out laughing. "You really are some piece of work, you know that? What do you think, those scumbags are my friends? That I can just make a call and set up a friendly dinner to discuss their latest shipment of dope? These people are stone cold killers. They'll shoot you in the head just to see if their gun is loaded. They'll tie you up, cut your fingers off one at a time, then shove them down your throat and choke you with them."

"Sounds like they scare you, Bobby."

"Hell yes they scare me. It's why I look over my shoulder every time I step out onto the street. They make the Mafia look like a book club. They murder cops, kids, women. And they specialize in torture, or did I mention that already?"

Sandor held up a hand to stop him. "Okay, so you can't make a dinner date with them, I got that. Just fill me in on who I need to get to, then take me over there. You're one of the best narcotics detectives in the department and you're not undercover. Which means they know who you are, am I right?"

"Damn right."

"Perfect. They operate clubs and restaurants and whatever. Let's pick a spot where I'm likely to make contact with one of the big players. They'll make you immediately, that'll move things along quickly, get me to the right guy."

Now Ferriello was staring at him in utter disbelief. "And what? You gonna tell them that you're with the United States government but they should believe you when you say that you're stopping by to warn them that the shipment of coke they're waiting on is contaminated with anthrax?"

"Not sure yet. You think that approach has holes in it?"

Ferriello was laughing again. "Holes? Even if they believe you, why will they care?"

"I can think of a few reasons, but let me lead off with the one I see as the biggest motivation for them to tread carefully here." He hesitated, having a look around the room. "I've never been in your office before."

"So?"

Sandor thought it over, then decided not to give his views on the interior decorations. He returned to the subject at hand. "I've been doing some homework on drug enforcement. Federal, state and local."

"Congratulations."

"You're undermanned and underfunded. You're fighting an uphill battle over a product that's cheap to grow, easy to refine, and more profitable per ounce than any other substance on earth. The chances of you ever winning this war are zero and none. You're raiding crack houses in Bed-Stuy while tons of coke and heroin and marijuana are smuggled into this country every year. Stop me if you disagree."

"Go on."

"The astronomical profits give these drug lords the ability to bribe police, local officials, even highly placed ministers in the banana republics where the dope comes from."

"I'm not arguing."

"The dirty little secret about narcotics is that middle America doesn't really care if you win the war on drugs. Inner-city blacks, Hispanics and other poor minorities, they're the real users of crack and smack and crystal meth. You contain the bulk of the damage in the ghettos and you've done your job."

Ferriello managed a weak smile. "You left out the coke parties in Hollywood."

"True, except our government wouldn't spend ten cents to stop Charlie Sheen or Lindsay Lohan from partying themselves to death. They certainly would like to stop suburban kids from smoking weed or snorting coke, but once again you're waging a campaign aimed at containment, not true victory."

"You've become quite the social philosopher Sandor. What's your point?"

"The point is, the narcotics trade has never been tied to terrorism." He waited a moment to let that concept sink in. "If the government believes that drug dealers are in league with terrorists the entire game will change. Think about it. If there's a biological attack on this country and the toxins got here through these narcotics smugglers, even the DEA will be dwarfed by the resources we'll mobilize. Homeland Security. The FBI. NSA. The entire United States military. Your entire department will look like Mayberry RFD."

Ferriello was shaking his head. "But narcotics already cause murder and mayhem."

"Yes, but to whom? Let's be honest. We've reduced crime in this country through technology and by ignoring the true victims. Statistically, who are the biggest victims of minority crime?"

"Minorities," the detective conceded.

"Right. As long as they're shooting each other in Watts and Newark and the South Bronx, Mr. and Mrs. America shake their heads, say, 'What a shame,' then sleep peacefully at night. You get a marauding band of crackheads invading Scarsdale and see what happens."

"You're not wrong."

"Thank you. Now multiply that outrage by a factor of a hundred million or so if those drugs are tied to a massive biological assault."

"I'm with you."

"Your Russian thugs in Brighton Beach might seem dangerous now, but wait till there's a public outcry and the army runs a dozen tanks and armored personnel carriers into their neighborhood."

"Come on, Sandor."

"You don't see that happening? Think about everything that's taken place since Nine-Eleven. Two wars."

"Overseas."

"What about the changes here? Wiretapping. Video cameras and surveillance everywhere. The left wing screaming about the abridgment of their rights."

"Don't leave out enhanced interrogation techniques. Your personal favorite, as I recall."

"I do what I have to do to save lives."

Ferriello sat back, his chair tilting toward the file cabinets behind him. "So where do you go with this? You try to convince these Russian pricks that they need to cooperate with you in order to survive?"

"As I said, I'm not sure, but if I'm going to locate this shipment I believe the way to do it is to get to them and work my way backward."

"What about locating the goods from the source?"

"We've got people on that right now."

CHAPTER FIFTY-EIGHT

OUTSIDE CARACAS, VENEZUELA

THE ELEMENTS OF tradecraft that make one man a successful covert operative or another an effective terrorist are in some ways two sides of the same coin. The ability to prepare, even for the unexpected. The knack for anticipating unforeseeable events. A talent for staying one step ahead of your adversaries. The need for maintaining secrecy, even from those one is tempted to trust. And, of course, the skills required to execute a plan.

In many instances your enemies come from several directions at once, creating an exponential increase in the level of difficulty being confronted. Such was the case now for Rafael Cabello. Without the support of the Venezuelan administration, Adina had to account for danger on three fronts. The first and most obvious, American counterterrorism, was expected. The second came from the narcotics traffickers he was dealing with, none of whom could be trusted, all of whom were dangerous, and each of whom was pursuing his own ends. Now, however, he also had to allow for a third possible interdiction—from powers within his own country.

Adina's failure to complete the ambitious attack against America's Gulf Coast was an embarrassment that still stung. Diplomatic posturing avoided an international disaster, since the involvement of the Chavez regime could never be proved or even formally charged. Yet those inside the Venezuelan dictator's tight circle of advisors knew how close Adina's actions had brought them to war with the United States. For all of the ranting and threatening Chavez had done over the years against the world's largest superpower, only a fool would believe he actually wanted any part of an armed conflict with the military behemoth to the north.

Now that Adina had embarked on a new plan of attack, he was careful not to reveal even a hint of his intentions to any but a few allies who remained close to Chavez. He assured them that his present efforts would be met with success, with no fear the source of the assault could be traced back to him or his country. As he sped toward a small airstrip outside Caracas, seated in the back of a nondescript sedan, he considered his situation. His refusal to share the details of his scheme now appeared prescient—he had come to realize he could not even trust that small cabal he once viewed as faithful to his cause.

———————

Adina was mulling over his next move when he and his two lieutenants reached the private terminal at Oscar Machado Zuluaga Airport. It was less than half an hour after they made their exit from the SEBIN headquarters, and he knew the sooner they were safely out of the country the better he would feel.

Alejandro spoke into the intercom and the security gate slid open. He drove through, heading directly for the tarmac, where a Cessna Citation Sovereign sat fueled and ready. Adina had arranged for the plane two days before, knowing the time for action was near. He could not risk using any sort of government aircraft, so he reached one of the president's wealthy partisans who remained sympathetic to Adina's political views. He set up this transportation, making it clear to the charter manager that a two-man crew should be on standby, ready to go on an hour's notice. At Adina's request he also dispatched a team of men to make some modifications to the interior of the plane's cabin, all of which had been completed.

As Alejandro brought the car to a stop outside the small terminal, the pilot and copilot were finalizing their inspection of the sleek aircraft. The young pilot turned and greeted the three men as they emerged from the sedan. "Just finishing up the preflight checklist," the pilot said, then introduced himself and his partner.

Adina nodded politely, but neither of his men replied, instead going about the business of unloading the car and carrying their bags onto the plane.

"Help you with those?" the copilot asked.

"No," Jorge said without looking up, hoisting a heavy duffel from the trunk.

Adina strolled over to the two young men. He was dressed with customary elegance, wearing a crisply pressed Italian suit made of a tan tropical wool, a white shirt without tie, and a colorful silk square in the pocket of his suit jacket. The only difference in his usual appearance were the touches he had applied just before leaving El Helicoide. His gray hair was dyed light brown. Contact lenses turned his hazel eyes dark. And he was wearing eyeglasses, with tortoiseshell frames and clear lenses.

No one had been able to get a photo of him for many years, but there were ways of creating virtual portraits from earlier pictures. His intention was to give himself a younger appearance for this journey, a change he had undertaken once before to create a passport issued by the Dominican Republic under another name. He was no longer Venezuelan nor was he Rafael Cabello.

"We should be leaving immediately," he told the two young men without looking at them.

"Not a problem," the pilot said pleasantly.

"Good," Adina replied with his thin, unpleasant smile.

"I was told you would have the flight plan."

Staring out at the hills in the distance, Adina said, "Yes. I have it."

The pilot hesitated. "May I see it?"

Now Adina turned to him. "It's in my bag. I'll give it to you when we get aboard."

The pilot nodded. "You'll be leaving your car here then? Will someone be picking it up or should I have it parked for you?"

Fixing him with his narrow gaze, Adina said, "Have it parked."

The copilot went into the nearby hangar and called out to someone about the car.

"Shall we?" Adina said, then began walking toward the plane.

The pilot, staying alongside him, said, "I've not even been told our destination."

"Mendez, in northeastern Mexico," Adina said. "There's a private airstrip there."

"I've been instructed to extend you every courtesy," the young man said.

"Good," came the reply, Adina not even breaking stride, "good."

CHAPTER FIFTY-NINE

MONTERREY, MEXICO

As Adina and his entourage went wheels up outside Caracas, Craig Raabe and Jim Bergenn were landing at the General Mariano Escobedo International Airport, just outside Monterrey, Mexico. Like Adina, they traveled on a private plane. Any sort of military transport would have marked them before they hit the ground, and flying commercial was not an option—they needed to get there quickly and they needed their weapons. Passing through a private terminal would resolve those problems and help speed them on their way.

Monterrey is Mexico's most successful and technologically advanced city. Raabe and Bergenn passed uneventfully through Immigration, identifying themselves as businessmen. This placed them comfortably and anonymously in the flow of visitors to a thriving metropolis known for its commerce.

On LaBelle's advice they chose this approach, forgoing the diplomatic protocol of checking in as foreign agents with the Mexican authorities. American DEA personnel had too often been disappointed by leaks within the law enforcement agency known as the Federal Police or, more commonly, the *federales*. LaBelle cautioned them not to involve the locals, at least not yet. If Bergenn and Raabe registered their presence at the headquarters of a large, cosmopolitan center such as Monterrey, there were too many ways for that information to be shared, too many ways for it to be delivered to the wrong people.

Instead, Labelle counseled them to maintain their pose throughout the arrival process. Once they picked up their rental car they could abandon any such façade, since they were going to bypass the city and immediately head east toward a town closer to the United States border. Their destination was a notorious little *pueblo* that, as LaBelle warned them, did not share the safe and secure reputation enjoyed by Monterrey.

Reynosa has a bloody history, owing to the narcotics traffic that passes through it on the way north. In 2010 the increase in violence among the competing cartels—as well as between the cartels and law enforcement—became so bad that the nearby United States Consulate temporarily closed its office. Corruption within agencies of the Mexican government is suspected to have been one of the reasons for that move, which was followed by the issuance of a travel warning by the State Department urging American citizens to stay away from the area, including Reynosa. A renewed warning was issued after the murder of an American citizen there in 2011, and in 2012 when the corpses of forty-nine decapitated bodies were found in an area near Reynosa.

"This is typical," Raabe said as Bergenn steered the car toward the rural horizon, the urban skyline of Monterrey disappearing in their rearview mirror. "Sandor goes to Sharm el-Sheikh and Moscow and we get a ticket to the armpit of Mexico."

"May I remind you, he almost bought it in both of those places."

"True, but Sandor tends to bring his own party wherever he goes."

Bergenn laughed. "I have a feeling we'll be having our own party in the next couple of days."

————————

At the conclusion of their briefing in Dallas, LaBelle told them he was going to entrust word of their mission to only one contact south of the border.

Felipe Romero was a DEA agent who had been under deep cover in Reynosa for the past two years. Mexican by heritage, American by birth, LaBelle described him as short and muscular, in his mid-thirties, with dark hair, dark eyes, and a pockmarked complexion that made him appear older than his years. He also warned them that Romero inhabited the treacherous middle ground between the reality of his position with the DEA and the counterfeit existence he was now forced to live.

"He's a serious guy," LaBelle said, "and with good reason." He described how Romero had lost a younger brother years ago to gang warfare on the streets of West Los Angeles. That had been difficult enough for a family being raised only by their mother, Romero's father having disappeared years before. But then his older sister was hit in the crossfire of a drug-related shooting, leaving her dead and landing his mother in a state mental facility. With nowhere to go, Romero joined the Army and turned his life around. When he finished his third tour of duty he signed up with the DEA.

"This is not just a job to Romero, that's what I'm telling you. This is a crusade. He will not deal well with anyone who gets in his way."

Bergenn and Raabe assured him that they understood.

"Good, because he's the best man I can put you together with down there."

———————

They were to meet Romero in an abandoned barn ten miles west of the Reynosa city limits. They arrived just before dusk and made one pass around the property.

The old farmhouse had all but collapsed, the roof caved in, the walls leaning at a precarious angle. A hundred yards or so behind it was the barn, a ramshackle structure that had apparently once been part of a functioning operation. Bergenn pulled the car around back where they got out and circled toward the front on foot.

There was no one there.

They were far enough from the road that they would not be seen, except by someone who might be looking for them, but they were still cautious as they entered the barn.

"This has got to be the place," Raabe said.

Bergenn nodded as he had a look around the musty interior. Then, from a shadow in the corner, a man stepped forward, an automatic in his outstretched hand.

"Don't say a word," he ordered them. "Just put your hands on your heads and stop moving."

The two agents did as they were told.

"You Romero?" Bergenn asked.

"What about 'don't say a word' was confusing to you, man? I'm holding the gun, I ask the questions here. Your names."

They told him.

"Who sent you here?"

"Why should we answer that without knowing who you are?" Bergenn replied.

"Because if I wanted to take you both down you'd be dead already."

"Dan LaBelle," Bergenn said.

"Describe him to me."

Bergenn did.

"He gave you a password."

Bergenn stared at the man. He was just as LaBelle had described. Stocky and strong and serious. "Freedom," he said.

"All right," he said, appearing more annoyed than relieved, "put your hands down."

"How the hell did you get the drop on us?" Raabe asked. "No car in the area. No footprints in the dirt here." He pointed to the barn floor.

"My car is in the woods, half a mile away. And I used some brush to cover my tracks in here."

"Nice work."

He frowned. "I don't know what you guys are used to in D.C. or wherever, but you have just entered one of the most dangerous places in the world. People here, they get a whiff of something wrong and they kill their friends, even their own family. No second chances, no mistakes allowed. You understand what I'm saying?"

"Yes," Bergenn said. "And just so *you* understand, we're field agents, not desk jockeys. So, do we get to ask questions now?"

"Felipe Romero, local runner for the Sinaloa Cartel." He recited the information as if it were his name, rank, and serial number. "Around here they know me as Pacquito. I've been in Reynosa for more than two years and I'm telling you as sure as I'm holding this gun, if you do anything to blow my cover, you'll become my enemy as much as any of them."

The two men from Central Intelligence nodded. "Got it," Bergenn said.

"So why are you here? DL didn't give me much."

"We're looking for information that can help us intercept biological weapons headed for the States."

"What's that got to do with me?"

"We have reason to believe a large shipment of cocaine has already been moved out of Venezuela. It may also contain a sizable quantity of anthrax."

The look on Romero's face told them he wasn't buying it. "Why would they take that risk? Chapo moves large quantities of junk, millions of dollars at a pop. What the hell would he want with anthrax?"

"Chapo?"

Romero treated them to another disapproving look. He was apparently someone who became easily annoyed. "Joaquin Guzman Loera, called El Chapo. Been the head of the Sinaloa Cartel since El Padrino was captured."

"Padrino?"

"Felix Gallardo. Ran things for years before they hunted him down."

"They also arrested Loera," Bergenn recalled, "but he escaped from a Mexican prison."

"Escaped? Yeah, he escaped all right. They say he had everyone in the prison on his payroll within two weeks of being locked up there. Including the warden. When he left, the authorities didn't even report he was gone till the next day, gave him enough time to get home and have dinner."

Bergenn nodded. "Since we took down bin Laden, Loera's become the most wanted man on the FBI and Interpol lists."

Romero did nothing to disguise his impatience. "What is this, man, you came all this way to give me yesterday's news?"

"No. We came here so you could help us locate the shipment. Tell us about Jaime Rivera."

Romero responded with a wary look. "DL must have told you that Jaime Rivera is the main reason I'm here. He runs the part of the operation that smuggles the drugs into the States. Works directly with

Chapo. The Gulf Cartel has been fighting for years with Los Zetas for control of this area."

"Because it's so near the Texas border."

Romero nodded. "When the Gulf Cartel got wind of Rivera's success rate in transporting the junk north, they made a pact with the Sinaloa crew."

"Rivera is really that much of a game-changer?"

"He's got an impressive track record. That's why I've spent two years trying to get to him."

"How close are you?"

"I've never met him," Romero admitted with a look of disgust. "Don't even know anyone who's ever laid eyes on him."

"Labelle said Rivera constantly moves his base of operations. Any idea where he is now?"

"If I knew I'd pay him a visit. Some of the runners think he's in the west, near Chapo. Others think he's gone north of the border because of the turf wars with Los Zetas."

"Wherever he is, Rivera is the man who arranges importation of the narcotics into the U.S.?"

"That's how it goes. My job is to stop him, but so far I can't even find him."

"Well then, it seems we're all looking for the same thing. How do we get started?"

"We?"

"We thought we'd pose as buyers," Raabe suggested. "Say we're with a syndicate in the Northeast."

Romero would have laughed, had the ability not been burned out of him long ago. "You two? They'll make you as cops in about thirty seconds. You want to get your heads blown off like that, you go ahead, but count me out. They'd shoot me too, just for being stupid."

The two agents shared a bemused look, then Bergenn asked, "What do you propose?"

"Let me do my thing. I'll check around, see if there's any chatter about shipments and where they're from. What you're looking for would be the larger variety."

"That's right."

"Okay," Romero said, then gave them a once-over. "Meanwhile, you look like two slices of Wonder Bread. You got something else to wear?"

"Oh yeah," Raabe told him.

"Good. I think you should get your bags and change right here. Head into town, check into the Hotel Esplendido, and sit tight. The less anyone sees of you right now the better. When I call, I'll say something about the girls being ready. Then we'll meet at the bar in the lobby."

"Got it."

"Anyone asks where and how we met it was at a place called La Taverna, on La Calle Fuente."

"La Taverna? There's an original name," said Raabe.

Romero was not smiling. "Just say we met having drinks this afternoon and started talking, got it?"

Both agents nodded.

"If they make you for feds, I can say I was getting a read on you, checking you out. Then you're on your own."

"Got it," Bergenn told him.

"And remember, Pacquito, right?"

"Got that too," Raabe said.

CHAPTER SIXTY

BRIGHTON BEACH, BROOKLYN

T HAT EVENING, AS Bergenn and Raabe sat in a small Mexican hotel room awaiting Romero's call, Lieutenant Detective Bob Ferriello was using his unmarked police car for the ride to Brighton Beach. Sandor had been clear in explaining his purpose to the narcotics detective. He had no intention of doing undercover reconnaissance. He was going to make his presence known, then work his way up the food chain as quickly as possible.

"This oughta be interesting," Ferriello said. He chose the nightclub Little Siberia as their destination, explaining that it was the location most likely to yield what Sandor wanted—a confrontation with someone in charge.

Brighton Beach is home to a variety of ethnic groups, and Brighton Beach Avenue is the main artery of the neighborhood. It is a wide street, perpetually in shadows cast by the angular canopy of elevated train tracks above. It boasts an array of retailers offering food, clothing, liquor and sundries, each shop catering to its particular landsmen. Contrary to a popular notion, there are more than just Russians in Brighton Beach. It just happens that the Russians rule the area.

Ferriello pulled into a no-parking zone on the avenue and snapped his visor down to display his police permit. In addition to earning him free parking, it warned the locals to stay away from his car. Sandor said he wanted to announce their arrival, and the narcotics detective was going with it.

Ferriello led the way around the corner to a nondescript building that looked more like a warehouse than a nightclub. They ascended a short flight of stairs to an unmarked entrance where two brawny types with shaved heads—reminiscent of Sudakov's men, Sandor noted—stood guard at the door. At Sandor's suggestion, Ferriello did not waste time with niceties. He flashed his badge and began to walk past them.

One of the sentries stuck out his arm, which was approximately the size of an oak log. "Private party tonight," he told them in an accent as thick as a Russian novel.

"Oh yeah?" Ferriello stared up at the man. "Well we're the friggen guests of honor, so get your arm outta my face before I throw a handcuff on it and drag you in for assaulting a police officer."

Sandor had never witnessed this side of Ferriello before. He was pleased to see it. He was also pleased to see that they had apparently come to the right place.

The Russian, meanwhile, was losing the staring contest. He slowly lowered his arm and said, "Guest of honor, eh? That's a good one."

"Glad you're amused," Ferriello told him, "now get the hell out of our way."

Which the man did.

Inside, if there was any sort of private party in progress it must have been happening somewhere else in the building. The scene here was much the same as at other clubs in New York except that the place looked as if it had been designed by someone who thought the décor at the Russian Tea Room was too austere. There was dark red velvet and smoked glass and black lacquer all over the place, giving an impression of something between a house of mirrors and a brothel. Which, Sandor assumed, was the point. Music was blaring, the bar was crowded, and people moved back and forth the way people do in these clubs, a mating ritual that becomes alluring, depressing or comical, depending on your point of view.

He and Ferriello headed for the bar, where a tall blond girl asked what they would have. She was considerably better to look at than the garish surroundings, and Sandor told her so.

She responded with a smile that had all the warmth of a frozen shot of Stolichnaya, so Sandor ordered that very drink. But Ferriello was not in the mood to waste time.

"Get me the manager," he demanded.

"Is something wrong, sir?"

"You know who I am?"

She shook her head.

"Your manager will. Tell him Lieutenant Ferriello wants to see him."

She hesitated, then negotiated a neat spin and walked away, giving Sandor an opportunity to judge the rear view. He dismissed the next thought, returning his attention to Ferriello. "I told you I wouldn't compromise you and I mean it. If things get out of hand I want you to leave. I can take care of myself."

"Trust me Sandor, nobody can take care of himself dealing with these animals."

"Maybe so, but if I have any chance someone is going to talk with me about this shipment, they're sure as hell not going to do it in front of a narcotics detective."

"As if they're going to spill their guts to you."

"It's all I've got right now. You're my path to meet the powers that be. Once I'm in you've got to get out."

Ferriello shook his head. "You may not be my favorite person, but I'm not leaving you here to be skinned alive."

"Yes, you are."

Ferriello was about to voice another protest when they spotted a tall man with wide shoulders making his way across the room. His strides seemed about two yards long and it was only a matter of seconds before the large Russian reached them and came to a stop in front of the lieutenant. He ignored Sandor as he glared down at Ferriello and said, "What?"

Sandor marveled at how much accent the man could work into a single syllable, and he told him so. Then, looking at the manager's smooth head as it glistened amid all the lights and mirrors, he wondered if baldness was some sort of job requirement for these people.

"I want to see Vaknin," Ferriello said.

The large Russian stood there glowering at the policeman without answering.

"He said he wants to see Vaknin," Sandor said.

The Russian turned slowly toward Sandor and fixed him with a look that was all business.

When he remained that way for a while, still not speaking, Sandor said, "I guess that's supposed to frighten me, the way you moved your head all slow like that."

Without taking his eyes off Sandor, the Russian asked Ferriello, "Who is this man?"

"Ask him yourself, Ivan. As you've already seen, he can speak."

"Ivan?" Sandor repeated, his gaze remaining locked with the Russian's. "Tell me, Ferriello, are you calling him Ivan like you might say 'Hey Joe' or 'What's up Charlie?' or is that really his name?"

Ivan reached out with a hand the size of a cinder block and grabbed a bunch of Sandor's shirt front. "I don't have to take any shit, not even from a cop."

"Maybe not," Sandor said in an even tone, "but if you don't let go of me right now you're going to find out exactly what you *do* have to take."

Ivan was still holding Sandor's shirt when he began to say something in response. He started with "Listen," but he never got the second word out. Sandor was three or four inches shorter than the Russian, but able to bring his right knee up and drive it hard into the man's groin. At the same time he thrust both forearms upward in a scissor move that broke the grasp on his shirt, then folded the knuckles of his right hand and hit Ivan with three quick chops to the throat.

As the Russian doubled over, struggling to catch his breath, Sandor nailed him just under his chin with his left knee, dropping the big man to the floor. Sandor now came down on him with all of his weight, spinning the Russian onto his back and pressing against the side of Ivan's neck with his right shin. He did a quick frisk and removed a Glock automatic from the shoulder holster under Ivan's jacket, which he held to the man's head.

It was over before it began, or so it seemed to everyone around them. One moment the brawny Russian was holding this stranger by the collar and an instant later they were both on the floor with Ivan gasping for air. Patrons began moving back as two other bouncers came running from across the room, but Sandor ignored all of that. His eyes were on Ivan, who was still heaving and panting beneath him.

"I didn't break your windpipe, at least not yet, so let's not get overly dramatic here. Just try and inhale slowly." He waited a moment. "That's it," he said.

Meanwhile, Ferriello had drawn his service automatic, a Colt 1911, and was standing with the gun at his side, his legs spread, waiting for the other two enforcers to get close enough to see the result of this brief but violent encounter. "Nobody should do anything stupid here," he warned them.

"I think your friend already did," one of them said.

Sandor's focus remained on the man he was holding down. "You know, Ivan," he said, "you and I have gotten off to a really lousy start. You agree?"

The Russian had composed himself enough to turn his head in Sandor's direction. "I don't care who you are," he said through clenched teeth, his breath still labored, "I'm going to kill you."

"I tell you what, we'll see about that later. Right now what I want is to meet your boss. That's all. No need for all the rough stuff, I just want to sit with the man. You got that?"

Ferriello was standing between the two bouncers and Sandor, his weapon still at his side. For a moment no one spoke and no one moved. Then the two beefy henchmen stepped apart as another man came up from behind them to join the scene. He was also Russian and muscular, although not as tall as the others. He was older and had a full head of hair. He was wearing a dark blue suit with a white shirt and red tie.

"What's going on here, Ferriello?"

"Vaknin," the policeman greeted him, then holstered his weapon. "Your manager here got rough with my friend."

"I saw what happened from my office," Vaknin said, then looked down at the men on the floor. "Would you two like to get up now?"

Sandor released the pressure on Ivan's neck and began to stand. But the big man was not done. He lashed out with his left fist, attempting to nail Sandor in the groin. Sandor managed to sidestep the blow, then kicked the Russian in the side of the jaw.

"Enough!" Vaknin commanded.

Ivan froze, still on the floor.

Sandor stood beside Ferriello. He handed the policeman Ivan's Glock, then brushed himself off. "Hope the big guy has a permit for that thing."

"You and your friend are disrupting my business and upsetting my customers," Vaknin declared in an angry tone that displayed absolutely no respect for the fact that Ferriello was a New York City police officer or that Sandor had just dispatched his manager without so much as wrinkling his own sport jacket. "Are you here to cause trouble or do you have some legitimate purpose?"

Sandor did not wait for his companion to respond. "That depends entirely on you."

"Who are you?"

"I'll tell you who I'm not. I'm not a policeman. And I'm not your friend. But I think you'll want to hear what I have to say." He looked around, then back at Vaknin. "In private."

Vaknin nodded slowly. Then he said, "Follow me."

CHAPTER SIXTY-ONE

BRIGHTON BEACH, BROOKLYN

SANDOR AND FERRIELLO followed the well-dressed Russian to the back of the large room. They were followed by the two bouncers, leaving Ivan behind.

Meanwhile, the loud music had continued playing and customers resumed doing whatever they were doing before. Sandor figured it was a place where this sort of action is not all that unusual.

To the right of the kitchen entrance was a door that Vaknin opened by punching in a series of numbers on a keypad that he blocked from view with his body. When the door swung open he bid them all enter, then followed them in.

The five men were now in a dimly lit antechamber. Straight ahead were four steps leading up to another closed door. The Russians were not moving anywhere, at least not yet. The two bodyguards had pulled out their weapons and held them to the heads of their guests.

"Now," Vaknin said, "before we discuss anything in private, you will hand me your weapons."

"You know I can't do that," Ferriello said. "And drawing a weapon on a police officer is a felony."

Vaknin responded with an impatient nod. "Yes, and I would like to see you prove it happened. In the meantime, your weapons."

Sandor ignored the automatic being pointed at him and turned to Ferriello. "This is where we say good night pal. I appreciate the introduction to Mr. Vaknin, but it's time for you to go." Ferriello began to shake his head, while Vaknin could not hide his surprise at the exchange, but Sandor cut off any further discussion on the topic. "I will give you my weapon," he told Vaknin, "then you have your men escort Lieutenant Ferriello out of here. Like I told you, we need to have a private discussion."

Ferriello said, "I'm not leaving," but Sandor was already reaching inside his coat with his left hand for the Walther PPK he was carrying. He lifted it from the holster by the butt of the gun, using only his thumb and forefinger, then dangled it for one of the bouncers to take away.

"I don't know who you are," Vaknin said, "but you take chances."

"That's the business I'm in," Sandor said, then turned to Ferriello. The policeman responded with a disgusted look before he followed the second henchman back into the club.

Once the door shut behind them Vaknin nodded to the remaining bouncer. The man took hold of Sandor's arm, then brought the handle of his Glock crashing across the back of Sandor's skull, knocking him to the floor.

———

When Sandor came to he found himself seated upright in a wooden banker's chair, his wrists and ankles bound with plastic restraints. They were tight against his skin. As he regained his bearings he saw that he was inside what was obviously Vaknin's private office. Sandor realized he was wet, which meant they had just thrown water in his face to revive him. He also realized his head hurt like hell. As his eyes began to focus he saw that he was facing Vaknin, who was sitting comfortably behind his desk.

"Was that entirely necessary?" Sandor asked. "You could have just invited me in and asked me to have a seat."

Vaknin leaned forward and rested his elbows on the large desk. "I saw what you did to Ivan," he explained, nodding toward the bank of monitors that showed the inside of the club from a variety of angles. "Ivan is considerably larger and stronger than you. And me, for that matter. I was certainly not going to take any unnecessary chances with you, especially since I still have no idea who you are or why you have come. You said that you wanted to speak privately and so I have arranged that." Vaknin then reached for a Glock that lay before him, taking it in his hand and pointing it at Sandor's face. "But just so we are clear, I am prepared to kill you if I feel it would best serve my interests. I do not care who you are or that you came here with a policeman. I only care about your purpose and whether or not you pose a threat to me. If necessary I will arrange your disappearance and never give it another thought. Are we clear?"

"Your English is excellent."

Vaknin bowed his head at the compliment. "Despite whatever you may think of the world I inhabit, I am an educated man."

Sandor craned his neck around, doing the best he could to have a look at the entire room. "Are we alone or is there someone in back of me I can't see?"

"We are alone, for now."

Sandor opened his eyes wide and then closed them, repeating the motion several times. "I don't suppose you have five or six Advil handy?"

"What is your name?"

"If I tell you, will that get me the Advil?"

Vaknin stared at him without speaking.

"Jordan Sandor."

"Mr. Sandor, while you had your brief rest in my office, I took the opportunity to speak with Ivan. As you can imagine, I'm unhappy with him and he, in turn, is angry with you. Whether or not I give him an opportunity to express his anger and thereby resolve my unhappiness remains to be seen. He told me that you are insulting and impertinent, and I can see that his assessment is accurate. But you have obviously gone to considerable trouble and put yourself in grave danger to have the opportunity to speak with me. I respect that and concede that I am fascinated by the effort, so please do not waste the opportunity. I am not known for my patience."

Sandor nodded. "How well do you know Ronny Sudakov?"

Vaknin sat back in his plush leather chair. "Why would that interest you?"

"Because he is about to put you and your associates at great risk."

"And why would he do such a thing?"

"I'm not certain that he is doing it knowingly. In fact, I suspect he is not aware of the problem he is creating."

"Come come, Mr. Sandor. You'll need to be less cryptic if we are going to continue this discussion."

"All right. I know that you are Timur Vaknin and that you are involved in smuggling narcotics into this country."

"Despite what your friend Detective Ferriello may have told you about me, if that were true he would have arrested me long ago."

"No, he would have arrested you only if he had sufficient evidence. The fact that you have been too clever to be caught does not disprove the ultimate fact. And, as you would say, let's not waste the opportunity we have to discuss this matter. I know that you are in the narcotics business and I also know that Sudakov is one of your principal sources for transporting the drugs."

"If that were so, why would he do me harm?"

"Have you ever heard of Rafael Cabello? Also known as Adina?"

"The Venezuelan?"

"Yes."

"A close associate of Chavez, I am told."

"A ruthless terrorist."

"One man's terrorist is another man's freedom fighter."

"I have never subscribed to the belief that murdering innocent people qualifies one as a freedom fighter."

Vaknin leaned forward again. "Ah, this is becoming clear now. You are obviously not NYPD, because Ferriello would never have left you as he did. And you cannot be DEA, since you would never have approached me in such a reckless manner. You are here because of Adina, the drug trade emanating from Venezuela, and the rumors that the money is being used to fund anti-American terrorism. Are you from Homeland Security?"

"Who I am should not be important to you. What *is* important is how Adina has infiltrated your business for his own purposes."

"And you've come here to save me? That really is amusing." Vaknin enjoyed an asthmatic laugh that ended as a cough. "Damn cigarettes," he said to himself, then returned his attention to Sandor. "Quite a story you're peddling. What might be the nature of the threat posed by Señor Cabello?"

"You're expecting a large shipment of cocaine that was processed in Venezuela and is being shipped to the States through Mexico with the help of Sudakov's people. There's no sense denying it. I've seen the shipment and I've met with Sudakov. What you don't know is that the cargo contains anthrax."

Vaknin was about to say something, then stopped.

"Whatever the DEA and the NYPD have been doing up to now to demolish your operation, not to mention to arrest you and your people, will seem like they've been chasing down a traffic ticket compared with the furies that'll be unleashed if it's suspected that you and your associates are engaged in terrorism. Now tell me, Mr. Vaknin, am I making *myself* clear?"

Vaknin rose slowly from his chair, then reached down and pressed a button on the underside of the desktop. Almost immediately, Sandor heard a door behind him open and then close.

"For the moment, Mr. Sandor, I am done answering questions," Vaknin said. "But you have only begun."

With that, Ivan came from behind Sandor's chair and stood looking down on him, a mirthless grin crossing his lips.

"Come," Vaknin said, "let's take our guest to the basement. I need some answers and I want to be sure he is motivated to tell us the truth."

CHAPTER SIXTY-TWO

BRIGHTON BEACH, BROOKLYN

Vaknin summoned two more men to his office and instructed them to tape Sandor's mouth shut, lift him—still tied to his seat—and carry him downstairs.

The men did as they were told. They slapped some duct tape across Sandor's lips, then hoisted him in the air and made their way out of Vaknin's room and down a set of stairs in the back of the old building to a dank, poorly lit basement. They carried him through a doorway into a small room, where they dropped the chair to the ground, sending a hard jolt up Sandor's spine. After Vaknin gave the nod, one of them ripped the tape from Sandor's face.

If they expected him to cry out in pain, they were disappointed.

The two henchmen exited the way they had come, slamming the door shut behind them, leaving only Vaknin and Ivan to deal with their prisoner.

Vaknin grabbed a metal chair from the corner of the room and sat down. "Now we can talk."

Sandor looked around. The room was a concrete bunker with no windows, the only light provided by an old fixture just above his head. There were a couple of other chairs and a table against the wall to his left. "Somehow I get the feeling you've entertained here before," he said.

"Yes, it's a convenient spot for quiet conversations. Both intimate and soundproof." Vaknin pulled a silver case from the breast pocket of his coat, took out a filterless cigarette, and fired it up with a gold lighter. He drew deeply and blew out an ugly cloud of smoke. "Now

Mr. Sandor, or whatever your name may really be, I am going to ask you some questions and I expect you to respond truthfully. I am going to ask Ivan to encourage you to be, uh, candid with me."

Sandor never saw the punch coming, but strapped in the chair there was not much he could have done even if he had. Ivan caught him in the side of the head with a right cross that rattled his teeth. Then, before Sandor could shake that off, the tall Russian moved in front of him and unleashed four quick jabs to the body. Bound as he was, Sandor could barely double over as the blows caught him squarely in the solar plexus.

When Ivan took a step back, Sandor did his best to prepare for another onslaught, tensing his stomach muscles and pressing his jaw against his shoulder to cushion the next shot. But Vaknin waved his man off to the side. "So, tell me who you are and why you are here."

Sandor was still catching his breath as he said, "I've already explained that to you. I'm here to prevent a terrorist attack."

"And you thought I would be likely to help you."

"To help yourself."

"So you said. And you are some sort of federal agent?"

"I am."

"But you came here with a New York City policeman. Who you then sent away."

"I asked him to bring me here to make this introduction."

"You came without a warrant. Without backup."

"I told you, I'm not DEA, and I'm not here to search your place. I'm here to talk with you."

"To that end you gave yourself into my custody. With a full awareness of who we are and what we do."

"That's right."

"You are a reckless man, Mr. Sandor."

Sandor had managed to shake his head clear and was doing his best to sit upright. "It's been said."

"Others must obviously know you are here. Explain why you would have come alone."

"If I brought a team of ten men with me, how likely is it that we'd be having this discussion?"

Vaknin nodded, then had another drag on his cigarette. "I see your point."

"You would have demanded a warrant, as you've just mentioned. You would have lawyered up. We'd have spent days going back and forth and you wouldn't have told me a damn thing."

"Agreed. But now that you are here, what is it that you expect me to tell you?"

"I expect you to tell me when and where the shipment from Sudakov is arriving."

Vaknin stared at him for a moment, then broke into his wheezy chortle. "Preposterous," he said, just before the laughter again turned to coughing. He gestured to Ivan with a casual flick of his wrist and his enforcer quickly stepped forward. He smacked Sandor hard across the face, backhand and forehand, repeating it until Vaknin ordered him to stop and retreat again into the shadows.

Having caught his breath, Vaknin said, "You are either very stupid or very crazy, Mr. Sandor. Certainly you have a better plan than simply asking me to incriminate myself in a combination of narcotics smuggling and terrorism?"

Blood flowed from the corner of Sandor's mouth as he turned to look for Ivan, who was standing somewhere behind him. "You and I are going to have another go at it sometime, pal. Sometime when I'm not all tied up."

"I suggest you direct your attention to me," Vaknin said, his tone having turned cold. "I warned you I am not a patient man and you are running out of time."

"You're a businessman, Vaknin. Assume for one second that I'm telling the truth. Assume we fail to intercept the shipment and it becomes part of an attack somewhere in the United States. You would have to agree that the consequences for you and your people would be catastrophic."

"But what if your visit here is part of some clumsy ruse to seize this alleged shipment of narcotics?"

"There is no risk to you. All you have to do is contact someone who can inspect the cargo. If I'm wrong you've lost nothing. If I'm right you have numerous options."

"Such as?"

"It depends on whether the toxins are mixed with the narcotics or separated from them in secure containers."

"I see." Vaknin puffed at his cigarette but said nothing more.

"You might also want to find out if someone in your organization is doing business with Adina."

Vaknin thought it over. "If I were insane enough to be involved in a terrorist scheme, why wouldn't I just kill you right now?"

"You would," Sandor said. "I'm betting you're a businessman and not a fool."

Vaknin abruptly got to his feet and turned to Ivan. "Check that he's good and tight."

Ivan appeared from the darkness again, this time to ensure that the plastic strips around Sandor's wrists and ankles were still firmly in place. "He's not going anywhere," the big man said. Then, for good measure, he lashed Sandor across the face with another backhanded shot.

"I'm telling you," Sandor said as he licked at the blood on his lower lip, "you and I are going to have a rematch."

"Brave words from a man in your position," Vaknin said, then turned to Ivan. "Tape his mouth again and come with me."

————

Left alone in the room, Sandor took a moment to assess Vaknin's next move. The Russian's first instinct would be to reach out to Sudakov, who was likely still somewhere on the other side of the world. If they spoke, there would be no reason for Sudakov to deny that the cargo in transit had been processed in Venezuela, but Sandor guessed he would not admit to any dealings with Adina. Sudakov would offer up a distorted version of the events in Sharm el-Sheikh. He would do his best to convince Vaknin that Sandor was nothing more than an agent working to dismantle their operation, someone they needed to eliminate.

If Sudakov was persuasive enough, Vaknin and his henchmen would return to this basement prison soon, and there would be very little in the way of further discussion. If Vaknin had any doubts, Sandor would have to work hard to enlist his help.

Or to force it.

Sandor knew that Vaknin was right, his story was indeed preposterous—a federal operative was asking a major drug dealer to compromise a large delivery of narcotics because it might be concealing biological weapons. And yet, why else would Sandor have come here alone and put himself at such risk? That was the riddle he hoped Vaknin could neither easily dismiss nor resolve based on Sudakov's assurances.

Sandor wanted to stir enough concern for the man to investigate further. Given Sudakov's reputation, Vaknin had every reason to determine if there was any chance Adina was somewhere in the mix. Whatever Vaknin learned and the action he took in response could be the source of Sandor's next lead.

But it would be useless until Sandor got himself free.

Vaknin wanted him alive, at least for now, and Sandor had done his best to provoke Ivan so Vaknin would not trust him alone with his prisoner. It had cost Sandor several hard shots to the face and stomach, but the strategy worked. Now, with no one watching him, he had a chance to find a way out of his restraints.

The plastic ties that held him were too tight and strong to be stretched or loosened, and he could not get to the blade he had hidden in the lining of his sport coat lapel. His only option was to break apart the arms and legs of the chair, and he knew he hadn't much time.

When Vaknin's goons dropped him to the floor it was definitely painful but potentially helpful. Whatever they had done to weaken the joints of the heavy, wooden chair would prove useful. He began rocking, the motion allowing him to slide the chair backward, closer and closer to the wall. When he was near enough, he drove upward with his legs, slamming the wooden back against the concrete, once, twice, then a third time. But it was no good. This was a well-made piece of furniture and it was not giving way. Figuring the legs had taken the hardest shot when they dropped him, Sandor maneuvered himself sideways, barely able to bring the chair off the floor with his ankles in harness. He began driving the left front leg into the cement wall.

Good thing this room is soundproof, he told himself.

After repeated *thump*s he heard what he had been waiting for, a distinctive *crack*. The restraints were cutting through his skin now, blood running down his shins, but he increased the intensity of his effort until the wooden leg finally gave way at the joint just below the seat and he tumbled to the floor on his side. He managed to bend his knee high enough to bring the broken leg of the chair into his left hand, then slid the wood from between his ankle and the restraint and got his left leg free.

Able to stand on that one leg now, he could generate far more force as he drove the side of the chair into the wall, smashing it again and again until he broke off the left arm and freed his wrist. From there he was able to pull out the blade from his jacket and cut the remaining ties.

He raced to the door of the room, not surprised to find it locked. He jimmied the knob, but it was a solid mechanism. There was no way he was going to kick his way through a metal door secured with a dead bolt and the blade was too large to help him pick the lock.

He picked up the largest remnant of one of the legs of the now-shattered chair. Together with his knife these were the best weapons available at the moment. He then lifted the metal seat Vaknin had used and placed it beside the door. Sitting down, he took a moment to check out his ankles and wrists. The bleeding was not bad; he could deal with it later.

Then he stood and had another look around the room. It was bare.

He stared up at the single light fixture, which hung above the spot where he had been seated. He used the wooden stick to shatter the bulb, plunging the room into total darkness.

He made his way back to the door, found the metal chair and sat down, then did the only thing he could as his eyes adjusted to the dark.

He waited.

CHAPTER SIXTY-THREE

REYNOSA, MEXICO

IN THE WORLD of espionage, counterterrorism, and intelligence gathering, infrequent moments of intense action are interspersed with long stretches of tedious inactivity. Just as Sandor could do nothing but wait for his captors to return, Bergenn and Raabe had to spend the evening in their hotel room, waiting for a phone call from Felipe Romero.

"At times like this I wish I still smoked," Bergenn said.

Raabe shook his head. "It's times like this I'm glad you don't."

It was nearly eleven when the phone finally rang. Raabe picked it up.

"I've got the girls," the voice told him. "You bring the money, I'll see you where we said." Then the line went dead.

Raabe hung up and looked over at Bergenn.

"Well?" Bergenn asked.

"He said he's got the girls, that we should bring money and meet where we said."

"So why the look?"

"I'm not sure, I mean we just met Romero, but I would tell you that was not Romero's voice on the phone."

Bergenn drew a deep breath and exhaled slowly. "All right, let's go find out."

They checked their weapons, each man chambering a round, then replaced the automatic handguns in their holsters. Bergenn pulled on a loose-fitting sport coat, Raabe a zipper jacket. They had a look around the shabby room, then took their passports and money, not leaving anything behind that could identify or incriminate them. They knew they might not have the chance to get back here.

"It's showtime," Raabe said.

Bergenn nodded.

They rode the elevator down to the lobby in silence. The cocktail lounge, just off to the right, was small and dark and uncrowded. It was easy to see Romero was not there. Neither man broke stride as they surveyed the room on their way to the bar.

The bartender approached, a short homely man with a crooked mouth. "What can I get you?" His English was clear, filtered through a Mexican accent.

Raabe ordered a Dos Equis, Bergenn a Tecate.

It did not take long for the beers to be served, no glasses. Not long after that a man came up from Bergenn's left and stood beside him.

"I understand you two are looking for some excitement tonight."

Bergenn scanned him up and down. He was a few inches short of six feet tall, trim, with an oily complexion and nervous eyes. He wore black pants and an oversized print shirt that was not tucked in, making it easy to conceal a weapon. "Maybe," Bergenn said. "We're actually waiting for someone else, said he could line up a good time for us."

The Mexican addressed the bartender by name and ordered a shot of Patrón and a short draft. Then, with a smirk, he said to Bergenn, "Well Someone Else ain't coming."

"Is that right?" Bergenn asked, trying to sound as if it didn't much matter to him one way or another.

"That's right. I'm in charge of your excitement tonight." The tequila and beer came and the man threw down the fiery liquor and chased it with the draft. "Time to go," he told them as he wiped his mouth with the back of his hand.

"I think we should wait for the other guy," Raabe said.

"I guess I'm not being too clear. Must be a language problem." He gave them a full smile this time, showing off surprisingly white teeth. "I'm here to take you to see the other guy." Then, before either of the Americans could respond, he added, "You should move it along before the fun's over. *Comprende?*"

"Where is he?" Bergenn asked.

"Not far. A short ride."

"What's his name?"

He showed off his gleaming smile again. "Calls himself Pacquito."

Bergenn nodded. "Yeah, that's the guy. What do you call yourself?"

"Miguel."

"All right Miguel, let's take a ride."

"Good," the Mexican said, then pointed to the bartender. "What is that expression you Americans have? I fly you buy."

————————

They followed Miguel out to the street, where he stopped and turned around. He moved close to them before he spoke, his voice barely a whisper.

"Look, I know you're both carrying, but if you think it's going to do you any good then you don't know Reynosa. All you're gonna do is piss people off, you understand?"

"If you think we're giving up our weapons then *you* don't understand," Bergenn said. "*Comprende?*"

"Hey man, I'm just telling you, is all." He pointed down the street. "That's my car over there."

"Uh huh. Well I tell you what, Miguel, I'm a little tired so why don't you go get your car and pull it up, right in front here?"

Before Miguel could reply, four men stepped toward them, appearing from the shadows and doorways of the dark street. Each one of them was carrying a handgun they were making no effort to conceal.

"Like I said," Miguel told them, "all you're gonna do is piss people off."

"Apparently," Raabe said.

Without another word, two of the men disarmed the agents. Then Miguel led them to his car.

————————

What Miguel had described as a short ride was a twenty-minute run beyond the outskirts of Reynosa. Bergenn was shoved into the backseat of Miguel's sedan, squeezed in between two of the armed thugs. Raabe rode with the other two in a second car, seated in the passenger seat with the barrel of an automatic pointed at the back of his head. Their journey ended at the entry gate to a small farm surrounded by a wire fence. There were two armed men on duty, each carrying an automatic rifle and an unpleasant attitude.

As the cars approached, the sentries leveled their weapons at the drivers. Miguel slowed to a stop and leaned out the window. After he exchanged a few words with the guards the cars were allowed to pass through. From there they drove on to the main house.

Both cars pulled up in front of the modest-looking home and Miguel got out. "You wait here," he told the others. He went inside, reappearing just a minute later. As he climbed back behind the wheel he said, "They want us to take our friends to the barn."

The barn, a hundred yards farther down the dirt road, was not unlike the structure where the two agents had met Romero earlier that day.

Bergenn and Raabe were prodded to get out, then led to the old wooden building.

Inside, the barn was illuminated by improvised spotlights strung from a couple of the rafters. Several men were milling restlessly about in what appeared to be an uneven circle, as if anticipating some big event they were tired of waiting for. And there, in the middle of the group, Felipe Romero, stripped down to his undershorts, was hanging from his ankles, upside down, blood running down his back and chest. Off to the side was a tall, muscular man with a dark face and dark eyes that shone under the intense lights. He was brandishing a short, sharp boning knife.

"Ah, Pacquito, your friends have arrived. To rescue you no doubt." He laughed, and most of the other men joined him in the merriment. "So *señores,* you have been waiting to hear from Pacquito, am I right?" Neither agent replied. "Well here he is. Not exactly what you had in mind, huh?"

Raabe spoke up first. "What the hell is this bullshit?" He looked around at the others, appearing more annoyed than concerned. "Who are you and why have you dragged us out here?"

"I am Mateo. And this is what the Chinese call the death of a thousand cuts. You know of this, yes?"

When neither man replied, Mateo lashed out and, with a few deft flicks of the wrist, carved two small X's into the flesh at the center of Romero's lower back. The man's body, which had been hanging limply in space, now convulsed as a new source of blood began to ooze from the shallow wounds. His muscles tensed, then gave in to his own weight, but Romero did not make a sound.

Raabe took a reflexive step backward. "Look, Mateo, I don't know who you are, or who you think we are, or what you and your buddies are up to here, but we'll take a ride back to our hotel right now and just forget we ever met. How's that?"

Mateo responded with a pensive look. "That would be fine, if you can explain how you came to know our man Pacquito and what business you have with him."

The two Americans assumed that Romero had not given up their cover. If he had, they wouldn't be having this discussion. Mateo obviously suspected something, but whatever it was it was not sufficient or credible enough for him to pull the trigger on the three of them. At least not yet.

Raabe pushed his way past two of the men to have a better look at Romero. They bristled at being shoved aside, but Mateo held up his hand, ordering them to let the American through. Raabe bent down and tilted his head to the side. Romero's torso was certainly bloody, but the cuts made so far did not appear anywhere close to lethal. They never do in this slow and painful method of bleeding a man to death. Romero's eyes were half shut and his face was flushed. He had been hanging there for too long.

Raabe stood and turned back to Mateo. "Yeah, we met this guy earlier today. He told us he could arrange to get us some goods." He cast a look around the group, then back at *el jefe*. "And some girls, if that's okay with you. Unless you happen to be with the Reynosa vice squad." He turned to Romero again, shot him a disdainful look, then directed his attention back to Mateo. "You got a beef with this guy, what the hell does that have to do with us?"

"Mm hmm, and where did you two meet our friend Pacquito?"

"What the hell do I remember? Some gin mill." Raabe paused. "I guess you call it a tequila mill around these parts." When no one smiled he turned to Bergenn, feigning the need for help. "I can't remember the name of the damn place."

"I can't remember the name either. The something-or-other tavern, over on Fuente, wasn't it?"

"Right," Raabe said. "The tavern on Fuente."

Mateo eyed each of them with obvious skepticism. "And you just happened to find Pacquito, willing to get you some product and some pussy, is that it?"

"More like he found us," Raabe said. "We just got to town, feeling out the local action, and he plopped down next to us at the bar." He looked around again for some support, as if they might be taking a vote at some point. "Are we done with this inquisition?"

"Maybe," Mateo said. Then he turned to one of his lieutenants. "Let him down," he ordered.

The reaction among the spectators was mixed. Some were clearly friends of Romero's and were relieved to see him crumple to the ground in a heap when the rope from which he was dangling was cut. Others seemed more interested in having the bloody proceedings continue.

A couple of the former group leaned over the barely conscious man. One gave him some water to drink.

Mateo, meanwhile, stabbed his boning knife into one of the wooden supports and stepped toward the Americans. "You two rolled into town, armed with automatics, looking like a couple of American cops, and you want us to believe you just happened to meet our boy Pacquito?" He turned his head to the side and spat on the ground, then got right up into Bergenn's face. "We're not finished here," he announced, then told his men, "Take their wallets, their money, whatever they've got with them, then lock the three of them up until I have some more time to look into this."

CHAPTER SIXTY-FOUR

OUTSIDE REYNOSA, MEXICO

Bᴇʀɢᴇɴɴ ᴀɴᴅ Rᴀᴀʙᴇ were herded from the barn to a nearby storage building. Romero was carried there. The two agents were shoved inside, Romero tossed to the ground, then the door was slammed shut and locked behind them.

Bergenn and Raabe immediately tended to the injured DEA agent, sitting him up against a wall in the dimly lit room. Even in his half-conscious state, Romero had the presence of mind to signal the others to come as close to him as they could. He whispered, "Be careful. They may have the room bugged."

Raabe did not hide his astonishment, spreading his arms and responding with a look that asked if this old place could really be wired for sound.

Romero nodded.

They resumed trying to stanch his bleeding, using their jackets to pat him down as they assessed the extent of the injuries. Whatever else Mateo may be, he was clearly good with a knife. The numerous cuts he had inflicted were all short, shallow, and designed to cause fast pain and slow bleeding.

As they bent over him, Romero managed to tell them what had happened in the past few hours.

After he had left Bergenn and Raabe and made his way back to town, he was immediately intercepted by three of the most dangerous enforcers in the local cabal. They told him that Mateo wanted to meet with him. When he asked why, he was given no explanation, but there was nothing unusual in this. What he found unusual was the show of force in collecting him and taking him to the farm. The second thing out of the ordinary was the tone of the questions.

Mateo, who was the regional head of their cartel, claimed to have information that Romero had met with two American *federales* that morning, and he was demanding some answers.

How could he have heard that already? It was as if Romero had been followed to their meeting place, but he knew that was not so, he had taken far too many precautions. He saw no evidence that he was being trailed to or from their rendezvous.

The two agents waited.

"I told them how we met at La Taverna on Calle Fuente. You wanted coke and girls, and I said I could deliver." He paused to take a breath. "He didn't even bother to ask me a second time. His men grabbed me and took me to the barn." He stared at them, his hard, sad eyes unblinking in the faint light. "You saw the rest."

"He was sure we were agents and that you met with us?"

"A hundred percent."

"Which leaves only one explanation," Bergenn said quietly. "Someone gave us up before we got here."

Romero's answer was a solemn nod. Then he mouthed the question, "How many knew?"

Bergenn and Raabe shared a concerned look. Then Raabe held up three fingers. Sandor. Byrnes. LaBelle.

"Then you need to know something else. About Jaime Rivera."

The two men were listening intently to Romero's raspy whisper.

"Lately I've gotten some information. I believe he's actually an American."

"I don't understand," replied Raabe. "Living inside the States, you mean?"

Romero shook his head "Worse. Working inside the government. Maybe even DEA."

"When were you going to share that little tidbit with us?"

"Only when I had to," Romero replied without apology. "I already told you guys, we've been working on this for two years and I've finally had a breakthrough. I can't afford to trust anyone."

"Your direct boss sent us," Raabe reminded him.

Romero offered no response.

"All right," Bergenn said. "Say Rivera is an American, possibly working from the inside. What else do we have on him?"

"We think he's a middleman, not the major honcho he's rumored to be. Loera may have set it up that way, have him appear more important than he is, get everyone spinning their wheels looking for this imaginary Rivera instead of chasing down the real players in Sinaloa."

"But if there's someone working from the inside to help move narcotics into the country, he *is* important."

Romero agreed.

"What about you?" Bergenn asked. "If Rivera is on the inside, how have you survived for two years?"

"Only a couple of possibilities. My cover is so deep maybe Rivera doesn't know about my assignment." The look on his face said he wasn't buying that one. "Or Rivera knows who I am, but taking me out would raise too many questions."

"You think it's likely he'd leave you in place for two years?"

Romero shook his head. "No, that doesn't make sense either. I think the explanation is simpler than that. Rivera knows who I am, but he also knows I haven't gotten close to him." He looked from one agent to the other. "Until now."

Raabe glanced at Bergenn, each thinking the obvious thought but neither man saying anything.

"Now I have intel that Rivera may work out of D.C. I've managed to track some calls lately. Disposable cell phones were used of course, but it looks like Washington."

"Assuming it was actually Rivera and not one of his deputies," said Raabe. "I assume you don't have confirmation since you're not even sure who this Rivera is, am I right?"

Romero nodded.

"Not much to go on after two years," observed Bergenn.

Romero reacted with disappointment rather than anger. "Like I said, that's why I can't trust anyone."

"So why are you telling us now?" Raabe asked.

Romero looked from one man to the other again. "It's not likely all three of us are going to make it out of here, that's why."

CHAPTER SIXTY-FIVE

BRIGHTON BEACH, BROOKLYN

Sᴀɴᴅᴏʀ's ᴇʏᴇs ʜᴀᴅ adjusted to the darkness. He stretched his muscles and took another inventory of his injuries, judging that no serious damage had been done from Ivan's punches, the blow to the back of his head, or the restraints that had cut his wrists and ankles.

When he heard footsteps coming toward him from outside the metal door he was ready for them.

It sounded as if there were only two men, likely Ivan and Vaknin returning. That would certainly make things easier.

Sandor listened to the dead bolt retract and the knob turn. He was standing now, and did not hesitate as the door swung open and the light from the hallway collided with the pitch darkness of the room. Before either of the Russians could react he leveled a blow with the hard wooden chair leg at the first man in. It was Ivan, and it caught him squarely in the neck. As he grabbed for his throat Sandor jammed the end of the wooden stick hard into Ivan's stomach, doubling him over and leaving him vulnerable to a third shot across the back of his head that sent him sprawling to the floor.

Vaknin had already turned and was running toward the stairway. Sandor leapt over Ivan's inert body and caught the Russian in three strides, bringing him to the ground with a nimble open-field tackle around the ankles. Having dropped his wooden bludgeon in the process, Sandor spun the man onto his back and held his knife to Vaknin's jugular.

"Don't move, don't make a sound," Sandor said as he reached

down and felt for a weapon. The man was unarmed, so Sandor pulled the blade away from his neck but kept him down by pressing his knee into the nerve just inside the crook of Vaknin's shoulder. "I came here to deliver a message, which I've done. Which means you've now had a chance to check me out. What have you been told."

"Nothing," Vaknin groaned.

"You're a liar. If you found out nothing you would have let me rot down here until you did. You reached out for Sudakov?"

He nodded.

"And?"

Vaknin glared up into Sandor's angry gaze. "I couldn't make contact with him directly. But his man says you're some sort of fed."

"I told you that myself. What else?"

"That you're dangerous." He hesitated, so Sandor drove the knee harder into the Russian's soft flesh between his pectoral muscle and rotator cuff. "That you need to be removed," Vaknin groaned.

They heard Ivan begin to stir from behind them.

"Get up," Sandor ordered Vaknin. As they got to their feet he took hold of Vaknin's left wrist and twisted his arm behind his back, forcing it up to his shoulder blade. He then pushed him forward until they were near enough for Sandor to kick Ivan hard in the side of his head, catching him in the temple and returning him to unconsciousness. Then he bent over and withdrew the Glock from Ivan's holster, finally letting go of Vaknin.

The Russian rubbed his arm and shoulder. "What do you want from me?"

"I've already told you. I want you to help me stop this shipment."

Vaknin gaped at him as if he was mad. "Even if I were that crazy, what could I do to stop it?"

"You could tell me its entry point in this country."

"I'd be signing my own death warrant."

Sandor lifted Ivan's Glock until the barrel was pointing directly at Vaknin's left eye. "You've already been told I'm dangerous. And you've already said that I'm reckless. You have a life-and-death decision to make right now."

Vaknin appeared to be giving it some real thought.

"My job is to prevent a terrorist attack, and I'll do anything it takes to accomplish that. You don't tell me what I need to know, the world is going to be short one more drug dealer, and I won't lose any sleep over it. *Ponyal?*"

Vaknin nodded his understanding.

"We're out of time here. What's it going to be?"

"If I tell you what I know, you would have no reason to ever say that you learned anything from me."

"None."

"Lower your gun, then." When Sandor did Vaknin relaxed slightly. "Sudakov is a different breed. I think you understand that."

"I do."

"But I can't believe he's become involved in terrorism."

"I'm not here to make you a believer, I'm here for information."

"I have nothing to do with Adina."

"Let's say for the moment I believe you," Sandor replied with growing impatience. He had that familiar ache in the pit of his stomach, the pain that comes from dealing with one sort of evil to catch another. "Just tell me how they're getting the drugs into the States."

Vaknin paused. Then he said, "Baltimore. The information I have is that the goods are coming by container ship into the Port of Baltimore."

"You're sure?"

"I have no details. I never have anything to do with the transport part of the business."

"The age of specialization," Sandor said with a look of utter disgust. Vaknin spoke about his drug smuggling operation as if he were importing computers. "When?"

"Not sure, but the share of these goods coming to New York should arrive no later than the end of next week. That includes the time it takes for the shipment into Baltimore and then the transfer here."

"Who brings it from Baltimore to New York?"

Vaknin uttered a weak protest but he was in far too deep now, and he knew it. "Transnational Truckers. They are the ones most likely to bring it north."

"And then?"

"We use different warehouses, usually in New Jersey. They notify me after the drop-off."

"I want the names and addresses of every one of them."

Vaknin said there were only three warehouses that would be trusted to receive this sort of shipment, and he gave Sandor the information.

"Is that it?"

Vaknin nodded.

"If any of this turns out to be bullshit, or if you warn your friends, then I'll be back for you."

"Warn them? How could I do that without admitting I gave you information about our operation? I told you already, I'm not suicidal. I'm going to tell them you attacked Ivan, took his gun, and escaped. Nothing more."

"We'll see. Now tell me how the hell I get out of here without having to put two in your head and then shoot my way through your nightclub."

———————

Vaknin showed Sandor the way out through the rear of the building, then pointed down an alley that would take him back to Brighton Beach Avenue. Sandor relieved Vaknin of the wad of cash in his pocket—there was no way he was going back upstairs to retrieve his own money and weapon. Sandor had also left behind a cell phone, but it was one of his disposable units with no memory card, speed dial numbers, or other encoded history.

It was time to move out.

To help accommodate Vaknin's claim that he and his bodyguard had been overpowered, Sandor hit him on the back of the head with the butt of the automatic, dropping him to the ground. He was sorely tempted to put one behind Vaknin's ear, but a deal is a deal, and he might need the smarmy sonuvabitch again.

Out on the street Sandor found a gypsy cabdriver leaning against his car smoking a Marlboro. "Manhattan," Sandor said, then flashed one of the hundred-dollar bills he had taken.

The driver immediately tossed the cigarette to the ground, got behind the wheel, and started the engine for the ride into town. Sandor settled into the back of the well-used Town Car and began to sort things out.

Vaknin had every reason to lie about the shipment arriving in the Port of Baltimore—even if he believed what Sandor told him he still wanted his narcotics delivered and by the nature of who he was and what he did, he was not inclined to help a federal agent. At the same time, he literally had a gun to his head and every reason to believe that Sandor was someone who, if he had been misled, would come back for him.

For now, it was the best lead Sandor had until he heard something from the other end of the food chain, which was presumably being worked by Bergenn and Raabe in Mexico.

Sandor did not give the cabdriver his home address, just in case anyone back in Brighton Beach became curious about where he went after he left Ivan and Vaknin on the basement floor. Sandor told him to take the Brooklyn Bridge into the city, then had him head up the East Side Drive to P. J. Clarke's on the corner of Fifty-fifth Street.

Inside, Sandor said hello to Mike McFadden, one of the bartenders he'd known there for years. He ordered a Gentleman Jack Manhattan, straight up, then asked to borrow McFadden's cell phone. After making two quick calls he downed the cocktail, left a generous tip funded with Vaknin's money, went back outside, and grabbed a taxi to his apartment on West Seventy-sixth Street.

———————

The first of the two phone calls he had made was to Bobby Ferriello.

Sandor let the detective know he had gotten out of Brighton Beach in one piece, thanked him for his help, and assured him he would have first dibs on the major drug bust that was almost certainly going down. Ferriello was pleased on all counts and, for a moment, their tenuous relationship felt as though it might actually rise to the level of civility.

The second call was to the Deputy Director's cell, and it was far less pleasant.

Byrnes picked up on the first ring and assured Sandor he had not awakened him despite the fact that it was nearly midnight. The

DD was still in the office working on a crisis down south. When Sandor said he was using a friend's phone—meaning his line was not secure—Byrnes ordered him, "Get to a proper line and call me back in the office."

Hence Sandor's quick departure from Clarke's. When the cab stopped in front of his brownstone, Sandor ran up the stairs two at a time, let himself into his apartment, and went to the safe that was hidden in the ceiling of his bedroom closet. He entered the code on the keypad, took out the metal box, and pulled out an encrypted phone. He powered it up and got Byrnes on the office line.

"I'm secure on my end," Sandor told him by way of greeting.

"Where have you been?" the DD demanded.

"Getting slapped around by the Russian mafia," Sandor replied. "I'll tell you all about it, but please fill me in on what's going on that has you in the office at this hour."

Normally the DD did not allow Sandor to set the agenda for their conversations, but tonight he made an exception. "Bergenn and Raabe are off the grid."

"How long?"

"Not long, several hours. But they were scheduled to report back and we've heard nothing."

"Any chance they're someplace where they can't safely communicate?"

"Possible, but we haven't even had any fail-safe signals."

"Did they meet the DEA agent LaBelle set them up with?"

"Bergenn reported in after they met him, name of Romero, working long-term undercover. They briefed him on our problem. He was going to find out what he could about the shipment, then circle back to them tonight."

"What about Romero?"

"He keeps on the down low, not unusual for him to remain out of contact."

"Damn."

"This entire operation feels like it's being pieced together with spit and string."

"Part of that is owed to how Adina operates."

"I can't disagree," Byrnes said. "By the way, we've heard some rumblings to the effect that Adina has worn out his welcome with the SEBIN in Caracas."

"Is that so?"

"We all know he had a disagreement with the moderates after his near-miss in Baton Rouge, but the pressure has been building. Since you forced him to destroy his compound, the rumor is that he was staying at El Helicoide. With Chavez ill they finally asked him to leave, but apparently he didn't take that very well. Had one of the ministers murdered, then made tracks out of the country."

"Why would he take out a minister?"

"Chatter has it that he and this minster were close, at least back when. He may have known more than Adina felt comfortable leaving behind."

"Typical Adina." Sandor thought it over for a moment. "If he's acting on his own he could be even more dangerous."

"You may be right. Tell me about the Russians."

Sandor briefed him on what he learned from Vaknin.

"Is it credible?"

"Don't know. I had a gun to his head, which tends to inspire people to tell the truth. I want to compare what he said to whatever Bergenn and Raabe find in Mexico."

"On the off chance this Vaknin was telling you the truth I should inform the authorities in Baltimore."

"Agreed," Sandor said, "but we want to be discreet about how we approach this. If these smugglers see us on alert down there it would be too easy for them to change destinations."

Byrnes agreed, then said, "The Director has me forming a task force. We're reading in the other agencies."

"Makes sense," Sandor said. This was one time they needed help. "I can see you've got your hands full, sir, but I have a request."

"What's that?"

"A company plane to get me down to Mexico. Right now."

CHAPTER SIXTY-SIX

MENDEZ, MEXICO

IN THE END, the simplest acts of evil are the most terrifying. With so many examples of inhumanity the world has been forced to witness in the past century, the indiscriminate murder of innocent people will always be the incarnation of man at his worst.

Which was the very purpose for which Adina devised his deadly assault on America.

Adina had no choice but to despise the United States. True democracy was anathema to his vision of a proper global order. Liberty, self-reliance, and basic freedoms are unacceptable to anyone who believes that power should be concentrated in the few; that the masses should be controlled through government-run businesses, health providers, and entitlement programs; and that the military should be used to maintain discipline if anyone begins to espouse a contrary view.

Lately, Adina had seen his countrymen growing soft in their allegiance to socialism. Oil profits were growing and the prospect of personal wealth was spreading like a cancer throughout the land. Adina witnessed the collapse of the Soviet Union, humiliated at the hands of the United States, and he was not about to allow his own country to fall prey to the same temptations and frailties.

He was determined to rally his people by raining fear on the Americans. Adina was convinced he could demonstrate how vulnerable and weak they were at their core. To that end he developed a plan that was as deadly in its execution as it was elegant in its simplicity. He had arranged a chaotic assault that would disrupt an entire city, leaving millions in a state of utter panic. Then he would unleash the anthrax attack, murdering tens of thousands of innocent people trapped in the midst of this bedlam.

He had come to Mexico to ensure that the shipment of his goods proceeded as planned, that nothing interfered with his accelerated schedule. There were details to be sorted out that required his direct involvement, such as coordination with the operatives waiting to be mobilized, the loyalists who would execute the assault.

He also had to prepare for any efforts by the Americans to stop him. Adina learned from his Russian contacts that the agent, Jordan Sandor, was still a problem. Efforts to eliminate him had failed, which meant investigations into everything Sandor had seen or done would be intensified.

So he traveled to Mendez, where the goods had already arrived and were now being taken to the shore for inclusion on a container ship headed for the Port of Baltimore. His next step was to sit with the local head of the Sinaloa Cartel.

———————

It took Mateo more than an hour to drive from the farm in Reynosa, where his men were holding Bergenn, Raabe, and Romero, to the country home outside Mendez where Adina waited for him. It was well past midnight when he arrived.

The two men had never met, having communicated through intermediaries over the past two months. Their greeting was warm, and Adina invited the Mexican to have a seat in the comfortable living room.

Adina was accompanied by Alejandro and Jorge. Mateo had brought three of his men for company. All five attendants were armed and alert.

"What a shame," Adina said as he lowered himself into an armchair opposite his guest, while the five sentries remained standing. "So much violence, so little trust."

Mateo smiled. "First things first, *compadre*. Since we have never met, we must each be sure we are who we say we are, no?"

Adina reacted by showing off his own treacherous imitation of a grin. "Ah, such caution. I admire this, I truly do. Even under such, how shall I say, secure circumstances." He then recited three passwords, and Mateo gave the proper reply to each one.

The two men nodded pleasantly at each other.

"So," Adina said, "I understand the goods have been delivered to your care?"

"They have."

"Then you have something for me."

Mateo lifted the suitcase he had set beside him on the floor when they entered. He placed it on the table, snapped open the two combination latches, and lifted the top to reveal the neatly arranged stacks of one-hundred-dollar bills. "The deposit," Mateo said, "as agreed."

Adina nodded toward Alejandro, who came forward to take the case and place it on the breakfront against the wall. "I presume you will have no objection to my man making a quick calculation of these funds."

Mateo responded with a throaty laugh. "He will be here for some time if he intends to count it all."

Adina nodded. "As I say, just a quick calculation."

"Of course."

"Good. Now that we have that part of our business out of the way, perhaps you will join me for some tequila."

Jorge went into the kitchen to arrange for the drinks as the other bodyguards relaxed, if only slightly.

"Are the goods on land or at sea at the moment?"

"Shall we say, they are in process."

"That's a bit vague for my taste," Adina told him. "I believe I'm entitled to know where my goods are right now."

Mateo blinked. "Still on the trucks. Ready to be taken to Matamoros for placement in containers tomorrow. From there the container will be taken to one of our freighters for a transfer at sea."

"Why the delay? Have things not gone smoothly?"

"As smoothly as they do in these matters. We have had a slight complication."

Jorge brought in a tray with a bottle and glasses. Adina poured. The two principals toasted their mutual success, then drank.

"Please go on," Adina told him.

Mateo placed his glass on the table between them and leaned forward. "Two men arrived in Reynosa today. From the States. We got word that they were greeted by one of our own men."

"Is that so?"

"Pacquito has been a good boy. But now we are being told he is a DEA agent." Mateo shook his head.

"Which he denies, of course."

"Of course. Claims he met the two Americans at a bar, tourists looking for drugs and women."

"Something that this Pacquito might normally provide?"

Mateo nodded. "He is only a soldier in our organization. We let our people make money on their own, provided of course those activities do not interfere with their primary obligations."

"So he would buy the drugs from you and resell them."

"Of course," Mateo said, as if any other possibility would be absurd.

"Have you discovered anything about the other two men to make you suspicious?"

"They drove into town this morning. Rented car. Not much luggage." He reached into his pocket, pulled out the passports he had taken from Bergenn and Raabe, then tossed them on the table. "These may be real or fake, who knows. But they were armed. Both of them."

Adina picked up the passports and had a look at the names. "What sort of weapons?"

"Automatics. Could be government issued or not. A Glock and a Walther P-99. The main point is that they didn't buy those in Reynosa, not within hours of arriving in town. I would have been told, believe me."

"Which means they were carrying when they came across the border."

"It would seem that way."

"So this Pacquito, he actually met them in a bar, that was the contact point?"

"No, that's the story all three of them are telling. When we got the call we were told they met at an abandoned farmhouse outside of town. Problem is that no one saw them, so we have no way of knowing if it's true."

"And I'm sure you were persuasive in questioning your man Pacquito."

"Extremely."

"And he still denies knowing these Americans. Beyond what he told you."

"That's right. In the face of death."

Adina rested his elbows on the chair arms and pressed his fingertips together. "Where are they now?"

"We're holding them at my farm. We put all three of them together."

Adina could not hide his surprise. "Why?"

"I want to know the truth about Pacquito. If he is a traitor, this will give him the chance to make his move. My men will take care of the rest."

"But the Americans, they may have value to us. I'd like to question them first."

Mateo thought that over. "I know your reputation, and I respect that. That is why I waited for our meeting before taking further action against these men. But you are in my world now, and betrayal is something that we must punish quickly and decisively."

Adina sighed. "Do whatever you like with this Pacquito, but find out what you can from the Americans. We cannot afford to have anything go wrong with our shipment."

Mateo reached out and grabbed the bottle, then poured each of them another shot. He threw his tequila back and fixed Adina with a look intended to inform everyone in the room who was in charge here. "The shipment is fine," he assured him. "As to questioning these *yanquis,* I'll see what I can do."

CHAPTER SIXTY-SEVEN

REYNOSA, MEXICO

INSIDE THE SERVICE shed on Mateo's farm the three Americans had no intention of waiting to see what their host had in store for them. They were huddled together, still speaking in whispers. The walls of their makeshift prison were constructed of wooden planks and, even if there were no electronic bugs, they might easily be heard from the outside, just as the three of them heard Mateo barking commands before he headed south to Mendez.

At one point, when they heard a car start up and drive off, Romero said, "Mateo just left."

"You're sure that was Mateo?" Raabe asked.

Romero, who was doing his best to regain his strength as the other two continued to work on his cuts, managed a painful shrug. "You heard him out there. He was giving orders before he took off. And his Escalade is the biggest vehicle here, makes the most noise. It had to be him."

"Where would he be going?"

"To meet someone. To figure out what to do with us." Romero closed his eyes for a moment. "He could have killed us already if he wanted to. You two must be right, there must be a shipment in play."

"Then why wouldn't he interrogate us before he left, find out what we know?"

Romero shook his head. "Not sure."

"So he's going somewhere for instructions."

"To see the man," Romero agreed.

"Jaime Rivera?"

"Could be. The good news is that he wouldn't go anywhere without three of his men."

"Why is that good news?"

"By my count that only leaves five of my former friends out there, plus the two sentries at the front gate. Of the five, two are probably in the house."

"So what are you suggesting?" Bergenn asked. "That we bust out of here and rush three armed guards?"

Romero looked up at them, his eyes bloodshot, his face gaunt. "If we wait, I can tell you our fate is certain. When Mateo comes back we will be tortured and then killed. Whether or not we tell them anything, it will not matter. And believe me, what you saw them do to me was nothing compared to the pain they are capable of inflicting. Remember, I have been here for two years. Even if I survive this night, I will never live long enough to forget what I've seen during my time here."

"It's late," Raabe said, nodding in agreement. "These guards are probably tired, hopefully a little drunk, and not expecting us to make a move." He looked to Romero. "What's your plan?"

The three men worked quickly and quietly, piling boxes of supplies and bags of grain, one atop the other in the rear corner of the small building. Romero rallied as best he could, using his energy more to direct the action than to lift anything.

There were various crates and burlap bags on hand, but unfortunately no tools. As Romero explained, Mateo was a sadist, not a fool. The space was loftlike, with a high ceiling, and the only things resembling windows were two openings a dozen or more feet off the ground. They were small, designed for ventilation and light, not for ingress or egress. Yet once the mountain of cartons and sacks was stacked high enough the three men could use them for their escape. They had no glass, just slanted wooden canopies on the outside that kept rain from pouring into the building.

Romero chose the window on the right since the voices they could hear seemed to be coming from the left, in the direction of the main house. This side would be darker and out of sight.

"The problem is the roof," Romero explained. "This is just a shed and it won't hold our weight."

"Not even one of us at a time?"

He shook his head. "Corrugated metal. It'll make a lot of noise and then you'll fall through like a dead weight."

"Bad choice of words," Raabe said.

Bergenn frowned. "So once we get to the window, we're going out and then straight down."

Romero nodded. "The drop will only be four or five feet. Just hang from the edge and then let go. The faster all three of us are on the ground the better."

Bergenn, who stood several inches taller than Romero, asked, "You going to make it okay?"

The young man forced a smile. "Hell, I'm going first."

Romero headed up the makeshift ramp and poked his head out through the rectangular opening, having a look around. It appeared he had guessed right, there was no one in sight. Better still, the lights from the main house were on the other side, blocked by the building, so he was in almost total darkness.

He forced himself through the small opening, the pain intense as the wooden frame of the window seemed to tear open every one of the cuts on his chest and back. He fought his way outside, managed to spin around, hung from the ledge for only an instant, then dropped himself to the ground.

The fall was longer than he anticipated and he could not stifle a groan as he collapsed in the dirt. Bergenn and Raabe heard him, which meant some of Mateo's men might also be on the alert. Raabe had scrambled up right behind Romero. He began working his long, lean frame out the window much faster and with far less effort, twisting into position and ready to make the jump.

Just then one of the guards came charging around the building.

For the next few seconds things seemed to Raabe as if they were happening in fast foward. Romero had not even gotten to his feet as the sentry was drawing a pistol from the holster on his hip, his full attention on the man on the ground. Romero lashed out with one of his legs, a futile attempt to take the larger man down as the guard began to level his weapon at Romero's head.

At that moment Raabe pushed off the side of the shed with his feet and let go with his hands at the same time. He plunged downward, landing on his back atop the guard and driving him to the dirt in an unconscious heap. He quickly spun around and, using a reverse choke hold, broke the man's neck.

Bergenn followed right behind him, engineering his fall closer to the building as Raabe grabbed the sentry's automatic. The two agents got to their feet but Romero was not moving.

"Go," Romero urged them in a hoarse whisper. "Go."

"Bullshit," Raabe responded, grabbing Romero under the arm and pulling him up. "We're all going."

But as Bergenn also lent a hand, two other guards came from around the rear of the building and fired the first shots, one of them hitting Romero in the thigh.

He cried out in pain as the two Americans dragged him around the corner of the building for cover. The fusillade continued, some of the rounds tearing through the wooden slats of the storage shed.

Raabe made a quick lunge back to the edge of the building and fired off two shots in the direction of the muzzle flashes aimed at them, then ducked back for cover. "Had to let them know we're armed," he said, and for the moment the onslaught subsided. "I guess there are no heroes on the other side of the wall."

Bergenn nodded, then ran the short length of the shed, toward the front, to have a look. He turned back to Raabe and said, "They can come at us from either direction. And we've only got one gun with limited ammo."

"No kidding." Raabe looked down at Romero. "How you doing, man?"

The DEA agent was on the ground beside him. "I'm dead" was his raspy answer.

Even in the darkness, the severe bleeding from his leg was apparent. Romero was trying to put pressure on the wound, but he was losing the battle.

"Damn," Raabe said. "We need to get a tourniquet on that right now."

"Forget it," Romero said. "Femoral artery, man. I've seen it before. I'll bleed to death before you run out of bullets." His voice told them he was already progressing from shock to a loss of consciousness.

Bergenn and Raabe shared a look, then Raabe said, "Screw it. I've got the gun. Jimmy, tie that thing off."

Bergenn ripped off his shirt, knelt down, and began to apply a tourniquet to Romero's thigh. He used a stick on the ground to tighten the dressing.

Meanwhile, another barrage of shots began.

"We're out of time here," Raabe said. "I've got to make a move."

Bergenn got up and stood beside him. "You took down one man so, by Romero's count, we have four to go, not to mention two at the gate. That Glock you're holding probably has a dozen shots left in the magazine, so unless you're Annie Oakley, you better have one helluva plan."

Raabe nodded, then dropped to the ground, stuck his head out just beyond the corner of the shed and had a look. Flames were bursting from the heated barrels of the automatics being fired at them. Using those as targets, he squeezed off three quick rounds, then pulled back.

"You hit anything?"

"I didn't hear anyone scream. You better check the other side again."

But even as Raabe spoke those words, it was too late. One of Mateo's men, armed with an AK-47, stepped out from the front side of the building and opened fire.

Bergenn was facing him. He never had a chance. In a matter of seconds his chest was torn apart by a dozen shots. He managed a final act of heroism, willing himself to remain standing for those final seconds of life so he could provide his friend a human shield, giving Raabe time to put two shots in the Mexican's face.

Both Bergenn and his killer fell to the dirt, dead before they hit the ground.

Raabe's instinct was to reach out for Bergenn, but that urge was trumped by his years as a professional. He charged past his fallen partner and grabbed hold of the dead guard's AK-47, just as a second man emerged from the shadows at the front corner of the building. Raabe, on one knee, took the man out with a four-shot burst.

He jumped up and raced to the rear corner again. It appeared quiet on that side. Spinning around he was confronted by another attacker making a flank move. Raabe opened fire with a series of shots aimed at the man's head. The guard fell onto his back, the assault rifle still in his hands as he shuddered, then gasped his last breath.

"Four down, three to go," Raabe said, assuming the men at the front gate had joined the assault.

He gathered up the second AK-47 assault rifle. After checking both sides of the shed again, he turned to Romero, prepared to hand him one of the weapons.

But the young man was dead. Somehow, in the crossfire, he had been hit again. In the darkness, Raabe could not tell if he had died from the first shot or the last. *What does it matter?* Raabe asked himself as he stood there, his back to the building, an AK-47 in each hand.

He took a moment to bend down and turn Bergenn onto his back. His friend's chest had been riddled with shots and he was covered in blood. He felt his neck for a pulse, knowing what he would find. "Shit," Raabe said aloud. He found himself wishing he could take dog tags from the necks of his two fallen comrades.

Then he stood tall again and checked the magazines in the two rifles, confirming he had plenty of ammunition.

All he needed now was a strategy.

CHAPTER SIXTY-EIGHT

REYNOSA, MEXICO

Craig Raabe had to make some quick decisions, and none of them was going to be easy. He was tormented at the prospect of leaving Bergenn and Romero behind. Good soldiers never abandon their fallen teammates to be desecrated by the enemy, and the thought of what Mateo and his men would do to these bodies made Raabe shudder. Sadly, he realized there was nothing to be done about that right now.

He had not learned much since arriving in Reynosa, but his responsibility was to escape from here, chase down Mateo and, more importantly, find whoever it was Mateo had gone off to see.

At the moment, Raabe had two basic choices. The first would be a frontal assault, trying to take out the remaining guards. On the plus side of that option, he was now fully armed and, even facing a three-to-one disadvantage, he was undoubtedly far more skilled than the men he would have to take down. Unfortunately, there were many negatives. The guards knew the layout of this property and he did not. They probably had called for reinforcements by now. And, despite the fact that he had two assault rifles, there was no way of knowing the size or scope of the arsenal he would be facing once he left the cover of this building.

His other alternative was to simply disappear into the night. That would give him a chance to make his way to safety or, even better, circle back and outflank his prey. The night was cloudy and dark and for the moment he was still behind the far side of the building, away from the lights at the main house. The field that stretched out directly behind him appeared to be planted with corn, and that would provide decent cover. Before he got there, however, there was unprotected ground he would have to cross, fifty yards or more, before he would reach the stalks. Obviously, the farther he got from the safety of the shed, the more visible he would become from angles to his left and right, assuming Mateo's men had positioned themselves on the points.

He concluded that the other play, coming out from behind the shed and rushing headlong at three invisible targets, was too reckless. Having made his choice he took a moment to discreetly check each corner of the building.

No one seemed to be coming.

Heading back to the center of the wall he had another look at Bergenn. He shook his head, drew a deep breath, and broke into a run dead ahead.

Raabe kept low and moved fast. Even in the darkness he knew his shadowy figure would eventually be spotted. And it was. Less than ten yards from the nearest line of crops he heard gunfire erupt from behind.

He veered off to the right, farther from the main house, then dove to safety as shots whizzed around him, some of them low and spitting dirt into the air. He clambered to his feet and, still in a crouch, headed deeper into the field, doing his best to become invisible, trying not to rustle the tall stalks as he ran. He was moving as quickly as he could, cutting left on a vector that would take him around the back of the main house.

Whether or not they were coming after him, he was not going away.

———

Just as Craig Raabe had said to Jim Bergenn minutes earlier, there were no heroes on the other side of the wall. Once the three remaining guards saw Raabe dive into the cornfield, none of them ventured forward. Instead they fell back to the relative safety of the front porch of the main house. There they took cover, watching for any sign of the American.

"He has one of the AK-47s," one of the men said.

"At least one."

"And maybe extra magazines."

"But he didn't return fire just now."

"Would you? Why waste the ammunition?"

"He's making a run for it."

All three nodded.

"What do you think we should do?"

"Maybe we should check to be sure the other two are dead."

They all looked at the distance between the main house and the storage shed, which appeared to have grown considerably now that there was an armed man out there in the darkness.

"They're dead. If they weren't, they would have taken off with that one."

The others nodded.

"What did Rico say? They sending anyone from Reynosa?"

The guard who had spoken with Rico nodded. "At least four men. He was calling them."

One of the others shook his head. "By the time they get here, that *maricon* will be long gone."

"Maybe," the guard said.

———————

Raabe continued to wend his way through the field, staying thirty or forty yards into the corn rows, keeping the main house in sight as he circled across the rear of the home toward the other side.

It was a bit incongruous, it occurred to him as he picked his way through the dense plantings, that a man like Mateo would be raising corn. It was understandable that he was not going to grow marijuana or coca leaves in plain sight. On the other hand, if an operational farm was a cover for his more nefarious—and profitable—activities, Raabe wondered who the man thought he was fooling.

He stopped for a moment, perched on one knee. There was nothing he could hear or see that indicated pursuit.

The night was oddly quiet after the explosions of gunfire.

Raabe stood a little higher, getting a better view of the house.

No one appeared to be moving.

Which was not necessarily a good sign.

They might be waiting for reinforcements, not to mention the return of Mateo and his henchmen. Why take their chances now when their three-on-one brawl might become ten-on-one? But Raabe had two weapons and limited ammunition. Time was not on his side.

He began moving again, running faster now, approaching the end of this field. As he came even with the far edge of the house he faced about the same fifty yards of open space he had rushed across to get to the safety of these cornstalks. Off to his right was another open area, unplanted ground with shallow furrows, nothing high enough or deep enough to cover him.

Well, he told himself, *the shortest distance between two points is a straight line.*

————————

Mateo was still with Adina when his man Rico received the call about shootings at the farm. Rico stepped forward, leaned down, and whispered into Mateo's ear, "We need to talk. Now."

Mateo knew his lieutenant well enough to realize that he would not have interrupted his discussion with Rafael Cabello unless it was truly urgent. He made his apologies and followed Rico outside. The two men stood so close their cheeks nearly touched.

"Trouble at the farm," Rico murmured.

"Tell me."

Rico related what he had heard.

Mateo told him to arrange for reinforcements. "And don't say anything to the others," he ordered. "Not until we're in the car. I'll wrap this up as soon as I can. You stay out here and make the calls."

Inside, Adina was waiting patiently to ask, "Everything all right?"

"Perfecto," Mateo said. "Just a misunderstanding, which I have rectified."

"Good. Now returning to the status of my shipment. Where were we?"

Mateo gave the appropriate assurances, did his best to seem unhurried, but soon said, "It is very late and I am anxious to attend to my guests in Reynosa."

"You will let me know what happens," Adina said. It was not a question.

Mateo resented the tone but, under the circumstances, he was in no position to argue. "Of course," he assured him. "You will be the first to know."

A few minutes later, after cordial goodbyes, Mateo and his three men were back in the car, racing for home.

———————

Raabe ran as low and fast as he could. To his amazement, there were no shots fired as he reached the back corner of the main house. The lights remained on inside. No one was patrolling this part of the grounds. It was clear they assumed he had simply run through the corn rows in the hope of finding safety and had continued beyond the confines of this farm. They were not in pursuit. It was also clear that these men, regardless of how ruthless, were not disciplined professionals.

Raabe stayed below the level of the windowsills as he made his way around the far side of the house. He was at the edge of the front porch, but he was not about to risk the noise he might make climbing up the three wooden steps. Instead, he checked behind him, then got on his knees and elbows, the two AK-47s secure in his hands, and crawled around to the front.

Now he could make out their voices. It sounded like there were only two men sitting on the porch, just above him, discussing what they should do before the others arrived. It was not clear if they were talking about Mateo and his men or reinforcements, but Raabe ignored their banter. Judging as best he could, he figured they were somewhere near the middle of the deck. There was no point in risking discovery by attempting to drag himself any closer. Instead he jumped to his feet and began firing before they knew he was there.

Raabe had been correct, there were two of them. He aimed for their chests, and neither one was able to get his weapon off his lap before Raabe strafed them with repeating shots from both rifles. Both men were driven backward off their chairs in a mangle of blood, torn flesh, and shattered bones.

Raabe dropped back down for cover, left to wonder where the third man might be. He did not have to wait long.

A hail of gunfire was unleashed, but they had no angle on Raabe. The shots seemed to be coming from somewhere on the main floor of the house but Raabe was protected by the front of the portico, which stood more than three feet off the ground. Raabe stayed low, leaving the floorboards to get the worst of it. Rather than retreat back around the side from where he had come, Raabe scampered forward. The firing stopped as he continued ahead, listening for any sound of the shooter.

All had become quiet again.

The odds were good that the shooter was repositioning himself, or possibly making a run out back to circle the house. Raabe was in no mood to wait. Having reached the far right corner of the porch, Raabe got to his knees and had a quick look.

Nothing.

Then the lights in the front rooms and the veranda went out. That would make it tougher for Raabe to spot his target, but his eyes had already adjusted to the dark. The other man's had not. He decided to use that momentary edge, rushing silently up the far steps and crouching below the first window.

The light switches had to be somewhere near the front of the home, which meant the man was going to make his move from there. Seconds later the barrel of an assault rifle appeared out the front door. Raabe remained in a motionless squat as he watched the man burst out into the open and begin firing over the side of the deck, spraying shots to his left and right. Raabe used both weapons, tearing the man to shreds. As the Mexican fell backward he kept his finger on the trigger, sending a series of shots into the air until he stumbled to the wooden floor and his weapon clattered to the ground beside him.

According to Romero's count, all of the men Mateo had left behind were dead, but Raabe was not taking any chances. He jumped off the porch and stooped low, waiting a long couple of minutes for another wave of attacks.

But none came.

Behind him were five vehicles, including a pickup truck and the two cars that had brought Bergenn and him here. He found the key for the pickup in the ignition and started it up. Then he stopped for a moment.

He was still not sure who might still be in the house, but he had no intention of leaving anything behind.

It did not take Raabe long to fire up the wooden structure, using shirts from two of the dead guards, gasoline from the cars, and matches he found in the truck. He grabbed some replacement magazines for the two assault rifles, then jumped in the pickup and spun to the back of the storage building. There he hoisted Bergenn and Romero in the truck's cargo bay, then took off.

There was no telling how soon Mateo and his men would return, or when someone else would spot the growing flames from the old house and come by. He was not even sure where he was going from here, but the first order of business was to get to a safe spot where he could plan his next move.

He floored the accelerator, racing away from the burning building, but did not get more than a quarter mile past the front gate of the farm when he saw headlights coming directly at him. He pulled the truck off to the side of the road, killed the lights, and took both reloaded AK-47s into a ditch ten feet or so ahead of the truck.

As soon as the oncoming car was within range he opened fire— this was not the time to wait and see who was at the wheel. The sedan veered off to its right and screeched to a halt. The driver then threw the passenger door open and dove to safety behind the car.

It appeared the man was alone, but in the darkness Raabe could not be certain. Whoever was there, they were not returning fire.

"Stand up and put your hands on your head," Raabe hollered across the road.

Then a familiar voice called back, "Only if you promise not to shoot me, Craig."

It was Sandor.

CHAPTER SIXTY-NINE

REYNOSA, MEXICO

Sandor stood beside the truck's cargo bay, staring at the bodies of Felipe Romero and Jim Bergenn.

"He never had a chance," Raabe said as he began to explain what had happened since he and Bergenn arrived in Reynosa the previous morning.

Still looking down, Sandor said, "Tell me as we go, we need to get out of here."

Sandor took the wheel of the truck. Raabe slumped beside him in the passenger seat and continued his account of being captured, their escape from the shed, and the shootings. When he was done he said, "Jim . . . ," as if there were something more he wanted to add.

"It doesn't seem real to me."

"Me either, and I was there." Raabe took a deep breath and said, "That's a star on the wall I never wanted to see." Then he became quiet.

Sandor allowed the silence to fall over them as they sped down the road. Then he asked, "What's the story with the fire?"

Staring straight ahead, Raabe said, "It seemed the thing to do at the time."

Sandor nodded. "Nice touch."

After a few more moments Raabe said, "I almost killed you on the road back there."

"Not really. I was using the night binoculars," Sandor explained. "I stopped a couple of times to try and get a look at the place before

I came busting in there. I saw the fire start and then you came bar-reling along."

"How the hell could I have . . ."

"You couldn't. Anyway, you did the right thing, you had to figure I was one of the bad guys. I thought about stopping, getting out and trying to wave you down, but you might not have seen who it was in the dark. I didn't want to stand there to find out if you were going to blow my head off. I kept low in the car, figured you would shoot me off the road. Best I could do."

Raabe nodded. "How did you find me?"

"Tracked you to your hotel. Bartender there took a hundred bucks to tell me how you and Jim left with one of the locals, guy who works for this guy Mateo. He watched through the front window when his friends showed up and they stuffed the two of you into a couple of cars."

"How did you find your way here?"

"Another hundred bought me directions to the farm. Said it was the place they were most likely to take you."

"He was right," Raabe said with a slow nod. "So where are we headed now?"

"Small airfield, about a half hour from here. We have a plane waiting."

"What about this guy Mateo?"

"I'll handle that with Byrnes. Our problem now is the leak. Only a few of us knew you were coming here. The DD, Bergenn, LaBelle, you, and me. Even Romero didn't know anything until you arrived."

"Which leaves LaBelle."

Sandor shook his head. "I've known him a long time. Hard to believe, but we need to know. I've got a lead on the shipment, but the source is less than credible. I'll tell you all about it on the plane."

"Give me the headline."

"Russian drug dealer in New York says this shipment is coming by container ship into Baltimore, then by truck to New York City."

"Why would a drug dealer tell you that?"

"I had a gun to his head."

Raabe nodded. "I guess that *is* a story for the plane. So we're head-ing to Baltimore?"

"No, Byrnes organized a task force to follow up on that. Our problem is the leak. If there's a hole in the pipeline we've got to plug it. Otherwise they'll keep making adjustments and we'll be chasing our own tail."

"So we're going to Dallas."

"Yes. We're going to Dallas."

A half hour later, when Mateo returned to his farm, the sun had not yet risen but the sky was alight with the bright flames of his burning house. The enormity of the blaze had already brought some curious onlookers from the neighboring areas but, since everyone knew whose property this was, none of them ventured past the front fence.

Mateo's driver pulled the Escalade into the parking area, a safe distance from the scattering embers and falling timber. Mateo and his three men got out, staring in disbelief at the inferno. It was too late to call for a fire truck. By the time they arrived only ashes would remain.

Mateo, who had not spoken a word as they approached this disaster, now gave voice to every imaginable profanity. His bodyguards raised their weapons and did their best to surround him, but it soon became apparent that whatever threat may have existed was now gone.

Having spat out the last curse, he led his men to the utility building where his prisoners had been held. They unbarred the front door and pulled it open. The shed was empty.

"Look at this," Mateo said, pointing to the pile of boxes and sacks his captives had used to escape.

None of his men spoke.

With Mateo in the lead they walked around to the side of the building where the captives had climbed out and dropped to safety. There they discovered the residue of battle—the bodies of three of his guards.

"*Mierda,*" he shouted out.

There was no sign of Pacquito or the two Americans.

Mateo was in something of a daze as he staggered back to his car, lost in a sense of dread he had not experienced since he was a mere soldier in the organization. He understood that the real damage here was not the destruction of his farmhouse or the death of his men. Even the escape of the three hostages was not critical in and of itself. No, the problem would be the consequence he would suffer for his incompetence. Not only would the cartel itself be outraged, but there might be graver reprisals if this debacle compromised the shipment arranged for Adina.

Overwhelmed by the realization of the peril he faced, he did not at first hear the noise as the troops approached.

Trucks and cars were pouring through his front gate and a combat helicopter rose above the horizon. Mateo's men, seeing that he was in some inexplicable stupor, grabbed him under the arms and began dragging him to the large SUV, but it was too late.

Several armored trucks in the vanguard of this assault screeched to a stop, blocking the front of the property. Someone with a bullhorn announced that they were *federales* and ordered Mateo and his men to throw down their weapons, lift their arms in the air, and give themselves up.

———

It was Deputy Director Byrnes who organized this welcoming party for Mateo.

After Sandor debriefed Raabe on the events at the farm, he grabbed his secure cell and called DD Byrnes. Byrnes agreed that if there was ever a time when the Mexican authorities could do something about the war on drugs—other than pay it tequila-scented lip service as they looked the other way—this was it. Mateo's traveling retinue was only three men, and he would have no way of knowing that his remaining force at the farm had been completely eliminated. His house was on fire, there would be no place for him to hide, and he was therefore vulnerable to capture.

When Byrnes placed the appropriate calls he was initially frustrated by the usual pushback—it was the middle of the night, they would need time to mobilize, there was no telling how many men they would require since Mateo may have called in reinforcements, and so forth. Byrnes remained calm, letting the wave of bureaucratic excuses wash over him as he was passed up the chain of command until he was finally patched through to the man in charge. Then he played his trump card. Mateo had just been involved in the kidnapping, torture, and murder of an American DEA operative; the kidnapping and murder of an American agent of undisclosed affiliation; and the kidnapping of yet another American agent whose fate was not being revealed, but who had survived long enough to tell the tale in graphic detail.

"Failure to take immediate and decisive action," Byrnes told the head of the local drug enforcement team who was now sitting up in his bed, fully awake, "is going to become a diplomatic shitstorm that'll land squarely on your head. Are you with me on this, *comandante*?"

"Yes," the man said. "I am."

So, just as Raabe and Sandor took off on the Company plane for Dallas, Mateo and his men were being handcuffed by the Mexican authorities.

In the moments before the *federales* arrived, Reynosa's top drug lord had been contemplating his fate at the hands of his former associates within the Sinaloa Cartel. Not to mention what might be visited upon him by Adina's people. They would begin with torture and end up using him for shark bait. Yet now, as he was taken into custody, there was a surprising serenity about him.

Suddenly arrest did not seem all that distasteful.

Mateo was pleased to be separated from his men and shoved into the back of one of the government SUVs. Looking across the yard at his three underlings, he was certain they would try to prove their machismo, preferring a long jail sentence to a betrayal of the *hermandad*.

Mateo, however, had already decided on a less repulsive course of action.

CHAPTER SEVENTY

DALLAS, TEXAS

THE MEETING WITH Dan LaBelle this morning was not going to be a friendly gathering in a swanky bar. Raabe cleaned up and changed clothes on the short flight to Dallas Love Field, the private airport outside the city. He and Sandor were met there by a local agent assigned to the Directorate of Support, and he drove them to the government building where LaBelle had his office. It was early and, after showing credentials that admitted them to the indoor parking lot, they found a guest spot and waited.

When LaBelle pulled into his designated space and climbed out of his car, Sandor was behind him, standing against one of the concrete pillars with his arms crossed. "Hello Dan," he said.

For a second or two LaBelle appeared disoriented. He was alarmed to find anyone waiting for him in this secure parking garage. Then he recognized his old friend. "Jordan. What the hell are you doing here?"

Sandor did not respond. He pointed to the sedan where Craig Raabe was sitting in the back, holding the door open.

"What is this?" LaBelle asked.

"Don't you know?" Sandor asked.

LaBelle glared at him. "I wouldn't have asked the question if I did."

"I'll do the asking this morning. Get in the car."

LaBelle hesitated, then stepped forward. "We know each other too long for me to be treated this way."

"I'll keep that in mind."

LaBelle got in the backseat alongside Raabe. Sandor sat in the front passenger seat and turned to face them. The local agent stepped out and made sure all the doors were closed.

Sandor asked, "What have you heard about the mission Raabe and Bergenn went on in Reynosa?"

LaBelle responded with a blank stare. "Nothing." He looked at Raabe. "I told you my communications from Felipe Romero are sporadic. We do everything we can to protect his cover." Turning to Sandor, he said, "I actually expected to hear back from you before I heard from him."

"Well you're hearing back from me now," Sandor told him. "Felipe Romero is dead. So is Jim Bergenn."

"What?"

"Bergenn and Raabe met Romero as arranged. Within hours your agent was taken by the Sinaloa Cartel and tortured. My men were captured. The point is, they knew we were coming before we got there. That right?" he asked Raabe.

Raabe had been studying LaBelle as Sandor gave him the news. If he was acting, he was very good. "That's exactly right. They knew about our meeting with Romero. It was pretty clear they also knew we were federal agents."

"But how?" LaBelle asked.

"That's our question," Sandor told him. "Only five people knew Bergenn and Raabe were going to Reynosa. The three of us, Bergenn and our DD. Even Romero had limited information, am I right?"

LaBelle nodded.

"And the way they took him down, it was obvious he hadn't been turned."

LaBelle said nothing.

"When you met Craig and Jim it was made clear you weren't to discuss their mission with anyone. Is that right?"

LaBelle nodded again, more slowly this time.

"So Dan, who is Jaime Rivera and what do you want to tell us about what happened in Mexico last night that cost us two good men?"

LaBelle sucked in a deep breath, then let it out like it was poison. "After everything you and I have been through I should be insulted, but I'm not. I can see how bad this looks."

"It looks very bad, especially when I toss Moscow into the mix."

"Moscow?"

"The meeting you set up for me with Vassily Greshnev."

"You two had dinner."

"You didn't hear what I was served for dessert?"

"What are you talking about?"

Sandor looked to Raabe, then back to LaBelle. "Did you check back with Greshnev after I saw him that night?"

"No. I figured I didn't have a need to know. If I did, you would have told me."

"After dinner I found an uninvited guest in my hotel room."

LaBelle said nothing.

"Someone set me up, which brings me to my second problem this morning. Only you, Greshnev and I knew about that dinner. Other than Craig, no one else even knew I was going to Moscow."

"You can't believe I had anything to do with that."

"Tell me what I should believe."

LaBelle hesitated, anger turning to a look of resignation. "You know how the bureaucracy works. I'm head of this office, but I'm still several rungs below the top level."

"What are you saying?"

"I'm saying that Vassily Greshnev is an important contact for us. Felipe Romero was a valuable asset."

"So?"

"So you report to Mark Byrnes and I have people I have to report to."

"Forget Greshnev for now. Are you saying you divulged information about the mission in Reynosa after you were told how sensitive it was, that it had to be kept strictly among us?"

"Look Jordan, you can get as indignant as you want, but no one knows better than you how this game is played. If I didn't report these things up the line and something went bad, my ass would be in a sling. Now you're telling me things did go bad. Think about it. If I didn't report the mission with Romero it would look like I was taking my orders from the CIA. Same goes for the contact I made for you with Greshnev."

"Whoa, whoa, whoa, when you say 'up the line,' how many people did you tell?"

"Only one. My director in D.C., Joseph Cleary."

Raabe said, "He's the DEA liaison on the joint task force Byrnes just formed."

LaBelle looked from Raabe back to Sandor. "Cleary is a good man. There's no way he's involved here."

"Well somebody tipped off the cartel that Bergenn and Raabe were coming, and that Romero was a mole."

"You know me a long time Jordan and I want you to look into my eyes when I say this. Romero was the toughest agent I ever worked with and I would never have given him up."

Sandor stared back at him without speaking.

"Well," Raabe said, "I can vouch for the fact that Romero was tough. They cut him to ribbons and he never admitted a thing. Then he helped us find a way to fight back. I wouldn't be here right now if it wasn't for him."

They were all quiet for a moment, the two men in the backseat waiting on Sandor.

He thought it over, then said, "Okay Dan, we're going to sort this out, so I hope you didn't have any big plans for today."

"Meaning what?"

"Meaning that you're coming with us to Washington. Right now."

CHAPTER SEVENTY-ONE

CIA HEADQUARTERS, LANGLEY, VIRGINIA

MARK BYRNES CALLED an emergency meeting of the newly formed task force, their second gathering in as many days. During their flight to D.C., Sandor, Raabe, and LaBelle briefed the DD on his secure line. When they reached Langley, LaBelle and Raabe were parked in Byrnes's office as the DD and Sandor walked down the hall to the conference room where the other members of the task force were filing in.

The panel included Joseph Cleary from DEA; John Chevalier from the Department of Homeland Security; Richard Bebon, who was Byrnes's opposite number at the FBI; and two men and a woman from the National Counter-Terrorism Center. Also attending was Peter Forelli from the NSA unit assigned to the White House, who joined them by videoconference.

Byrnes began by asking Sandor to summarize the latest developments in Mexico and to review, for those who were not present the previous day, the information he obtained in Brighton Beach. Then the meeting was opened to questions.

Bebon, from the FBI, went first. He was tall and slim and, despite being in his early sixties, sat up ramrod straight, his early years in the military having never been forgotten. "Let's start with the intel Sandor got from this Russian in New York. You have any independent reason to believe it's credible?"

"No sir, no independent verification yet," Sandor admitted. "However, before I posed my questions I created an environment that would be likely to persuade someone to tell the truth."

Bebon held up his hand. "Spare us any description of the environment you created."

"Understood."

"Since you were the one who developed the intel I just want to know if you believe it's at least possible these toxins are actually coming by ship into the Port of Baltimore."

"It's possible, nothing more. As I also reported, we believe the transport of the cocaine that includes the anthrax is being organized by Roman Sudakov. Use of a container ship would be the preferred method, and I've learned that they typically offload in a port other than the final destination for the goods. Based on what Vaknin told me, the narcotics are ultimately headed for New York City. Logic would dictate that the anthrax is therefore also intended for use in New York City."

"So Baltimore makes sense as the port of entry," Bebon said.

"Yes sir. But we have new information, resulting from the raid this morning on the farm outside Reynosa. The Mexican authorities are working with people sent from the DEA in Dallas, jointly interrogating the men taken this morning. So far the local head of the cartel down there, name of Mateo, is offering some cooperation."

"Credibility?"

"Yes, credibility is again an issue, but this man has his own motivation to be truthful."

"Go on."

"The activities at his farm last night are probably known already to the others in the pipeline for this shipment. Same with his arrest. Once a man like that is taken into custody, he's as good as dead to the cartel. Mateo refused to speak to the *federales*, insisted that he would only speak to our people. He said Mexican security is leaky as a sieve."

"Man who wants to save his own hide is likely to tell the truth," Bebon said.

"Mateo says that the cartel would assume we'll turn him," Sandor went on. "As a result they would almost certainly make a last-minute change of plans for the destination of this shipment. His best guess is that they would pick another port, such as Newark."

"New Jersey? Didn't you just say they don't choose a port near the final point of distribution?"

"These are unusual circumstances. And please keep in mind that Adina is involved. Knowing how he works, as soon as he got word of trouble he would do everything he could to reroute the cargo. He believes in misdirection, as we've seen before."

"Well then," Bebon said, "let's stop and inspect every damn container coming from Mexico into Baltimore and Newark for the next few days."

Chevalier, from DHS, spoke up. "You know it's not that easy Dick. First, the container ship may not even be coming from Mexico, they can transfer these boxes out at sea. The ship could have embarked from anywhere. And the number of vessels and containers sailing into those harbors is mind-boggling. There's no one in this room that doesn't understand these ports are the Achilles' heel in protecting our country, not just from terrorism but from narcotics, smuggling . . . you know the deal."

Bebon shook his head in disgust.

"And what if this drug dealer is wrong? What if he's lying?" Chevalier asked. "What if it turns out they chose a different port altogether?"

Cleary, the Assistant Administrator from DEA, returned to the subject of the interrogations in Mexico. "When did you receive word this Mateo is cooperating? I haven't heard a thing about it."

"Just came through," Byrnes lied. "I'm sure you'll be getting a full report as soon as you get back to your office."

Cleary nodded, unhappy there were developments within his own agency of which he was unaware. "We lost a good agent down there," he said.

"And I lost two of mine," Byrnes said, lying for the second time. He had told the group that Bergenn and Raabe both died along with Romero, all three bodies having been discovered by Sandor. Byrnes told Sandor he found it impossible to believe that anyone in this group would have betrayed them, but if there was any such possibility he agreed, there was an obvious advantage in claiming there were no survivors from the shootings in Reynosa.

Sandor had never known Byrnes to speak untruthfully—a total anomaly in his profession—and he marveled at how easily the DD helped spin their story. Barely able to suppress a grin, he reckoned he might have to rethink his unquestioning trust in the man.

Meanwhile, Cleary responded by telling the group, "This is tragic all the way around."

"Yes," Sandor agreed. "What we can't understand is how the mission in Reynosa went so wrong so fast. The only ones who knew our people were meeting Romero were the Deputy Director, Dan LaBelle in Texas, and me. The operation was a secret."

Cleary gave a dismissive shake of his head. "There are no secrets in this business, Agent Sandor, you know that. Reporting along the chain of command comes with the territory."

Sandor studied him for a moment but said nothing.

"The important thing now," Cleary told the others, "is to figure out how we turn this to an advantage in stopping the shipment. We know Mateo is a major player in the Sinaloa Cartel. When I get back to my office I'll speak with LaBelle. He and his team will make a deal with him if he really has information that can lead us to these narcotics."

"And the anthrax," Sandor reminded the group.

Bebon piped up again. "I don't give a tinker's damn what kind of deal they make, I wouldn't trust a drug dealer like that from here to the door."

"I agree," Chevalier said.

Cleary dissented. "From Mateo's perspective, anything he can do to trade for his safety at this point is better than being put back onto the street."

"Which leaves us where?" Bebon asked. "It sounds like we're running out of time."

"I agree," Sandor said. "Two or three days at the most. If it were up to me I would keep pressing this Mateo for information. Find out if the drugs are already at sea or if there was time to reroute them. Was Baltimore the original port? Is Newark the likeliest destination now?"

"What we've heard so far," Byrnes jumped in, "leads us to conclude that all of our efforts should be focused on Newark."

"Abandon the work in Baltimore?" Chevalier asked.

"Exactly," the DD told him, his third lie of the meeting.

"With all respect," Cleary said, "I don't think that's your call to make. We've got jurisdictional issues we can't gloss over." He looked around at the others, and a couple of them were nodding in agreement. "We appreciate the efforts your agent has made and the fact that you convened this task force. But the CIA cannot be calling the shots on this."

"He's right," Bebon weighed in. "And we need to read in the Coast Guard ASAP."

"I've already made a call," Chevalier from DHS told them.

Byrnes held up his hands, showing them both palms and a friendly smile. "No disagreement here. Just keep me in the loop and let me know what you want from us."

Peter Forelli, who had remained silent throughout, now spoke up from the video screen on the far wall. "Sounds like you guys are on top of this, and I'll report that to the President. Be sure you copy the NDI and keep us posted."

With that, the meeting was adjourned.

CHAPTER SEVENTY-TWO

CIA HEADQUARTERS, LANGLEY, VIRGINIA

Byrnes escorted the group to the nearest bank of elevators, then led Sandor back to his office, where LaBelle and Raabe were waiting.

"How did it go?" LaBelle asked.

"Not sure," Byrnes admitted.

They took their seats around the conference table.

"We laid it out just as we planned," Sandor said. "We gave them every reason to think that Baltimore is no longer the intended port."

"I felt lousy doing it, too," Byrnes said. "Especially with Bebon in the mix."

"It'll only be a couple of hours," Sandor said. "By then we should know something. Worst case, we can tell them we had misinformation."

"*We*, Sandor? I'm the one who's going to have to explain why I misled the FBI and DHS."

Raabe interrupted. "You might not have misled anyone, sir. LaBelle's office received a call from his team in Mexico. We waited till you got back to patch them in."

"Do they know you're here?" Byrnes asked LaBelle.

"No. I picked up the message from my assistant," the DEA agent explained. "She thinks I'm still in Dallas."

"It's best if it stays that way for right now," Sandor advised, and the others agreed. Then he turned to Raabe and said, "They also think you died down there with Romero and Bergenn."

Byrnes pointed Raabe and LaBelle to chairs in the corner of the room where the video camera would not pick them up. A few seconds later the screen glowed to life with the image of one of the DEA agents participating in the interrogation of Alphonso Mateo. They were at a secure location in Monterrey.

"I'm Deputy Director Byrnes, this is Agent Sandor. He just returned from Reynosa. He was responsible for setting up the apprehension of Mateo."

"Jake Scovell, assigned to Dan LaBelle's unit in Dallas."

"What have you got for us, Agent Scovell?"

"The subject has been surprisingly candid. It's no secret in this part of the world that his capture renders him expendable. There are exceptions, of course, for the few that are really in charge."

"Such as Loera."

"Exactly. Mateo is not in that category."

"So he's singing?" Sandor asked.

"Like a choirboy."

"Let's have it then."

Scovell nodded. "Yesterday Mateo received a tip that Romero was working for us. He ordered Felipe and your men to be locked up, holding them for leverage while he went to a meeting outside Mendez, about an hour away. He was going there to make a down payment on the cargo we're all concerned about."

"Go on."

"The meeting was with Rafael Cabello."

"Adina," Sandor said through gritted teeth. "He was there?"

"Yes sir. Mateo says he was checking on his delivery."

"Why would Adina go to Mexico himself?" Sandor wondered aloud, but Byrnes shot him a look that said the topic would be handled later.

Scovell, meanwhile, told them he had an answer to that question. "Mateo claims he gave him the deposit he was owed on the narcotics. We're still trying to confirm the amount."

"Great," Sandor muttered.

"Mateo says that Adina was aware there was trouble back at Mateo's farm."

"How?"

"They were in the middle of their discussion when one of Mateo's bodyguards got a call. Mateo did not want to be interrupted, but the man said it was urgent. That's when he learned the three prisoners had gotten free and taken out one of the guards."

"Mateo repeated that to Adina?" Sandor asked.

"No, he says he didn't. He'd already told him about the two Americans coming to Reynosa, bragged about having them locked up. After the call he did his best to say everything was fine, but he could see that Adina guessed otherwise. Mateo says he gave every assurance that the delivery was on track, then hightailed it back to his place. We know what he found when he got there."

"Where was Adina going?"

"Mateo doesn't know. He had come to Mendez by private plane, so he could be heading anywhere."

"At the time of the Adina and Mateo meeting, what was the status of the shipment?" Sandor asked.

"Mateo says it was on a truck headed to Matamoros for placement in a container. The *federales* already have a detachment trying to hunt it down, but it's probably too late now. They move goods all over the map, switching trucks, then hiding in warehouses and garages and barns. And then there's the problem with the Mexican authorities. We have no jurisdiction, so they won't let us join the hunt. I don't have to tell you about the level of cooperation we get down here. I'm thrilled they're letting us do the interrogation."

"Based on Mateo's demand."

"True. He's looking for a deal from the U.S., not the Mexicans."

"Stay on top of it," Byrnes said. "We're not just dealing with narcotics here, Scovell."

"We're clear about that sir. Problem is, this is way above my pay grade." Scovell hesitated. "I got word from my boss, Dan LaBelle, to give your agency my full cooperation. I was also told not to report anything up the line here at DEA until I hear back from him. I'm a bit uncomfortable with that, to say the least, but I trust LaBelle and I'm running with it. But when it comes to making deals with a guy like Mateo on behalf of the United States government—"

"I understand," Byrnes interrupted. "You just tell him that you're getting authority from your superiors. Meanwhile, keep him talking."

"Yes sir. I'll get back to you as soon as I have more."

After the DD shut down the video link, LaBelle and Raabe stood and joined them back at the table.

"Jake's a good man. I hate to put him in a bind like this."

"He's not in a bind," Byrnes said. "He's helping us work out of one."

LaBelle nodded. "I guess that's right."

The DD turned to Sandor. "You've got something to say. It's written all over your face."

"Well, for starters, I wouldn't count on the Mexicans to locate the goods. They wouldn't tell you if the container was sitting in their parking lot."

"They're not as bad as that."

"No? Ask LaBelle here. Anyway, that's not the issue. They're not going to catch up with the shipment, that's going to be our job, and the way to do that is through Adina."

Byrnes sat back and waited.

"He never goes anywhere close to the action unless he has a trap-door to jump through. Look at St. Barths. He was there when he engineered the attack on Fort Oscar and the downing of that airplane, but he was on a yacht and safely out to sea by the time the shooting started. Knowing the hunt is on for this shipment, why would he go to Mexico, less than an hour from where the drugs are being loaded for transport?"

"Maybe he didn't know we're getting close," Raabe suggested. "At least not until he met with Mateo and found out Jim and I were in Reynosa."

Byrnes agreed. "The money he received, if this Mateo is telling the truth, was a pretty strong incentive. We know he's become increasingly unpopular in Caracas. He might have needed the cash to fund his scheme. It may be as simple as that."

Sandor shook his head. "If it was about picking up money he could have made other arrangements."

"That may be true," Byrnes conceded. "So why do you think he would have taken the risk? There had to be a reason for him to go there."

Sandor looked around the table, then fixed his gaze on LaBelle. "According to Mateo, Adina came in on a private plane, flew into Mendez, which is within striking distance of both Reynosa and Matamoros, the two towns most likely to be involved in the transport of these goods. That's no accident. Then factor into the equation that Rafael Cabello is a meticulous planner who leaves nothing to chance."

"So?" LaBelle asked.

"So, I think he went there to pick up his anthrax and take it into the States himself."

CHAPTER SEVENTY-THREE

MENDEZ, MEXICO

MATEO WAS NOT wrong. Neither was Sandor.

Mateo told the interrogators that Adina suspected there were problems when he witnessed Mateo's reaction to the phone call that interrupted their meeting. When Mateo refused to even admit there was trouble, it only made things worse.

Adina had traveled to Mexico to pick up the first installment of the money he was due for the narcotics. As Sandor guessed, the Venezuelan was also persuaded it was time for him to take control of the anthrax.

Before arriving in Mendez, Adina had engaged in an encrypted exchange of testy communications with Sudakov. Once Mateo and his men hurried off to deal with whatever had transpired back at the farm, Adina resumed his correspondence with the Russian.

Adina began by admitting that his shipment contained other materials, having nothing whatever to do with the narcotics. It would be best, he suggested, if he could remove those few parcels and then have the drugs sent on their way.

Sudakov was livid at the deception. "It is apparent this is the cause for the publicity our party has been generating," he wrote.

"Publicity was certainly not my intention," replied Adina.

"You should have told me someone else was coming to the party," Sudakov texted back.

"My apologies," Adina replied. "I will have them removed from the table immediately."

Now that Sudakov realized the rumors about toxins being included in the cargo were true, he wrote, "I understand this party-crasher is ill. Is there any chance the disease is contagious?"

"Absolutely not. I am going to oversee the removal myself."

After several additional rants, Sudakov signed off. While Mateo had only given a vague description of the location and progress of the goods, Sudakov provided specific information. Unlike the careless Mexican, Sudakov and Adina shared a penchant for precision and an appreciation for detail.

In less time than it required Mateo to reach his farm, Adina met with the truckers who were carrying the narcotics. They were waiting in a warehouse, not far from shore, where all the goods were to be packed into a huge metal box and taken to sea on a trawler for transfer onto a container ship. The goods were surrounded by sacks of Colombian coffee, designed to frustrate drug-sniffing dogs and to give it the appearance of a legal cargo.

After the exchange of appropriate code words supplied by Sudakov, Alejandro and Jorge went about the tedious business of opening the casings until they found what they were looking for—the airtight suitcases constructed of hard plastic that were situated deep inside the recesses of the large packages. They still bore the seals that were placed on them in the lab near Barranquitas.

With the help of the drivers and their armed accomplices, everything was then closed up and the trucks sent on their way.

Adina and his men took the anthrax and drove through the night, back to the airstrip near Mendez.

CHAPTER SEVENTY-FOUR

WASHINGTON, D.C.

THE DEPUTY DIRECTOR deployed two teams to tail Joseph Cleary when he left the task force meeting at Langley. The decision was made with some reluctance—it was simply not in Byrnes's DNA to believe a highly placed agent of the United States government could really be a traitor. Even after John Covington's duplicity, not to mention the treachery of Vincent Traiman, the DD preferred to see their betrayal as an aberration, not a commonplace risk. But Dan LaBelle had been adamant in his assertion that he told only one person about Bergenn and Raabe meeting with Romero in Reynosa. And that one person was his boss in Washington, Joseph Cleary. Now that Mateo was spilling his guts, they knew he had received a tip that two federal agents were coming to town, and that they were there to meet Pacquito, who was actually an undercover operative for the DEA by the name of Felipe Romero.

That was the only reason the DD went along with Sandor's plan to deceive members of the task force—it was clear that someone inside the DEA was working with the Sinaloa Cartel.

Byrnes had told three lies in that meeting. The first concerned the cooperation of Mateo. He assured Cleary that he would be getting a report, but Byrnes arranged to cut him out of the loop until this was resolved. That maneuver took the intervention of Peter Forelli, the only one in the group who knew what Byrnes was up to.

The second lie was the claim that both Bergenn and Raabe had died during their attempted escape. As long as Cleary thought the

two CIA agents and Romero were all gone, he should have no concern that any of them had the chance to pass along any intel. That left
only Mateo for him to deal with.

The third, and most critical fabrication, was that Baltimore had
been abandoned as the likely port of entry for the shipment, and a
decision had been made to focus on Newark.

That set of facts was intended to force Cleary's hand, along
with the question posed by Sandor. He asked the gathering how
things could have gone so badly for Bergenn, Raabe and Romero so
quickly in Mexico if no one outside their inner circle knew of the
mission. Cleary, being the representative from DEA, was forced to
reply, making a vague reference to the regular chain of bureaucratic
reporting, obviously covering himself for the moment when LaBelle
was compelled to reveal that he had told his boss the three men were
meeting.

Now that their web had been spun, Byrnes had several concerns.

What if Cleary had been telling the truth? What if LaBelle was
really Jaime Rivera? The DD could not ignore the fact that LaBelle
had chosen to meet with Bergenn and Raabe outside his office. That
he did not read in anyone else from his own staff about the contact
about to be made with a field agent who had been risking his life
undercover for two years. Or that Felipe Romero reported only to
him.

The DD did not have the history with LaBelle that Sandor shared,
and he told his agent not to count on that relationship if the answers
they got were not what he expected.

––––––––––

The two teams dispatched by Byrnes from the National Clandestine
Service had no trouble following Cleary. They were all experienced
agents. The NCS was the section of the CIA to which Sandor was assigned although, as the DD was so fond of pointing out, it often seemed
that Sandor roamed Langley as if he were in a department of his own.

Both teams used their own cars, not the so-called unmarked
vehicles so easily spotted in Washington. There were two men in each
vehicle, operatives well practiced in shadowing a moving target. The

drivers knew how to fall back when they got too close, allowing the other team to take the lead. The agents in the passenger seats were operating electronic eavesdropping equipment that would pick up any phone calls made or discussions the subject might have in a face-to-face meeting.

Cleary was driving his own sedan. He was alone, but he made no phone calls. Only twice did he do anything resembling evasive action as he proceeded along the roads back to the capital, but it soon became apparent he was not heading toward his office. Instead he proceeded to a public garage adjacent to the shops at Crystal City. He parked, then made his way on foot to another car, an unoccupied black sedan, a couple of dozen spaces away.

The two surveillance vehicles veered off in different directions, then circled back to positions within the range of their audiovisual monitoring devices.

Cleary had a key to the other car. The four agents watched as he entered on the driver's side, then sat there and waited. Perhaps someone would be meeting him, perhaps he wanted to gauge any activity in the area. Meanwhile, they called in the license plate of the black car and had it traced to a shell company in Virginia.

After ten minutes Cleary removed a telephone from the glove box and powered it up. It was a disposable cell with international capability. He then made three calls.

Byrnes was waiting with Sandor when LaBelle was led back into his office, this time flanked by two agents from the Directorate of Intelligence, or DI.

LaBelle wore an unhappy look.

"What have you got?" Byrnes asked.

The DEA agent took a seat, but the duo from DI remained standing. The senior man began his report.

"The subject left Langley but did not return to his office."

"I assume," Byrnes interrupted, "the subject you're referring to is Joseph Cleary, Assistant Administrator of the DEA?"

"Yes sir."

"Proceed."

"He was alone," the man from DI continued, then gave details of the surveillance by the four agents from DCS.

"Tell me about the phone calls," Byrnes said.

"The calls were made from a disposable phone that had been fitted with an encryption program. Our software cut through it."

"Well done, I'm sure. Now, the calls?"

"Yes sir. The first was to a cell phone in Mexico. We fixed the location just outside Monterrey. The second was to a mobile number in Egypt, somewhere offshore, on the Red Sea. The third call was placed to a landline in the Cayman Islands. The private number of an executive in a bank there." The man looked up. "Do you want me to read each of the transcripts, sir?"

"We can read those ourselves," Byrnes told him. "Summarize them please."

"Well sir, the first two conversations were somewhat oblique, but we believe we have a clear read on the substance. In the first, the subject conveyed a warning that someone being held in custody in Monterrey is posing a serious danger. The subject directed that the threat be neutralized. Then the subject addressed a second problem." The man from DI shot a quick look at LaBelle. "He wanted Agent LaBelle found and removed."

Byrnes glanced over at the DEA agent. He understood why La-Belle looked as if he had just heard of a death in the family. "Did he say why?"

"In effect, he said that LaBelle was the only surviving connection between the subject and the incidents in Reynosa."

"Anything else on that call?"

"No sir."

"Go on."

"The second call was quite brief and had to do with a possible change of destinations. They appeared to be discussing a delivery. The subject advised that the attention being paid to the primary drop-off point had now shifted to a second location, so their original plans should not be altered."

"Nothing about the shipment containing toxins?"

"At the very end, the subject asked something vague about that, but the man to whom he was speaking said the issue was under control."

"That was all they said on that subject?"

"Yes sir."

"Just to be clear," Sandor jumped in, "when he answered the question he did not deny there were toxins in the shipment?"

"No, all he said was"—and now the agent thumbed through his copy of the transcript—"the matter is 'under control,'" he quoted.

Byrnes nodded. "And the third call?"

"The subject was making financial arrangements. It's all in the transcript there. At the conclusion of the discussion he said that he would be seeing this banker soon."

Byrnes rubbed his face with both hands, then said, "I don't suppose there's anything else in those transcripts about a planned attack."

"No sir, I certainly would have pointed that out."

Byrnes nodded.

"After the third call the subject left the vehicle, got back into his car, and headed home. The teams from NCS want further instructions."

"Of course," the DD said. "First I'd like you to take Agent LaBelle down the hall. Make him comfortable while we sort out a few things." He turned to LaBelle. "I'm truly sorry about this. I'm going to call Bebon at the FBI. I'll tell him we have a credible report that your life has been threatened and that we need a protection detail. I saw in your dossier you have a wife and children."

"I do."

"We're going to attend to that right now." He stood and so did Sandor and LaBelle. "I'll be back to you in a few minutes," he told the man from DEA. After the agents from DI led LaBelle out of the room, Byrnes went to his desk and picked up the phone. He was patched in to both surveillance teams and asked for status. When he was told that Cleary was in his house, Byrnes said, "Do not let him out of your sight. If he makes a move, report in immediately. Be prepared to take him into custody."

Then he called Bebon at the FBI.

What began as an unauthorized mission to assassinate Rafael Cabello had since grown into an international, multi-agency initiative to prevent a terrorist attack. When Sandor discovered anthrax was being manufactured at Adina's Venezuelan compound there was no clear indication of how, when or where the toxins might be used. The CIA had enlisted the resources of several federal departments, from DHS to the Coast Guard, and there was still only the sketchiest evidence even confirming the existence of the plot.

Until now.

Sandor and Byrnes were seated at the small conference table in the DD's office debating the importance of Cleary's phone call to Egypt.

"That had to be Sudakov he was speaking with, just look at this transcript, it's obvious. And Sudakov confirmed there were toxins in the shipment. You know I'm right sir."

"I *believe* you're right, Sandor. There's a difference."

"Not in terms of what we need to do."

"If you're wrong—if we're wrong—this is going to be one hellacious black eye for the Agency."

"Then let's bring Cleary in, find out what he knows."

"Don't worry, we will. I just want to wait a bit. Right now we have to hope he has them believing we're tracking this shipment into Newark and ignoring Baltimore. That should keep them on course for Baltimore. If they find out we've arrested Cleary we'll be doing ourselves more harm than good."

They were interrupted by a knock at the door and Raabe was ushered in by Byrnes's assistant. Raabe was showing signs of both grief and fatigue after all that had transpired in Reynosa, but for the moment he managed a satisfied look as he held up a sheaf of papers. "SIGINT," he announced. "We have chatter out of New York."

Byrnes pointed him to a chair. "Talk to us."

Raabe sat, placed the paperwork on the table, then looked up and said, "Upper Manhattan. The boys from the NCTC have been working with our people, reviewing data from the past two months. They've identified communications between Venezuela and what they think might be a sleeper cell in Washington Heights. It's a big enclave for Latin Americans, as you know. The exchanges had been totally benign, back-burner stuff. The DEA was contacted a few weeks ago when some calls from Mexico figured in the mix. NCTC thought it sounded like it might be about narcotics, so we weren't even notified."

"And now?"

"There's been a lot of recent activity domestically. NCTC is still taking the lead, our people are trying to keep their jurisdictional hands clean. Anyway, they picked up a lot of talk about a big party in the next couple of days."

"That's it?"

"No. It gets better. They mentioned a guest of honor coming to town. But guess where they have *not* been calling lately?"

"Venezuela," Sandor said.

"Bingo. There hasn't been a call to or from Caracas since the rumor that Adina had flown the coop."

"What do the most recent exchanges sound like?"

"They're discussing the time frame for their little bash. Seems they want to make it sooner. Since then the chatter has died down and their attempts at coding discussions have become more intense."

"Do we have addresses on these people?" Byrnes asked.

Raabe shook his head. "They use nothing but disposable cell phones. S and T triangulated the locations, that's how they nailed Washington Heights as the general area."

"I don't suppose anyone mentioned an anthrax delivery," Byrnes smiled hopefully.

"Not quite," Raabe said as he started thumbing through the papers, "but have a look at this." He found what he was looking for and passed it to the DD. "Here it is in Spanish with the translation. The key line says 'the confetti will be here soon, should be quite a party.' And how about this one?" He passed a second sheet to Byrnes.

The DD took it and read the highlighted section aloud. "'They'll never be able to blow out the candles on this cake.'" He looked up. "You figure the confetti is the anthrax."

"It's one way to read it," Raabe said.

"What about this reference to candles?"

"Not sure," Raabe admitted. "We've got our analysts on it, poring through every line of transcript from the last sixty days. One thing seems certain though. Taken together, those references aren't talking about a cocaine delivery."

Byrnes was not convinced. "Let's see what else NCTC turns up. Context is crucial. Couldn't confetti be coke and the candles be a reference to crack?"

"That's not how we read it, sir."

"I'm not a cryptologist," Byrnes said with a frown as he placed the papers on the table. "What do you think Sandor?"

Sandor had been shuffling through some of the other pages. He looked up and said, "Adina never plans anything straight ahead. Craig may be right, this may be a reference to anthrax, and maybe it's not. What bothers me is the mention of fire. You don't spread anthrax by burning it."

"So you're saying a biological attack may not be the only thing he has planned."

"Yes sir, that's what I'm saying."

"All right, I'll call downstairs, get our people on these transcripts, too. I also want to speak with DHS on this. I need to report to the task force about Cleary."

"And I need to get to New York," Sandor said.

CHAPTER SEVENTY-FIVE

WASHINGTON HEIGHTS, NEW YORK CITY

W<small>ASHINGTON</small> H<small>EIGHTS HAS</small> grown to define the entire upper portion of Manhattan, an area stretching from the Hudson River on the west, the Harlem River on the east, the Spuyten Duyvil canal—which separates the island from the Bronx—on the north, and Harlem to the south. A region once dominated by Irish-Americans and Jewish immigrants, in the past half century it has become home, almost exclusively, to Hispanics from virtually every country south of the Rio Grande.

Many who consider themselves true New Yorkers never see any more of the neighborhood than they might glimpse during a quick visit to the Cloisters museum or the sprawling medical facility sitting atop the east bank of the Hudson. This separation of the Heights from the rest of the city is owed in part to the deteriorating quality of life driven by the rampant narcotics trade there. The residents of the area who are peaceable and law-abiding have to deal with gang warfare, street violence, and the inevitable crime that results from a society where illegal drug use is rampant. Given the number of welfare recipients, minimum-wage workers, and day laborers, it is not surprising that an undercurrent of angry, anti-establishment sentiment can easily be cultivated. Just as *jihadists* nurture anti-Western hatred in their impressionable children, anti-American socialists promote the politics of blame as they deride the capitalist ethic of hard work and achievement, preaching the easy life promised to all by entitlement programs.

Adina himself would be pleased with the rhetoric being spread.

Proponents of these self-defeating morals argue, "Your unfortunate circumstances are not your fault, they are the fault of those who have more than you, who take advantage of you, who expect you to educate your young, build a family unit, and work hard for what you get. Who are they to tell you how to live? What do they know of your struggles? Why not take what you feel entitled to instead of what they tell you that you need to earn?"

A battalion of willing radicals is not hard to assemble in this cauldron of poverty, rage, and substance abuse. Controlling them and relying upon them is another matter entirely.

Miguel Lasco was sitting at the back table in a dimly lit bar on Staff Street, just off Dyckman Street, on the northern edge of Washington Heights. Six of his key men were with him.

They trusted the owner of the tavern, who was also its full-time bartender and part-time lookout. Nevertheless, they leaned forward when they spoke, their voices hushed.

"We have to cover a lot of ground," Lasco said with a concerned look.

"Don't worry, we're putting our best men in the tunnels," one of the others assured him.

"Understood," Lasco said. "But the GW alone, with lanes upper and lower. That's going to take a lot of cars right there."

The others nodded their understanding. The building in which they were meeting was practically in the shadow of the George Washington Bridge.

"The tunnels are still the key," another man reminded him.

"Of course," he said, "but the man told us from the start, we have to hit every bridge. All or nothing. He told us that right from the beginning."

The others nodded.

"This is our moment. This is what we've dreamed of." Then Lasco added with a conspiratorial grin, "And the payoff will make it all worthwhile."

They became silent.

"Day after tomorrow you'll have all our groups in place?"

The others said they would.

"We've got to make sure the drivers don't have any details till that morning. They're good boys, but we cannot afford to trust anyone outside this circle. Agreed?"

The others agreed.

"Tomorrow they've got to line up the remaining cars. Where do we stand on that?"

The man in charge of securing the vehicles made his report. They were still fifty cars short, but he was confident it was not going to be an issue.

"You better be right, my friend."

"I'm not worried about the cars," he replied. "I'm worried about discipline," he admitted. "We can't have these young studs getting stoned or drunk or flapping their gums between now and then."

"And what about afterwards?" another in the group asked. "There won't be one of them who'll be able to keep his mouth shut. Bragging, if they don't get caught, ratting us all out if they do."

Lasco agreed. "Our job is to get this done and then get the hell out of here."

"With the money," the man responded.

"Of course."

"And when does Mr. Green show up, eh?"

"When the goods arrive," Lasco told them. Then he leaned as close to them as he could. "Tomorrow," he whispered.

CHAPTER SEVENTY-SIX

EN ROUTE TO NEW YORK CITY

Aᴅɪɴᴀ ɴᴇᴠᴇʀ ʟᴀᴄᴋᴇᴅ a contingency plan. Since the incursion into his compound he harbored suspicions that his anthrax would not make it all the way to New York as a stowaway within the cargo of narcotics. On some levels, he believed that was for the best. Let the authorities focus on intercepting the cocaine; he could still get the toxins through. He now had possession of the deadly cases. All he had to do was to get them to Manhattan.

The radar systems and tracking technology along the border between Mexico and Texas had tightened since 9/11. Any plane not filing a proper flight plan, or deviating substantially from the assigned vectors, would soon be met by F-16s that were constantly ready to be scrambled and deployed.

A private plane coming from south of the border would be met by Customs wherever it set down and subjected to careful scrutiny.

A crossing by car was out of the question.

Small, unmanned devices could be flown north carrying the toxins. The goods would then be dropped in the Texas desert, where they could later be retrieved by use of their electronic homing system, but Adina dismissed the idea out of hand. The UAV could fail. The tracking mechanism might fail. The packages might be found by someone else before he and his men got there.

Use of an ultralight was another possibility, having one man carry the toxins and fly under the radar. The plane would set down in the Texas flatlands where the pilot would be picked up by car and taken to a private airfield someplace nearby. Adina's charter would meet him there, having flown in without the dangerous baggage and already passing through customs. Since the next leg of their journey would be domestic, Customs would no longer pose a threat. Again, however, they faced the concerns of an unreliable aircraft. There were also too many moving parts in that plan for Adina's taste, not to mention the possibility that the crossing would be picked up by the enhanced radar.

The overriding concern was the danger in any means of crossing from Mexico directly into the United States. Adina knew trouble was brewing and the arrival of the American agents in Reynosa meant the Border Patrol would already be on high alert.

Fortunately Adina had already planned a safer, if more circuitous, route.

The Cessna jet took off from Mendez, landing less than two hours later at La Isabela International Airport in Santo Domingo. Newer, smaller, and better equipped to deal with private jets than Las Americas Airport, it was the perfect spot for Adina to refuel and then embark for his trip north.

Charter flights landing in the Dominican Republic usually meant the arrival of wealthy tourists, so inspections were perfunctory at best. No one with any sense was smuggling anything *into* the country, and the government had no interest in what you might be taking out.

Once the brief inspection was concluded, Adina told the pilot and copilot to get some rest. They would be leaving soon.

"I'll need to file a flight plan, sir. This is an international airport."

Adina nodded. "We'll find you in the lounge and let you know. Leave the air-conditioning on in the cabin." It was clear he wanted the crew off the plane, so they went on their way. When they were gone Adina took a seat in the cabin, facing Alejandro and Jorge. "You are both satisfied the cases will not be found?"

"They did a good job modifying the storage bins," Alejandro told him. "They replaced the lining with removable panels, then made it look like there's fabric sewn on top of that. The cases are airtight and the goods are odorless. If they try and run any sort of interior detection, the plastic cases will blend in with the fuselage."

"And we're just three visitors from the Dominican Republic," Jorge chimed in, reaching into his pocket and holding up his counterfeit passport.

Adina nodded thoughtfully. "They're looking for a container ship from Mexico on its way toward Newark. Whatever those agents discovered in Reynosa, they'll assume the goods are traveling by sea and cannot arrive before day after tomorrow, more likely the next morning."

"Which means they'll be too late."

"We hope so" Adina said. "Alejandro, go tell our young pilot he has three gentlemen who would like to fly nonstop to Stewart Airport, in Newburgh, New York."

CHAPTER SEVENTY-SEVEN

ARLINGTON, VIRGINIA

SANDOR HAD TO get to New York. With time running out he knew the best place for him now was at the point of attack. He also knew that chasing Adina from behind was not going to get it done. He needed to get in front of the situation.

On his way to Manhattan, however, he had a couple of stops to make.

Commandeering an Agency car, he took Craig Raabe and Dan LaBelle and drove toward Arlington, Virginia. Whatever he was going to do when he got there—which he had not yet decided—these two men had earned the right to be present. As he approached his destination he contacted the teams Byrnes had in place. Sandor told them he was going to meet with Joseph Cleary and that they should remain at the ready but take no action unless he called them in.

A few minutes later he arrived at Cleary's home, pulled into the driveway, and turned the car off.

"You two wait here. I'll let you know when I'm ready for you."

Raabe placed a hand on his friend's arm. "I still think this is a lousy idea."

"Me too," Sandor admitted, then got out of the car.

As he strolled up to the front door he had a look around. The house, an old-style split-level, was situated on a quiet suburban street. At this time of night there was not much going on, which was for the best. If Cleary had allies watching the people who in turn were watching Cleary, the two NCS teams would have spotted them.

Sandor rang the bell and waited.

When Cleary came to the door he was still in his work clothes, although his jacket and tie had been removed and the sleeves of his shirt were rolled up. The man looked as if he was busy. "Sandor," he said, not hiding his surprise.

"There's been a development. We need to talk." Before Cleary could respond, Sandor walked past him into the small foyer.

Other than the overhead Cleary had switched on when he answered the bell, the lights in the house seemed to be off, except for a room off to the left.

"Family asleep already?"

"My wife took the kids to see her sister. With everything going on I figured it was a good time for her to get away."

"Get away?"

"I'm up to my eyeballs with the situation we have here. Thought it would be best."

Sandor nodded. "No distractions. Makes sense."

"Look, I'm in the middle of pulling some data together. What's the new development?"

The two men were facing each other beneath the harsh glare of the brass and glass light fixture. They stood about the same height and Sandor had positioned himself directly in front of Cleary, so they were eye to eye.

"No small talk, Cleary? No offer of a drink or anything?"

The man's eyes narrowed slightly. Then he glanced toward the front window. In the darkness he could not see if there was anyone else in Sandor's car. "What are you up to?"

"You know the old expression, 'Lie down with dogs and get up with fleas'?" Cleary did not respond. "Looks to me you're as flea-bitten as an old hound."

"What are you doing here?"

"I'm having a conversation with a dead man walking."

"I'm calling your boss right now," Cleary said, then began to turn toward his office.

Before he could complete the about-face Sandor grabbed him by the wrist, spun him back around, and was showing him the business end of his Walther PPK.

"Like I said, I'm here to have a conversation, then you can call whoever you want."

Cleary did a reasonable job of maintaining his composure, actually managing a sneer as he said, "I know all about you, Sandor. You're a renegade with a terminal discipline problem, and right now you're way over the line. Pulling that weapon on a senior government official is going to earn you time in federal lockup."

"You're scaring me to death, Cleary. Is that an intimidation technique they taught you when you went through the initiation rites for the Sinaloa Cartel, or did you work up that little act on your own?"

Cleary glared at him without speaking.

"I have to admit, I may be a little myopic on this issue, but I simply cannot see how a man in your position can betray his own country."

"Betray my country? You're insane."

"Am I?" Sandor gestured with his weapon, pointing toward Cleary's office, then gave the man a shove to get him moving. He followed him into the room, then had the man from DEA sit behind his desk. Sandor remained standing as he poked through the papers that were spread out.

Cleary smirked at the effort. "You're delusional."

Sandor moved beside Cleary and opened the top drawer. A revolver sat atop some documents. Sandor removed the gun and stuck it in his waistband.

"I think it's time for me to make that call to Mark Byrnes," Cleary declared, a touch of arrogance having returned.

When he reached for the phone, Sandor slammed down hard with the butt of the Walther, nailing Cleary's hand. "Not just yet," he said as the man yanked his arm back with a pathetic yelp. Sandor pulled out his cell and hit a button. Raabe answered on the first ring. "Come on in, both of you. The front door is open."

When Raabe and LaBelle joined them in the small room, Cleary could do nothing to hide his surprise at seeing his agent from Dallas. "What is this?" he demanded.

LaBelle stared down at him without answering.

Cleary turned back to Sandor. "If you claim to have some right to be here, I want to see a warrant and I want to call my lawyer. If not, the three of you need to get the hell out of my house right now."

LaBelle was still looking at his boss as he said, "You were the only one I told about Bergenn and Raabe going to see Felipe. You were the only one who could have given them up."

"Other than you, that is."

No one replied as Raabe removed a digital recorder from his pocket, hit PLAY, and they all began listening to the recordings of the three phone calls Cleary placed just a few hours earlier.

Halfway through the first conversation Cleary said, "I want to call my lawyer. Now."

"Sorry pal," Sandor said. "This is a matter of national security. You're not making any calls to anyone. You told your friends that we're looking for the shipment to arrive in Newark, that Baltimore is the safe bet. That was our play, and it suits us fine. You're not meeting with some shyster who'll be passing along any messages. We don't even want your friends down in Mexico knowing you're in custody. You're being held incommunicado until this is over."

"I have rights."

"Of course you do, although I voted to take you out right here, but some people think you'll be more valuable alive. We'll go visit them and see about your rights."

For a moment no one spoke as the tape of Cleary's phone calls continued playing.

"You'll hear it all enough times, believe me," Sandor told him as he reached out and turned off the machine. "So what was it all about? Greed?"

"Greed?" Cleary's voice was thick with anger. "You have no idea what you're talking about, you pathetic little policeman. You have no sense of what it's like to spend your life fighting a battle no one will ever let you win." He shook his head, as if the truth were so obvious. "People want to use narcotics, it's a fact of life. No one can stop the demand and it's too profitable to shut down the production. So I spend my days shoveling sand against the tide, and for what? My agents are murdered, the governments in Colombia and Mexico sabotage every viable plan to stop these criminals, and at the end of the week I take home less money than some twenty-six-year-old punk banging computer keys on Wall Street who doesn't produce a single useful thing in the world."

Sandor burst out laughing. "That's it? That's all you've got? A speech about the poor frustrated bureaucrat who couldn't deal with the harsh realities of the world for another day?" Cleary started to move, but Sandor leveled the barrel of the automatic at his face. "Ah, ah, ah," he said.

Cleary stopped.

"So that justifies you joining their side?"

Cleary responded with a look as cold as death. "You can't prove a thing. Those calls don't mean anything."

"We'll see. Meanwhile, I still haven't heard how you can justify the murder of thousands of innocent people. How does that factor into your mantra of self-pity?"

"Your fairy tale about anthrax, you mean?"

"Fairy tale?"

"Why would the cartel risk polluting a cargo of narcotics worth millions of dollars to import biological weapons?"

"You tell me."

Cleary stared at him as if he were speaking to a moron. "They wouldn't."

"But Adina would."

Cleary began to say something, then stopped.

"Gentlemen," Sandor said to his colleagues, "please give us a moment."

LaBelle turned to leave, but Raabe hesitated. "Jordan . . ."

"It'll be fine. I think Mr. Cleary wants to tell me something privately."

Neither Sandor nor Raabe paid any attention to Cleary's protests.

"I'll be right outside," Raabe said, then followed LaBelle out and closed the door behind them.

"So," Sandor said as he turned back to Cleary, "you want to tell me about the anthrax?"

"I already told you. The Sinaloa Cartel is not in the business of terrorism, except to the extent it protects their business interests.

There's no reason they'd be transporting biological weapons into the United States."

"So you say, but I don't believe you." Sandor had been holding the automatic at his side. Now he pointed it at Cleary's face. "You know about the toxins, and I want you to tell me about them right now. By the way, I'm not interested in any long-term interrogation." He cocked the hammer on the PPK.

"You're not going to just shoot me, Sandor."

"Don't bet on it. You've already called me a renegade, and I've already told you I'd just as soon see you dead as listen to anything you have to say. At least I'm offering you a choice." Sandor leaned on the desk, the barrel of the Walther not more than two feet from Cleary's eyes.

"I don't know anything about anthrax," Cleary said, his voice less certain now. "There are rumors of a big shipment coming from Venezuela. They say Adina might be involved. The only thing I've heard about anthrax comes from you."

"That's all you got?"

"That's all I know."

Sandor nodded. "Who else you working with in the DEA? You don't look smart enough to be doing this on your own."

"I want to call my lawyer."

"You keep saying that and I have to tell you, it's really annoying." Sandor moved the gun to within a foot of the man's eyes. "You're sure there's nothing else you want to tell me first?"

"Screw you."

Sandor stood up and removed Cleary's revolver from his waistband. Without another word he calmly walked around the side of the desk, fired a shot into Cleary's knee with his automatic, then fired a shot from Cleary's revolver into the ceiling.

The door burst open and Raabe came rushing in with his gun drawn. Cleary had fallen out of his chair and was on the floor, writhing in pain.

"It's under control," Sandor said with a shrug. "He went for a gun in his desk drawer, I wrestled it away from him, but when I grabbed his revolver both weapons went off." He didn't even bother to look down at Cleary as he added, "Unfortunately, he seems to have been hit in the leg."

The sound of the gunshots also brought one of Byrnes's NCS teams onto the scene, the other two men holding their position outside.

Sandor repeated his story, then said, "Don't bother with an ambulance, it'll attract too much attention. Just walk him outside between the two of you, then take him to the Gables and lock him down." He had another glance at Cleary, then said with a smile, "We wouldn't want some pain-in-the-ass innocent bystander getting in our way."

Cleary, barely able to string words together, did manage to spit out a disjointed string of expletives.

Raabe turned and glared down at him. "If I were you, buddy, I'd shut the hell up and be thankful his gun only went off once."

CHAPTER SEVENTY-EIGHT

BALTIMORE, MARYLAND

Sandor left Raabe and LaBelle with the men from NCS and drove to his next stop, a restaurant called Chazz, on Aliceanna Street near the harbor in Baltimore. Cleary had warned his cohorts that Newark was under watch, leaving Baltimore a relatively safe harbor. That meant no one in the Coast Guard or DEA wanted to give any sign that security had been tightened around the port. Sandor arrived alone, choosing this Italian restaurant, renowned for its authentic coal-oven pizza and casual attitude, as a suitable place to meet with DEA Agent Evan Walters, designated by the task force to spearhead the efforts here.

Walters was waiting at the "owner's table," which sits in an alcove against the far back wall of the main dining area. Sandor had barely taken his seat when the man staked out his territory. "I want to be clear, I'm only seeing you as a courtesy. I don't want some spook acting outside his authority to screw up our operation."

"Nice to meet you too."

"We've got a full Coast Guard presence in Baltimore, my team is on full alert, and the locals will back us up as needed. So, what else can I tell you to get you on your way?"

"I'm glad to see the era of interdepartmental cooperation is alive and well in Charm City."

Before Walters could respond, a waiter came by with menus.

"We won't be eating," the man from DEA told him. "Just bring me a club soda with lime."

"Jack Daniel's, rocks," Sandor said. After the young man ambled off to get the drinks, Sandor said, "I assume you've been fully briefed about the danger of the toxins in this shipment."

"Of course."

"We don't know if the narcotics have been contaminated, which we doubt, or if the poison is hidden inside the cargo, which is more likely."

"Please tell me something I don't already know."

"All right," Sandor said, leaning forward and lowering his voice. "If it weren't for me, you wouldn't even have a clue these goods are on their way here. So save the tough-guy act for someone you can impress."

Walters was a thickly built, broad-shouldered man, at around forty just a couple of years older than Sandor, and apparently just as ready to mix it up. For a moment it looked as if he was going to come out of his chair and across the table, but he apparently thought better of it. Instead he said, "I've been warned about you, Sandor. A loose cannon if ever there was one, which is exactly what we don't need right now. So unless you've got something to tell me that might help with this assignment, I'm outta here."

Now Walters did begin to rise, but Sandor fixed him with a dark look that warned him to sit his ass back in the chair. The man was somewhere between standing and sitting when Sandor said, "You've got some major leaks in your agency relating to this shipment. My guess is that you haven't been read into that part of the program."

Walters lowered himself back into his seat. "Has this been confirmed up above or is this a story you just invented?"

"We're not sure if we've identified everyone involved. The only reason I'm even discussing this with you is that Dan LaBelle says you can be trusted."

"Is that why you're here?"

"I'm here to tell you that you need to watch your back on this operation. We can't afford to have anyone warning Adina or Sudakov that we're still targeting Baltimore."

When the waiter returned with their drinks, the looks on the faces of his two customers told him he best not ask if they'd changed their mind about ordering food. He quickly left them alone again.

"This mole in the agency, is it someone highly placed?"

"I can't tell you that," Sandor said, "but it doesn't matter. The concern is that he may not have been working alone."

Walters nodded.

"You'll be hearing back from LaBelle or an agent in my department, Craig Raabe. You're not to discuss this with anyone but the three of us."

"Got it."

Sandor drank down half of his whisky. "You're going to have to play this pretty close to the vest within your own agency."

"I guess so."

"You know a Russian dealer in Brooklyn, Timur Vaknin?"

"I know of him."

"He's likely the buyer here, at least for some of the cocaine, if that information helps."

"It might."

"I also have intel that the trucker supposed to take the goods away is Transnational."

Walters gave an appreciative nod. "That will definitely help."

"Good," Sandor said, then drank off the rest of his whisky and stood. "I've got a flight to catch."

CHAPTER SEVENTY-NINE

NEW YORK CITY

SANDOR WAS GLAD to be back in his apartment.

The Company plane made the short flight from the BWI Airport to Teterboro, New Jersey, where a car was waiting to take him home. Now he had time to do some stretches, shower, put on clean clothes, and draw a few deep breaths.

He went to his bedroom, unlocked the panel in his closet, and took out the metal box where he kept his weapons, emergency funds, and other tools of the clandestine trade. He was already armed with the PPK so he strapped on an S&W .38 snub-nose revolver in an ankle holster, took extra ammunition, then replaced the box and began pacing from room to room while he waited for a phone call.

Craig Raabe was still in D.C., coordinating the information being gathered. LaBelle had also stayed behind. Based on what they had put together so far, Sandor was convinced of three things. First, he believed Adina's target was New York. Baltimore and Washington were possible, but the intel developed from the discussions coming out of Washington Heights pointed to an attack somewhere in Manhattan.

Second, the information Raabe got in Mexico, as reinforced by the ongoing interrogation of Mateo, indicated a short timeline. A container ship from the western reaches of the Gulf of Mexico was likely heading up the east coast of the United States and would arrive in Baltimore in less than two days.

His third premise was far more speculative. He did not believe the anthrax was still inside the shipment of narcotics.

This was one time, he admitted to himself as he paced from one room of his apartment to the next, he hoped he was wrong. If the toxin was still within the cargo container it should be easier to intercept. It would also give them these next two days to identify the ship carrying the contraband. If he was right, he feared the means for a widespread biological attack was already inside the country.

It would be classic Adina, like the unmanned subs he launched in the Gulf Coast that were nothing more than a diversion from the real destination of the weapons that had already been smuggled into Louisiana. And that was only one example of how the Venezuelan terrorist played chess. Even if the rumors were accurate about Adina having become persona non grata in Caracas, and the analysis in Langley was correct that he needed to cash in on the narcotics shipment, Sandor was still certain of the man's priorities.

He would be focused on the attack against the United States and would do everything he could to make that happen.

The airports were being watched, but the photos of Adina being circulated were only computer enhancements of old pictures. The border authorities from Texas to California were on alert, but it was a mammoth job with all of the traffic coming across every day. Worst of all, it was likely that Adina had sent the toxins by messengers, possibly through more than one route, staying away from the epicenter of his assault, making detection even more difficult. Added to this dilemma was the fact that anthrax is a virtually odorless powder and—unlike an explosive device—would not be easily identified by X-ray.

He went to the kitchen, grabbed a bottle of water, and drank down the entire thing. Then his cell phone rang.

"Sandor?"

"It's me. You get the warrant?"

"Done," Bobby Ferriello told him.

"Perfect. When will you be ready to go?"

"We're ready now," the narcotics detective said. "We have a SWAT team prepared to move into position."

"We don't want to make a bigger scene than we absolutely have to. No way of knowing who else is watching."

"Understood."

"I'm on my way."

Sandor picked up his old Land Rover from the garage down the street and took off for Brooklyn. When he arrived at Ferriello's precinct he was not shown to the lieutenant's office, but to a large space on the floor above. There were more than twenty officers present, ten of them in full combat gear.

Ferriello was standing with a couple of uniformed men, studying a map and a series of photographs all pinned to a fabric board against the wall. Sandor was escorted in and greeted by Ferriello. "I have to admit, the way things were left at Vaknin's place I wasn't sure I'd ever see you again. At least not all in one piece."

Sandor nodded. "When they had me down in their little dungeon I wasn't so sure myself." He had a quick look around. "Your war room?"

"Something like that. Hey everyone," Ferriello announced to the group, "this is Sandor. He's with the feds, riding shotgun with me." The brief introduction was followed by a series of quick nods and hellos, then Ferriello led Sandor to the map. "These are the positions they'll take," he explained as he pointed to buildings in Brighton Beach. "Three two-men SWAT teams on these rooftops, the other four men will be deployed at ground level. Once we get inside, no one is leaving the place without one of our men having a bead on him."

"Everyone understands that we want to avoid a show of force unless it's necessary, right?"

"Absolutely."

"We need to take Vaknin, get his computer, his records, whatever else we find. We're running out of time, but we also can't afford to scare his friends away."

"Understood." Ferriello paused, then added, "A lot of the men and women here have been waiting a long time to nail this guy. We're happy to get the chance."

"That's good," Sandor said. "Then let's try not to screw it up."

Ferriello forced a smile. "Damn, and I almost forgot why I hate your guts."

The heavily armed SWAT teams rolled out first. Their job was to reach their positions without being seen, then signal the all-clear. They traveled in a single, unmarked van.

Sandor rode in Ferriello's sedan, leaving a couple of minutes later. Four plainclothes officers trailed them in two other cars for street-level backup. Those four, Ferriello, and Sandor were issued Kevlar bulletproof vests, which they now wore under their shirts.

Several uninformed officers remained in the conference room to monitor communications.

It was not long before the SWAT team leader radioed that they were in place.

Ferriello, who had been sitting three blocks from their destination, pulled out and made the turn onto Brighton Beach Avenue. He parked and led Sandor to the now familiar entrance to Little Siberia.

The two beefy types at the front door were the same pair they had met just a few nights before.

"Hello boys," Sandor greeted them as he and Ferriello reached the top of the short staircase. "Remember us?"

One of the two large skinheads began to say something, but Ferriello was not in the mood, not tonight. "Stand down, asshole," he told the bouncer.

"Wow," Sandor whispered as they walked through the door and then past the red velvet curtains that led to the bar, "you on some sort of adrenaline high?" When Ferriello grunted his response, Sandor warned him, "Take it easy partner. We may have a long night ahead."

Ivan was already on his way across the room, obviously having been given a heads-up from his men out front. He was scowling at Sandor by the time his long strides got him there.

"I owe you," he snarled.

Before Sandor was able to offer his view of their relationship, Ferriello reached in his pocket and pulled out the search warrant. "This is only going one of two ways, Ivan, easy or hard. This warrant says I can do basically whatever the hell I want here tonight and believe me, I've got the manpower to do it." Ferriello kept his voice down.

For the moment, he wanted this to stay a three-man discussion. "You follow?"

Ivan gave up the eye-lock with Sandor and turned to the lieutenant, but he did not answer, he only blinked.

"I don't need to break up your bar, ruin your business, and haul you and all your weight-lifting friends into lockup, but I will if I have to. You paying attention here?"

"What do you want?"

"We know where Vaknin's office is. Mr. Sandor was a guest there the other night, as you may recall. You're going to take us there to see Vaknin and we're all going to sit down and talk. Right now."

"Vaknin is not here," the big man told them with obvious satisfaction. "You have wasted your time."

"I don't think so," Sandor said. "The warrant gives us access to the entire premises, with or without your boss at home. We'll just pay his private room a visit."

"I do not have the code or the key," Ivan told them, another apparent triumph.

Sandor shook his head and then smiled in that way he knew could really irritate people. "I don't want to get off on the wrong foot with you again, Ivan, but I think you may be lying to us. So here's how we'll do this. You've got sixty seconds to take us to the office because, if you don't, twenty cops are going to bust in here with everything from battering rams to plastic explosives and by the time we get done, this place will be a wasteland and you'll be doing twenty years in a federal penitentiary for kidnapping a federal agent." When Ivan responded with a blank look Sandor said, "That's right, remember the other night when you tied me up and threw me in the basement?" Sandor paused. "That look you're giving me, is it indigestion or a language problem?"

"We are not done, you and I."

"Maybe not. Meanwhile, it's just like Lieutenant Ferriello said, this can only go one of two ways. So what is it going to be, door number one or door number two?"

CHAPTER EIGHTY

WASHINGTON HEIGHTS, NEW YORK CITY

MIGUEL LASCO HAD received word. Everything was in place for tomorrow.

He was with three of the men in his inner circle, looking over the cars they had parked on the upper floor of a multistory indoor garage on Payson Avenue. Since the economic decline in this area, it had become an underused building. It was on the selling block various times, offered as a potential warehouse, a teardown for apartments or offices, or even for use in its current configuration. There were no takers. No one was going to demolish this old brick structure and invest in new residential or commercial construction, not at this location in this neighborhood. It remained a garage, barely generating enough revenue to pay the real estate taxes and throw off a few dollars to the elderly man in Florida who owned it.

This week, however, the upper floor was chock-a-block with stolen cars, each of which had a new license plate attached, some expired, some exchanged from other cars, enough of a disguise to allow the limited use to which these automobiles would be put in the morning.

"We have all we need then," Lasco was saying.

"Yes, with the cars the other men already have, there are plenty."

"Good."

For a moment none of the four men spoke. Then Eduardo, his closest confidant, said what all of them were thinking. "We have done a great deal of work on faith. We have involved many young men. Some may not live through tomorrow. We have been given promises and we have made preparations. Now we must arrange the most dangerous part, rigging the cars and making them ready. So where is the money? And where are the drugs?"

Miguel responded with a somber look. "I have to make a couple of calls. Give me a few minutes."

CHAPTER EIGHTY-ONE

BRIGHTON BEACH, BROOKLYN

Ivan chose the easy path, at least for now. He led Sandor and Ferriello across the floor, unlocked the panel door by punching a code into the keypad, then took them upstairs to Vaknin's private office.

It appeared Ivan had been telling the truth. Vaknin was nowhere to be found.

Ferriello told Ivan to have a seat. Sandor drew his Walther and aimed it at the Russian's head as the narcotics detective handcuffed Ivan to the chair.

"This is false arrest," the man protested.

"Write the Kremlin," Sandor suggested, then relieved Ivan of the Glock in his shoulder holster. "Now, where is Vaknin hiding?"

"I don't have to tell you anything. Your warrant only gives you the right to look, it does not require me to talk." He managed another of his defiant looks, which were starting to get on Sandor's nerves. "I will say nothing more. I want a lawyer."

"Of course you do," Sandor said, giving him a pat on the head. Then he turned to Ferriello. "The team leader would let you know if they saw anyone leaving?"

"Absolutely."

"Including the back exit I used the other night?"

"Of course."

"Do me a favor, check with them anyway while I return this call to D.C."

As Ferriello radioed SWAT command to confirm that there had

been no sign of Vaknin coming or going, Sandor phoned Raabe for an update.

"I was just calling you."

"So I saw," Sandor told him. "I'm in the middle of something here. What gives?"

"We've identified a call from the Heights."

Sandor turned his back to Ivan and walked to the corner of Vaknin's office. "Go ahead."

"There's suddenly very little communication back and forth, as if everyone was ordered to go radio silent."

"But you said you heard something."

"There was a short call from a disposable cell somewhere in upper Manhattan—get this—to an airborne cell."

"Airborne as on an airplane?"

"We triangulated the coordinates. Somewhere over the Atlantic, east of South Carolina."

"Can FAA identify the flight?"

"Negative. Too much air traffic, no way to establish altitude or vector. As I say, it was a short call."

"Any way to tell if it's commercial or private?"

"No way to be sure, but our guess is private. The call was incoming, so it couldn't be made to one of those old credit card phones on the plane. And receiving a call on a commercial flight is a tricky business."

"Unless you have a satellite phone and duck into the men's room with it."

"Possible but not likely."

"Tell me about the call."

"The discussion was in Spanish. There were no greetings, no names. The caller wanted to know if everything was on schedule. Guy on the other end was clearly not happy, said the number was for emergencies only. Said everything was on schedule, not to call again until contact was made. The caller pushed the issue, said people were getting nervous that the package had not arrived. He was told to assure everyone that everything was on schedule."

"He repeated that phrase?"

"He did."

"What else?"

"Nothing. That was it."

"That really was a short call. What about voice ID? Or pinpointing the caller's location?"

Raabe reported what they had so far. The audio was full of static. Even after the recording was enhanced, voice recognition was useless. The best they could do on the source of the call was someplace in Washington Heights, toward the west side. "But there was a second call from the same number, immediately after that one. To a cell somewhere in the South Bronx."

"Go on."

"This conversation was in English. Same caller, telling someone that everything was on schedule. The guy on the other end said, 'Allah be praised,' and hung up."

"That was the entire conversation?"

"That was it."

"I take it you have more."

"Oh yeah. Did some cross-checking and DHS weighed in. They've been keeping an eye on a mosque in the South Bronx with suspected Al Qaeda connections. Right near the site where that call was received. The group has been quiet, so DHS has been monitoring without making contact."

"I would say it's time to make contact."

"I'm on it," Raabe said and hung up.

Sandor returned his attention to Ferriello, who was busy going through papers in Vaknin's desk. "The hell with that," Sandor said, "you can be sure he didn't leave anything in writing that'll help. I'll grab his laptop, you take Ivan, and let's get the hell out of here."

"What about finding Vaknin?"

"Somehow he knew we were coming for him. It's written all over this goon's ugly puss. Leave your people in place to wait for him, we've got other work to do right now."

They left Little Siberia the way they came in, right through the main room. Ferriello went first, followed by Ivan with his hands cuffed behind his back, and Sandor trailing. Sandor wanted to make a show of their departure in the hope that another of Vaknin's lieutenants would call to tell his boss the police were gone.

As soon as they reached Ferriello's car, the narcotics detective radioed the SWAT commander to advise what they were up to and to have the teams hold their positions in the hope Vaknin would appear. Then Sandor shoved Ivan in the backseat of the sedan and climbed in after him.

Back at the precinct they threw the Russian in lockup and returned to the war room. Sandor laid out everything he had learned from Raabe.

"So," he concluded, "we're fighting this on two fronts with almost no time left. The biological weapons are on their way, and may be coming by air. The drugs are still likely to be arriving by sea. But either or both of those assumptions could be wrong."

The captain in charge of this detail thanked Sandor for the briefing, then said, "You realize that most of this is way beyond our authority."

"I do. The task force in D.C. has been in contact with the local FBI, DEA, and DHS offices. I just wanted you to be up to speed, especially with all the help the lieutenant has provided." He nodded in Ferriello's direction. "I'll keep your unit advised captain, and I would appreciate any word you get on Vaknin. He may know more about what's going on than the last time I spoke with him."

"We'll keep the SWAT team in place for the next few hours. If he doesn't show we'll shut his operation and that may flush him out."

Sandor nodded. "Good. Now I've got to head to Federal Plaza to see what the task force has drummed up."

"Not without me, you're not," Ferriello said as he got to his feet.

Sandor looked to the captain.

"Already approved," the silver-haired officer told him. "Bobby will be our on-site liaison. If that's all right with your department."

"Right now we can use all the help we can get."

CHAPTER EIGHTY-TWO

STEWART AIRPORT, NEWBURGH, NEW YORK

JUST AS HE had assured Miguel Lasco, Adina was on schedule. His flight from Santo Domingo made a stopover in Wilmington International Airport in North Carolina to clear Customs and Immigration. The forged passports he procured for Alejandro, Jorge and himself easily passed muster—after all, they were created by the Venezuelan government. A thorough inspection of the plane disclosed nothing improper—neither the cases of anthrax nor the cash from Mateo was found inside the specially constructed bins along the interior of the plane's fuselage. The three well-dressed visitors from the Dominican Republic were sent on their way without any untoward delay.

The United States is a huge country, Adina reminded himself, with too many harbors, too many airports, and too many miles of border to effectively monitor every unwanted activity. For nations as well as people, size can create both strength and vulnerability.

The jet was soon approaching Stewart Airport, north of Westchester County in New York state. Adina realized the security would be tight at the area's major airports—LaGuardia, JFK, and Newark. Smaller venues nearer the city, such as White Plains and Teterboro, received many private and charter flights, but they would also be closely watched. A couple of hours north of midtown Manhattan, Stewart provided the perfect point of entry.

While on the ground in Wilmington, Adina received word that Mateo had been captured and turned by the *federales,* and was now cooperating with the American DEA. There was a concern the cocaine shipment was now in serious jeopardy. However that played out, Adina was especially pleased to have received the down payment provided in Mendez. There might even be a collateral benefit from the Mexican's betrayal, since he would cause the authorities to focus on the cargo ship heading up the eastern seaboard rather than the journey Adina had undertaken with the anthrax already in hand. Mateo knew nothing of the Venezuelan's primary objectives or the fact that the anthrax had been removed from the cargo container, so he had nothing to tell them about that.

Meanwhile, Adina decided to make some minor modifications to his plans. The new details were put in place and he was about to discuss them with his lieutenants when the pilot came from the cockpit and joined them in the main cabin.

"Gentlemen, we'll be reaching the airport soon and you will need to put on your seat belts and make yourselves comfortable for landing."

When the young man lingered, Adina asked, "Is there something else?"

"Yes sir, there is. As you know this is the fourth leg of our trip in the past two days. Our time in the air has already exceeded our permitted flight time."

Adina responded with a knowing smile. "There are two of you up there. Don't you take turns getting some rest?"

"Of course, sir, but as a two-man crew there are certain limitations."

Adina, maintaining his thin-lipped smile, asked, "Is there a point to this? You aren't suggesting my men come up front and land the plane, are you?"

Alejandro and Jorge gave their best impression of laughter and even the pilot smiled.

"No sir. I was just wondering where we might be going from here. More important, when you expect to leave." Adina's smile vanished as he stared at the young man. The pilot broke the uncomfortable silence by saying, "I've flown this sort of itinerary for, uh, dignitaries before. I just find it's helpful to get some idea of the timing."

"I see," Adina replied, his tone sounding now like a concerned parent. "You have no need to worry, you'll have all night to rest up. We will be leaving around dawn."

"Thank you."

As the pilot turned to walk away, Adina added, "You and your colleague will be properly rewarded for your tireless effort."

The pilot stopped and looked back. "Well thank you, sir," he said. Then he disappeared behind the closed door of the cockpit to share the good news.

It was dark when they landed, which was for the best. As the crew went about their business, checking in at the private air terminal and making plans for where they would sleep that night, Alejandro and Jorge picked up the two rental cars they had reserved. When they returned, with the plane to themselves, Adina watched as his lieutenants opened the storage compartments, pulled out the false panels, and removed the hard plastic suitcases containing the anthrax.

The tarmac was quiet as they quickly placed the six cases in the trunk of one of the sedans, locked the car, then joined Adina again inside the jet.

"You have more than enough time to reach the hotel, no need to speed or draw attention to yourselves." They nodded. "As soon as I have word from you that you are in place, I will initiate the signal to have them send their men to your room. They will have the detonation devices, but I want the two of you to ensure they are securely fitted to each of the units before you leave."

"Of course," Alejandro said.

"Once you are comfortable they know what to do you will return here, but no earlier than sunrise. We do not want to encourage any unnecessary questioning by the locals. We will aim for a takeoff at seven, but as long as we are in the air by seven thirty we will be fine."

"Understood."

They then took some time to review the various signals they had arranged, so that no telephone discussions would be required unless an emergency arose.

"I will meet with this mercenary Lasco, then I will be at the motel." The two men nodded, then they all stood and Adina shook hands with each of them. "Tomorrow we will enjoy a great victory," he told them, then sent them on their way.

CHAPTER EIGHTY-THREE

FEDERAL PLAZA, NEW YORK CITY

SANDOR AND FERRIELLO took their cars to the CIA field office in downtown Manhattan. After checking in with the assistant director in charge and saying a quick hello to a couple of agents Sandor knew, they were shown to a small conference room where they phoned Raabe on a secure line.

"Please tell me you have something new."

"We do, but it doesn't seem to fit," Raabe said.

"Go ahead."

"The group at NCTC has gone back, reviewing earlier phone calls, analyzing the discussions. There's an incredible amount of chatter about the need for cars."

"Cars?"

"Over a hundred of them in one conversation."

"Why would they need all those cars to spread anthrax?"

"That's what I mean," Raabe said. "It doesn't fit. If you're going to spread anthrax, you do it in some sort of confined space. Indoors is obviously the ideal environment, but it could work in a stadium or some other outdoor location with a concentration of people."

"Not the best choice, though. A gust of wind can clear the stuff out before it does maximum damage."

"Exactly. So why would Adina arrange for a hundred cars? Or more?"

Sandor thought it over. "Let's assume one or more of them is going to be the means of delivering the anthrax. What if the rest of them are being used as decoys? This way, if we get too close, he'll have all the cars scatter, making it impossible for us to know which one is carrying the goods."

"No way. I mean, if he had a hundred identical cars with identical license plates, maybe I could buy that. But there's nothing in these transcripts to indicate they need a particular model or type of vehicle."

Sandor nodded, then looked to the police detective. "I'm putting you on speaker," he told Raabe. "Bobby Ferriello from the NYPD is here." Then Sandor asked what Byrnes thought about this.

"He's stumped too. Thinks it sounds more like a carjacking ring than a plot by Adina."

"But there were calls about this back and forth to Venezuela."

"Until recently."

"And a call today to a private plane."

"Right."

Sandor nodded. "This is classic Adina. He's got a secondary plan, maybe even something to cover the first. Or the other way around. Do we have anything at all on the location of all these cars?"

"Not yet. As I told you, the phone calls came from Washington Heights. We managed to pinpoint one of the early calls to a coffee shop on 207th Street. Not very helpful. The best guess here is that they're somewhere in that neighborhood, but keep in mind they might not even all be parked in one place. The discussions were vague, but the message was that they need vehicles. They may be coming from all different directions."

"Damn."

"You said it, brother."

"What about the lead in the South Bronx?"

"The DHS is on it. As I told you, they've been keeping an eye on that mosque."

"Anything interesting going on there?"

"I was coming to that. They had a gathering of their congregation tonight, a closed-door session. Supposed to be a discussion about improving multi-cultural relationships in the community."

"Don't tell me when the meeting broke they went running to a local parking lot and jumped into a hundred cars."

"No, wise-ass, but I did get word that six of them left the place around twenty minutes ago and headed for the subway."

"What's so unusual about that?"

"Spotter said they appeared to be a bit nervous, heads on a swivel, that sort of thing."

"We having them tailed?"

"DHS has people on it and your friends at the FBI have been notified."

"The DD's task force was told?"

"Everyone's up to speed. This may be nothing more than six guys going to town for the evening, but our leads are thin so we're tracking everything."

"Descriptions?"

"Six men, all look to be in their twenties or thirties. Two black, four appear to be Middle Eastern. Casual dress. No indication they're armed."

"Of course not. If they're involved in anything here, then they're on their way to make a pickup, not a delivery." Sandor turned to Ferriello. "Any thoughts from an experienced street cop?"

Ferriello hesitated. "Six suicide bombers on their way to be fitted up?"

"It's a stretch, but I have a sick feeling in my stomach telling me the same thing."

"Maybe not, though," the detective said. "Get back to the cars for a second. They would make sense if they're using them to split up a large delivery of narcotics in the next couple of days. The shipment we're after may be more than a ton of product. Once it gets here, spreading the risk would be smart."

Sandor, who had been leaning over the speakerphone in the middle of the conference table, decided to have a seat. "Maybe," he said. "But then you've got a hundred runners chasing around town with millions of dollars of coke. Not sure that would sit too well with the Russkis in Brighton Beach."

"Good point," Ferriello admitted.

"So how do the boys from the mosque fit in?"

"Hold on," Raabe said. They listened to him have a brief discussion with someone in the background, then he returned to the phone. "Our six friends just took the number-four train into Manhattan."

"We're already in Manhattan. I'm heading for the car; let me know when you find out where they get off."

"Will do," Raabe said and hung up.

Sandor hit the OFF button on the circular speakerphone, then looked up at Ferriello. "It may be a nothing lead."

Ferriello nodded.

"Maybe it's time for you to get back to Brooklyn."

The policeman shook his head. "You heard my captain. You're stuck with me."

"Then we have two serious issues you need to understand. First, my agency has no jurisdiction here. Second, we're dealing with terrorists, and I'm not interested in taking prisoners."

"We've met before," Ferriello reminded him. "And I might be helpful to you, since I do have jurisdiction."

"You're already way out on a limb. Staying there is not likely to be a wise career move."

The detective laughed. "Are you kidding me or what?"

They looked at each other for a moment without speaking. Then Sandor said, "All right, don't say I didn't warn you."

"I won't."

Sandor stood up. "Then let's go."

CHAPTER EIGHTY-FOUR

NEW YORK

ALEJANDRO AND JORGE made the drive into Manhattan without incident. At this time of night there was not much traffic heading south, and both had been to New York before so they had no trouble finding the hotel in Times Square.

The building was enormous, rising more than fifty stories above Broadway, with a huge covered parking facility in the center. The north side of the building was connected to a theater featuring live performances. To the south, the building featured a large, multilevel movie complex.

Alejandro pulled up to the sign in the midst of the reception area that said "Stop Here," where he was immediately greeted by an African-American valet. Alejandro gave the name on his bogus passport, the name in which their reservation had been made. Then he and Jorge climbed out of the rented sedan.

"Will you be staying with us long?" the pleasant young man asked as he jotted the license plate number on the parking receipt.

"Three nights," Alejandro said, knowing that he would be gone in just a few hours.

"It'll be a pleasure to have you here. Need help with your luggage?"

There was no way around this, as Adina had warned them. They should not be juggling six thirty-pound cases, not without drawing unwanted attention to themselves. "Yes, that would be helpful," Alejandro said, then reached inside the car and hit the button that popped the trunk open.

The valet grabbed one of the brass trollys and wheeled it to the rear of the car. "Cool luggage," he said.

Jorge was standing beside him to oversee the transfer of the hard plastic suitcases. "Yes," he said, forcing the friendliest tone he could manage. "They hold up very well when the airport baggage handlers start tossing things around."

The young black man nodded. "Six, huh? Don't they whack you for extra bag charges? You oughta just get yourselves a couple of big ones."

"Good idea," Jorge said, then watched as the cases were placed on the trolley.

"I'll check in," Alejandro said. "You can stay with the luggage."

Jorge nodded.

"Don't worry," the valet said with a wide grin, "I got your stuff covered."

"It's not you we're worried about," Alejandro told him. "This is New York, right?"

The young man laughed, then led them to the sliding electric doors.

"By the way," Alejandro said, "we'll be needing the car again in a couple of hours. Just so it doesn't get buried in your parking lot." He held out a twenty-dollar bill.

"Like I said," the valet told him as he made the money disappear with the dexterity of a pickpocket, "I've got you covered."

————

As Alejandro was checking in at the front desk of their midtown hotel, Adina was using the navigation system in his rented car to find his way to meet Miguel Lasco. His destination was a restaurant, just off Interstate 684 in Westchester County, located in what appeared to be a large old house that had once been the main residence of a country estate. He pulled into the parking lot, turned off the car, and waited. There had been no indication he was followed, but taking an extra minute or two was the sensible move.

Convinced he was safe, he got out, took hold of the attaché case he had brought with him, climbed up the steps to the veranda, and entered the front door.

Lasco had no idea what Adina looked like, but Adina had a description of the small, dark-skinned man. He spotted him seated in a booth, just off the bar area.

"I see my friend there," Adina told the hostess who was standing in the small foyer, then walked past her.

As Adina approached, Lasco started to get to his feet. Adina sat him back down with a firm look and an almost imperceptible shake of his head. When he reached the table he laid the case on the bench and slid in behind it.

"It is a great honor to meet you," Lasco said in a hushed voice.

Adina frowned. "It is always sunny in Caracas."

"Ah yes," Lasco replied with a look that said he had forgotten himself. Then he gave the required response. "Except when the clouds come from the north."

"Good. You are Lasco. My name need not be spoken."

"Of course. I was not sure you would come yourself."

"I believe you are due that respect," Adina lied. He would have preferred not to have come to the United States at all, but changing circumstances required the involvement of both him and his men to ensure the success of this operation. He was frankly disgusted at the notion of playing the role of bag man to this greedy little Venezuelan, but with Alejandro and Jorge in the city he had no other option.

"Thank you," Lasco said.

A waitress appeared and Adina requested a glass of their best red wine. Lasco already had a beer in front of him.

"Will you be needing menus?"

Adina had no interest in dining with Lasco, but he suddenly realized he had not eaten all day. "Give us a few minutes," he replied, sending her off for the wine.

"Things are in place," Lasco said. "Everyone is ready."

"I should hope so," Adina said as he gently patted the attaché beside him. It contained a portion of the cash given to him by Mateo. "This mission is well planned and well funded."

Lasco did his best not to look in the direction of the case. "Our friends in the Bronx are also prepared." He hesitated before adding,

"We were surprised to hear that some of them will be meeting with your men tonight."

Adina concealed his anger. Lasco had no need to know men were being sent from the mosque in the South Bronx to meet with Alejandro and Jorge. Ever the master of compartmentalization, there was no need for Lasco or any of his people to be told about the anthrax attack. They had a different task. Providing them information beyond that would only create unnecessary danger. "There are various matters to be addressed tonight. Nothing is being kept from you that would affect your role."

Now Lasco could not resist peeking at the attaché.

"Nor is your role being diminished in any way, if that is your concern."

Lasco's face said there were other concerns. "These couriers from the mosque, I have been told they are carrying detonation devices."

"They are," Adina reluctantly admitted. Another breach in the chain of communication. "Why should that be a concern for you or your people?"

Lasco drew a deep breath. "Please be assured that our respect for you is of the highest order. We have taken risks and will be taking even greater risks, as you know. But our young men," he continued, his voice even quieter now, "they are not suicide bombers."

"Please," Adina said with some alarm as he quickly looked around them, "be careful."

"My apologies." Lasco lowered his voice to a whisper. "All I am trying to say is that we have designed an operation from which all of us should walk away unscathed. The last-minute introduction of detonators, for purposes that have not been shared with us, is a matter of grave concern to the members of my inner circle."

Adina sat back against the hard bench. The assault to be carried out by Lasco involved numerous automobiles, some of which had been rigged with combustibles that would only be triggered once his drivers were safely distanced from the point of attack. He could understand why the sudden appearance of detonators, especially in the hands of extremists, was troublesome. Perhaps Lasco's men feared they were to be made human sacrifices as the final stages of this terrorist strike were played out.

Adina actually began laughing just as the waitress brought his wine and placed two menus on the table.

Interrupting what she thought to be a jovial exchange between two friends, she said, "We have some specials, if you'd like to hear them now."

"Later," Adina said as he waved her away, then turned back to his companion. "I see why you are worried, I do, but be assured you have nothing to concern yourself about. The detonators are intended for another target entirely." He was not about to divulge his plans for the six Al Qaeda operatives or the use of those timers with the cases of toxin.

It was evident that Lasco was not satisfied. "I take it you are not prepared to tell me about this other phase of your operation."

Adina looked him squarely in the eyes, quickly gauging the impact of either refusing the man's request or granting it. He said, "I trust you, and you must trust me. These items have nothing whatever to do with your objectives." Now it was his turn to lower his voice. "Once you have accomplished what you set out to do, I have men setting up these devices within the financial district," he lied. "To add to the destruction."

Lasco nodded, wanting to believe him. "The financial district," he repeated.

"Don't you see, once your men have done their job, that area will be especially vulnerable. We could not bring those sorts of devices through Customs, so we enlisted the aid of our friends in the Bronx." As Lasco mulled it over, Adina added, "I entrust this information to you and you alone. For the security of my men, it would be best if you did not tell anyone else."

"Of course. You have my word."

Adina tried to appear relieved at having put Lasco's mind at ease. What Lasco was thinking, however, was something else entirely.

"Now let us talk about something pleasant. You have something for me," Adina said as he gestured at the paper bag beside Lasco. "And I have your money."

CHAPTER EIGHTY-FIVE

NEW YORK

Timur Vaknin received word from his bouncers that it was safe to return to his nightclub. The authorities had made their move, as expected. Ferriello had arrived in the company of that annoying federal agent Sandor, this time brandishing a search warrant. After rummaging around his private office, they took Ivan in handcuffs and left.

Sudakov was an imbecile, he grumbled to himself as his driver turned onto the street behind the old building that housed Little Siberia. What sort of fool would endanger a hugely profitable business by becoming involved with the likes of Rafael Cabello? Did Sudakov really believe that the infamous Adina had abandoned terrorism for narcotics smuggling? What a jackass.

Now Vaknin and his club were being targeted by every federal authority from the FBI to the DHS. His organization and their operations had been placed under a microscope as never before.

Sudakov, you stupid bastard.

The car came to a stop by the alley that led to the basement entrance. Vaknin needed to get to his office to see what had been taken and, perhaps more important, what remained. Not even Ivan knew of the existence of the safe he had installed beneath the floor. Hopefully that was intact, along with all the cash he kept there.

Taking the driver with him he strode quickly down the long, dark passage, removing the key from his pocket as he approached the rear door to the building.

———

From the rooftop across the street, the lookout for the third SWAT team spotted him. "We have visual confirmation," the officer advised into his microphone.

"Is it Vaknin?" the team leader asked.

"That would be affirmative. Looks just like his picture. Walking toward the rear entrance with one other man."

"Let's move out," the leader ordered.

Within moments Ferriello's backup team, which had been parked down the street, was on foot with guns drawn, circling to the back of the building. The nearest SWAT team raced down from their third-floor rooftop for backup.

The four men from NYPD converged on the Russian just as he was putting his key in the basement door.

"Don't make another move, Vaknin," the lead officer said. "You're coming with us."

———

Sandor chose Ferriello's car for their transportation, just in case they needed to get through any sort of secure area that became cordoned off. Even though it was unmarked, Ferriello's car was credentialed. Trying to get through in Sandor's old Land Rover would have wasted time.

They were sitting curbside in Foley Square, waiting for more information on the whereabouts of the six men from the South Bronx. Sandor looked around at the streetlamp-lit plaza, where any number of vans and trucks were parked. The scene provoked the thought that regularly haunted him—how do you protect a country as large and trusting and open-armed as the United States of America when any sick bastard can load a vehicle with explosives or biological weapons or even containers of gasoline, and then detonate it to murder and maim innocent people?

"It's a sick world," he said more to himself than to Ferriello.

"Tell me about it," the policeman agreed.

Then Craig Raabe called.

"Talk to me."

"The six suspects exited the subway at Times Square," Raabe told him. "Crowded this time of night, so it's been easy for the boys from DHS to keep tabs. They followed them directly to a hotel on Broadway." He recited the name and address.

"That's good work," Sandor said. "Where are they now?"

"In the lobby. Just got word one of them is on the house phone."

"We're on our way." He gave Ferriello the address and the detective threw the car in gear and pulled away.

"I've got more," Raabe said. "A possible lead on Adina."

"Go."

"Hold on, the DD is joining us for this. Also patching in Bebon from the FBI."

After a short pause, Sandor could hear a door closing in the background, then Byrnes was on the call with them. "You there Dick?" Byrnes asked the man from the Bureau.

"I'm on," Bebon said.

"Go ahead," the DD told Raabe.

"We got a hit from the CBP. They've been helping us with the airports, checking out private flights. We just got word that three men with passports from the Dominican Republic landed in a Citation at Wilmington this afternoon."

"Wilmington as in North Carolina?" Sandor asked.

"Check. The passengers and crew went through Customs without a hitch. Flew on to Stewart Airport, up in Newburgh. We confirmed arrival about four hours ago."

"Photos? Descriptions?"

"Hispanics. One middle-aged guy and two young bucks. We have photos, just had them circulated to everyone. You'll get them on your phone."

"No one's had a picture of Adina for more than ten years," Sandor reminded them. "For all we know he's had plastic surgery."

"Listen up," Raabe said. "There was nothing suspicious about this flight, the crew, or the passengers. Nothing unusual found on the plane. But try this one on for size. Once we had the intel, we brought in State. One of our big boys contacted his opposite number in Santo

Domingo. Grabbed some mucky-muck away from dinner and had him run down the three names on their passports."

"Don't tell me. All phony?"

"Bingo. But the folks in Wilmington insist the passports were in order."

"Meaning they could have been created by someone on the inside."

"Tinkers to Evers to Chance," Raabe said. "Maybe someone in Santo Domingo owed someone in Caracas a favor, and Adina needed an ID that would get him through Immigration."

"Forgeries straight from the source. And the in-flight phone call that was intercepted . . ."

"Was to an airplane we fixed as someplace off the coast of South Carolina."

"So the timing fits?"

"Like a glove. The call was made less than an hour before this Citation touched down in Wilmington."

As Ferriello sped north on Centre Street he was getting the gist of this new intel. "Where are these three now?" he asked.

Raabe heard the question. "According to some guy working in the private terminal at Stewart, they picked up two rental cars and took off about three hours ago. The older man stuck around for a while, then left by himself. The other two left together shortly after they touched down."

"I don't want to rely on 'some guy,'" Sandor said. "Sir, if this is Adina," he said to the DD, "there's no one in that airport that'll be safe if he suspects we're onto him."

"I have a team on the way there now," Bebon told them.

"Sir, with all respect, when your men approach they'll need to keep an extremely low profile until we have more information. That sonuvabitch can smell trouble from a mile off."

"Understood," Bebon agreed.

"I assume the jet is still there," Byrnes said.

"Correct," Raabe told them.

"Any flight plan filed for a departure?"

"None," Raabe said. "But the guy inside the terminal said the crew mentioned they expected to leave in the morning."

"How big is the crew?"

"Two men."

"Get me the names, I'll have them checked out," Bebon said. "Find out if they're legit or part of Adina's team."

Sandor broke in again. "We've got to let the tower know that plane should not be permitted to take off under any circumstances. Use whatever excuse they have to."

"Done," Bebon responded.

Sandor still didn't like the way things were playing out. "We need to lock the place down without Adina or his men getting a whiff of what we're doing. That's not going to be easy."

Before anyone could respond, Ferriello's phone buzzed. He connected the call, listened for a moment, then turned to Sandor. "They've got Vaknin," he said.

"Keep me posted on what goes on up there," Sandor said. "They've taken Vaknin into custody and I need to hear what he has to say."

"Get back to us right away," Byrnes said.

"We're getting close to the hotel. I'll report back."

CHAPTER EIGHTY-SIX

NEW YORK

REGARDLESS OF THE fact that Manhattan is the world's most famous island, people tend to forget that it is, in fact, an island. It is joined to the outside world by four tunnels and sixteen bridges.

The Holland and Lincoln tunnels connect to New Jersey. The Brooklyn Battery Tunnel leads to Brooklyn, the Queens Midtown Tunnel to Queens.

The regal George Washington Bridge is the only over-water connection to New Jersey. Three bridges lead back and forth to Brooklyn: the eponymous Brooklyn Bridge, the Williamsburg Bridge, and the Manhattan Bridge. Only one leads directly to Queens, the 59th Street Bridge, with the Triboro Bridge connecting Manhattan with both Queens and the Bronx. Ten other bridges connect to the Bronx: the Henry Hudson, 225th Street, Alexander Hamilton, University Heights, 181st Street Washington, 145th Street, Macombs Dam, Willis Avenue, Madison Avenue, and the Third Avenue bridges.

This arrangement had long been a source of fascination for Rafael Cabello. There was obviously no airport on the island, only a couple of heliports, and a handful of water taxis and ferries. What if every one of those bridges and tunnels were suddenly and violently destroyed? Or temporarily obstructed? Where would people go, how would they escape? How would they react to the sense of isolation?

A thrilling rescue by water followed the destruction of the World Trade Center towers, but that was a unique situation, and the damage to those skyscrapers was confined to a limited area of Manhattan. If, however, every bridge and tunnel around the island were rendered impass-able in a coordinated strike, panic would reign as droves of New Yorkers would instinctively flee toward the subway and train systems. They would crowd into terminals, flood stairwells, and squeeze into subway stations.

Which would render them absolutely vulnerable to a biological attack.

That was the genius of Adina's plan, inspired by Hurricane Sandy, when he saw the chaos after some of Manhattan's bridges and tunnels were closed. He would now shut them *all*, a first devastating wave of terror that would set the stage for a second, even more deadly assault.

He mulled over the details once more as he sat alone, enjoying a relaxed dinner. Miguel Lasco had gone on his way with his money in hand and the assurance that his share of the cocaine would be deliv-ered in just a few days. The important thing, Adina reminded him, was to successfully implement the first phase of this operation.

Lasco admitted that he was still worried about the involvement of this group from the Bronx, but Adina did what he could to allay those concerns. He explained again they had nothing to do with the scheduled assault on the bridges and tunnels, which was the truth.

Finishing his main course, Adina had a look down at the paper bag Lasco left with him. It contained the loaded revolver and additional ammunition he requested. Ironically, Adina was not personally vio-lent. He actually found physical altercations repugnant. Nevertheless, he felt an unmistakable sense of relief knowing that he had a weapon available—just in case he needed it.

When his cell phone vibrated, Adina pulled it from his pocket and had a look. It was Alejandro, leaving the signal that confirmed he and Jorge were in their hotel room, all six cases in hand.

Adina nodded to himself, certain that all the pieces were in place. He called the waitress over and ordered dessert.

———

Before tonight Lasco knew Adina only by reputation. Now that he had met the man he was certain one part of his legend was true—Rafael Cabello was a very dangerous man. It was in his face, the way he moved, his cool reserve. And in those narrow, green, snakelike eyes.

Lasco was driving south on I-684, his only companion the attaché case Adina had given him, which contained more money than he had ever seen in his life. He did not dare open it in the restaurant, not with Adina watching. Outside, as soon as he got in the car, he had a quick look at the carefully prepared stacks of one-hundred-dollar bills.

Yet regardless of the money, he was not happy with news of detonators being supplied by those lunatics from the Bronx. Truth being told, he was never pleased about their involvement. When he was first approached by Adina's emissary he was assured of having the preeminent position in coordinating and executing this attack. It was not until weeks later that he was informed of the *jihadists* and how they would be playing a secondary role. He never trusted them—who in his right mind would trust a religious extremist?—but for so long as he felt he was in charge he assumed he could handle them. Contact with their leader was limited, which was both a matter of caution and consistent with the intended level of their participation.

Now, in the face of what he had learned, he knew that if the source of these funds had been anyone else he might consider a last-minute change in plans. But it was Adina, and so that was impossible.

Early this morning his men were going to drive cars and vans and trucks to their appointed spots on every bridge and tunnel into and out of Manhattan. Once there they would slow down and then arrange a series of intentional collisions across every lane, three cars deep, bringing all traffic in both directions to a complete standstill.

The drivers of those vehicles would then leave their wrecks and jump into the lead cars that would stay ahead of these crashes, providing their means of escape. Before heading off, they would ignite strips leading to the trunks and cargo bays of their smashed vehicles, all of which were filled with gasoline and other explosive materials. The fuses were primitive, no high-tech items required. It would reduce the risks of detection or something going wrong. They would be set off, leaving behind them a fiery wall of destruction.

News of the detonators was a game-changer. Why were they needed? Was this some sort of double-cross?

His people saw themselves as freedom fighters, adversaries of the

American capitalist machine, enemies of the privileged elite. They were most definitely not suicide bombers. That insanity was left to deranged zealots who believed their greater reward would come in heaven.

Lasco had no specifics on these devices. Were they timers, radio activated, IFR? What were they really going to be used for? Lasco did not believe for a moment the story about explosions in the financial district. Adina had a plan he was not sharing. Did he intend to remotely ignite the vehicles his men were driving before they could make it safely away?

That possibility turned his stomach inside out. He knew Adina had lied to him, or was at least withholding the truth. Which left him with an agonizing choice. Defying the man seemed absolutely out of the question, but sending all these young men to their deaths seemed equally impossible. Should he share his fears with the other men who had organized this with him? Or should he just move forward, warning them all to remain alert?

Lasco drove on through the night, not sure of what he would do when he returned to the garage in Washington Heights, but certain that he now understood what it meant to shake hands with the devil.

CHAPTER EIGHTY-SEVEN

NEW YORK

Ferriello continued to weave in and out of the uptown traffic on his way to Times Square. His cell phone was turned to the speaker mode as he and Sandor listened to news of Vaknin's capture.

"We brought him back to the precinct," the SWAT team leader explained, "but the feds want him at Federal Plaza. And fast."

"Where is he now?" Sandor asked.

"He's sitting in the captain's office. Won't say a thing, already demanding to see a lawyer."

"Naturally. I assume you explained that he's not going to be allowed to talk with anyone but us as long as we're facing a credible terrorist threat."

"We certainly did. By the way, we took his driver too, or whoever he is. Tossed him in a holding cell."

"Not anywhere near his pal Ivan I hope."

"Hey Sandor, we may not be federal agents, but we didn't just fall off the back of a potato truck."

"Sorry, no offense intended."

"Yeah."

"Just a lot of intel coming at us all at once."

"Always the way, right?"

"Unfortunately," Sandor said. "How would you guys feel about my speaking with Vaknin?"

The SWAT team leader chuckled. "Ferriello told me about you and Vaknin. Fast friends?"

"Something like that."

"Hang on, I'll clear it with the captain. And Sandor."

"Yes?"

"FYI, we'll have to tape the call."

"Got it."

A couple of minutes later they were connected to Vaknin, who was told that Sandor and Ferriello were on the line and that the conversation was being recorded. The first thing the Russian said was "I still have a headache from where you hit me."

"Hey pal, my wrists and ankles are still bleeding from your plastic handcuffs. Just in case I decide to have you prosecuted for kidnapping a federal agent I've taken some nice photos of the cuts."

Vaknin grunted into the phone.

"We'll have plenty of time to compare bruises later. Right now I want you to tell me everything you know about what's going down tonight."

"You mean, other than the raid on my club and the police illegally arresting me and my employees."

"Yes, other than that."

"I don't know a thing," Vaknin said without hesitation.

"Look, whatever happens, your situation is going to turn from bad to really horrible if you withhold information. Don't be an idiot Vaknin, you're in the business of narcotics, not terrorism."

"I want to speak to my lawyer."

"You're not listening to me. We've got your boy Ivan in lockup. Once he found out this was about a terrorist attack he made a deal."

"Pizdet."

"So you say."

Vaknin huffed and puffed into the phone. The man definitely needed to stop smoking, Sandor noted yet again.

"We have your computer."

This time Vaknin answered with a loud snort. "So what? You going to arrest me for cybersex?"

"I'm going to hold you incommunicado until you tell me what you know about Adina's plans."

"You're not listening to me, Sandor. I know nothing about Rafael

Cabello or his plans, it has nothing to do with me. How much clearer can I be than that?"

"You reached out to Ronny Sudakov again. What did he tell you this time?"

"You tapped my phones?"

"Let's just say a little birdie told me."

"Rubbish. If you listened to the conversation you already know what that moron said."

"Indulge me."

There was silence, then Vaknin spoke up again. "He admits he became involved with Adina, but insists it was only business."

"The business of narcotics."

Vaknin did not respond.

"So, he was dealing with a known terrorist, but he claims terrorism was never on the agenda."

"So he claims."

"And you're also just a businessman, is that it?"

"I am not a terrorist."

"So *you* claim." Sandor looked to Ferriello, then said to Vaknin, "In the interest of saving your own hide, you don't have a thing to tell me about what's been planned?"

"If I knew I would make the deal, wouldn't I?"

Ferriello shot Sandor a look that said he didn't like the man but he believed him.

"All right," Sandor said with a nod, "enjoy the hospitality of the Brooklyn Narcotics Squad. We'll get back to you."

When he punched the END button he saw that Craig Raabe had sent him an email with images attached. They were the passport photos of the three men who had flown from Wilmington into Stewart Airport a few hours ago. He opened them, one at a time. The first two meant nothing—he had never seen Adina. But when he got to the third image he said, "Damn! I know this guy."

"Who is he?"

"A goon I saw in the jungle in Venezuela. He's one of Adina's henchmen."

CHAPTER EIGHTY-EIGHT

NEW YORK

Six young men from the South Bronx were seated in the suite booked by Alejandro and Jorge. The two Venezuelans remained standing. The hard plastic cases containing anthrax were lying on their sides on the large glass cocktail table. Beside them were the six devices these men had brought with them.

The detonators had been made for attachment to the base of the cases with a strong strip of adhesive that would bind the mechanism to the plastic. The suitcases each had four short, circular supports so, when the cases stood upright, the timers and explosive charges would not be visible.

Jorge was going about the business of securing the detonators in place as Alejandro reviewed their plans.

"The important thing is to switch the timer on only when you are certain no one is watching you. By the time you reach your destinations there will be a lot of activity in the streets, a lot of people running and a lot of police. You must make yourselves appear part of this panic, you understand?"

They all nodded and one of them said, "This has been explained to us in great detail."

"Good. It is still important to review things one more time."

Again, the six nodded as one.

"You should arrive at your designated locations before seven thirty this morning," Alejandro told them. "We are setting all the timers for five minutes. This is not much time, but we cannot afford to have the bags discovered before they are ignited. Once you switch them on you will probably have to fight through a crowd to get clear."

"We understand," another of them said.

"Two of you will be going to Grand Central, two to Penn Plaza, and two into the main Times Square subway station. You all have your assignments?"

They nodded.

"Each of you knows the best place to leave the cases?"

"We have been carefully instructed," the first man told him.

"Good." Alejandro thought carefully about the next statement. "You all understand that this is not a suicide mission. There is no reason any of you should stay behind when this poison is exploded into the air."

This time they did not nod. They began nervously looking from one to the other. The first man, who was apparently the senior member of the group, spoke up again.

"Our responsibility is to make sure that these explosives are ignited and the maximum possible damage done." He stared at Alejandro, his eyes dark and unblinking.

Jorge glanced up from his work on the cases, but said nothing.

"Is it your plan to stay with the cases until they detonate?" Alejandro asked.

"The devices have a button that allows them to be exploded, bypassing the timer," the young man said. "We will assess the situation when we arrive at our designated positions, but each of us is prepared to die for Allah if we find it would be best not to risk leaving the bag behind."

Jorge looked up again. This time he said, "Once you initiate the timing sequence, there doesn't seem to be a way to stop it. Even if the case is found within the five minutes, the explosives are still going to blow."

The young Muslim said, "Unless the detonator is detached from the case. Then it will be nothing more than a small blast, not likely to harm anyone but the person disarming the bag."

Jorge shared a quick look with Alejandro. Neither man responded.

"It won't matter," the Muslim assured them. "We will do what we must."

Alejandro thought it over. "You will make the decision, it is up to you. Just remember, even if someone finds the bag they are not likely to risk trying to remove the detonation device. They would have no way of knowing an attempt to disengage the mechanism wouldn't cause the whole thing to blow up."

"Allah will be served," the young man replied.

This time when Jorge turned to Alejandro the message in his eyes was plain—*let's get this done and get the hell out of here.*

CHAPTER EIGHTY-NINE

NEW YORK

FERRIELLO BROUGHT HIS car to a stop down the street from the hotel, just west of Broadway. It was after eleven at night, but in Times Square there is no such thing as darkness.

He and Sandor got out and walked down the block for a meeting they had arranged in a quick call to the counterterrorism unit on site. They were greeted by two FBI agents and two uniformed members of the NYPD.

After exchanging IDs, Ferriello asked, "What've we got?"

The senior federal agent briefed them. "We showed the passport photos at the front desk. The two younger men in those pictures arrived about an hour ago and checked into a suite they have reserved for three nights. They went upstairs, forty-fifth floor. No phone calls out, both of them still in there."

"Any sign of the third man in the photos?"

"Negative."

"Bags?"

The agent nodded. "We spoke to the bellman who handled them. Said they had several matching hard-shell cases. All the same size. He said the guests were unusually anxious about how the bags were being handled, never let them out of their sight, forked over a large tip when he placed them in the room."

Sandor and Ferriello shared a concerned look.

"We're dealing with an incredibly toxic substance," Sandor told them. "You remember when someone sent a gift of anthrax to that newspaper building in Florida about ten years ago?" The others nodded. "That place is still contaminated. You can't even go inside to this day without wearing a hazmat suit."

"Understood," said the senior FBI agent.

"And that was a whole lot less of the powder than they have here tonight."

No one said anything for a few moments.

"Our two friends have any visitors yet?" Sandor asked.

"I was just getting to that," the FBI agent said. "The six men from that mosque in the Bronx arrived together, two African-American, four Arab-American. Our men tailed them directly to this hotel. Got here about twenty minutes ago and began doing a lousy job of trying to look like they weren't together. They walked through the lobby and outside again, circled around the front, then they all came back and one of them used a house phone. From there they stopped at the hotel security station in front of the entrance to the bank of elevators. One of the guards made a call, got an okay from the men in the suite upstairs so he let them pass."

"The suite on forty-five?"

"That's right."

"They all still in there?"

"Far as we know," one of the police officers said. "We have men posted on each end of the floor."

"Good. These six guys from the mosque, were they carrying anything?"

"Not in their hands," the FBI agent told them. "They were all wearing coats or jackets, but we were told not to approach them. No idea what they might have underneath or in their pockets."

Just then the radios on the belts of both NYPD officers buzzed. One of them grabbed it and hit a button. "Go," he said.

The voice that came through was a whisper, barely audible over a stream of static, the message one word. "Movement."

They all took off at a run toward the hotel entrance.

The two plainclothes policemen who had been dispatched to the forty-fifth floor did not have much time to prepare. One of them rode the elevator to forty-six, got off, raced down the stairs, and remained in position, hiding in the stairwell at the end of the long hallway. The other officer was given a busboy uniform and a food cart. He made the quick change, took the elevator to forty-five, and was now doing his best to look busy, staying away from the peephole of the suite from which he might be spotted, but remaining in the corridor.

They were ordered not to engage the suspects, advised that they were extremely dangerous and might be armed with explosive devices.

When the door to the suite opened and Alejandro and Jorge emerged, the officer posing as a waiter turned his back to the Venezuelans and gave the one-word report into the mic beneath his lapel.

"Movement."

Then, looking back in their direction, he offered a pleasant, "Good evening gentlemen."

But neither of Adina's men was buying the act. Why had a busboy suddenly turned away from his cart as soon as they entered the corridor? Why was he just standing there in the hallway? And something about his pants and shoes were off.

In response to the greeting, Alejandro showed off a broad smile and strolled toward the elevators. As he passed the undercover policeman he caught a glimpse of the bulge under his jacket, likely a weapon, and he was taking no chances. In one lightning-quick move he produced the razor-sharp knife he was concealing inside the loose cuff of his jacket, spun and grabbed the officer by the hair from behind, then yanked his head back and drew the blade hard and deep across the front of the man's throat.

The officer slid to the floor, blood pouring down his neck and onto his chest as the life flowed out of him.

Jorge was reaching inside the busboy jacket for the officer's gun when another man emerged from the stairway entrance at the far end of the hall. The second policeman had witnessed the attack and now instinctively stepped out, automatic in hand, and took aim. But battles involving life and death do not allow for indecision. Whereas a trained law enforcement officer is hindered by the rules he has learned about the use of deadly force, a cold-blooded killer such as Jorge had no reason to hesitate. He fired twice, and the second policeman was dead before he was able to get off a shot.

The sound of the gunfire reverberated along the corridor. When someone opened a door and began to ask what was going on Jorge cut him off.

"NYPD," he hollered out in an authoritative voice. "Everyone stay in their rooms with the door locked. Someone call nine-one-one, we have an officer down."

Meanwhile, Alejandro let himself back into the suite, where the six young men were all standing, frightened looks on their faces. "Nothing to be concerned about," he told them, "but you cannot stay here as planned. You must get out of the hotel and find somewhere else to wait. It should not be a problem."

The group leader, in a calm but firm tone, said, "They have found you, which means they will find us."

"No, Jorge and I will lead them away from here. They have no way of knowing about you. We will cause as much confusion as possible to give you the chance to get away."

"But . . ."

"Listen to me. We'll take the stairs to the right, it will buy time and give you the opportunity to escape. Split up, take the elevators or the other stairs, go to different floors, then begin to leave, one at a time. Don't go to the lobby yet, and don't all move together."

The young Arab shook his head. "The cases will give us away and our mission will be ruined."

"No," Alejandro insisted, then hesitated. "If any of you are stopped, you know what to do." He pointed at the bags containing the anthrax.

Now the young man nodded.

"Good luck," Alejandro said, then ran back into the corridor to find Jorge, who had hustled down the corridor and was removing the automatic from the second dead policeman.

"Here," he said, tossing Alejandro the weapon as he also took the officer's radio and extra ammunition. "Let's go."

CHAPTER NINETY

NEW YORK

B<small>Y THE TIME</small> Sandor and Ferriello reached the hotel lobby there had been no further word from either officer stationed on the forty-fifth floor. Sandor knew they could not take the chance of initiating contact—there was no telling if either officer might be near the hostiles and, in a building this large with its dense metal infrastructure, even the best radio system was likely to generate static. The risk of the communication being overheard was simply too great.

Still, it had been too long since they got word that the suspects were on the move. Sandor crossed the lobby to have a look at the digital screen alongside the large bank of elevators. The NYPD officer who was monitoring that area confirmed that none of the elevators had stopped on the forty-fifth floor since they received their radio call.

As Sandor worried over the delay, the FBI agent in charge and the NYPD antiterrorism liaison approached.

"Report of a shooting on forty-five was just called in to nine-one-one by a hotel guest, said he saw two men on the ground before someone ordered him to close his door and call in the emergency."

"No one's heard from either officer?"

The head of the antiterrorism unit shook his head. "We have to assume they're the ones in trouble."

Ferriello, who had positioned himself across this cavernous entry hall, joined them. "Bad news?"

"The worst," Sandor said, then told him.

"What now?" the NYPD liaison asked.

Sandor looked around, as if there might be an answer somewhere within this forty-foot-high lobby. "We've been watching the elevators, none have stopped at forty-five since we got word they were on the move. This is a huge hotel with stairs on both ends of the building and all sorts of exits."

"You think they're all coming down forty-five flights of stairs?"

"Maybe," Sandor said. "They might split up, stop on different floors, try to force their way into another room and wait us out. Or try to get into one of the theaters on either side of the building and leave from there. We need to keep a strong presence in the lobby, with men at both stairwell exits. And the elevators of course. But we can't all just sit here and wait for them to show up."

"I'm calling in my entire unit," the man from the FBI said. "This is no longer an undercover op, Sandor. Whatever the joint task force thinks is going on here, we now have credible information of a terrorist threat, with the likelihood two police officers are down."

"Damn right," the man from NYPD agreed.

Two uniformed police officers standing near the reception desk came up to find out what was going on, just as Sandor was saying, "We've got to try and avoid causing a panic here. This mess could pour right out into the middle of Times Square."

"Nothing to be done about that now. We've got to respond with every available resource, and with all due respect for what you've done up to this point, this is an FBI matter now, with support from the NYPD and DHS."

"Okay," Sandor said, "but remember that in addition to the two shooters, you've got six hostiles likely carrying anthrax that may be rigged to explode anytime and anyplace."

"Understood."

Now Sandor stared the man down as he said, "I'm still going to do my thing, you all right with that?"

"Do what you need to do," the lead agent from the Bureau told him.

"Appreciate that," Sandor replied, then reached out and unclipped the radio from the belt of one of the uniformed officers. "I'll need to borrow this. We've got to assume they took the radios from your two men, so get word to everyone that you're using a secondary frequency."

The policeman looked to his superior, who nodded. He then took the radio from Sandor, switched it to an emergency setting, and handed it back.

"Thanks," Sandor said. "I'm going up the north set of stairs." He pointed to the rear of the lobby, then turned the radio off. "Don't want this squawking once I'm inside."

"Understood."

"Your men can cover the other side, but I'll take that one alone."

"The hell you will," Ferriello said.

Sandor shot him a glance that said this was something he had better think over. "Don't do anything you'll regret later."

Ferriello returned the serious look. "I almost never do."

"Almost never is a pretty good track record. Let's go."

———————

Forty-five flights was going to be a lot of stairs to climb, but Sandor took off at a run across the lobby. Ferriello drew a deep breath and followed him to the stairwell entrance. Sandor opened the door, held it as they passed through, then shut it behind them as silently as he could. From there he led their ascent.

Each of the first eight landings had metal doors with no handles. They were marked NO RE-ENTRY, emergency exits for the theater on the other side. On the first landing Sandor had a quick look at the door, confirming it would be easy enough to force open if the terrorists chose this way out of the hotel.

Ferriello nodded his understanding, then the two men moved as quickly and as quietly as they could, guns drawn, taking two steps at a time. Sandor stopped and held out his hand when they reached the tenth floor. Ferriello nodded gratefully, leaning forward with his hands on his knees as he tried to catch his breath.

They listened, but there was nothing to hear except the detective's wheezing.

"You need to get to the gym more often," Sandor whispered.

"Tell me about it."

Without another word, Sandor took off again.

When they stopped after ten more flights they were both winded, but this time they heard something other than their own panting. It was only a faint noise, coming from ten or more floors above them, but the sound was unmistakable. Footsteps. Moving toward them.

Sandor held a forefinger to his lips, then pointed to the corner of the landing, beside the hinged side of the fire door. Ferriello nodded and took that position. Then Sandor slowly and silently climbed up the next set of stairs.

The floors were separated by two flights, each consisting of fourteen steps, each running in the opposite direction of the one before. That created a small landing at the midlevel turn, the spot where Sandor chose to wait. He crouched in the corner beneath the dim light, his Walther in hand. However many of the eight men were coming, his plan was to draw their fire, take out as many as he could, then hope that the backup from Ferriello would be enough to finish the job.

He realized a prolonged shoot-out might give one of the hostiles a chance to release anthrax from one of the cases, but there was no choice now. He figured it would be better to have it explode in a stairwell than in the middle of the hotel lobby.

Then he looked above him at the air vent in the ceiling.

Damn! If the toxins got loose in here there was no telling how the circulation system might spread the deadly powder throughout the building.

He didn't need to just kill these bastards, he needed to kill them before they had that chance.

With the sounds of the men from above growing louder, Sandor stood and quietly descended the flight of stairs where Ferriello was crouching. He got as close as he could and whispered his concerns. "Don't hesitate and don't worry about hitting me. We need to take them all out before they can release any of the anthrax."

Ferriello nodded and Sandor hurried back to his position, just fourteen steps above.

Alejandro and Jorge decided that the theater below provided their best chance of escape.

They had studied the layout of the building when they arrived, comparing it to the information Adina had provided. They reviewed various contingency plans, just in case the couriers from the Bronx were somehow compromised or the two of them were otherwise discovered while still in the hotel. Making their way into the theater and then out to the street was clearly their best option.

They hurried down the stairs, each holding the Glock automatics taken from the dead policemen. They also had the radio, but thus far there were no communications coming through on the officer's two-way.

When they reached the twenty-fifth floor they stopped and stood still, listening.

Nothing. No indication the police were coming for them from below, at least not yet. No sounds of any of the six young men from the Bronx using the stairs above them.

"When are those idiots going to move out?" Jorge whispered.

Alejandro shrugged. "Maybe they took the other staircase. Or the elevators."

Jorge nodded. That was not their problem now.

They started off again.

The high, narrow stairwell was silent from top to bottom except for their soft steps as they ran. They were only a dozen or so flights from entry to the theater as they made the turn on the twenty-first floor.

Their eyes had adjusted to the dim lighting, but even so it took a moment for them to make out the figure squatting in the corner against the wall. The Venezuelans had their weapons at the ready, but they never had the chance to react.

Sandor's training was in special ops, not law enforcement.

The sound of gunfire exploded as Sandor fired shot after shot into their chests. Alejandro managed to squeeze off two wild rounds that ricocheted off the concrete walls as he stumbled forward. Jorge sent one shot above Sandor's head before falling facedown and sliding to a stop at the bottom of the stairs.

After the earsplitting reverberations the stairwell fell silent again. Ferriello had raced up the steps, where he found Sandor standing over the taller of the two men. Alejandro had tumbled all the way to the landing, his gun having clattered to the floor. He had been shot three times but was still breathing.

"Only these two," Ferriello said.

Sandor nodded. "Check the other one," he said as he replaced the magazine in his PPK.

"Dead," Ferriello confirmed.

Sandor knelt beside Alejandro. "You hear that? Your pal is dead, so now you have a choice. You tell me what I want to know and I can get you medical help. Otherwise I'll let you die here too. Your call."

In addition to the gunshot wounds, the large man seemed to have broken several bones in the fall down the staircase. He could hardly move, but he did manage to curse at Sandor in both Spanish and English.

Sandor nodded patiently. "I've seen you before you know. Adina's retreat, down near Barranquitas."

The man's moribund eyes could not hide his surprise. "That was you?"

"The one and only. Nice little operation you had there."

"He is going to kill you, *maricon*."

"Let's worry about me later. In case you haven't noticed, you're the one dying right now, so how about it? You want to live, you've got to answer some questions. Like where's the anthrax and where are they going with it?"

Alejandro managed a nasty smile, then in a raspy voice told Sandor where he could shove his questions.

"We know all about the six boys from that mosque in the Bronx, and we know about the cases you brought here. This hotel is surrounded so none of them are getting away. Why not do yourself a favor and cooperate. Then I'll call in a medical team and this won't have to be the last night of your life."

Alejandro stared at him without responding and Sandor could see the man was not long for it.

"Okay, let's start with an easier question. What is Adina doing with all those cars? Why would he need all those cars to spread anthrax?"

Once again the man's eyes revealed his surprise, although his energy was waning fast. He lifted his arm, took hold of Sandor's shirt, and pulled him close. With his voice barely a whisper, he said, "You don't know, but you'll find out." He twisted his mouth into one last smile. "Just wait a few hours. You'll find out."

Then his grasp weakened, his hand fell away, and he was dead.

CHAPTER NINETY-ONE

NEW YORK

Ferriello took the radio from Sandor, switched it on, and reported their situation.

"We heard the gunshots," came the response, "the staircase is like an echo chamber. The situation is already getting out of hand in the hotel and the theater on that side. People running all over the place," he was told.

"The two officers on forty-five?"

"Both dead. We have men up there now, that floor has been locked down."

"What about the six hostiles with the cases?"

"No sign of them yet."

"What about the rear stairs?" Ferriello asked.

"The entry on forty-five is also secure. We have a four-man team heading up from the lobby. There may be some movement above. Our men are proceeding with caution."

Sandor took the radio. "Have a team get up here, we're just above the twenty-first floor. Secure this stairwell. We'll grab an elevator and head to forty-five and then come back down the other side."

"Copy that."

"Be sure your men shoot to kill. If any of this anthrax is released, the air ducts are going to turn this entire building into a gas chamber."

Without awaiting a response Sandor led Ferriello through the door and into the corridor of the twenty-first floor, where people were peeking out from their rooms to see what all the noise was about.

Sandor did not hesitate. "Get back inside," he hollered, then fired a shot into the ceiling to punctuate the order. One door after another slammed shut.

Sandor punched the elevator's UP button and waited.

"What's the plan?" Ferriello nodded

"We start at forty-five, check the suite, then go looking for these bastards."

Ferriello nodded.

"Look on the bright side," Sandor told him as the doors slid open and they stepped into the elevator, "running downstairs is a lot easier than running up."

———————

Alejandro had suggested that the six men from the Bronx split up, but for now they remained together, huddled on a landing on the forty-third floor in the north stairwell. They had not heard the shooting on the other side of the hotel and had no way of knowing the fate of the two Venezuelans. The oldest among them, who acted as the group's leader, was a Lebanese who had abandoned his given name and now called himself Abdullah—servant of Allah. Abdullah drew them together in a tight huddle and spoke softly.

"We must move in three groups now. It will give us the best chance of completing our mission." The others nodded. "Once we are safely away from the hotel we can all separate and head to the places of our destiny." Again, the other five silently agreed.

There were still a few hours before the scheduled attacks. One of them asked if it made sense to try to force their way into another room to wait it out right there. The hotel was enormous. There had to be a place to hide. Perhaps Alejandro was right, perhaps the manhunt would be directed at the two men who had murdered the police officers, not at them.

Abdullah shook his head. "No, it is too risky to involve others. Someone might hear us or see us and make a call. No, you four will remain with us for a few more floors, then you will enter the corridor here and take the elevator down to the basement. Split into two groups and take different elevators. Do not stop at the lobby. You will certainly find a way out from the lower level. You will come with me," he told the sixth man. "We will continue down the stairs."

————

When Sandor and Ferriello stepped off the elevator on the forty-fifth floor they were greeted by an FBI agent wielding an assault rifle. After displaying their IDs, they were escorted down the hall to the door of the suite where two uniformed NYPD officers were standing guard. The hallway was crowded with law enforcement personnel along with staff from the medical examiner's office who were attending to the two fallen policemen.

Sandor was told that both officers were already dead when the medics arrived.

Inside the suite they found a forensic team scouring the place. The captain in charge of the investigative detail reported that there was not much there. All the men and all of the cases were gone. Nothing in the place had been used—not the beds, the minibar, not even the bathroom. The only thing left behind were six clear pieces of plastic that had been tossed in a wastebasket in the sitting area.

"Let me have a look," Sandor said.

Already bagged and tagged as evidence, they were held up for him to see. Each strip was several inches long and roughly three inches wide.

"What do you make of them?" Ferriello asked the head technician.

"They each have a residue of some kind of bonding agent. Appears to be fairly strong. We'll test them to see what type, but my best guess is that they were the backing to some sort of adhesive strip. No telling what was on the other side, of course."

Sandor shook his head. "How about a lightweight device, rigged with some sort of plastic explosive?"

"Anything is possible. As I say, it appears to be a strong compound. How did you make that leap?"

Sandor did not respond to the question. Instead he thanked the captain and told Ferriello it was time for them to move. As they hurried out of the suite and down the corridor, Ferriello repeated the investigator's question.

"Think about it. Adina got these cases of anthrax past detection in Wilmington. Clear, odorless powder encased in plastic. Sad to say, but not all that difficult to conceal on a private jet. Six detonators would have posed a different risk, might have set off some alarms or shown up on some detection devices. The couriers from the Bronx probably brought the detonators."

"Which they attached to the cases right here."

"Seems that way."

"Which means we're dealing with cases loaded with anthrax that are set to explode."

"That's how I see it."

They reached the entrance to the far stairwell. "What about all the cars then? That guy back there said we would know in just a couple of hours."

"That's the piece I can't figure out. If they're going to ignite six packages of anthrax, why would they need all those vehicles? They have enough anthrax to kill tens of thousands of people, depending on where they detonate those things."

"Maybe that's the key," Ferriello suggested. "Maybe the cars have something to do with where they intend to set them off."

"Maybe," Sandor agreed. "If we find the cases we won't have to deal with that problem."

————

When the six men from the Bronx reached the thirty-seventh floor, Abdullah decided they had gone far enough. They opened the fire door and had a look into the hallway. It was deserted. They entered the corridor, quietly pulled the door shut behind them, and gathered around once more to listen to their leader's determined voice.

"We cannot wait, there is no way to complete our mission if we do not get free from this place now."

"Can we use our phones?"

"Who would we call?"

"The imam. For advice."

Abdullah shook his head and gave him a somber look. "Would it be fair to ask for advice from someone who knows even less than we do of this situation? No, it would not. We have delayed long enough for those men to get away. Hopefully the police are following them. It is time for the four of you to get on the elevators and find your way out of here. The longer we wait the more dangerous it will become. And remember, my friends, we have the means of escape in our own hands." He held up his case for emphasis. "We must be prepared to do whatever must be done."

––––––––

Just before they entered the south stairwell, Sandor took the radio from Ferriello.

"All hands please listen up. We are seeking six hostiles. Each is carrying a hard-shell bag containing biological weapons we believe to be anthrax. The cases appear to be fitted with detonators. Repeat, the containers these six men are carrying are fitted with devices that might be ignited at any time. Upon encounter do not hesitate. Do not give them any opportunity to detonate. Shoot to kill, but be careful not to fire at the cases." He handed Ferriello the radio, saying, "Leave it on this time," then pulled the door open and started down the stairs.

There was no sound within the stairwell as Sandor and Ferriello descended. They had already passed the thirty-seventh floor when the two-way crackled to life.

"Now hear this, we have located the six men carrying the cases. Security cameras in the elevators show two each in the two elevators. They just got on at the thirty-seventh floor heading to the lobby. One elevator is two floors ahead of the other."

Sandor grabbed the radio again. "Sandor here. Do not let them go directly to the lobby. Repeat, stop the elevators on each floor if you have to, but do not open the doors, just do whatever you can to slow them down. Bring a shooting team to the twentieth floor, we'll meet you there."

Someone immediately acknowledged.

"What about the other two hostiles?" Sandor asked.

"Two returned to the south stairwell," came the reply.

Sandor switched off the radio so he and Ferriello could listen for any activity in the stairwell below. When they heard nothing they took off at a breakneck pace until they reached the door marked "20," pushed through it, and hurried into the corridor. Four men in FBI jackets had just arrived from the north side of the building and were in place.

"Fire as soon as you have the shot," Sandor said as he ran toward them. "We cannot afford any of these devices to be detonated. Am I clear?"

"We have those orders," one of the men confirmed.

"And don't hit any of the damned cases."

For a moment they were all silent, listening as the first elevator approached. Then it came to a stop before them.

When the doors slid open none of the agents hesitated, unleashing a fusillade that tore through the two terrorists where they stood. As the cases fell harmlessly to the floor in a haze of smoke and blood, Sandor rushed in to pull them away, fearing one of these men might yet have that final ounce of life necessary to hit the triggering mechanism. As he suspected, Sandor found the detonators taped to the bottom of each case.

Moments later the second elevator arrived and the gruesome scene was repeated with the same lethal ferocity.

That left two men and two IEDs filled with anthrax.

CHAPTER NINETY-TWO

NEW YORK

THE TWO ELEVATOR doors had been jammed open as members of the bomb squad secured the four recovered cases. Officers moved up and down the corridor, ordering curious guests back into their rooms.

"Time to go," Sandor said.

He and Ferriello moved out of the way and went back to work on the radio. "This is Sandor. Any sighting of the other two hostiles?"

"Negative," came the reply.

"The last sighting was the south staircase?" Sandor asked.

"Affirmative."

"Got it covered," Sandor said. "Have your men start up from the lobby, I'm coming down." Then he turned to Ferriello. "Ready?"

Ferriello nodded. "I'm right behind you."

"Much appreciated."

———

Sandor and Ferriello entered the stairwell again and headed down. After descending a few flights they heard something and both men came to an abrupt stop.

Sandor listened, now able to make out what sounded like a young man saying prayers in Arabic. The prayers grew louder as Sandor hurried down another three flights, where he stopped, the young man now in view.

He was standing with his back to the corner of the landing. He appeared to be in his mid-twenties, slight of build, with an olive complexion and fine features that were drawn tight in a mask of tension as he stood there trembling.

There was no sign of the anthrax.

Sandor stepped forward now, startling the young Arab. "They're about to send ten guys in here to blow you away." Sandor looked around but still did not see the case. He stuck his Walther inside his waistband. "We can talk first, maybe that doesn't have to happen. Okay?"

The prayers stopped. After a moment of silence the young man said, "I have nothing to say."

Sandor moved closer. The young Arab cringed but did not try to run. "Where's the case?" Sandor demanded.

At first he made no reply. Then he resumed praying.

"Your friend take it?"

The praying continued, but the look on his face provided the answer.

"So, you went yellow at the last minute, huh?"

This time, when the young man stopped praying, he glared at Sandor.

Sandor stepped forward and grabbed him by the neck. "Where'd he go?"

The young man did not answer, but Sandor caught the nervous sideward glance in the direction of the staircase below.

Sandor turned to Ferriello. "See if you can get anything from him," he said, "I'm going after the last of these scumbags." Without awaiting a response he handed the policeman the radio. Then he drove his elbow into the side of the terrorist's head, not waiting to watch the would-be assassin crumple to the ground in a whimpering heap as he took off down the stairs.

————

A few floors below, Sandor reached the metal doors that served as emergency exits for the movie house. He checked the first one, then continued down another flight. The door on that next landing showed signs of what he was looking for. It had been jimmied open, likely with a knife.

The last terrorist was going to make his way out to the street from the theater.

Pulling out his switchblade Sandor easily managed to trip the lock and made his way inside.

It was a huge theater and, at this late hour, the seats in this upper section were empty. His eyes adjusting to the darkness, Sandor stayed in a crouch as he made his way toward the back row, almost tripping over a uniformed security guard who was sprawled across the carpeted steps, clutching at his side, blood spread across his white shirt.

"Got a warning call on my radio," the guard said in a raspy voice. "I tried to stop him,"

"Hang in there pal, help is coming," Sandor said. Then he spotted the sixth terrorist making his way across the aisle, one case in each hand, hurrying toward the emergency exit on the far side of the building that led to fire stairs exiting onto the street.

Sandor did not hesitate. Staying low, his gun drawn, he sprinted through a row of seats until he closed in, just as the man reached the door. Sandor stood tall and called out to him. "You make one more move and you're a dead man."

Abdullah turned, his expression calm, a look more of curiosity than alarm. "I can make these explode any time I want," he said.

Sandor knew that the man was at a disadvantage, holding a case in each hand. From what he had seen from the cases recovered in the elevators upstairs, he knew the terrorist would have to drop one of them to get to the detonator. That was the only edge Sandor needed. "You have a choice," he said as he moved nearer.

"Don't come any closer."

"Okay." Sandor stopped, quickly doing the calculations on angle, timing and—most critical of all—the man's access to the triggering device at the bottom of the case. "I'm Sandor. What's your name?"

The young man responded as if the question came as a complete surprise. "Abdullah. My adopted name is Abdullah."

"You have any idea what you have in that case, Abdullah?"

"Yes. I do."

"Want to tell me?"

Abdullah thought about it, then said, "It is retribution for the acts of all the infidels."

"The infidels?"

"Yes."

Sandor nodded. "You grew up here in New York City?"

"The Bronx."

"Uh huh. So the infidels, they include all of those people you went to school with who aren't Muslims?"

"Don't play word games with me."

"I'm not playing games. I just want to understand who you expect to kill and why."

"I want to punish all of those who do not adopt the word of Allah."

"And you think Allah would want you to randomly murder a lot of people, including yourself? Including a lot of other good Muslims?"

He responded with another look of confusion.

"What you have in that case is going to kill everyone in its path, not just infidels. You give any thought to the innocent Muslims you're going to slaughter?"

Abdullah paused, then said, "They will die for the good of Allah."

"What about the people who haven't adopted the word of Islam yet? They'll die before they have the opportunity to choose your faith."

He shook his head. "There is no choice, there is only Allah."

"You're wrong Abdullah, you have a choice. You can put those cases aside and walk away to follow whatever path you want in life."

"That is not a choice, and I do not want to talk with you anymore. I only want to leave here and reach the moment and place of my destiny."

"You meeting with one of those cars? Is that the place of your destiny?"

Abdullah responded with a look of disgust. "I have nothing to do with the cars. The cars are for cowards, those who feel the need to survive, who are not willing to make the ultimate sacrifice for their faith."

"Do they really expect to survive the attack?" Sandor still had no idea what the cars had to do with the anthrax, but it seemed the right question, especially when Abdullah responded with a bitter laugh.

"They won't be anywhere near the place of my destiny," he proudly declared, then realized he had said too much. "I told you I don't want to speak with you anymore. Go away," he demanded, his voice rising as he held up the two plastic cases.

"All right, take it easy," Sandor said. "But before I go . . . ," he continued, then was done talking. He fired a shot that caught Abdullah in the chest, causing the young man to stumble backward and drop one of the cases. From there Sandor would have been pleased to aim at his legs, then rush forward and grab the bags. But Abdullah managed to hang on to the second case and was already reaching for the detonator at the bottom. Sandor had no choice but to fire twice into the young man's forehead.

Abdullah jerked back and hit the wall. Then he slid to the floor, dead before the second lethal case fell harmlessly to the ground in front of him.

The few late-night patrons in the main section of the theater below reacted to the sound of the gunshots by screaming for help and running frantically toward the exits. Sandor grabbed the two cases and hustled back to the fallen security guard. There he found Ferriello already kneeling beside the man, applying first aid.

"FBI has the punk upstairs. He should give us some answers," the narcotics detective said. "Told me his pal was heading for this theater."

"Okay. I'll get these bags to the bomb squad, then I've got to make a call."

CHAPTER NINETY-THREE

CIA HEADQUARTERS, LANGLEY, VIRGINIA

CRAIG RAABE WAS standing in a situation room located on a sub-basement level in Langley. Before him were a collection of murky images on several clear video monitors, known as transparent OLEDs. It was still a couple of hours before dawn, but he, a team of technicians, and three NCS agents were watching satellite photos of cars, SUVs, and vans pouring out of a garage on Payson Avenue in the upper reaches of Manhattan. A number of FBI and NYPD vehicles were closing in, but it was too late to stop any but the last few of the vehicles.

The door to the room opened and Deputy Director Byrnes walked in. "What have we got?"

"The tip on the location of this garage was right on the money," Raabe told him. "We're just a little late, and we still can't make any sense of it."

"Hold the thought," the DD said, "I've got Sandor on the line." He walked to one of the workstations, arranged a call transfer, then flipped Sandor onto speakerphone. "Go," he ordered.

"All six cases have been recovered and none of the toxin was released, that's the main thing," Sandor responded. "The FBI bomb squad has already secured the anthrax. It was messy, but we got it done."

"How messy?"

"Five couriers down. I also had to take out two of Adina's men. They brought the goods to town and were on their way home."

"You get anything from either of them?"

420 JEFFREY S. STEPHENS

"One was DOA. The other survived just long enough to say some nasty things about my mother. Otherwise not much. I asked him about the cars and he laughed at me. All he said was that we would know in a few hours."

"That seems right," Raabe told him. "We just watched them leave an indoor garage in Washington Heights."

"They all look like they're heading to the same place?"

"Don't seem to be, that's part of the problem. They're moving in all different directions."

The DD interrupted. "Let's get back to what happened in Times Square."

Sandor's voice came over the loudspeaker again. "There were six couriers from that mosque DHS identified in the Bronx. They arrived at the hotel, met with Adina's goons and picked up the cases. It looks like they brought the detonators, attached them to the base of each bag with an adhesive strip, and they were ready to go when we arrived. Four were terminated by the FBI, NYPD and me. A fifth gave up when the shooting started. Then I went after the last one."

"So five are dead?" Byrnes asked.

"Affirmative."

"And both of Adina's men."

"Completely."

"Doesn't anyone take a live prisoner anymore?"

"Ferriello took the sixth man into custody. Wasn't as loyal to Allah as he thought he would be when the moment of truth arrived."

"And?"

"He had some assigned location for igniting the case. Won't say where, and doesn't seem to know anything about the cars. The bomb squad says the devices were rigged with timers, but none had been set. The detonators also had panic buttons, they could have blown them whenever they wanted."

"Hence the decision not to try and take them alive."

"That's how I saw it, sir. Odd thing about the last guy, he spoke like he intended to be a martyr. He didn't seem to have any intention of setting the timer, he was going down with the ship. Said the men driving the cars are a bunch of cowards, not willing to die for Allah."

"So he mentioned the cars."

"I asked him, but that was all he would say."

Byrnes turned to Raabe. "What do these vehicles look like they're up to?"

Raabe shook his head. "No clue. If Adina's plan was to have those six men explode anthrax all over town, why would he need the cars?"

"A diversion," Sandor suggested. "Maybe the cars are supposed to do something before the anthrax is released. The drivers couldn't know that these six lunatics have been stopped, not yet. The hotel here is in a state of panic, but it's also in lockdown."

Byrnes had a chilling thought. "We saw Adina work his bait-and-switch in Baton Rouge. What if those cases aren't holding the anthrax?"

"I had the same thought," Sandor reported. "We already had one opened and tested by experts from the Bureau. These are the real goods. The anthrax was packaged at the center of the case, surrounded by a plastic foam. The case was hermetically sealed, totally airtight. The lab techs had a tough time getting it open, but they say the stuff is pure."

"And deadly," Raabe said. "I also got the word on that, sir."

"What if there's more anthrax than we thought?" Sandor asked. "What if Adina has a contingency plan?"

"Maybe we should let the media know a terrorist plot to release anthrax has been terminated," Byrnes suggested. "Maybe if the drivers hear that on the radio they'll pull back. The last of those six men told you the drivers are cowards, they're not out there to die for a cause."

"Any word about terrorism to the media right now is going to increase the panic here, which is already growing. Remember, we've had multiple shootings and a huge law enforcement presence right in the middle of Times Square."

"I understand."

"Not to mention that we still want Adina. We need to delay any report of his plot failing for as long as possible."

"Wait a minute," Byrnes said, "if these drivers are not doing this for a cause then they must be doing it for money. What if the cars have nothing to do with anthrax? What if it's all about the narcotics being shipped in?"

One of the other agents in the room, from NCS, said to Byrnes, "We may be about to get an answer, sir." He was holding out a phone to the DD. "I have Assistant Director Bebon from the FBI on the line for you."

Bebon was patched in and placed on the speakerphone.

"My men got to the garage in Washington Heights in time to stop a few of the cars," he said.

"We saw some of the action via satellite," Byrnes reported.

"We have those drivers in custody. More important, they grabbed a man inside the building who appears to be in charge. Name of Miguel Lasco. We've already brought up the dossier on him. Venezuelan dissident. Anti-American rabble-rouser. Arrests for narcotics trafficking but no convictions. The critical part is that he's willing to talk."

———

Lasco's willingness to talk was due in part to the fact that he saw no way out and in part to his fear of Adina. His agreement to cooperate also came with the usual demands for immunity and protection. Since the situation in New York was at code red and most of the vehicles were already gone, the lead agent on the ground had little choice but to get permission from D.C. to promise Lasco whatever he wanted—provided the information was in time to prevent a disaster.

NCTC linked in and quickly verified through voice recognition that Lasco was on several of the early calls they had recorded between Washington Heights and the area near Barranquitas, Venezuela. He was a key player in whatever Adina had orchestrated for all these vehicles and admitted that a large shipment of cocaine was expected in New York in the next few days. More crucial than that, he claimed to know where the cars were going and what they would do when they got there.

But, if he was to be believed, he knew nothing about an anthrax attack.

The interview was being conducted in Lasco's office on the ground floor of the garage. By the time he finished explaining what was about to happen, the two agents interrogating him and the third who was recording the exchange were all speechless. The senior man had rushed from the room, phoned Bebon, and hastily arranged this conference call, which included everyone on the task force who could be found at this hour of the morning.

"With so many of us on the line," Bebon told them, "this will go much better if no one interrupts my agent. I'll ask the questions as needed. Now go ahead," he ordered.

"There are over a hundred cars involved," the agent began. "Most have already left from this parking garage, the rest are coming from an outdoor lot in the South Bronx, near the mosque we discussed earlier. The drivers have all been assigned bridges and tunnels, covering every means of entering and leaving Manhattan. The earliest departures are heading to New Jersey, Brooklyn and so forth. They'll be turning around and coming back to the city at the appointed time."

"What is the appointed time?" Bebon asked.

"Oh-seven-hundred today, sir. The plan is to obstruct every means of ingress and egress on Manhattan Island. At the arranged time the drivers will maneuver themselves into positions in each tunnel and on each bridge so they are side by side, covering all lanes, three deep. As they reach the three-quarter point on each bridge or inside each tunnel they will slow their vehicles, then the trailing cars and vans will intentionally turn and collide with each other. The second row of drivers will do the same. This will form an impassable roadblock, with hundreds of rush-hour vehicles brought to a stop behind them on each bridge and inside every tunnel. Then the drivers of those disabled vehicles will get out, light preset fuses, and jump into the lead vehicles, which will have stopped to pick them up and drive them away."

"The fuses. What are they intended to ignite?"

"The vehicles that will intentionally crash into the others at slow speeds have their trunks and cargo bays filled with gasoline and some other explosive materials, all pretty much garden-variety stuff. I'm not sure what that will do on the bridges except to make clearing the wreckage more difficult and possibly impact the cars stopped just behind them. But the air drafts and ventilation systems in the four tunnels are another matter." He paused. "It could turn them into raging infernos for all the people stuck behind them."

"And they're planning to do this on every bridge and every tunnel, in both directions?" Bebon asked.

"Yes sir, every one."

For several seconds no one spoke. Then Bebon said, "We need as many boots on the ground as we can organize, and I mean right now. We're looking for more than a hundred cars and vans with no special markings mixed up in what will become a typical rush-hour morning in New York City. I'll get out an APB. We need to stop them."

———

When Bebon opened the call to questions everyone began speaking at once. Craig Raabe picked up the phone that had connected Sandor, cutting him off from the chaos.

"You get all that?"

"I did. I'll report all that information to the team here, but there's nothing I can do on my end to make a difference. I need to get out of here, and I'll need your help."

"You going north?"

"I am, and in a few minutes every helicopter in Manhattan is going to be spoken for. I need a ride, and I need it now."

CHAPTER NINETY-FOUR

EN ROUTE TO STEWART AIRPORT

As Bobby Ferriello sped Sandor crosstown to the Twenty-third Street heliport, Craig Raabe made the necessary calls to commandeer a chopper. It was after 6 A.M.

"FBI is already on their way to Stewart," Sandor said as he loaded the magazine for his Walther. "I want to be there too."

"Understood," Ferriello said. "You want company?"

Sandor looked up at the police detective. "Thanks, but you're going to have your hands full here."

Ferriello nodded.

"And you've already done plenty."

"Wouldn't have missed it for the world."

When they reached the landing port the helicopter was waiting, the rotors already spinning in the predawn darkness.

"Hey," Ferriello said as Sandor opened the car door, "maybe you're not so bad after all."

"Sure I am," Sandor said with a smile as he shook his hand, then climbed out of the car and ran toward the entry gate, where he flashed his credentials and disappeared into the chopper.

———

It was just before seven as Sandor approached Stewart Airport. During the flight he remained in regular contact with Raabe, who gave him updates on the efforts to prevent the attacks in Manhattan.

The NYPD, aided by the Fire Department and every federal agent the task force could muster, were doing their best to intercept vehicles that had been identified by the satellite photos. Attack helicopters had been dispatched from Fort Dix in New Jersey to assist in spotting and stopping them. There were emergency cars and trucks stationed at the entrances to every bridge, and, after the task force contacted the Port Authority, a command decision was made to completely shut off all four tunnels on both sides. The move was wreaking havoc with the early traffic, but at least the most serious threats of death and destruction would be averted—igniting gasoline in the open air would be far less damaging than the creation of a ventilation-swept blaze in the confines of a long tunnel.

All of the major television and radio stations were already covering the story, and this time they didn't have to gin up the fear factor. The military had stepped in, grounding every news helicopter in New York, but enough video footage had already been shot to fill the airwaves and Internet. The headline was that despite all the manpower devoted to the effort, some of the cars and vans had gotten through. It was too late to stop them all, and hell was breaking loose all over the city.

Three of the drivers had arrived at the Henry Hudson Bridge before the roadblocks had time to set up. The drivers botched their attempt at a controlled collision in the southbound lanes, all of them traveling too fast. When sparks flew at the impact, the containers of fuel they were carrying exploded. The drivers attempted to flee on foot, but they were covered in burning gasoline and they died at the scene.

"That's the good news," Sandor said, and Raabe agreed.

Unfortunately, the resulting fireballs carried to the cars of innocent drivers immediately behind them, but all of those people were saved by the rescue vehicles that were just arriving on site.

Similar explosions occurred on the 59th Street Bridge, the University Heights Bridge, and the Macombs Dam Bridge. The drivers of the booby-trapped cars managed to escape the fires, but they could not outrun the authorities. Meanwhile the blasts there caused fatalities and injuries to those unlucky enough to end up behind them.

"How many innocent people dead?" Sandor asked Raabe.

"So far six deaths have been reported. Also a lot of people require treatment for third-degree burns. Whatever they put in there with the gasoline, and however they rigged the stuff, the reports say it was like liquid fire flying through the air."

"Bastards," Sandor said.

"Why would Adina have tried something so complicated, involving so many people? What was the point?"

"I have a theory," Sandor told him.

"I'm all ears."

"What if these attacks were timed to occur before the anthrax was going to be set off? Even if he only succeeded in hitting half the bridges and tunnels, what would people do once word got out?"

"They'd run for trains and subways and try to get out of Manhattan."

"Which means the major terminals and stations would be jammed with people still coming into town during the morning rush hour and people trying to get out. Perfect spot to set off the anthrax blasts."

"Which means we've stopped him there." Sandor paused. "But maybe it's not over yet."

"This is one time I hope you're wrong."

"Me too," Sandor admitted. "Keep me posted," he said, then signed off.

CHAPTER NINETY-FIVE

NEWBURGH, NEW YORK

Adina was seated on the edge of the bed in his motel room, transfixed by the images on the television screen as he listened to the on-site reporters.

Explosions had occurred on the Henry Hudson Bridge. People, their clothes on fire, ran from their cars. Rescue teams were already on the scene. A few other bridges had been hit with similar casualties, but coordinated attacks on Manhattan's major bridges, as well as her tunnels, had been prevented.

Of more concern to him were the vague and seemingly unrelated reports of a series of violent incidents at a Times Square hotel.

Adina looked at his watch. He had been up all night, still dressed in his clothes from the day before. It was nearly seven and he had not heard from Alejandro or Jorge. Twice he had risked sending them the prearranged signal from his cell.

There had been no response.

He stood and paced the small room for a moment, already knowing what he must do. He pulled out his phone and called the pilot.

The young man answered on the second ring, already awake and prepared for the early departure Adina had predicted.

"It's time for us to go," Adina told him.

"We're here at the airport, we'll be all set."

"I'm just a few minutes away."

"I need to file a flight plan."

"Of course. We'll discuss that when I arrive," Adina told him, then rang off.

He turned off the television and walked to the nightstand, where he picked up the pistol Lasco had given him and secured it in the waistband of his trousers.

Then he lifted the seventh case of anthrax and headed for the door.

CHAPTER NINETY-SIX

STEWART AIRPORT

A short time later Sandor's chopper set down at the far end of the airport, where he was met by two FBI agents.

After introductions he asked, "What've we got?"

"The suspect just arrived and got on the jet," one of the men said as he pointed toward the private air terminal several hundred yards away. "He boarded alone. We did not interfere. We were told to take no action until you arrived."

"The crew on board?"

"Got on just before he did. Two men. Requested a takeoff back to Wilmington," he said, checking his watch, "five minutes from now."

"What has the crew been told?"

"The tower told them there was going to be a slight delay."

"Any indication of their level of involvement?"

"No, we have no information on whether they're hostiles or not. We're treating the situation as if they are."

"All right. I need a mechanic's uniform. Then have the tower tell them they spotted something and they need to send a man aboard."

The two agents looked at each other, then the second man asked, "Spotted what?"

"What the hell do I know? An oil leak on the ground. A flat tire. Have them come up with something."

"Look, we were told this is your operation, but we've already got a dozen men all over this airport. Why don't we just rush the plane in force? Or tell the crew they all need to disembark?"

Sandor shook his head. "I've got my reasons. Trust me on this."

———————

Ten minutes later, Jordan Sandor, dressed in a dark blue mechanic's coverall, strode across the tarmac and up the stairs onto Adina's jet. He was surprised to find the cabin empty.

"Hello?" he called out.

"In the cockpit," a man replied.

Sandor stepped forward toward the entrance of the small cockpit, where he was greeted by the barrel of a revolver pointed at the side of his head.

"On your knees" Adina said, "your back to me, hands on your head."

"Look buddy . . ." Sandor began, but Adina cut him off.

"Do not waste my time with whatever fairy tale you've invented for this occasion. Just do as I say or I will shoot you where you stand."

Sandor did as he was told.

"You," Adina said to the copilot, "go into the cabin and pull the hatch closed. And remember, I can see you from here." Keeping the pistol trained on Sandor, Adina allowed the young man to pass, then positioned himself in the doorway so he had a view of all three men.

The copilot pulled up the steps and secured the hatch.

"Back here," Adina snapped. When the copilot returned to his seat, Adina said, "We will now take off, gentlemen."

"I don't think so," Sandor disagreed, his back to the man.

"Excuse me?"

"This airport is surrounded by federal agents. Apache helicopters are hovering on the perimeter, out of sight, standing by with orders to shoot this plane down if it gets so much as three feet off the ground."

"Nonsense," Adina snarled.

"That so?" Sandor craned his neck around to have a look at him. "If you want to shoot me, go ahead, but I'm your only chance of walking out of here alive."

Adina's eyes narrowed. "And who would you be?"

"No one important, except that I can tell you what's been going on while you've been waiting to fly back to a hero's welcome in Caracas."

Adina pointed the gun at Sandor's forehead but said nothing.

"The attacks on the bridges and tunnels were prevented. Your two henchmen are deader than yesterday's cigar. And all six cases of anthrax have been recovered."

"What is that charming expression you Americans have? Ah yes, 'Perhaps you did not get the memo.'" Then Adina reached behind the pilot's seat and held up the seventh case of anthrax.

Sandor said nothing.

"Yes, I see in your eyes you recognize this custom-made luggage."

"What do you intend to do with it?"

"That, of course, is my concern. For now, what I do not intend is to stand here and waste time when we should already be in the air."

"Not happening, anthrax or no anthrax."

"Once we tell them I have this case on board, they may not be so anxious to shoot down this plane and release a deadly cloud over the entire area."

"And who's going to tell them you have anthrax on board?"

"You are, of course."

"Not me, pal."

For the first time, Adina's arrogance faltered. "If you are so certain they will shoot this plane down, why did you come aboard? You'll die too."

"No, because we're not taking off. I came here to take you into custody."

"You really do have a death wish."

"Not at all. No one here is going to die, not this morning."

Adina displayed his venomous smile. "So, why the ludicrous costume? I knew you were not a mechanic when I saw you coming toward the plane."

"Not really my style, I admit, but I wasn't sure how you'd react if I showed up in full military gear. I just didn't want you shooting me before I got up the stairs. I needed to get inside so we could talk."

"You've achieved that limited success."

"The way I calculate things, you only have a few ways to go. You force these boys to take off and the Apaches will blow us all out of the sky. Whether or not the anthrax is released, or how effective it will be in killing innocent people will no longer be our problem, will it? On the other hand, if you fire a single shot at any one of us, that sound will bring a SWAT team rushing onto this plane and you'll be cut to ribbons before you take your next breath. But, if you hand me that suitcase and let me walk you out of here then you become a political prisoner."

Adina nodded slowly, as if something had just become clear to him. "With diplomatic immunity."

"Your old pal President Chavez will see to that, won't he?"

Adina began to say something but stopped. Then his eyes widened slightly as he said, "You're Sandor, aren't you?" When he received no response he said, "Yes, of course you are."

Sandor shrugged. "So what's it going to be?"

"Why would you have come aboard and risked your life to do me this wonderful favor?"

"Because you're better off to me alive than dead."

"I could kill you right now and still walk away."

"Would I be here if that were true?" Sandor shook his head. "No, I already told you. They hear a gunshot and they'll move right in with six-shooters blazing. You may have diplomatic immunity from Venezuela, but I have my friends right nearby." He got to his feet, not even looking at the pistol that Adina was still holding on him. "We also have a five-minute deadline before they shoot their way in here, whether or not you fire that thing."

"How do I know I won't be shot as soon as I step outside?"

Sandor shook his head with a look of utter disgust. "If we wanted to shoot you, twenty men would have stormed the plane by now."

"I want to speak with my embassy. Right now."

"Of course you do, and as soon as you give yourself up you'll be afforded all of your rights."

"The American way," Adina said with obvious contempt.

Sandor ignored him and turned to the two young men. "Time to go boys. While Hamlet here does his Act Three soliloquy, no sense you getting nailed in the crossfire."

They gave Adina a nervous look but did not move.

"Go ahead," Sandor told them, "he's not going to shoot you."

After some tense moments of silence Adina said, "Go."

The two crewmen got quickly to their feet and hurried out to the cabin, where they opened the hatch and leapt down the stairs.

"Well then," Adina said as he and Sandor stood facing each other in the confines of the small cockpit, "how do you propose to ensure my safety?"

"That's entirely up to you. If you like, you can use me as a shield when we walk off the plane."

Adina sighed. "I have no doubt I'll be taken alive, Mr. Sandor. As you suggested, I have knowledge of too many things your people want to hear about. They'll shove me into a rat-infested hole in Guantánamo, or perhaps transport me somewhere overseas where your associates can ignore your laws and my rights."

"You really think the State Department is going to risk that sort of diplomatic brawl with your pal Chavez?"

Before Adina could reply, Sandor lashed out with his left forearm, sweeping up at Adina's gun hand. At the same instant, he drove the heel of his right hand hard under the Venezuelan's chin, knocking him backward against the bulkhead. Adina lost his grasp on the case of anthrax as he fell, but he was still clutching the revolver. Leaving no time for the stunned terrorist to react, Sandor was on him, twisting the gun from his hand and pressing his left arm against Adina's neck as he gained control of the pistol and held it to Adina's temple.

Kneeling atop him, his teeth gritted tight, Sandor said, "I could have killed you as soon as I walked in here, but there were witnesses. And I just had to hear you whine about diplomatic immunity, at least once."

Adina, gasping under the pressure on his throat, was barely able to answer. "You aren't going to kill me," he rasped, once again summoning that reptilian smirk. "You can threaten me, but without the fear of death you have nothing."

"Well then," Sandor replied with a flash of his own cruel smile, "you have sorely misjudged me." He stood and stared down at Rafael Cabello. "But just so you know that I play fair, I'm going to give you the same chance you gave every one of those innocent souls you've taken." Then Sandor reached under his overalls for his own gun, leveled the Walther, and fired three shots into Adina's face.

CHAPTER NINETY-SEVEN

TWO WEEKS LATER, CIA HEADQUARTERS, LANGLEY, VIRGINIA

SANDOR, RAABE, AND Byrnes were back inside the situation room from which the task force organized by Byrnes had coordinated their efforts during that deadly night and morning, two weeks before.

Everyone involved agreed that the damage control had been extraordinary, given what had been put in place. Once again, however, Sandor could not shake the sickening feeling that he should have somehow done more.

The deaths of Adina, his two men, the five couriers from the Bronx, and the various drivers who had died that night were of no consequence to Sandor—they were the rightful casualties in a cowardly and pointless war of their own making. Yet innocent people had also perished on the bridges that could not be protected in time. Two police officers were murdered in the hotel. Countless others were injured.

And for what?

Sandor had been roundly congratulated for his role in preventing an anthrax attack the experts were now estimating could have taken more than twenty thousand lives.

Numbers, Sandor told himself. *When will we learn that no one has the right to measure human life in gross numbers? Human lives must always be counted one at a time.*

Jim Bergenn. Felipe Romero. Lillian Mindlovitch.

Two days after the task force stopped the worst consequences of the catastrophe Adina had planned for Manhattan, the DEA

seized the large shipment of Adina's cocaine as part of a joint operation with the Coast Guard in the Port of Baltimore. They had also
shattered the myth of the elusive Jaime Rivera; uncovered the mole
within their agency, Joseph Cleary; had Alphonso Mateo still singing
like a canary; and not only vindicated Dan LaBelle, but were arranging his promotion.

Sandor knew the part he had played in all this, but he was also
mindful of the large pile of IOUs he had racked up along the way. Farrar and Hasani in Sharm el-Sheikh. Ferriello in Brooklyn. Greshnev
in Moscow. Carlton in Curaçao. Vauchon in St. Barths.

There was also the expected dustup over the death of Adina.
Sandor reported to Byrnes that he had acted in self-defense. He
explained that once the crew left the plane he and the Venezuelan
got into an argument, Adina threatened to release the anthrax and
then waved the gun at him once too often. He had no choice but to
protect himself.

To which the DD replied, "And I assume you're going to stick
with that story?"

"I am sir."

"Three shots in the head was protecting yourself?"

"Can't be too careful in a close-quarter gunfight, sir."

"Anything else you want to tell me, Sandor?"

"Just a question sir?"

"Yes?"

"If a mass murderer starts sniveling about diplomatic immunity,
does shooting him qualify as justifiable homicide?"

Byrnes was not smiling when he asked, "Is that going to be your
full report, Sandor?"

"Yes sir. Except for the last part. That won't be included."

The usual diplomatic scuffle followed, but this time the suits at the
State Department surprised both Sandor and his boss when they cast
aside political considerations and told the powers in Caracas to go fly
a kite. One of them actually said in a memo, "If it is their intention
to idealize the murderous acts of a genocidal criminal like Rafael Cabello perhaps they can get Andrew Lloyd Webber to write a musical
about him, but as far as we are concerned this matter is closed."

When Byrnes gave him the news, Sandor smiled and said, "Go figure."

Of all the things he had done in his career—good and bad, right or wrong—the removal of Adina from the living was something he would always be proud of.

———

At the moment, Sandor was concerned about one more piece of unfinished business.

He was standing shoulder to shoulder with Craig Raabe, Byrnes right behind them, as they studied a transparent screen display of satellite photos from the north shore of the scenic resort town of Agios Nikolaos in Crete.

It was late in Greece, after ten at night, and none of the three men spoke as they watched the outlines of two figures position themselves near the rocks beside the shore at the base of a large hilltop estate that rose majestically above the sea. A few hundred yards out, sitting at anchor in the Aegean, was a large yacht that Sandor knew only too well.

The two figures now lay very still among the rocks and remained that way for what seemed a long time.

"You should have let me do this," Sandor murmured, as if to himself.

Byrnes placed a hand on his shoulder. "No way."

They became quiet again as they watched a group of men and women leave the main house and walk down a long, winding set of stone steps that led to the shore. There they boarded a tender that carried them out to the yacht. Once the motorboat was tied off at the stern they began climbing up a narrow set of stairs to the rear deck.

Even in the gloaming, the name on the stern was clear. *Odessa*.

The three men in Langley continued to observe without speaking. Without any sound it was eerie as the minutes ticked by, infrared lighting allowing them to follow the images of the group climbing onto the large yacht as the two men near the jetty remained perfectly still. Suddenly there was a brief flash from where the two figures were positioned behind the rocks. Then, an instant later, the head of one of the men boarding the yacht jerked violently, and he fell backward into the sea.

It was over.

Sandor took a deep breath, then turned away with a mixed sense of satisfaction and sadness, knowing that he had kept his promise to Farrar and a silent pledge to Lilli.

NEW YORK CITY

Two days later Sandor telephoned Bill Sternlich to say he was back home. Sternlich offered to meet him for a drink, but Sandor declined.

"Not today, Bill. I have something to take care of. Some other time." Sandor took a cab crosstown to Manhattan's Upper East Side. The building was a classic four-story tenement, no doorman, no elevator. Old-school New York. He had called in advance, spoken with the building superintendent and explained his business. He met the man out front, a squat, dark-skinned Hispanic wearing a tired expression and a stained gray T-shirt. The man did not seem all that impressed when Sandor flashed his federal ID, but he did give his full attention to the green and beige picture of Benjamin Franklin he was handed.

The super held out the key. Sandor took it and said, "She's not coming back."

The short man blinked. "That right?"

"I'll have someone send the landlord a formal notice. Then you can clean out the apartment." Sandor took a deep breath and let it out slowly. "We haven't been able to locate a next of kin. You ever see her with anyone?"

The super shook his head. "Some different guys, you know how it goes with a good-looking girl in this town."

"Nothing steady?"

"Nah. Nice girl, though. Always friendly." He shook his head. "Gone, eh?"

Sandor nodded.

"Sorry to hear it," the man said, but he did not ask how or why.

"Sorry to have to tell you," Sandor replied. He turned from the super and climbed the front stairs, entered the building, and headed up three flights to apartment 3E. He paused there, key in hand, then unlocked the door.

The apartment was small, the sort of place he figured Lilli Mindlovitch would have lived in. The foyer was just large enough to accommodate both Sandor and the open door. The area that passed for a living room could barely contain a modern-looking love seat, a round-backed chair, and an étagère that held a television, some books, and an assortment of photographs .

Sandor had a look at the pictures. Lilli with friends, Lilli as a young girl, and Lilli with an attractive older woman he assumed was her mother. For a moment he thought of his own mother, then decided to let that go.

He turned away and checked the kitchen, which was so tight he could hardly move without bumping into a wall or a cabinet. The refrigerator was emptier than his, which was saying something. The bathroom was even smaller than the kitchen, but it was neat and clean and full of shelves holding every sort of cream, cosmetic and lotion.

He went back to the living room and picked up one of the photos. It was unmistakably Lilli as a teenager, which was not all that long ago. She was standing on a beach someplace with a big smile that was framed by her long, windblown hair.

There was no reason for her to die, Sandor told himself. Too many people die for the wrong reasons. Some, like Lilli, die for no reason at all. He had another look at the photo, then carefully replaced the picture on the shelf, as if it were important that it be placed in the same spot he found it.

He stood there for a moment, looking around one last time, bearing witness to all that remained of the existence of Lilli Mindlovitch. Then he knew there was nothing more for him to do, that it was time to leave. He headed for the door but stopped and went back to the living room. He picked up one of the more recent photographs, deciding he would keep that one, telling himself it would be fine. There was no one left who would care.

As he turned to leave with the photograph in hand, he pulled out his cell and dialed Sternlich. "Hey Bill," he said. "Let's go get that drink."

THE END